P9-CME-181

Look for the next book in the
Love Letters series . . .

Eternally Yours

Coming soon from Jove

continued on next page . . .

DEAREST BELOVED

CHRISTINE HOLDEN

JOVE BOOKS, NEW YORK

DEAREST BELOVED

A Jove Book / published by arrangement with
the author

PRINTING HISTORY
Jove edition / November 2001

Visit our website at
www.penguinputnam.com

ISBN: 0-515-13228-4

A JOVE BOOK®
Jove Books are published by The Berkley Publishing Group,
a division of Penguin Putnam Inc.,
375 Hudson Street, New York, New York 10014.
JOVE and the "J" design
are trademarks belonging to Penguin Putnam Inc.

PRINTED IN THE UNITED STATES OF AMERICA

10 9 8 7 6 5 4 3 2 1

With profound thanks to God,
for His blessings are abundant.

Acknowledgements and Thanks:

Greg Williams, rising football star, and a staunch supporter.

Claude Walls, your kindness, encouragement, and consideration is boundless. We love you.

Vernon Clark, adopted son and brother. All our love.

Tracy Doucette and Stacy Jackson, romance readers and supporters. Thank you for giving Zoey an extraordinary start in school!

Eric Paulsen, news anchor extraordinaire and a true friend of novelists of all genres.

And last but certainly not least to Miles F. McWilliams Sr., it's a pleasure working with you every day. Thank you for imparting your knowledge and experience to me.

1

Faint strands of the boisterous music playing in the ballroom drifted down the long hallway of the earl of Pembishire's home in Berkeley Square. It curled into the warmth of the elegant study where Lady Arielle Stanford and her dearest friend, Lady Georgette Wagner, had retreated in search of privacy and a moment's peace from their chaperons, Lady Agatha Stanford Wilford and her husband, Dr. Morgan Wilford. Most of all, they had retreated away from the curiosity seekers who had come to pay homage to Hunter Braxton, the marquess of Savage.

Few had actually seen Savage since his victorious return from Waterloo after helping to defeat the Corsican. However, Pembishire and his wife were friends of Savage, and the countess had promised to deliver the man tonight for all to see, admire, and drool over—given that he was rumored to be a man of immense wealth.

But Arielle had discredited the tasteless discussions of his possessions; she didn't care that his features supposedly made one wonder how a man could truly be *that* handsome. Besides, knowing how exaggerated facts became in their retelling, Arielle's only purpose for allowing her sister to drag her here was to see Georgette.

She hadn't seen Georgie in three months because she had been too busy tending to her own scandalous dreams to get away. Now she was sorry she hadn't suggested she and Georgie get together some other time. Boredom at the mundane conversations in the ballroom overtook all enthusiasm.

Restless, she sank deeper into her comfortable wing chair and raised her half-filled champagne glass in salute. She took a sip, then sighed. "Georgie, tell me again why you brought me in here."

"Really, Ellie," Georgette huffed, thrusting a hand through her upswept black hair. "Isn't there anything else in the entire realm that interests you besides medicine? Of course, I believe that's something to take your mind off the unfortunate circumstances of your birth."

"Oh, Georgie," Arielle said with a chuckle, setting her crystal flute down on the small mahogany table next to her. "Don't go on so. Just because I'm determined to become England's first female physician doesn't mean that it's my *only* interest." In truth, though, in her single-minded determination to pursue her dream of becoming a doctor, she had ignored, even forgotten, every one of her other interests. "As for my patrilineage," she continued, her mood turning solemn, "and as ambiguous as my feelings are for Thomas at times, he is the only father I've ever known." If not for her father's explosive temper, she never would have discovered her illegitimacy. But at the age of eleven, six years after her mother's death, Thomas, angered by Arielle's determination to care for a bird with a broken wing that she'd found, had labeled her as the bastard that she was.

He'd wanted her to get to a fitting to have a gown made for a dinner party he was giving for one of her sisters. She'd wanted just a few minutes more to bandage the bird's wing. From that war of wills, her entire life had changed forever. In one vicious tirade, she'd finally realized Thomas's treatment of her varied between fatherly love and angry resentment.

Georgie drained her own glass of champagne and set it aside, drawing Arielle's attention back to the conversation. Georgie rubbed a hand over her belly in a way that made Arielle curious, but spoke again before Arielle questioned her. "The man who sired you was married at the time of your mother's mistake, if I remember correctly."

"That's what it was, you know, Georgie?" Arielle said softly, hugging herself. "A mistake. Mama never would have betrayed Thomas, unless she was seduced and coerced into doing so. The one thing I remember about Mama, besides her love and protection toward me, was her great love for Thomas." She paused momentarily, caught up in the emotion of missed years of her mother's support and guidance. "If you don't mind, I really don't want to discuss my parentage."

"Of course, Ellie. I am so honored that you've shared your secret with me all these years."

Arielle smiled. "You know none of that matters to me anymore. Medicine is what motivates me."

"I understand that Agatha practically needed wild horses to drag you away from the books Quentin gives you."

Folding her arms and raising her chin in defiance, Arielle sat straighter in her chair. Her sisters couldn't keep anything to themselves. "Where did you hear that?" she asked, already knowing the answer.

"Agatha told me," Georgette said with a mischievous laugh.

"Agatha couldn't keep a secret if she were in imminent danger of losing her elegantly coiffed head," Arielle stated without rancor, rising from her seat. "Perhaps we had better rejoin the others before Lady Shepperton sends a brigade to seek us out."

"Of course," Georgie agreed, coming to her feet. "But first I must tell you why I asked you in here."

"Exactly why did you?"

"To prove a point, Ellie."

Arielle frowned, unsure what her friend meant. "What point?"

"The chaperon point, silly. Look around you," she said, indicating the empty room with a sweep of her manicured hand. "Our chaperons are so busy with their own interests they've forgotten all about us."

Theirs was a special circumstance; Arielle's family served as chaperons for them both, which made Georgette subject to the same attention, or lack thereof, that Arielle normally received from her kin. "So?"

"So? So Eric and I have taken advantage of our time alone numerous times."

"Georgette!"

A dazzling smile lit Georgie's pretty features, her un-blemished complexion pinkening. Unremorseful, she shrugged and rubbed her stomach again with a protective, motherly gesture that Arielle witnessed whenever she made house calls with Quentin.

Gasping in horror as comprehension dawned, Arielle looked at her friend's flat belly. "What are you saying?" she asked.

"That I am with child."

Silence met Georgie's matter-of-fact statement. Arielle and Georgette had grown up together, daughters of two best friends who in turn became best friends. They were both the youngest members of large families and had lost their mothers six years apart—Arielle at six and Georgette at twelve. But that's where their similarities ended.

Arielle had never believed in love and babies and wed-dings the way she should have. She didn't want to give up her life and have her ideas and beliefs molded into one unequivocal opinion—her husband's. Georgie, on the other hand, thought differently. She believed there was a man for every woman, and that man would be her other half, the missing link to eternal love, the mirror of her soul.

Apparently, Georgie had found that man in Eric.

A twinge of envy hit Arielle, surprising her. But she ignored it and rushed to her friend. At a loss for words, she embraced Georgie tightly. "Wh . . . I . . . Oh, Geor-gette!"

"Calm down, Ellie," Georgette said softly, patting Arielle's back. "Don't go into apoplexy."

"B-but aren't you the least bit concerned? Think of the scandal!"

"*You're* worried about scandal, Lady Dr. Stanford? A gentlewoman with aspirations to lower herself to the working class?" Georgette asked with a laugh, stepping out of Arielle's embrace and shivering dramatically. "You mightn't ever recover your good name. On the other hand, Eric and I love each other, Ellie. So where's the worry, darling?"

Suddenly melancholy, Arielle worried her bottom lip.

"There you are!" a melodious voice chimed.

Lady Julia Shepperton, the countess of Pembishire, breezed in, her burgundy and silver gown a glaring testament to her hourglass figure. An exquisite woman, she had chestnut hair, gleaming gold-green eyes, and a smile pasted upon her painted lips. Her superior look spoke volumes. She had overheard part of the conversation—if not all of it.

Arielle smiled, as patently false as the countess. "Julia," she said, standing in front of Georgette, who had paled upon Julia's surprise entrance. If Julia chose to drag Georgie's name through the mud, no one could stop her. As merely a baron's daughter, Georgie mightn't be so lucky as to weather the damage a countess could do her in society, especially if Eric didn't stand by her through the storm. But hopefully Julia wasn't that hypocritical, given the affair she was presently engaged in with Arielle's father. "How rude we must appear to you. Deserting the festivities you've planned for everyone."

Julia smiled, her catlike eyes devoid of friendliness. "Nonsense, little Arielle. I understand completely your interests. You'd much prefer to be traipsing around with the good doctor than circulating amongst your own set. No wonder no man wants you." She patted Arielle's shoulder. "Be at ease, darling. You're not rude, just naive. In case you didn't know, everyone needs a pause now and again, even from one of my parties."

Arielle shrugged away from Julia, her heart pounding with hurt, her cheeks burning with indignation. She hated the countess's smug reminder that, even now, two years after her debut, she'd found no one who would want her enough to marry her despite her dreams.

"I would say *especially* from one of your parties, my lady," she retorted, as sugary as Julia, knowing she only left herself open for more of Julia's taunts.

The countess arched a fine eyebrow. "My dear Arielle, whatever do you mean? In the event you find fault, I'll certainly scratch your name off my list."

Georgette jumped in quickly. "You're most understanding, Lady Pembishire. It's been ages since Arielle and I have seen one another. We needed a moment alone together and it was wonderful."

"I can only imagine," Julia said, looking down her nose at Georgette. "However, I thought you would be interested in the imminent arrival of Lord Savage, my guest of honor."

The tension was thick enough to choke them. Georgette cleared her throat. "Isn't that the reason we're all here? To meet the elusive marquess?"

"Indeed," Julia announced and departed the chamber.

Arielle and Georgie followed slowly in the wake of the countess's expensive perfume.

Ignoring the fine paintings lining the wall, Georgie whispered, "Perhaps meeting the marquess will focus your passion on something other than medicine. Namely *him*."

"You're incorrigible, Georgie," Arielle returned in exasperation. "No matchmaking!"

When Georgie didn't respond, they fell into silence. But Arielle prayed her friend took her seriously. In the two years since she'd come out, she had had numerous suitors, none of whom impressed her. She was realistic enough to know that she'd probably turn into an old maid. Yet Georgie wasn't a realist by any stretch of the imagination. She acted on impulse and lived on her dreams. It would be just like her to try to get Arielle and the marquess together and expect it to work out.

Her friend truly was incorrigible, but she needed protection from the viperous tongue of Lady Pembishire. Because of Georgie's association with Arielle, Julia might choose to humiliate Georgie and announce her pregnancy to the world. Especially since Julia so enjoyed spreading gossip.

Perhaps Arielle could talk her father into convincing Julia to be discreet in this matter. Yet her father would never do it. Thomas never did anything Arielle asked of him. His need to have her at his beck and call for assistance in whatever project he was currently involved in, was the only reason he hadn't married her off yet to one of her suitors.

She had pleaded with Thomas to help her gain attendance at the Royal College of Physicians, but he had turned her down without considering her request. Without even listening to what so compelled her to seek entrance.

"You'll ruin our good name, Arielle!" he'd shouted in his usual overbearing manner. "And I won't be a party to that. Do you hear me, girl?"

"I understand perfectly, Papa," she'd snapped back.

She'd refrained from shouting that his affair with the countess of Pembishire was just as scandalous. Thomas hadn't a clue that she knew his secret, but she'd seen them in the throes of passion in her father's office on Christmas Eve and still blushed at *what* she'd seen. Her father had no right to be so judgmental and callous. He completely disregarded her need to study medicine.

Still, she wouldn't allow him to deter her. She'd thought having a powerful man like her father behind her would aid her quest. But she'd just have to find another way to follow through with her plans.

They reached the ballroom. The musicians had taken a break, but chatter buzzed through the chamber. The popping of a champagne cork reached her ears, followed

shortly by the tinkling of glasses. Trilling laughter erupted
and Arielle groaned.

She really wasn't up to this evening and couldn't wait
for Julia to introduce the marquess so she could make her
excuses and slip away. Arielle had a lot of thinking to do.

"Excuse me," Julia said politely. "I see my husband
gesturing for me."

"Where is the marquess?" Georgie inquired, craning her
neck to see the man of the hour.

A frown marred Julia's features as she too glanced
around the crowded room. "I don't see him. Hhmmm . . .
that's strange. His arrival was noted by two guests."

"Perhaps we are overlooking him in the crowd, Julia,"
Arielle offered.

"Nonsense. Hunter is a tall man, quite hard to miss.
Now, excuse me," Julia said, going in the direction of her
husband.

It wasn't long before Georgette went to Eric's side and
Arielle found herself standing with other guests and sipping champagne as they listened to Julia apologize that
the marquess wouldn't be attending after all. Instead of
holding her public embarrassment against him, however,
she stood and expounded upon the merits of her honored
no-show.

Bored almost to tears, Arielle's mind drifted as she perused the room, looking for the marquess. Apparently, the
two guests had been mistaken. She noted Agatha and
Morgan seemed engrossed in Julia's words and she
smiled. It had been her sister and physician husband
who'd introduced Arielle to Dr. Quentin DeVries, nearly
three years ago. And it was Quentin who had piqued Arielle's long-standing but latent interest in medicine. He
had honed that interest to a fine point, impressed by her
genuine compassion, surprised by her innate knack for the
healing arts. Now, becoming a doctor was an all-
consuming dream of hers.

A dream that couldn't come true unless she became
licensed. Due to a relatively new law, it was illegal for

her to practice the type of medicine she wanted to without becoming licensed. It was impossible to become licensed without having proof of training. And it was unheard-of that highborn women attended universities.

She swallowed hard, her dilemma inescapable. Needing a diversion, she glanced to where Georgie and Eric stood. It was obvious they only had eyes for each other. Arielle chuckled to herself. Georgette was right. If she and Eric wanted to steal away at the moment, no one would gainsay them. Their chaperons, Agatha and Morgan, weren't paying the slightest bit of attention to Arielle or Georgette. Even *she* could steal away if she wished.

With a sigh, Arielle refocused her attention on Julia's droning voice.

"Of course we have all heard of Hunter's heroic deeds at Waterloo. But few of us know how benevolent he really is. He has consistently aided the poor with both money and goods. And he has made many a dreamer's wish come true."

"How wonderful," a listener expressed. "Those qualities in anyone are commendable alone, Lady Shepperton, but you forgot to include his fabulous wealth!"

"Well, that is a plus for all the unmarried hopefuls here," Julia said brittlely, her displeasure at the vulgar comment obvious in the rigid stance of her body. She cleared her throat. "That aside, however, the expected introductions must wait for another time since his lordship is . . . er, unavailable at the moment. He has been detained at Braxton Hall. But this doesn't mean the party is over. Please enjoy yourselves further. My dance card, for one, is still filled."

On cue, chuckles rose from the crowd before the circle of listeners, mostly women, began to disperse. Arielle wondered where the men had gone to; apparently so did their wives.

"Where has Harvey disappeared to?" an annoyed matron asked her friend.

"I think they all went to the card room. Come, Thea, we shall search there."

Watching as the women left, it came to Arielle that Eric, Morgan, and three other gentlemen seemed to be the only men in the room.

"Arielle," Agatha said as she walked up to her and put her arm around her. Morgan, Eric, and Georgie were right on her heels. "I'm sorry his lordship didn't show. I truly wanted you to meet him."

Annoyance flickered through Arielle and she glared at her sister. "Why?"

"Because he's very handsome and could very well change your present thinking about medicine," Georgie offered.

Agatha drew in an agitated breath. "I have no one to blame for that but Morgan for introducing Quentin to her."

"Me?" Morgan pointed a finger at himself. "I believe it was on your insistence that I did so."

"Oh, go have a cigar or something," Agatha snapped, waving him away.

"A spectacular idea, love," Morgan said with a smile. "Join me, Eric. I don't want you to hear my wife belittle me to her sister."

Big, strapping Lord Eric Astor, heir to an earldom, glanced at Georgette. His topaz gaze swept her with a steamy look, then he said, "May I?"

"Go on," Georgie said and laughed when he bowed with drama before following Morgan in the direction of the card room.

Arielle smiled, taking notice of who was really in charge in that relationship. She wouldn't be averse to having a relationship with someone who understood her need to aid the sick and become a doctor.

Because of current strictures, however, that would never happen. She had no one to marry her and no prominent person who'd be willing to help her. . . .

Arielle paused, Julia's words flooding her senses. *He*

has made many a dreamer's wish come true.

Of course! The marquess of Savage.

She'd pen a note to him, asking his help. What harm could there be? Chances were he'd laugh at such a high-handed request and simply ignore her. Then again, maybe he'd take her seriously and help her. She wouldn't know unless she tried her luck. As soon as she got home, she'd write him a letter and have it hand-delivered the first thing in the morning.

"Come along, Ellie." Georgette pulled her toward the refreshment table. Patting her belly, she winked at Arielle. "I'm famished."

"You two go ahead," Agatha said. "I'm going to find Julia."

After trying unsuccessfully to leave the festivities early, Arielle fidgeted for the next two hours, her idea nearly causing her to go into apoplexy for want of implementing it. Finally, Agatha gathered their party together and announced it was time to depart.

She arrived home not long after and hurried to her bed-chamber. A soft light glowed in the cheeriness of the bright yellow decor. Her fireplace remained unlit but the chill hanging in the air hardly touched her. Excitement thrummed through her body, warming her blood and pumping through her veins. She sat at her desk, stacked high with medical books. Before she forgot the words jamming together in her head, she took paper and pen from the top drawer and began.

Most Honorable Lord Braxton . . .

Arielle wrinkled her nose at how pretentious the letter was starting off, even if it was the correct way to address him. Yet she doubted someone so willing to aid the poor was worried about pretenses.

Hoping she made the correct decision, she grabbed another piece of paper and started over.

Dear Lord Braxton,
   I regret that I did not meet you at the earl of Pembishire's party tonight. However, I heard grand

*things about you, your bravery, your benevolence,
and your willingness to help in making one's
dreams come true. I have an avid interest in gaining
entrance to the Royal College of Physicians. I suppose I should tell you that I am a woman. Please
don't be shocked by my brashness. To become a
doctor is my passion and I have no one else to help
me but you. I await your reply with great anticipation.*

*Yours truly,
Lady Arielle Stanford*

2

"Your missives, milord. Including this special post. Delivered by a private liveryman."

Hunter Braxton, marquess of Savage, watched as his butler set a small stack of letters and pamphlets within reach on the dining table. But Wilfred kept the special envelope in his hand, holding it out as Hunter glanced at the delicate penmanship on the expensive parchment. "Undoubtedly another invitation," he said with a sigh, taking it from the retainer and dropping it on the pile. "I'll read it with the others."

With distaste, he eyed the bowl of porridge he'd been served a short while ago and pushed it aside, then smiled at his nearly bald and clean-shaven servant, and rubbed his eyes.

Hunter could use companionship, but he was tired of being used as the main attraction for a social climber's party.

"Thank you for bringing these in, Wilfred," he told the short, stocky man, one of the two servants he'd kept on during his years out of England.

Hunter had known Wilfred and Geoffrey since he'd been in leading strings and he shared a genuine affection for both men. It stood to reason he'd retain them no matter what. Certainly, his eight-year absence away from home had proved that point.

They were both retainers whose original positions were blurred by the lines of time. While he had been away serving king and country, they had been dutifully serving him, caring for his estates, managing his household. In his stead, they'd made monthly visits here, to his ancestral seat, Braxton Hall, on the coast. They chose to live at Hunter's London town house on Park Lane on the western border of Hyde Park. Hunter didn't know their exact ages, but Geoffrey and Wilfred had been old when he was a child. They were nothing less than ancient now.

Yet, whenever he broached the subject of their retirement, they balked at the idea. It didn't matter that he intended to give them each a large settlement and monthly pension, along with their choice of living anywhere they desired—even with him. They wanted to remain at his side and run his household as they had for as long as he remembered.

And, in truth, Hunter would be lost without them. To him, Geoffrey and Wilfred were so much more than mere servants. They were his family and the only constant since his uncle died after having raised Hunter as his own son.

Wilfred removed the bowl of untouched porridge. "It wasn't to your liking, milord?"

"Wilfred, I ate enough porridge in the army to satisfy a lifetime."

"Perhaps his lordship would prefer sausage, kippers, and eggs," Geoffrey announced, pushing a cart into the dining room. Thick whiskers, once chestnut brown but now white, vibrated beneath the man's frown as he glared at the porridge in Wilfred's thick hands. "We thought the porridge would have been a good start to your breakfast, my lord, but decided you needed something more substantial. A growing lad like yourself."

Hunter repressed a smile. At thirty-three, he was hardly "a growing lad" any longer. "You shouldn't have, Geoffrey." But his mouth watered and his stomach grumbled at the tantalizing aromas of the fresh baked bread, fried eggs, sausages, kippers, and baked apples with clotted cream.

His belly rumbled again, and satisfaction gleamed in Wilfred's dark eyes. "I'll get your tea, milord."

"Thank you." Hunter surveyed the dishes that Geoffrey set before him on the small table, then dug in with relish when he was served. Hungry also for company, he almost made the mistake of calling Geoffrey and Wilfred in to dine with him, but they were sticklers for protocol regarding those matters and would never accept the invitation.

At least tonight, he'd be surrounded with dozens of people, all terribly curious about the mysterious marquess of Savage, the man who had all but shunned society for most of his life; the man who was amongst the most eligible bachelors in the realm. The man with the secrets of his past plaguing him.

When he finished his meal, Hunter stood and took the stack of letters. He went into the long hallway and ignored the peeling walls and dull floors. Most of the manor needed remodeling. Although Geoffrey and Wilfred looked after things, they hardly saw to its upkeep. Braxton Hall had been shut down for eight years and it showed.

Hunter had come here only once since his return last August. Now that the buzz of the Christmas holidays was past, he'd decided it was time to tackle the huge task of bringing the estate up to par. It would be costly and time-consuming, but it would give him a chance to explore his options.

It was well past time to take a wife. He had to decide, however, if he wanted to risk the good name of a nobleman's daughter if his past ever came to light.

In his study, he sat at his desk and dropped the letters before him. Frowning at the moldy, closed-in scent, he opened the window nearest him, despite the air's chill, then returned his attention to the letters. He glanced at the first pamphlet on the stack of letters, an announcement of a public gala taking place in the near future at Vauxhall Gardens.

Due to the attention he'd have to give Braxton Hall for the next several months, he really didn't care about galas, public or private. No, *especially* private, he amended. And

especially not an affair given by his friend's wife, Julia
Shepperton.

How Douglas was able to abide that woman for so long
was certainly beyond Hunter. He once had, but only
briefly and years ago. Their affair had been strictly sexual
and he'd soon gotten tired of her demands. Apparently,
age hadn't mellowed her. He'd been back from his cam-
paigns less than a week when she'd invited him to a small
intimate dinner. A "welcome home" party, she'd said.
Hunter had arrived to find a bevy of unwed hopefuls lined
up, vying for his hand in marriage. That repulsed him to
no end. He certainly wasn't a prized stud to be put on
display!

God only knew what the scheming woman had planned
this time. At least she'd been honest enough to inform
him of its magnitude. Yet the only reason he'd accepted
the invitation as her guest of honor was because of Doug.
He wouldn't insult his friend's overbearing wife by refusing her.

Which meant he was in for a long night.

Browsing through a few more letters, he found perfumed notes of greetings and invitations to parties given
by high-ranking peers. Which didn't impress him at all
since he had no intention of attending a single one of them
after tonight. Not for the next several months, at least.
And there was nothing and no one to make him change
his mind.

He suspected the contents of all the letters were pretty
much the same—all requesting his presence at some function. The repetition of it all bored him. Yet courtesy demanded that he open them all. That way, no one would
be left out when he sent his regards and regrets.

Picking up another envelope, he remembered this one
being delivered by "special post." Really, it hadn't been
delivered any differently than the rest. The only thing unusual about it was the word *urgent* scrawled across the
top.

With a sigh, he unfolded the letter. The same delicate

penmanship that was on the outside greeted him as he
started reading.

Dear Lord Braxton,

He paused at the greeting, surprised but appreciating
the simple style. A small smile pulling at his lips, he
started over.

> *Dear Lord Braxton,*
> *I regret that I did not meet you at the earl of*
> *Pembishire's party tonight. . . .*

Hunter froze as the sentence sunk in. *Tonight?* Gazing
at yesterday's date, he scowled. Last night? Cursing
roundly, he hurriedly read the rest of the letter. Bloody
hell. How could he have made such a blunder? Julia's
party had been last night.

He'd missed it!

He imagined the gaggle of disappointed women, hov-
ering on Julia's every word as she expounded upon his
doings, waiting faithfully by every entrance to the town
house. All of them certain he would put in an appearance
to choose one of them for a courtship.

The impact of that scene settled into him. He'd missed
it! There was a God after all, he chuckled to himself.
However, he'd pen a letter to the Sheppertons and explain
the mix-up. Douglas was an understanding man, and Julia
could not hold a grudge against him.

A breeze from the open window fluttered the forgotten
letter in his hand. His first thought was to set it aside, but
the writer had made a request of him. Hunter reread the
letter and frowned.

Lady Arielle Stanford.

He'd never heard of her. But, he'd been away . . . a lifetime. And before that, he hadn't circulated amongst the
ton very much. He didn't know many of them, yet it
seemed as if everyone knew him. Added to that was Julia's propensity to stretch the truth whenever she spoke
of him.

True, he had given aid to those who asked it of him, but he wasn't a fairy godfather, out to save the world. He was merely a wealthy man, and a high-ranking lord, out to do his part in aiding the poor and downtrodden.

Her stationery and writing told him Lady Stanford was well-off and refined. Her signature told him she was titled. Beyond that, he knew nothing of her. Hunter did know, however, about dreams. His own remained unfulfilled. He had absolutely no one to help him turn his dream into reality. For all the wealth that he had, all the power he could wield for others, he was helpless in his own quest—to discover the facts surrounding his birth.

Now, he had the chance to help someone else, a lady of quality with no one else to turn to. Her letter was brief, but he felt it came from her heart.

Obviously, the poor woman was desperate. What woman would risk revealing to a stranger her deepest desire otherwise? He imagined she was a spinster far beyond marriageable age who'd finally decided to pursue her life's wish. Or maybe she was just frightfully unattractive and wanting to become a physician served as her way to gain her independence.

She deserved his help and he'd try to aid her in her quest. Besides, her letter saved him from making a fool of himself by showing up at the Sheppertons tonight.

Still, Hunter wondered why a woman of her standing would consider a male-dominated profession. A profession that she had virtually no chance of penetrating. She was setting herself up for heartbreak.

Had she considered the scorn and prejudices she'd suffer if she happened to succeed in her goal of being accepted into the university?

Pity for the unfortunate woman engulfed him. Without further ado, he took pen and paper from his drawer and began writing.

> Dear Lady Arielle,
>   Thank you for your letter requesting my help to gain attendance at the Royal College. Before I can

lend my assistance to you, however, I propose that
we meet at your estate at your earliest convenience
to discuss why a lady of good breeding is interested
in becoming a physician.
 I look forward to your reply.

> *Most cordially yours,*
> *Hunter*

He sealed the letter, penned a letter of apology to Julia,
then sent Geoffrey to deliver both missives.

That done, he pulled out the list of supplies he needed
to begin working on the estate. He was anxious to restore
Braxton Hall and put his life together. Or at least make
sense of the circumstances surrounding his birth.

His *illegitimate* birth.

He really had no time to make the dreams of a desperate spinster come true. He had too many of his own to
see to.

3

"Arielle, are you listening?" Dr. Quentin DeVries asked with annoyance, his hands firmly on his hips as he frowned at her.

Her dear friend had every reason to be irritated with her, Arielle thought, carefully focusing her attention on Quentin and the postmortem examination he was performing. This was the sixth time she'd sat in on the procedure. The first time she'd actually fainted and she wasn't the fainting type; the second time she'd thrown up. After four additional sit-ins, she ignored the slight queasiness she experienced at the sight of organs and tissues laid open.

She knew she was there to learn, but her thoughts continued to stray. She'd had a restless night, reproaching herself during most of it for her brashness in sending Lord Savage the letter.

If only she could retrieve it!

Too late, however. By now, Lord Savage had no doubt received it. What must he think of her? A highborn lady seeking to enter the field of medicine. Besides laughing himself into spasmodic fits over the letter's contents, he was likely too busy to concern himself with her plight.

At loose ends, Arielle moved from the opposite side of the table, stopping next to Quentin. He was pleasantly handsome, with a thick mop of brown hair, chocolate brown eyes, and a slim, lanky body. He was also one of the kindest people she knew. In the two and a half years since she'd met him, he had become a trusted confidant.

She wouldn't ever want to do anything to offend him. "Forgive me."

"I realize you have a lot to contend with at the moment," he said without inflection. Not waiting for a response, he raised a perforated appendix he had just extracted from the patient. "This poor gentleman suffered from perityphlitis. You can see the suppuration in the organ. It correlates with his previous illness, wouldn't you say?"

"I suppose so," Arielle conceded slowly, studying it. On previous occasions, she had seen other appendixes that had been undamaged and knew this one was diseased. "It looks like inflammation and peritonitis had set in as well."

"Indeed it does." Quentin carefully laid the infected organ on a tray covered with a white towel. "These types of examinations are a window to future diagnoses and treatments, Arielle. I believe surgery might have saved this man's life."

Arielle raised an eyebrow at that suggestion. "Surgery? Isn't that a rather radical step? After all, you are a physician and not a surgeon."

"Yes, I am," Quentin agreed, his attention on the exam. "However, if this man had had his appendix surgically removed, his life might have been saved. What did he have to lose by trying the procedure?"

"Nothing, I suppose," Arielle said quietly. "And I can understand your desire to perform the operation. He was your patient and he trusted you. I only wonder, should I face such a dilemma would I live up to my calling?"

Quentin gazed at her briefly and smiled. "Of course you would. Licensed or not, instinct would guide you."

"As well as the lessons I've learned from you."

"Yes, which includes these postmortem exams. I tell you, Arielle, until I started performing these, the notes that I had taken were meaningless."

"I'm sure they were, Quentin," Arielle said softly, envious of the education he had received. She could go through her entire life waiting for Oxford, Cambridge, the

Royal College, and the other universities to allow her to walk their hallowed halls as a student. Or she could forget all sensibilities and send the marquess another letter requesting his aid if he didn't respond to her soon.

She sighed, her interest in Quentin's current study sorely lacking. Restless, she walked to the window and gazed out. A gentle rain had fallen for most of the morning, reminding her that her life wasn't as she wanted it to be. She wanted acceptance from her family, attention from her father. She wanted an office of her own, where patients near and far visited her. She wanted love and happiness, which she knew she could never have. What man would want her?

Leaning her head against the windowpane, she closed her eyes to ward off her dejection. First and foremost, she wanted to become a doctor.

"Quentin, will we ever marry?" she asked abruptly, the question rising out of the ashes of her despair. "I mean, we respect each other's opinions and we admire one another. We can very well marry for our careers."

"Of course, sweet," he said from behind her, no inflection of surprise in his voice. "Who else would want us?"

Turning to face him, she found his head still bent at his task. Her heart sank at his dry resignation. Who else would want them indeed? *More to the point, who else would want me?* She was more than certain Quentin could make a love match. "When will it take place? You know you're like kin to me."

"I cannot answer that, Arielle. I thought to ask you upon your twenty-first birthday, when your father could put up no opposition." He shrugged, still busy at his task. Finally pausing, he looked up. His dark gaze searched her and he smiled with bittersweet poignancy. "I have a lifetime of work that I want to share with you, but I also have desires of my own that I am determined to see happen. Until that time, I can't ask for your hand."

"I know. We once spoke of opening a hospice for the poor."

"Yes, we did. And we can still do that. It just won't be soon." Without further comment, Quentin returned to his work.

Arielle watched her friend work, admiring his skill and determination, hoping that she could one day match them. Yet her confusion over conflicting desires tormented her. She wouldn't wait forever to become Quentin's wife. She wanted to become a mother and share all the things with her sons and daughters that she had been deprived of by her own mama's death.

Those thoughts led her to believe that she wasn't as dedicated as she told herself. How could any lady balance the demands of being a wife and mother *and* still be productive in a career? Women weren't meant to do both. Her sole purpose in life was supposed to be the care and concern of her husband and family.

Not any determination to set a different course for herself.

4

Thomas, Viscount Stanford, watched from his study as his youngest daughter made her way back home. His jaw tautened as she paid the driver, then rushed toward the front door. Thomas knew full well that she'd spent her day with Quentin DeVries, but didn't feel the need to expend his precious energies trying to stay her hand.

Raising five daughters without a wife had been difficult enough. Being left with the youngest, who had nothing of him in her, yet who was most like his beloved dead wife, and thus a reminder of her horrible secret, was almost more than Thomas could bear.

He wanted Arielle always near him and at the same time, far, far away. It was madness, he knew, but there were times when he couldn't look into Arielle's face without remembering the beginning of her life. At other times, he remembered she was the daughter he had raised in his wife's stead, and he loved her as fiercely as he did his other girls.

It shamed him to admit his indecision and so he handled it by leaving Arielle to her own devices as much as he possibly could. But he hated that she spent so much time with Quentin. He'd hoped that she'd have gotten her fill of the sick and infirm by now. Instead, her determination to become a physician grew deeper and deeper.

If he didn't do something soon, she'd shame him before the entire ton. As it was, rumors were starting to spread.

"Maisy, I'm famished. Would you mind preparing a meal for me?"

Arielle's voice addressing the housekeeper swirled to him through the ajar door.

"Of course, my lady."

"Thank you. I'll be in the dining room."

Thomas listened to Arielle's retreating footsteps. For a moment, he considered letting her eat alone, but he was hungry as well. Besides, it might do some good to show a little interest in Arielle today. His debts were deepening dangerously and she might just be the key to everything.

Arielle sat at the gleaming dining table with her father. Partial sunshine filled the small chamber, glistening through the spotless sash windows.

It had surprised her to see her father in residence so late in the afternoon, but she didn't question his reason. Besides, her disappointment at not finding a response from the marquess of Savage took away any interest in her father's affairs.

"Arielle, my dear, is something troubling you today?"

Guilt swept through Arielle. She could never tell him that she'd attempted to obtain the marquess's help. Her father would never understand. He was adamant against her becoming a doctor and made her feel unworthy of his love every time she mentioned it. Still, she'd never hidden anything from him before. "Of course not, Papa."

Absently trailing the spotless mahogany table, she smiled again, searching his eyes, hoping to find a bit of understanding. Of course he knew what troubled her. He *always* knew what troubled her. He just didn't give it much regard. "What could be troubling me?"

Thomas swiped a napkin across his mouth. "I haven't seen Quentin around here," he said pointedly. "Have you and the good doctor finally seen the folly of your misguided dreams?"

"Oh, Papa," Arielle answered, allowing her annoyance to surface in the tone of her voice. Speaking this way to her father was rare for her, but well justified at the moment, she felt. If he'd been more willing to listen to her, she never would have turned to the marquess of Savage for help. The humiliation she felt at her actions would never have come about. She had tried everything she could think of, without success. When that didn't work, Quentin stepped in for her. But the one person who should have been proud to do whatever he could, consistently refused. "Must you always be so contentious? You've always known how I feel about the field of medicine. Quentin and I—"

"Your sister should never have allowed her husband to introduce you to Quentin DeVries. The man is feeding your dreams with false hopes, Arielle. I keep hoping for the day you acquire a little sense. You must get the silly notion of becoming a physician out of your mind, my dear." Thomas glared at her. Leaning back in his seat, his bulk spilling over the sturdy wooden arms of the chair, he looked down his nose at her.

Arielle bowed her head, resenting her father and his words. He had the ability to make her feel a dozen years younger, like a six-year-old child who sought permission for a treat instead of an eighteen-year-old adult who wanted help to achieve a life's dream.

"Not only is it an impossible dream, it's a scandal in the making, child. You are a gentlewoman and shouldn't lower your standards in hopes of becoming part of the working class. I rue the day I ever consented to your friendship with DeVries," he finished, his voice cold and hard.

Ignoring the hurt flooding her, Arielle swallowed hard. She should be used to her father's scathing criticism of her. Lately, it occurred more frequently and she knew he had some type of problem worrying him. A problem that went much deeper than his ridiculous affair with Julia Shepperton. Arielle knew it had to do with their finances. He had spent a small fortune redecorating their town house in the latest styles, while still enjoying his usual visits to the gaming hells. Mounting debts made his dark moods easier to understand. But it also deepened his derision toward Quentin. Yet no matter how much Thomas needed to lash out, she couldn't allow him to mock her.

She stared at him with the same intensity with which he looked at her, disregarding his ugly frown of distaste. "It isn't a silly notion, Papa," she said softly. "It's what I want to do."

Thomas sighed. "Perhaps *silly* was a poor choice of words, child," he said in a more reasonable tone. "I certainly did not mean to disparage your hopes."

"I understand, Papa," Arielle replied, buttering a biscuit. "You were missed last night," she went on, changing the subject while she was still ahead. "Although the marquess didn't put in an appearance either."

"Really? Poor Julia must have been awfully disappointed."

Unable to stop the memory of seeing her father's and Julia's bodies entwined on the floor, Arielle cast him an accusatory glance at his sorrowful tone. "Why, Papa?" she snapped, before she could stop herself. "Because of the marquess's absence or yours?"

Thomas's green eyes widened, then narrowed; a blush crept from his neck and into his face. "How dare you!" he sputtered in surprise. The guilt on his face confirmed what she already knew. "What are you implying, young lady?"

Could she really sit there and accuse her father of such improprieties, even if she had seen them with her own eyes? No, she couldn't. He was her father. And he was human, which meant he wasn't perfect. Besides, she truly loved him, even though his overbearance made him hard to abide at times.

"I beg your pardon, Papa. I'm very observant, you know? It must be a doctor's curiosity that makes me so," she told him with a smile, sipping her warm tea.

Thomas's color deepened. Instead of assuaging him, she'd managed to stoke his always simmering temper. "And what have you observed?" he demanded.

Setting her cup down, Arielle cleared her throat and studied her hands. She shrugged at her father's question. "Just that you and Julia have spent an inordinate amount of time together. And at the oddest hours too." *And in the oddest positions,* she added silently, though wisely keeping that thought to herself.

"Why . . . you . . . I never . . . Arielle!"

Arielle forced a lighthearted giggle, unable to do much else. Long ago, she'd discerned the difference between how he treated her and her sisters. They had been sheltered and shielded. She, on the other hand, knew too much, too soon. Growing up, she'd envied her father's reverence for her four older sisters. Arielle believed that her father loved her as he did her sisters, but in a different way. In them, he had no resentment. For her, he always had a reminder of the past.

"Papa, don't give yourself a stroke. You're both adults. But you should certainly be more discreet around one another."

Sadness enveloping him, Thomas lowered his head. "Arielle, child. I—I don't know what to say. We thought we *were* being discreet," he said regretfully. "I'm . . . I've been very lonely since the death of your mama."

Outside of his clubs and his gambling, Arielle had long been aware of the solitary life her father had led for the past twelve years without a wife to share it with. Yet she wouldn't excuse his inappropriate behavior with a married woman. Nor would she continue to condemn him. At the least, he needed her understanding, and wondering about her own future made it easier to give. In twelve or fifteen years, when she was well past her marrying years, would she too pine for companionship?

"It's all right, Papa," Arielle said tenderly. "Sometimes we fall into unfavorable situations. I wish to see you happy."

Thomas reached over and patted her hand. "Thank you, child," he said gratefully.

"By the by," Arielle went on, her thoughts settling on

Georgette. Her friend was a bit too flighty for her own good and needed all the protection she could get. Hopefully Thomas would help with this, at least. "Last night Julia overheard a conversation, between Georgie and me, that was meant solely for my ears. I trust she too will exercise discretion in the matter." She rose from her chair and threw her arms around Thomas's shoulders, her father's expression nearly causing her to collapse in laughter. Yet it conveyed his understanding that Julia's silence would ensure her own.

"I believe there's a form of extortion somewhere in that statement," Thomas said with a weak smile, his guilty look only intensifying.

Arielle laughed and kissed his cheek. Somehow, she'd reached a turning point with her father this morning. No, he still hadn't agreed to help her—he was as adamant as ever regarding that. Yet she had stood up to him and talked openly with him about Julia Shepperton. It wasn't a true test of what she hoped was a new beginning between them, for he had asked nothing of her, but it was a start.

"Excuse me, milady," the housekeeper said, coming into the breakfast room, holding an envelope. "This letter was just delivered for you."

Reaching for it, Arielle's heart skipped a beat. "Thank you, Maisy," she said, squelching the urge to rip it open and study it. Finding no telltale waxed seals or crest burst Arielle's anticipation. Addressed only to "Lady Arielle Stanford," it gave no clue as to who sent it.

The hope that it was from the marquess rose within Arielle and her heart pounded. Such wishful thinking. He'd certainly not make a point of responding so promptly, if he intended to respond at all.

Thomas stood from his chair and pushed it under the table, then kissed her on the cheek. Looking over her shoulder at the envelope, he said, "Probably a request from your doctor friend, wanting you to join him in a house call, Arielle."

That was entirely possible, Arielle thought, shaking her

head slowly at the weariness and distaste in her father's voice. But this wasn't Quentin's handwriting.

"I'm sorry we quarreled, my dear. Have a pleasant day."

He walked past her and quit the room.

Following Thomas through the doorway, Arielle called, "You too, Papa," then she went into the parlor. There, she settled into the nearest chair and opened the envelope as fast as her shaking hands allowed. Then she began reading.

Her eyes widened at the words.

Not only had his lordship read her note, but he'd consented to help her. Of course she'd meet with him at her earliest convenience!

Rising to her feet, she twirled around the room, holding the letter close to her heart. Unadulterated joy lightened her step, swelled her heart. What a genuinely caring man. What a kindhearted, philanthropic soul. She'd cherish this letter, these words, *his* words, forever. It was the answer to her dreams, the key she needed to open a new world to her.

It was everything she'd ever hoped for.

It didn't matter that he wanted to meet with her to discuss her true motives. That was to be expected. He couldn't very well lend his assistance without being sure of her intentions.

Before I can lend my assistance to you was what Arielle concentrated on. Once he met her and she satisfied his concerns, he most definitely *would* lend his assistance. She'd be honest with him and tell him how much the field of medicine meant to her. He wouldn't deny her when she poured her heart out to him. He couldn't.

She gazed at his closing. *Most cordially yours, Hunter.* With that simple friendliness, she felt as if she already knew him. She didn't doubt that their meeting would go well.

Hardly able to contain her joy, she made her way to her bedchamber to write the marquess her reply, and a squeal of delight escaped her.

5

Dear Lord Hunter,

   Needless to say your ready response nearly left
me speechless. Thank you for consenting to aid a
maiden's most fervent dream. I accept your invitation to meet with you. However, we must do so at
your estate. For reasons I'd prefer not to mention,
it wouldn't be wise to have you call upon me at my
home. I am free every day except Mondays and
Thursdays. All other days, I can prepare myself for
availability at a moment's notice. Again, my sincere
thanks.

                                   Yours truly,
                                   Arielle

   Hunter chuckled at the close of the letter. Arielle. She
certainly didn't stand on ceremony. Quickly, she'd
grasped his intimation on informalities and followed his
lead. Yet beyond her seeming dislike for titles, there
wasn't much he could gather about her from her letter.
Except, maybe, that she sounded somewhat desperate.
But, then again, any "maiden" whose most fervent dream
was to become a doctor had to be desperate.
   He doubted she was a maiden. No young woman of
quality would risk her reputation and come unchaperoned
to a gentleman's estate.
   Hunter gazed around the barren walls of his receiving
parlor. The room was bare too, with most of the furniture

stored in the attic. He'd been in the midst of starting the long process of selecting color schemes for each room when Wilfred brought Arielle's letter to him.

Hunter stared at the fluid handwriting, as if the words, and their patterns, could whisper interesting tidbits about their owner. Lady Arielle Stanford intrigued him. The neat and meticulous writing intrigued him.

Neat and meticulous.

With a curse, Hunter looked around the empty chamber. The room could be called many things, but never neat and meticulous.

Despite her bluestockinged aspirations, she had been born a peer's daughter. As such, she didn't deserve to walk into Braxton Hall and see it in this condition. It was rotting, peeling, cracking, and disreputable. He didn't even have a housekeeper to dust.

That, however, would change immediately. Of course, he couldn't make Arielle wait until Braxton Hall was remodeled and redecorated. That would take months. Possibly years.

He'd wait another few days before extending an invitation to her to visit Braxton Hall. He'd tell Wilfred and Geoffrey that they needed to hire two women within the week.

Then, when the fascinating spinster walked in, she wouldn't find any improprieties with him. Even if *her* dreams left a lot to be desired.

For the next week, Arielle did naught but focus on her impending meeting with the marquess of Savage. A meeting that had yet to be scheduled. Unlike his first answer, he hadn't sent such a quick response this time.

Now, on the eighth day of her waiting, Arielle thought she might go mad. She had barely taken a walk outside in all that time, anticipating a reply and wanting to be there to send an answering yes that same day. Could he have been serious in his intention to help her? Or had he sent the response to teach her a lesson for disturbing him in what could only be to him a frivolous request?

To escape her mounting frustration, she decided to visit Quentin. He lived in the other end of town, so Arielle hired a hackney to take her there.

After paying the driver, she made her way toward the small building Quentin used as his residence, while thoughts that Hunter's letter was a cruel jest persisted. Still, Arielle knew she shouldn't, or couldn't, give up hope yet.

She smiled grimly as she reached the small gray door.

Quentin came from a family of good means and he could afford to live much better than in this densely populated section of London. But her friend wanted to be near the patients who so desperately needed him. The over-crowded, poorly built houses were breeding grounds for disease and death. But Quentin ignored all of that, for the sake of his patients.

Arielle's admiration for him ran deep and she was anxious to inform him of her wait for an answer from the most celebrated lord of the realm.

She raised her hand to knock, but the door swung open before she could. Quentin plowed right into her. If he hadn't grabbed her arm to steady her, she would have toppled over.

"Arielle! What are you doing here today?"

"Quentin, I didn't realize I needed an appointment to see you," she jested at the sound of his surprised voice.

"Never!" Quentin assured her, stepping onto the sidewalk and closing the door behind him. "Is someone ill—is it you?"

"Neither," Arielle told him, falling into step with him as he began walking. "I—I just needed to get away, and I thought I could lend a hand today."

"I can always use an extra pair of hands, Arielle. Especially ones as delicate as yours."

"Thanks for the compliment, Dr. DeVries," Arielle said

with a chuckle, "but I think you should know that I may
have found a patron—"

"A patron?"

"Yes. A patron. A benefactor." Arielle only hoped to
call it true.

"That's great tidings, Arielle. I knew your father would
come around to your way of thinking."

Arielle laughed at Quentin's assumption. "I declare,
Quentin. Your conjecture is solidly off the mark."

A brow raised. "I beg your pardon?"

"My father is steadfast in his decision against aiding
me. My benefactor, hopefully," she added as much for
equilibrium as for fairness, "is none other than the marquess of Savage."

Astonishment lighting his eyes, Quentin halted and
stared at her. "Surely you jest!"

Shaking her head, Arielle giggled and related to him
how the idea had come to her to seek his lordship's help.

"There should be no doubt in Lord Savage's mind that
you possess the cold nerve to become a physician," he
said, his amusement evident in the crinkling of his eyes
as he smiled. "Especially since that same unflinching
nerve penned such a request to him."

His statement irritated her. He'd never understand just
how deeply she'd agonized over her decision. "I never
said I didn't flinch," she snapped. "But one must do what
has to be done."

"I know," Quentin soothed, starting forward again.
"And I'm quite proud of you. Your determination will
bring you far. I've heard great things about the marquess.
If it's within his power, I can look forward to my friend
and colleague Dr. Arielle Stanford to aid me in my profession."

"Dr. Arielle Stanford," Arielle repeated in awe, imagining the sign with those words. "Dr. Arielle Stanford. I
can hardly credit such a miracle truly happening."

Quentin patted her on the back, his brotherly affection
welcome. "Your patience and faith have served you well,

Arielle. And your dedication is the miracle," he told her as he stopped in front of a shabby wood and concrete structure. "Reaching your goal will be well worth the wait."

Arielle focused on the building looming before her, realizing it was the home of Mrs. Portia Beecham, one of Quentin's patients.

Unlike her own world, no trees and gardens graced the houses. Here, filthy streets and crowded living conditions stole such serenity. The wails of young babies and the language of ruffians replaced the songs of birds and the delicate conversation of ladies and gentlemen out for a pleasure ride. Even the crisp air that Arielle loved seemed thick with misery.

But she knew there had to be a better way for these people. With more sanitary conditions, disease could be contained. With better nourishment, survival rates for the impoverished would increase. She knew too that if more physicians were available to the poor, there mightn't be as many sick and dying.

There was so much she wanted to do, so many ideas she had to share if she but had her chance. So many other obstacles stood in her way. First and foremost, she had to find a respectable medical school that would accept her as a student. Now that the government was requiring physicians to be licensed in order to practice, it was of the utmost importance to do so. Though she suspected that the law was too new for all doctors to comply, she knew she would have to remain within the boundaries of the law at all times if she wanted the smallest chance to succeed.

Everything depended on his lordship's success. Was he truly the answer to her prayers?

She smiled. "I suppose I have no choice but to wait," she thought out loud.

Quentin squeezed her hand then knocked on the door. A little boy answered. Tory's sad, round eyes in a too-thin face were always the first thing Arielle noticed about

him and today was no different. He smiled when he saw
Arielle; she stooped down and hugged him.

"How are you?" she asked cheerily.

"Fine, milady," the child answered. He didn't give her
a chance to respond before continuing. "Me mum is bad
off t'day."

"Is she out of her horehound syrup, lad?" Quentin
asked, brushing past them and stepping into the dark interior.

"Aye, Dr. DeVries," Tory answered, holding Arielle's
hand as they followed Quentin inside.

"Tell your mum that Arielle and I will return shortly.
We're going to purchase her medicine and then return to
check on her."

Arielle smiled brightly, focusing on the child and thinking about the widowed woman who lay beyond the thin
bedchamber door. She tousled Tory's thick curls. "Why
don't you and Dr. DeVries walk to the apothecary and
purchase whatever you need while I go chat with your
mother, lamb." She pulled out some pound notes and
handed them to Tory, who promptly handed the money
to Quentin.

Quentin looked pleased at this development. "Anything
else, my lady?"

"Yes. I'm sure Tory's mother and siblings would like
a nice meat stew tonight. While you are examining her, I
will prepare dinner—"

"You're full of energy, my lady." Quentin laughed.
"Calm yourself."

"You're right," Arielle agreed. "Just pray there's a letter awaiting me when I return home."

Quentin placed a hand over his heart and turned his
gaze heavenward. "I pray," he said, full of mischief.

Dodging the playful swat Arielle threw his way, Quentin took Tory's hand and departed the gloomy room, talking animatedly to the child.

Her friend would make a wonderful husband someday—
devoted, reliable, funny, and lovable. They had a lot in

common, but their friendship grew through their similar interests and yet her feelings for him had never developed further. He was, and always would be, a dear and important friend to her.

She knew, too, that he would marry one day. Unlike herself. Her life's chosen path wouldn't allow her to find a husband who understood her desires and still found *her* desirable. She wanted love and marriage and babies. Truly, she did. But she wanted something else, something the world found repugnant, distasteful, and scandalous because of her sex.

Yet it was something she couldn't give up.

Unless the marquess had changed his mind about helping.

Sighing deeply at that depressing thought, Arielle opened the bedchamber door. Mrs. Beecham's wracking cough suddenly pushed Arielle's problems aside. She smiled at the frail woman, "Where are the others?" she asked, referring to Mrs. Beecham's five other children. "I saw Tory, and he left with Dr. DeVries."

Portia Beecham's light brown eyes widened when she saw Arielle. "I thought I heard yer voice," she said in her raspy voice. Her thin shoulders shook as another cough seized her. "The others left a time ago. Tory is still young enough to want his mum's company sometimes."

"He's six now?" Arielle asked as she sat next to the woman on the small cot and felt her forehead, finding it slightly warm.

"No, milady. He's seven an' a half."

"His birthday is in July."

"Aye," Mrs. Beecham said proudly. "Ye remember!"

"At least I remembered that, if I didn't remember his age," Arielle said with a laugh. She brought her hands to Mrs. Beecham's stomach and began pressing. "Tell me if it hurts any place that I touch."

"No," Mrs. Beecham repeated several times as Arielle did her examination, knowing Quentin would repeat it for his own observation.

"Good." Arielle stood and leaned over the frail woman. "Can you sit up?"

"Aye, milady," Mrs. Beecham answered with a cough, bracing her arms to do just that.

Without hesitation, Arielle put her arms around Mrs. Beecham's shoulders and gently pulled her into a sitting position.

"Thank ye kindly."

"Anytime," Arielle answered, situating the only pillow Portia possessed. Then she opened the window, allowing fresh air into the confines of the sickroom.

Mrs. Beecham sat up and waited until Arielle returned to her place on the bed and continued her examination.

Without hesitation, Arielle placed her ear next to Mrs. Beecham's back. "Breathe in deeply." She listened, then instructed the woman to do it again several more times, front and back. "Your condition hasn't gotten any worse. But it seems you have a slight fever today. Is anything else out of the ordinary?"

"No. I don't have much o' an appetite. Might be a good thing, huh, milady, since we don't have much food left?" she chuckled sadly. "Rot it all, don't go gettin' no ideas, milady. I see the wheels in yer head creakin'. I ain't accepting no charity, as much as I appreciate yer kind heart. Ye have enough on yer shoulders already. It's unfortunate enough ye insist on buyin' us a meal whenever ye come and preparin' it with yer own hands—"

"Don't get overwrought, Mrs. Beecham," Arielle soothed, having heard this argument countless times before. She berated herself for not instructing Quentin to buy more food for the family. Hopefully, he knew to purchase a few extra things. "Is there anything else I should know about?"

"I'm a wee bit tired."

"More so than usual?"

"Aye. I'm supposin' it's due to worryin' over my oldest. She's expectin', ye know?"

"No, I didn't," Arielle said softly. "When?"

"Maura thinks she's about two months along." Mrs. Beecham leaned back on her lone pillow, her forehead wrinkled. "She's fifteen."

As poor as they were, the odds of either Maura or the baby surviving weren't good. She knew that the Beechams were a proud family, left virtually penniless after Mr. Beecham's death when the hackney he drove over-turned and crushed him. Arielle couldn't allow them to continue in such a manner, despite Mrs. Beecham's resistance. Determination that the family *would* accept her help settled into her. She would think of a way to see that happen.

"Does Quentin know?" Arielle asked, her mind turning.

"No, Dr. DeVries doesn't know. I jus' found out three days ago, rot it all."

"Don't worry, Mrs. Beecham. All will be fine." Arielle started for the door. "I'm going to get a cool cloth to place on your forehead."

As she walked to the cabinet in the small kitchen, Arielle knew with startling clarity that she had to find a way to legally help these hopelessly poor and desperately ill people. Her patients needed her and she had to convey that to Lord Hunter Braxton, the marquess of Savage.

6

Dear Lady Arielle,

Forgive my tardiness in getting back to you. As I have accomplished some degree of order here at Braxton Hall, I feel it is now presentable enough to invite a lady of your standing to afternoon tea, to discuss your request. Please be advised that Wilfred, my retainer, will be at your door tomorrow at one o'clock. I will be looking forward to our meeting.

Cordially,
Hunter

"Arielle, are you all right?" Thomas's concerned voice drifted through the open door that connected his study to the parlor where Arielle now stood. In fact, she'd just arrived and found Hunter's letter.

"Yes, Papa, of course," she answered quickly, tracing her fingertips over the bold writing. "I—I stubbed my toe on the piano leg." Small untruth, Arielle thought, rejecting completely that it was an outright lie. She couldn't very well tell her father that she'd meet with the marquess of Savage or the reason for the meeting. *Especially* not the reason for the meeting. Not yet anyway. He would surely forbid her to see him.

She gazed at the letter again, reverence and appreciation curving her mouth into a smile. The marquess had merely wanted to tidy his home before he invited her. How very sweet of him, she thought, holding the letter tightly to her breast.

"Arielle?"

"I'm fine, Papa," she emphasized, answering the unspoken concern in his tone. She had never been better. An hour ago, she'd left Mrs. Beecham resting comfortably, then she'd returned with Quentin to his office to discuss how best to proceed with Portia's care. Returning home minutes ago, she'd discovered the letter on the table in the parlor. And until her father's voice had broken into her uncontained joy, she hadn't realized she'd screamed.

After waiting for days to hear from the marquess, she only had to wait a few hours more for her opportunity to convince him to help her. Tomorrow at one. She'd be ready at noon, in case the retainer arrived early.

Hearing her father moving around in his study, she glanced toward the connecting door, swallowing any guilt she felt at the small deception she planned for the meeting. She'd tell her father she was with Quentin.

Although it was against Thomas's better judgment, as he often pointed out, he did grant Arielle permission to accompany Quentin on his visits to patients. Arielle knew her father's hope that she'd get her fill of the sick and infirm served as reason enough for his disgraceful lack of discretion and authority. But he couldn't know how wrong he was. Her visits only served to strengthen her resolve.

Even if it wasn't a problem for her to sneak off to Braxton Hall tomorrow, Arielle was loath to betray Thomas's trust. However, she consoled her conscience, she already had his permission to go out unattended. Even if it *were* only to go with Quentin to visit his patients. His only stipulation was that she not use the Stanford carriage during these times. Yet, when she returned from her outings, Thomas never questioned her. For all he knew, she might have gone to rendezvous with a secret lover.

Sometimes, Arielle wished her father *would* question her whereabouts with Quentin. It would at least show his interest in her, even if he wasn't interested in what she wanted to do.

However, his disregard for her affairs now proved fortunate. And Arielle certainly wouldn't worry about her sisters' opinions. Unless their father requested that one of them chaperon her to some function, they generally ignored her as well.

"Milady," the housekeeper said, stepping into the parlor. "Dinner is served."

"Dinner? Already, Maisy?"

"Yes, milady. Your father is waiting for you in the dining room."

Arielle glanced at the clock on the mantel. Eight o'clock. How had the time passed so quickly? Almost too excited to eat, she made her way to the dining room anyway. Her father stood by the table, a plate piled with food at his place. As she approached, he held out her chair for her. "Papa, did I keep you waiting?" she asked, taking her seat.

"No, my dear," he assured her gently. "Maisy just summoned me to the table." He situated his bulk in his spot at the head of the table, then grabbed a seed roll from the basket of warm bread that sat near him. "How's your toe?"

Tasting her claret, Arielle frowned. "My toe?"

"The one you stubbed a little while ago," he reminded her, buttering his roll.

"Oh! *That* toe." She sat her glass down and crossed her fingers for the new lie she told. "There's no need for concern, Papa. The pain is long forgotten."

To distract his attention, her gaze meandered to the food-laden sideboard, then back to Thomas. He ate contentedly, satisfied at her explanation. She went to the sideboard and uncovered the soup tureen.

Aromatic steam curled up. The scents of pigeon, bacon, ham, chestnuts, sweet herbs, and other unknown ingredients married extremely well, watering her mouth and rumbling her stomach. Happily taking a bowl, she dished herself a small serving of the chestnut soup and returned to her seat.

"Papa, are you not up to snuff? You don't seem your usual self this evening."

Thomas looked at her, anguish clouding his eyes. "You must understand, Arielle, Douglas has completely ignored Julia," he blurted unexpectedly.

Her initial shock that her father broached this subject with her again, and in such a manner, stole her ability to speak. She tightened her lips in disapproval, not wanting to know what went on between her father and Julia. Although she'd seen it with her own eyes, hearing her father speak so openly about it only served to annoy her. He seemed to be of two minds. When it suited him, he spoke to her about clearly unsuitable subjects, yet he adamantly refused to help her because of the shame it would bring upon him. What about the disregard he visited upon her regularly? Was there any father in the whole of the realm who would have a conversation about his mistress with his daughter?

Thomas stared at her intently, silently demanding a response from her.

"So she turned to you," Arielle guessed, determined not to judge him. Determined not to point out to him that Douglas's neglect of his wife didn't give Thomas license to dally with her.

"Yes," Thomas replied, "she turned to me."

Merely nodding, Arielle ate her soup, wondering where this conversation was leading.

Apparently nowhere, she thought with a sigh, as Thomas continued in a lighter tone. "By the by, Julia said you can certainly rely on her discretion over the conversation she overheard between you and Georgette."

"The lady is quite affable and most considerate."

"Of course she is," Thomas said. He laid his fork aside and narrowed his eyes at her. "Exactly what did she overhear, Arielle? You girls aren't planning some sort of mischief, are you?"

Arielle smiled. Wouldn't he be surprised if he knew the truth! To him, she shook her head. "Certainly not, Papa. We're not small girls anymore. We're fully capable of taking responsibility for our actions."

"That's a relief," Thomas said, picking up his fork again and digging into the greens on his plate. "As long as your secret doesn't affect our good name."

Arielle didn't know whether she wanted to laugh or cry at that statement. It really saddened her to know that her father was as shallow as everyone else in their acquaintance, that his main concern was the sullying of the Stanford name.

"Arrest your fears, Papa," Arielle told him. "We are not involved in childish acts. I promise you."

The worry creasing Thomas's features relaxed somewhat and Arielle pushed aside thoughts of her father, his problems, and her secret wish that what she did truly mattered to him. Looking forward to her meeting with his lordship, Arielle continued her meal on a hopeful note. When it ended, her father bid her good night and headed for his club.

She watched him go, sympathizing with his need to alleviate his loneliness, but it didn't compare to her need to fulfill her dreams.

Tomorrow couldn't arrive soon enough.

7

The big gray and burgundy carriage approached Braxton Hall with slow dignity. In spite of Hunter's reservations at meeting the spinster, the afternoon companionship of a gentlewoman appealed to him. Especially one who didn't seek to have him tie the knot with some eligible young miss. Neither would she be there to scrutinize him after having heard any undue rumors that might persist after all these years about his mother's good name, which always led to speculations about his questionable birth. Perhaps the lady might even suggest a few ideas to speed up the remodeling of his manor.

The two women he'd hired, Dora and Beatrice, had tidied and cleaned the parlor as well as they could, considering its moldy condition. The room had been airing out since early morning, its stuffy, closed-in odor almost gone as the afternoon breezes filtered in through the half dozen open windows. It was an unseasonably warm day.

Just before the conveyance containing Lady Arielle advanced to the main entrance of the manor, Hunter removed himself from the doorway. He returned to the parlor for a last-minute assurance that everything was in order.

In all his memory, he didn't recall any true entertaining going on at Braxton Hall. His most abiding memory of Braxton Hall involved the midwife who'd attended his own birth. The midwife who'd revealed to him, on his tenth birthday, that he was a bastard.

Uncle Proctor had summoned her to aid a servant who

had miscarried. After tending the woman, the midwife had found Hunter in his bedchamber and told him the words that would haunt him from that day forward.

"All the wealth in the realm won't hide the stain of a by-blow, lad. Find your true mark in this world. It ain't as a Braxton, although that was your mother's name. I don't know what your real father's name was."

Hunter never discovered the woman's real purpose in revealing his parentage to him. Her tone hadn't been malicious. Nevertheless, hearing those words killed something deep inside him.

Taking the circumstances of his birth into consideration helped Hunter make some sense of his uncle's seclusion. But the possibility that having a bastard nephew in his presence was what really caused the man to all but sever his social ties caused Hunter untold regret. Whatever the exact reasons, Proctor *had* become a recluse, and as a result, so had Hunter. Which made his present mood quite understandable.

He felt like a schoolboy meeting his teacher for the first time. Nervous. Anticipatory. Curious. Because of his years amongst a regiment of men, he easily traversed the rounds in the ton. This meeting, however, was something completely different. This meeting was taking place at his home, without the benefit of dozens of people surrounding him. Certainly rumors ran rampant about him whilst he was out and about and certainly he was scrutinized. This situation, however, left him open to an intensely personal scrutiny that he normally avoided whenever he circulated as the mysterious marquess of Savage.

Bloody hell, Arielle Stanford was a mere woman. An unfortunate, probably unattractive, spinster, well past marriageable age. Someone like her should pose no problem enrolling in the university.

"Beggin' your pardon, milord," Wilfred said from the doorway. "The young lady has arrived."

Unease rippled through Hunter at the wry amusement

in Wilfred's voice as he said *the young lady*. Hunter turned just as his retainer spoke again.

Wilfred gestured with his hand toward a vision standing beside him. "Lady Arielle Stanford is here to see you. Milady," he continued, unperturbed that his employer literally stood with his mouth agape, "Lord Hunter Braxton, the marquess of Savage."

The vision curtsied unsteadily, then straightened to her full height, which wasn't very tall. Free of curls, her hair hugged her shoulders and back in long, golden waves. Her face was pale, her skin as smooth as porcelain. Wide, luminous eyes, green as liquid emeralds and under sweeping lashes, fastened on him as the sweet scent of rosewater swirled toward him.

Shock quickened Hunter's heartbeat, rippled along his nerve endings, coupling with the unease he'd felt earlier. *This* was the spinster he was expecting? No, it simply couldn't be. Not when her intoxicating fragrance hypnotized Hunter. Her fragile youth amazed him. And her delicate beauty as she stared at him fascinated him.

An unrecognizable emotion stirred deep in Hunter's gut, just as she curtsied again.

"Thank you, my lord, for your consent to aid me. . . ."

Her voice trailed off as he continued to stare, his surprised brain hardly able to fathom the incredible beauty before him. He wanted to believe this was some type of cruel joke, that this girl, this promising young woman, didn't truly intend to closet herself away in a medical school and then waste her life mired amongst the sick and infirm. But she'd spoken with such sincerity, her green eyes so honest, that he knew it was true—she *was* the "spinster" he'd corresponded with.

An uncomfortable silence grew between them, stretching into minutes as Hunter weighed his possibilities.

He couldn't, in good conscience, help her throw her life away. Just from her letters he knew she was educated and entitled to place "Lady" before her name. Her father held at least a low-ranking title. All that, however, was inconsequential. With her beauty, she'd have a sterling match in terms of marriage in no time at all. That's what she should've been thinking about.

She lowered her lashes, covering those incredible eyes from his view. Embarrassed at his boorish behavior, Hunter cleared his throat. "Forgive me, my lady," he managed, "I hadn't expected you to be so young." *Or so beautiful*, he silently added, his heart beating a mad rhythm. "Are you quite certain you are old enough to make such a momentous decision that will encompass your whole future?"

Arielle drew in a shaky breath, barely aware that the butler was taking his leave. Handsome beyond her wildest dreams, Savage was tall, broad-shouldered, and slim-hipped. Ink black hair framed a face with an aquiline nose, dark eyebrows, and a bold, chiseled jaw. His sinfully black hair, cut short and gleaming like onyx, and his brilliant blue eyes, cerulean blue, as blue as azure, and fringed with long, thick lashes, combined to assault her senses.

She wasn't sure what she'd been expecting, but it wasn't this godlike man who was looking at her with such disbelief and uncertainty. Apparently, she wasn't what *he'd* been expecting either.

"My lady?"

Hunter's deep, strong voice seeped into her mind and she remembered his question about her age. Her heart pounded, a heady excitement she'd never experienced fanning out into her. "Uh, I—I'm eighteen, Lord Savage."

"Hardly old enough to make such a rash decision," the marquess snapped. "And, please, call me Hunter."

Arielle became aware that she stood just inside the parlor door. Her heart somersaulted, and for more than one reason. His impossible handsomeness seriously upset her balance and he sounded for all the world like he was about to renege on his promise to help her.

She cleared her throat. Her entire future depended on the next few moments and her ability to convince the marquess to keep his word. No easy task, considering she could think about little else at this moment other than the heated looks he gave her. "Hunter, I assure you this decision is anything but rash."

He smiled at her, mysterious and seductive, then took her by the hand and led her fully into the parlor. Delight shimmied through her at his touch, but he seemed not to notice as he said, "Please have a seat, Arielle, and excuse my manners. In truth, I expected to see an older, more settled woman. Not one in the bloom of youth."

Appreciating his honesty, Arielle sat on the sofa and waited until Hunter seated himself across from her before she spoke again. She asked the question she most dreaded the answer to. "Will that play a part in your willingness to aid me, my lor—Hunter?" she queried with a firmness she didn't feel.

He was possibly her last chance, her *only* chance, to gain acceptance to a medical college. Her heart would break if he backed out now, after he'd raised her hopes to such a high degree.

His silence returned—the silence that indicated his second thoughts and his disapproval. The very air around them thickened. Then, he smiled.

Its reassurance brightened his features and lightened her heart.

"I'm not one to make promises lightly, Arielle," he said softly. "However, I was quite taken aback upon seeing you."

"How so, my lord?"

She'd never met a man who'd so quickly and thoroughly intrigued her more than the marquess had. Looking at him filled her head with romantic nonsense. As if a man of his stature would even consider having her to wife.

Or to bed.

Heat crept up her neck at her improper thoughts. But having studied many of Quentin's medical texts, she knew the functions of the human body better than she should and thus knew what lovemaking entailed. She knew too that there had to be a certain amount of attraction on the part of both parties for sex to take place. While there certainly wouldn't be any problem with the attraction bit on her part, Savage wouldn't want a learned, university-bound woman to carry his heirs and bear his name.

Hunter drew in a breath, catching her attention. "I was misled by your letters."

Her heart sank, her upset showing itself in her crest-fallen look, for he quickly added, "Through no fault of yours, of course. I—I just thought you were a different sort."

She ignored the way the breeze blowing through the opened windows lifted his silky straight hair, ignored the brilliance of his eyes as a shaft of sunlight reflected in their depths, and instead considered his statement. She regretted not informing him earlier of her age and her marriageable status. She'd thought only to focus on the goal she'd sought to attain for so very long.

Sighing, she folded her hands in her lap and regarded them. Without looking up, she replied, "An older sort, perhaps?"

Hunter laughed softly and she couldn't help but smile in return. "Er . . . yes. But, though I may have briefly recon-sidered upon first seeing you, I still intend to help you."

"Thank you," Arielle said shyly. Gratitude toward his sincerity prevented her from questioning what had made him change his mind back to his original intent.

To get her mind off of her host, she scrutinized the room with new awareness. She'd failed to take full notice of just how bare the chamber was when she entered.

The huge windows had no dressings. It was obvious from the wallpaper that the walls had been washed down. Some places in the paper were missing altogether, and Arielle guessed it had been peeling before the cleanup. The water and vinegar used to clean it only served to strip it away completely. Other parts of the paper had overly bright streaks of cleanliness that trailed to the original dinginess.

She noticed the place in the ceiling where the chandelier should have been and met her host's uncomfortable gaze. At that moment, she realized how incredibly rude and obtuse she was being by studying the room in Hunter's presence.

"My lord . . . Hunter . . . forgive me. . . . I wasn't looking . . . I was just thinking—"

Not allowing her to finish, Hunter cleared his throat. "I suppose you are used to better, my lady." He gave a short, embarrassed laugh. "In the short time since my return, I haven't really gotten into restoring the manor. Or hiring a full staff. My deepest apologies for the unbecoming appearance of my home."

Arielle thought she'd dissolve where she sat. Never in her memory had she been at a loss for words, but she didn't know how to tell Hunter that she'd been studying the manor and thinking how much she'd enjoy adding her own special touch to it. A statement like that would certainly come out the wrong way. At the same time, she thought it odd that the marquess of Savage would be concerned over her reaction to his home. Why should her opinion matter to him?

Perhaps it wasn't her. It was simply the fact that the manor was in deplorable condition and he'd be embarrassed for any visitor to see it. Arielle fully understood the reasons for the manor's condition. It hadn't been inhabited for a number of years. Still, she wondered what had become of the tapestries and other furniture that must have once occupied it.

She swallowed hard when she realized she was looking around again and Hunter saw her doing it. Embarrassed now for the both of them, Arielle refused to direct her attention around the chamber again. That left only Hunter to look at.

She smiled at him. "I don't see the need for apologies, Hunter. I suspect after a few months of occupancy here, all will be up to snuff."

"Indeed it will, my dear."

"And of course such a matter calls for a housewarming?"

His blue eyes regarded her with keen interest. She'd never noticed much on a man, much less his eyes, but Hunter's were quite ... fascinating, particularly when they were looking at her as if she were the most beautiful woman in the world and his alone.

"Most definitely. Perhaps you can be persuaded to attend. It would make such an occurrence more tolerable—"

Arielle laughed at his choice of words. "Tolerable?"

"Yes," he grumbled. "By the time Braxton Hall is put to rights, I will have many obligations to fulfill. I do loathe the pretentiousness of the ton's parties. But in order to stay in touch, one must tolerate such pomp."

He really didn't sound as if he enjoyed his position—a foreign concept to her when her father and sisters enjoyed theirs so much. Even she, who was bound and determined to set a different course for herself, enjoyed, every now and again, the lavish parties and breathless whirlwind of London.

"Of course," Arielle said.

A moment of silence followed, but this time it wasn't filled with discomfort and unease. Just friendly awareness. Meeting his gaze, Arielle wondered what really went on behind the blue regard.

"Are you hungry? Wilfred was supposed to have tea and crumpets here by now."

Arielle considered lying, just to enjoy his company longer, then decided against it. "I'm not really hungry," she admitted. "But I'm sure Wilfred will be here soon."

"I have no doubt," Hunter agreed.

And because she wasn't hungry, due to the breakfast she'd had and the jumble of emotions knotting her belly now, she'd have to leave so he could enjoy his meal.

He stood to his full, magnificent height and her breath caught, even as she lamented the dismissal she was about to receive. She stood, too, and the top of her head barely reached his shoulders.

An odd urge to kiss him stole into her.

"Arielle?"

The husky sound of her name falling from his lips brought her to her senses. She'd never be so wantonly presumptuous as to kiss him. If he wasn't feeling the same way, it would ruin everything, including, possibly, her name.

"Yes?"

"Allow me to show you the whole of Braxton Hall. That is if you care to see it?"

"I would be honored," she blurted with uncontained enthusiasm.

Whatever prompted the invitation, Arielle felt privileged to have received it. She hadn't expected such hospitality from him, or such accordance. As they left the parlor and passed a line of stern-faced paintings that hung in a long row on the wall in an even longer hallway, Hunter explained that they were his ancestors.

"They never left their vigil of the estate," he explained proudly. "Even in my long years of absence."

"I'm sure they were happy not to have been stored away somewhere," Arielle said with a laugh. "They may have grown . . . er, restless."

"As in restless enough to haunt this hallowed estate?"

"Please, my lord," Arielle said, shivering dramatically. "Do not even think to tease me about such things. I'm not fond of ghostly experiences."

"Have you ever had any?"

"Certainly not! And the moment I do is the moment I never return to the place where it happens."

"Then my ancestors will indeed behave. They'd never intentionally send a beautiful young woman away," Hunter said as he took her hand, his familiarity not in the least insulting however improper it might have been.

"Come along, Arielle. We'll start in the kitchen and finish up in the attic. By then Wilfred should be through with whatever he's preparing for us."

"Very well," Arielle said. "I can barely contain my anticipation."

Of course, her anticipation should have been all for what he intended to do. It shouldn't have had anything to do with prolonging her visit with him.

She needn't have worried about their visit ending anytime soon, Arielle realized a half hour later, with only half the tour completed. The manor was simply huge, with a dozen bedchambers, four of which had connecting sitting rooms. At first, she hesitantly offered a tip or two on what she would do were she the one refurbishing such a beautiful home. As time progressed, she realized he was more than happy to hear her opinions after he asked her for them when she remained silent. From that point on, she didn't hesitate to speak freely.

The attic, which Arielle saw more as a storage room, was stuffed with furniture, all covered with graying, dusty sheets. She wanted to have a peek at what was hidden to see if any of it was worth saving, but Hunter didn't give her the chance. He guided her back the way they'd come up and finally, after four flights, they arrived at the parlor again.

The tour had come to an end.

His expression unreadable, Hunter dropped into the wing chair again. "Any advice for the receiving parlor, Arielle?"

"Doing this up in vivid yellow colors would be the height of fashion and it would welcome visitors instantly," Arielle suggested, still standing.

Hunter gazed about. "Vivid yellow? It's worth considering. Will you also consider taking a seat again? Or do you prefer to stand?"

Arielle laughed at the husky amusement in his voice, as she went to the sofa and sat. Her heart raced and her whole being thrummed. It was an experience so new and different, it frightened her. His nearness and the wonderful day she'd spent in his company made it hard for her to remain calm.

Around the silence, Arielle's mind wandered to erotic thoughts. Imagining herself in Hunter's arms heated her cheeks. The whole business of being alone with him affected her in a strange way. Yet, he seemed quite relaxed and hardly bothered by it.

In all her memory, she had yet to enjoy such a day with Quentin. They held one another in the highest regard, but with him the hustle and bustle of learning new medical techniques, reading medical texts and journals, performing an autopsy on some poor cadaver, or simply visiting the infirm were the only things that interested him.

On the other hand, Hunter's world was vast and varied, and he had allowed her a glimpse into his life.

"I'm very impressed with your home, my lord," she said finally. "I have no doubt that Braxton Hall will one day be restored to the former glory you undoubtedly knew growing up here."

"Despite its present deplorable state?" he asked with a raised eyebrow, obviously mistaking her comments as an aspersion against his ancestral seat.

"Of course that isn't what I meant," Arielle began defensively.

Hunter laughed softly. "Relax, my lady. I didn't take offense. I'm well aware of the work that must be done to restore its beauty."

"It won't take that long, my lord," Arielle stated, rising from her seat and walking slowly around the room. "If you already have in mind what you want." She most certainly did.

"Not really," Hunter admitted. He smiled like a guilty little boy. The effect nearly stole her breath. "I want to take my time and therefore can't seem to make up my mind."

She waited, hoping, wishing that he'd ask her to extend her help. But the question never came. Instead, inscrutability returned to his very blue eyes as he watched her. She cleared her throat, frightened at how easy it might be to lose herself in the intensity of his look. "I suppose we should get to the reason for my visit."

"We should. Do you really wish to do this, Arielle? Do you really wish to give up the chance at marriage for the field of medicine?"

His words were husky and provocative, the insinuation in them giving her a heady, feminine feeling.

"Must I choose, my lord? Why can't I have both?"

Short, mocking laughter pierced her, as surely as if he'd taken a scalpel to her. In their brief acquaintance, she thought he understood what she wanted. Apparently, she'd misjudged him. But she couldn't forget that he might be her last chance. She couldn't allow the wild, unfamiliar attraction flaring between them to sway her.

"You're far too smart not to already know that answer." He stood abruptly, moving toward her.

He stopped mere inches away from her, so close that she smelled the faint scent of his cologne, saw the pounding pulse point in his neck. A long finger dipped beneath her chin and tipped her head back, his touch like the gentle fluttering of a butterfly's wings.

His mouth pressed against her own, the contact of his firm lips exploding within her. He wrapped his arms around her, pulling her closer to him, urging her mouth open. When she complied, the wet silkiness of his tongue found her own and she melted against him. His kiss teased and caressed, moving temptingly over her mouth. Incredible sensations swept through her. A feeling so new and erotic it made hot tingling flames race through her veins, moisten her loins, robbing her of her breath, just as he gently set her apart from him.

"Will you be content to never know a man's touch? I think not."

"How dare you presume to tell me what will and won't content me, my lord?" she snapped, forcing her unwanted desires at bay, embarrassment coursing through her. He'd used a kiss to make a point, not because he felt any attraction for her. She'd mistakenly assumed differently, but she wouldn't do so again. "I want to become a licensed physician, hence my contacting you. I will allow nothing and no one to stand in my way, least of all you."

He drew back as if she'd slapped him and nodded curtly. "Then it shall be as you wish, my lady. There's no need of any more convincing. I will help you."

His features were cold and unapproachable, his words as frozen as the earth outside.

She nodded, telling herself how glad she was at his agreement. But something had happened here today to her. Something she didn't want to explore. The remembered pressure of his lips still burned her mouth, the taste of him embedded in her brain. But he wasn't the friendly, approachable lord he'd been upon her arrival. He was distant and tense.

Just then, Wilfred appeared. "My lord, lunch is served."

"I—I'd better take my leave, Hunter," she said, her legs shaky.

"You're over an hour away from London. Please, stay and have a meal with me."

Knowing how unwise it would be not to take that advice, Arielle soon found herself dining on a light meal of asparagus in cream, boiled chicken and sauce, and buttered oranges. They discussed more about the manor and the grounds, which were in as much need of landscaping as the house was in need of redecorating. But, all too soon, the time for her departure arrived.

When she arrived home later that night to an empty house, she realized the day had been as perplexing as it was pleasurable. The only hope she harbored that Hunter still intended to help her lay in his telling her he would have an answer for her as soon as his time permitted. Hopefully, it would be sooner rather than later.

Mrs. Beecham and her family needed her. Undoubtedly, Mrs. Beecham's pregnant daughter, Maura, would feel more comfortable to have Arielle as her physician rather than Quentin. Although it would take years for her to become licensed, she at least would be enrolled in an accredited school. Hopefully, it wouldn't be seen as such a violation of the law were the authorities ever to discover that Quentin allowed her to care for the Beechams unassisted.

Sitting down at the small desk in her room, she sighed. The fine cherrywood furniture overflowed with textbooks, journals, and notes. She pulled one particularly thick book from the stack and opened it.

She read a few sentences and stopped. Usually she was quite good at absorbing whatever she read in one of these books. Tonight, however, she felt restless and agitated. She walked to her window and gazed out into the night.

Thick fog hung in the winter air, shapeless, dense vapors that hid everything from view. Leaning her head against the window frame, Arielle shivered slightly, despite the blazing fire going in the fireplace. She pulled her night wrap tighter about herself as an image of the marquess of Savage formed in her mind.

She wondered what he was doing at that exact moment. Was he thinking of her as she was of him? Had he enjoyed himself today as much as she had? She'd write him a thank-you note in the morning for showing her such a grand time, but at that moment she really wasn't up to it.

If only Hunter had been a doddering old man, well past the prime of his life, he wouldn't have affected her so. But she couldn't have both her career and him—or any man for that matter. She either had to content herself with having a good, respectable marriage and a houseful of babies or she had to allow Hunter to do as she'd first requested and get into the school.

Her heart skipped a beat; she knew that once a position was secured for her at the college she'd never see Hunter again. That thought caused her to feel a loss of something that was never really hers to lose in the first place.

And that something was Hunter Braxton.

8

Thieves, liars, murderers, bastards, and whores, the lot of them! The entire Braxton line should have been banished from the realm. Their titles had come about nefariously and their men were larcenous rogues. That's why John Price, duke of Ridgeley, had refused to make any attempt to see his grandson. But he was an aging man now and he needed to make amends.

Yet he couldn't do it alone. It was doubtful the boy would even see him at this late point. Especially since that boy was a thirty-three-year-old man with an impressive military record and the wealth of the dubious Braxton titles behind him.

Standing upon the cliff where his estate was located, the old duke glared down at the tempestuous North Sea. The roiling winter storm was as intense as his own emotions. Heavy black clouds hung low in the brewing sky; the icy mist draped him with bitter cold. The deafening roar of white-capped waves crashing upon the rocky shoreline below couldn't drown out his regret and sorrow.

With a sigh, John huddled further into his heavy clothing. For some reason, his son, Fenton, had always loved winters upon the North Sea. From time to time, John visited the cliffs that jutted out over the water, seeking nearness to his lost son. But his solace was elusive and he knew he would miss Fenton until the day he died.

Just as Proctor Braxton had undoubtedly missed his sister, Roxanne, when she'd died in childbed, delivering Fenton's son, nine months after his death.

How fair was it that a man with his entire life ahead of him, and an expectant wife, would be killed in an accident? Why did such misfortune have to fall upon John's only son?

He had searched for answers to those questions for years and never found any. Had he allowed his grandson into his life, he might have found some relief from his endless torment. But he'd been eaten up with bitterness, hatred, pride, condescension—deadly sins for certain. So much so that when Proctor swore to raise Hunter as his son and never allow John to see the boy, he had pretended not to care.

It was just like that bastard Braxton to do such a thing, he'd told himself. He'd even sworn that Roxanne had seduced his son and gotten with child purposely to ensnare the Ridgeley heir.

Roxanne Braxton, however, was a sweet, caring woman, who'd been caught in the bitter rivalry between her brother and the father of the man she loved. It hadn't had anything to do with Fenton and Roxanne. And certainly not their son, Hunter. But the machinations of two selfish men had made it so.

"Your Grace?"

John turned at the sound, not at all surprised to see his loyal servant standing on the stone pathway, a few feet from him. "You've always walked so softly, Edward. I didn't hear you come out."

Edward bowed. "Forgive me, Your Grace. But Cook has prepared warm scones and hot tea for you."

"Are you trying to get me indoors?" John asked, chuckling.

"You're very wise to us, my lord. However, it is quite chilly out here. You could catch your death."

"Quite right," John agreed, starting toward the house. "I wouldn't want to succumb before I've laid eyes on my grandson."

"Quite right, Your Grace," Edward echoed, following behind him.

John smiled faintly. Edward had become his friend and confidant over the long, lonely years. He was always there when needed. However, his loyal presence was no longer enough.

Now, John wanted to know his grandson. He wasn't getting any younger. Although he wasn't expecting to meet his Maker anytime soon, he wanted to be sure that his line was secure. John wanted to pass along his rightful titles to Hunter, but he doubted Hunter would welcome him with open arms after all these years. Which meant it was time to involve himself in society again and find out exactly who was closest to Hunter Braxton, his heir.

*D*ear *Arielle,*
    I beg your forgiveness for having so carelessly kissed you. I am certainly more of a gentleman than that. Despite the ambiguous end to our meeting, I truly enjoyed your visit and haven't forgotten the reason for it. I went this morning to inquire about that position for you, but the board of Regents is absent and will reconvene in a fortnight. I will be in London on a business matter this coming Friday and would consider it an honor to call upon you that afternoon. If you agree, a reply will not be necessary.

                  Most cordially yours,
                  Hunter

Leaning back in his chair in the study, Hunter read over the letter for a second time, undecided whether to send it as he'd written it. Arielle had made a surprising impression on him. His first meeting with her, six days ago, still stunned him. Images of her lovely face flooded his mind constantly. He hardly fathomed that she truly wanted to waste such youth and beauty in a medical college, where even the staidest of young *men* entered. And she was anything but staid.

He had promised to help her gain entrance, and he would abide by that promise. But he'd also try to dissuade her from her intentions. He wondered about her family. Especially her father. Was she so headstrong that they all left her to her own willful devices?

Yet he couldn't freely question her without expecting to have to offer a few answers himself, and she was certainly more than willing to question him. He was just as willing to offer ridiculous excuses for the lack of knowledge about his real father.

He only knew that Proctor Braxton was his uncle, not his father. He knew that his uncle had sequestered his only sister, Roxanne, away on a far-off estate during her pregnancy, where Proctor had joined her. When he returned to Braxton Hall, it was with the infant he claimed was the son born to him by a wife who'd died birthing his heir.

Proctor had loved Hunter enough to last an eternity, loved him better than some fathers would have. Loved him enough to seclude him from the rest of the world when rumors began circulating about Hunter when he'd been enrolled at Eton.

Yet his uncle Proctor had hated Hunter's unknown father just as fiercely, so much so that any questions Hunter had of the man went unanswered. After a while, the topic of his father became a forbidden subject, one that Hunter knew better than to broach.

One that also had Hunter leaving home upon Proctor's death. But there came a time in every man's life when he had to stop running. For Hunter that time came when he survived the horrors of fighting against Napoleon's armies.

But with his decision to return home came a few realizations as well. First and foremost was the fact that he shouldn't ever marry. It would be fine for him to be known as the bastard marquess, but humiliating for any wife. Secondly was the fact that even though he could never squelch his natural curiosity to discover who sired him, he'd have to be as discreet as possible about his inquiries. He might never have a wife, but he'd always have a mother. He would go to any length to protect her name—even if that meant eventually giving up the quest of finding the identity of his father.

Uncle Proctor had been the one man who could have saved Hunter years of unnecessary speculation if only he'd given over and answered just one of his many questions. Knowing for certain that he was illegitimate rather than guessing at it would have at least armed him for whatever lay ahead. Now, however, the uncertainty left him more vulnerable than he cared to admit.

Vulnerable to the likes of Lady Arielle Stanford and the bitterness that might ensue if he allowed her to get too close to him. But he wanted to know her better. He wanted to change her mind about wanting to enroll in medical school.

Perhaps in the fortnight before the board returned, he might be able to.

He was a noble fool, thinking such thoughts. Like Arielle, most young ladies now on the "marriage mart" were much too young to know about the Braxton scandals and therefore too uninformed to make a sound decision if he thought to pursue one of them.

A vision of Arielle rose in his mind. The softness of her body as she relaxed in his arms. Her flushed cheeks and endless eyelashes as she responded to his kiss. Her green eyes flashing in outrage as he asked her if she could give up the pleasure of marriage for the pursuit of a medical license. The sweetness of her voice as she asked why she couldn't have both.

It might have been selfish of him, but had he been her husband, he could never share her. He'd place her upon a pedestal and revel in her wit, admire her beauty, listen to her opinions. But he wasn't so open-minded that he'd allow her to become a doctor. Ladies didn't do such things. They took care of their families and their households.

Why was Lady Arielle Stanford so bloody different?

And what difference should it make to him? She was just passing through his life, on her way . . . to a university.

Hunter stared at the letter again. It was better for both of them if he kept his promise. Still, he wanted to meet her family and find out how it was they would let her go unattended to a gentleman's home. He wanted that answer as much as he wanted to see her again.

He turned over in his mind the afternoon she'd spent with him. He remembered how easily she laughed, despite the clearly serious side of her nature. She'd enthusiastically expressed her opinion about how she thought his manor should be decorated. Chuckling to himself, he admitted how much he'd liked her suggestions.

Egads, Arielle Stanford seemed so perfect. The kind of woman he'd gladly surrender his freedom to. That is, if he didn't carry the slur of his illegitimacy. No matter how attracted he was to Arielle, he couldn't consider matrimony to anyone.

Perhaps it was best that she be accepted into the university. That would certainly assure her spinsterhood. It wasn't as if her life's status should concern him. That's what she had a father for. But with her chosen profession, Hunter knew that at least she wouldn't end up in the bed of some lecherous lord who would never appreciate her.

Annoyed at the thoughts he had no business entertaining, he rose from the seat at his desk. Folding the letter, he stuffed it into an envelope and called for Wilfred.

Hunter told himself the length of time he'd endured away from home helped fuel these unaccustomed yearnings. In his absence, he'd had encounters with many a beautiful woman, but he'd never been as affected by any of them as he was by Arielle. Well, he'd just have to regain control of his wayward emotions.

"You called, milord?" Wilfred asked, entering into the room.

"Yes, Wilfred," Hunter said, pushing his disturbing thoughts aside. He handed Arielle's letter to the retainer. "Deliver this missive to Lady Arielle Stanford posthaste."

A hint of a smile curved Wilfred's mouth. "It's as good as done, milord," he said with a small bow.

Wilfred strolled from the room, looking as pleased as punch, and Hunter suddenly wondered if he were making the biggest blunder of his life.

9

Brisk winter temperatures and unusual sunshine cloaked the London afternoon. The warm, blazing fire in the Stanford drawing room hardly alleviated the cold hanging in the air, but Arielle didn't care. She fidgeted around, unable to sit or remain calm, her nervousness warding off the chill of the day. If Maisy hadn't remarked upon the temperature, Arielle wouldn't have noticed it.

She was awaiting Hunter's arrival, as anxious as a debutante preparing for her entrance into society.

When Wilfred brought the letter yesterday, she'd just returned from aiding Quentin with his patients. But once she'd turned Wilfred over to Maisy to give him a warm meal and a basket to tide him over on the way back to Braxton Hall, Arielle had rushed to her bedchamber, letter in hand.

As she read the letter, a gamut of emotions ran through her: giddiness that Hunter even thought to apologize to her, crushing disappointment at the delay for an appointment at the university, and excited delight at Hunter's request to see her.

It was certainly acceptable to her. She had only to get her father's permission to receive his lordship. Although she was more than certain Thomas would agree to Hunter's attendance of her, she'd better ask anyway. He had absolutely no idea that she was even acquainted with the marquess and finding out offhandedly might cause a scene.

Unfortunately, Arielle had been asleep last night when

he'd come in from his gentlemen's club. And despite her early rising, she'd still missed him and had no idea when he'd return from wherever he'd gone so early.

She prayed for Thomas's return the entire morning. When she realized that wasn't forthcoming, she considered sending a missive of regrets to Hunter, but quickly decided against that. She had no idea when the opportunity to entertain him in her home might present itself again. If ever. Besides, it was very likely that he'd already left Braxton Hall by now and wouldn't receive her note anyway.

Now, with Hunter's arrival imminent, she was sure she'd go into apoplexy. Not that she hadn't been alone in the company of a gentleman before. On numerous occasions, she'd been left alone with Dr. DeVries. But he was only Quentin to her family, and to herself as well. Quentin, with his unquestioned decency.

Other than that, her father would never approve of her entertaining a gentleman without a chaperon. No matter that he was the heralded marquess of Savage. *Especially* because he was the heralded marquess of Savage. Before a great nobleman like that, Thomas would want his household to appear as proper as any other titled home would.

Well, it was too late to correct the situation's late hour. She'd just have Maisy stand someplace unobtrusive in the parlor to give some semblance of propriety. The housekeeper's presence should be enough to satisfy all parties involved. Although she'd long ago stopped caring about propriety, she didn't want her father to get suspicious about her acquaintance with Hunter.

Going to the window once again, Arielle looked out just in time to see a black curricle, the golden Braxton crest emblazoned on the side, stop in front of the town house. A few moments passed before Hunter's tall, elegant figure stepped out, his blue Carrick swirling about the wide breadth of his shoulders.

His stride was purposeful and confident as he moved toward the entrance. She sucked in a calming breath as he came ever closer. If he had looked up, he might have noticed her watching him and glimpsed the wonder on her face. Was he really that handsome or was her mind playing tricks on her?

Arielle's heart raced. This wasn't supposed to be happening. Whatever *this* was. Although she couldn't put a name to it, she only knew her excitement was supposed to come from the marquess's ability to get her into medical college.

Not from the man himself.

She watched as he withdrew a timepiece and frowned. It had been less than a minute since he'd knocked, but still, he was supposedly expected. She thought to rush to the door herself and open it, but that would be the height of bad taste when they had a household staff to do it.

Still, she started toward the entrance hall and saw Maisy making her way there.

"Oh, Maisy," she blurted, rushing forward.

"Yes, milady?" the housekeeper answered, staring at her with raised eyebrows.

"That would be the marquess of Savage at the door. Since my father isn't here, I'll need you to make your presence known in the parlor while I converse with his lordship."

"As you wish, milady," Maisy said kindly, then went to open the door.

Not wanting to seem anxious, Arielle returned to the parlor and sat on the sofa.

"Lord Braxton to see Lady Arielle." Without warning, Hunter's huge frame suddenly occupied the doorway. A smile froze on her face.

"My lord . . . er, Hunter," she squeaked, her gaze following Maisy, who took a seat in the far corner of the room. "Do come in."

Hunter advanced toward her, and Arielle held out her hand.

"Hello, my dear," he said, bowing over her hand and kissing it with the utmost decorum.

It was the barest brushing of his lips against her skin, but the effect would have been the same had he gathered her in his arms and kissed her with hot passion. Hypnotized by his touch, by his scents—of leather and spicy cologne and male, Arielle allowed him to keep her hand in his, her body deliciously warm and heavy.

"You appear flushed," he said softly, huskily. He swept her with an intimate look, but said loud enough for Maisy to hear, "Is my arrival untimely?"

"Your arrival is perfect," Arielle told him, surprising herself at how steady her voice sounded.

Maisy scraped her chair across the floor, whether by design or accident Arielle wasn't sure, but it had the desired effect. Hunter put a little more distance between them and glanced in the housekeeper's direction. He smiled in perplexity at Arielle.

Unsure of how this appeared to him, she returned his smile, then looked at Maisy. "Whatever are you doing here?"

Maisy had become like a mother to her in the short while the woman had been working there and she doubled as Arielle's personal maid—further indication of her father's financial woes. That, and the fact that besides their respective carriage drivers, Maisy was only one of a small staff of six. But she was very protective of Arielle and had no qualms about speaking her mind, which she did now.

"I'm here, milady, as your chaperon, in case you've forgotten."

Arielle blushed. It was no less than she deserved for playing the game she had. "Of course."

"I think it is only right that your housekeeper remain," Hunter inserted, scanning Arielle appreciatively.

The memories of their brief kiss intruded upon Arielle's better sense and she nodded firmly. "Maisy has a full day ahead of her, my lord. I am quite used to fending for myself." *What am I doing?* She nodded to Maisy. "That'll be all for now. We'll have refreshments shortly. I'll ring for you."

Maisy scowled, but took her leave. Arielle explained to Hunter the reason she'd been there in the first place.

Hearing Arielle's explanation, Hunter understood better how Arielle had been able to visit his estate unchaperoned. Because of her family's neglect, her liberties were unhindered.

A seething dislike grew inside Hunter toward her father. How dare the man neglect her so! "What of your mother?"

"She died of consumption when I was six." Arielle smiled to cover the sadness in her voice.

"Do you remember her?" he asked, wondering if he were bringing about bad memories.

"Some things. She had the most gentle voice. I have vague memories of going into her rooms and falling asleep in her arms. But I'm unsure if that's wishful thinking or true recollections."

"Did you ever ask your father?"

Arielle shrugged. Yet the careless gesture didn't mask the hurt in her lovely eyes. "I might if he ever truly listened to me," she said ruefully. "I have four older sisters. When Mama died, the eldest, Ellen, was within two years of making her debut. After that it was Kate, then Agatha, then Emma. Once all the girls had been introduced, then . . ."

"The weddings began," Hunter guessed.

"Exactly, my lord," Arielle said with a laugh. "Ellen's wedding to Laurent actually took place just before Kate's. As the baby who was born five years after the last of them, I was rather left to my own devices."

"It's a them and a me, is it, then?"

"No, no," she denied, more out of loyalty to her family than anything else. Perhaps, too, a small amount of shame that she was somewhat of an outsider to her own family. "Agatha and her husband chaperon me quite often."

"And what of your father?"

"Papa truly loves me," she explained, hearing Hunter's derision and guessing at the reason. "But I'm the only one of his daughters who is capable of fending for herself."

"Perhaps because you have no choice," Hunter suggested.

"Perhaps so," she said quietly. Who knew how she might have turned out had her mother lived or had her father actually remembered her existence more often.

Hunter watched the forlorn look descend on Arielle's features. He hated seeing the sparkle of her eyes dim and the corners of her mouth turn downward in sadness. The thought for an outing to cheer her up came to him.

Besides, she'd be thoroughly compromised if it were discovered he had been alone with her in her home. He hoped that the housekeeper was still within earshot. After all, she didn't know if he had come for a rendezvous with Arielle or not and it was simply appalling that no one cared enough to see that didn't happen.

Hyde Park would be a perfect place to visit Arielle while protecting her reputation. Although that reputation would still be exposed to suspicion, no one would voice it aloud. There would be no proof that they hadn't come across each other on an afternoon ride.

"Arielle, it isn't proper for us to be alone together in your home."

"I—I know, Hunter," she said, her tone deflated. Shifting her weight, she looked down at her feet. "Forgive me for the predicament I have put you in. This seeming compromise would have us unwillingly wedded without second thought. I thought Papa would have been here and—"

"Shhh," Hunter comforted, gently placing a finger over her lips to silence her. The warm mouth beneath his fingertip was soft and inviting. But he ignored his urge to kiss her. "I don't intend to leave just yet. I merely have a solution. We wouldn't be alone in Hyde Park, would we?" he asked with a grin.

She nodded vigorously, the cloud of melancholy lifting instantly. Her ready acceptance didn't surprise him in the lcast. From thc timc of hcr first lcttcr to him, hc'd alrcady perceived her daringness.

Without further ado, he took her hand and, like two naughty children, they hurried out of the door to the waiting carriage.

10

Once Hunter had handed her up into the curricle and followed in behind her, he steered the pair of black horses toward Hyde Park. Familiar sights went by in a dizzying array of scenery as Hunter handled the vehicle with vigorous skill. She quite enjoyed the cold air whipping about her cheeks and ruffling Hunter's black hair. She wanted the ride to go on forever, but all too soon Hunter reined in the horses on a curving edge of the park. This spot was secluded, hidden from the view of any passersby.

"Would you like to remain here a moment?"

With him looking so devilishly handsome, Arielle embraced this quiet moment after the exuberance of their departure from Stanford Manor.

"This is perfect for a brief escape," she said breathlessly.

Hunter loosened the reins, then stepped down from the curricle and helped her out. A brisk breeze passed around them, swirling through the tall, ancient trees.

"Are you cold?" he murmured, brushing the back of his hand against her cheek.

Arielle leaned into the caress, feeling as though she belonged no where else but there with him. "Not very," she replied.

"Are you up for the theater tonight? Pembishire and his wife have invited me. Julia would be a chaperon of sorts for you," he said, adding, almost as an afterthought, "if you have no one else."

Hunter's question caught her completely by surprise.

She had never expected this outing, let alone an invitation
to the theater. Arielle considered how she'd endure an
evening in Julia Shepperton's company, but she'd spend
time with the devil himself to be near Savage.

"I would be honored, my lord."

"The Globe has the Royal Shakespeare Troupe on
hand."

During a few comfortable moments of silent strolling,
Arielle digested the events of the day. Upon awakening
this morning, she'd seen to some correspondence that
needed answering, with little expectation of a relaxed day.
She'd believed she and Hunter would spend some time at
Stanford Manor, then he'd leave. But that wasn't the case.

Sighing contentedly, Arielle relaxed against the trunk
of a large tree they'd stopped under. Hunter leaned beside
her, persuing her profile, then he placed his hand on her
shoulder.

A moment's surprise touched her, then she hesitantly
glided her hand along his arm, enjoying the presence of
him, the companionable silence, the friendly closeness.

Capturing her hand in his, Hunter brought it to his lips
for a kiss. He scowled suddenly, breaking the moment.
"Why, your hands are freezing, Arielle!" he said, alarmed.
"Where are your gloves?"

"They are in the parlor at home," she answered, realizing her mistake immediately. "I forgot them."

Hunter pulled her away from the tree and back to the
curricle. Her heart sank.

"That does it. Can't have you catching your death."

She smiled at him, wondering how her request for Hunter's help had gone so awry. She still had days to go
before the Board of Regents resumed their seats. And her
priorities were already shifting.

Arielle could have kicked herself for forgetting her
gloves. With Hunter so near, she hadn't been affected
by the chill in the air—it had gone virtually unnoticed.

Unfortunately, her hands told a different story. They *were* a little bit cold, but not enough to garner such a reaction from Hunter. She could have stayed under that tree in a blizzard, and forever, as long as Hunter was with her.

Now that she was indoors, however, she felt a marked difference. Heat emanating from the various fireplaces throughout the house made it cozy and warm. Regretfully, Hunter had made his good-byes in the entrance hall, promising to return in several hours so they could attend the theater.

Finding that her father was still absent, Arielle asked Maisy to prepare a bath immediately and proceeded to relax in the steaming water.

But when the water grew cold, Arielle stood and summoned Maisy.

"Are you ready to get out, milady?" the housekeeper asked. She had Arielle's night wrap draped over her arm.

"Yes, Maisy. It's time, don't you think? I was beginning to wilt."

Smiling in agreement, Maisy nodded and cloaked a night wrap over Arielle's shoulders.

"The marquess is quite a handsome man," she remarked as she guided Arielle to the small dressing table in the bath chamber.

Arielle sat and Maisy began brushing the tangles from her damp hair.

"A girl could easily lose her heart to him," the housekeeper continued.

Arielle laughed nervously. "Rest assured, Maisy, that I haven't and I won't. I'll let nothing deter me from my dreams."

"Aye, child, so you've said before. I'm simply wondering were they real dreams or a way out of your loneliness."

"That's not fair, Maisy," Arielle said, pulling away and rising to her feet. "You know how important it is to me to help save people's lives. It is not something to be taken lightly."

Maisy placed her hands on her hips and glared at her. "Give me an honest answer, child, and I'll beg off. Would you prefer to be in childbed birthing his babes yourself or would you prefer to be helping another woman bring another man's son into the world?"

"You know the answer to that very well, Maisy!" Arielle said heatedly.

"Indeed I do, little one, but I'm not so sure that you do," the housekeeper returned just as hotly. "If you can honestly stand there and tell me you'll cancel your theater outing with the marquess should Quentin call around with an emergency, *then* I'll tell you I didn't know the answer. Otherwise—"

"Your otherwise can hardly be credited. Just because I'd refuse to go with Quentin tonight doesn't mean I'd do so again. I haven't been to the theater in ages."

"A fact you ignored until Savage invited you."

"It's no use talking to you tonight. You simply refuse to understand my new friendship."

Maisy gazed at her tenderly. "Perhaps I do, pet," she said softly. "Now sit and let me brush the tangles from your hair. We can't have your hair a hopeless mess for your big theater outing tonight."

Arielle did as she was told, escaping Maisy's presence as soon as possible and going to her bedchamber.

She refused to give any credence to Maisy's words, however, afraid that if she did she might find more than a little truth in them.

Arielle glanced at the clock on the mantel and saw that there was still much time to go before curtain call at the theater. She hadn't any idea where Hunter was at the moment, but a couple hours remained before he would return for her. Meanwhile, the bed looked very inviting. And after the exhilaration of the day and the warm bath, fatigue hit her full force.

A nap would be just the thing to renew for this evening's outing.

* * *

At his town house, a myriad of paperwork spread before him, Hunter rubbed his eyes, unable to concentrate as he contemplated the day's events. He really hadn't planned to invite Arielle to the theater tonight. He'd only intended to discuss her plans for the college. Then he'd seen her again and her presence, her loneliness, simply overwhelmed his common sense. He really couldn't abide not seeing her again as soon as possible, so had given in to the impulse and invited her out with him and the Sheppertons. Arielle's ready acceptance delighted him.

Now he had quite a night planned for them and couldn't wait for it to get under way.

The rare sunshine of late afternoon turned into gray shadows of dusk until finally a night sky claimed the last vestiges of evening. Stars dotted the indigo heavens and a full moon added a brilliant glow, a dizzying madness that made him wish for impossibilities and gave sense to his wildest illusions.

The perfect night made it easier for Hunter to hope the time he'd spend with Arielle later would be a continuation of the day. She had been utterly delightful. So much so that he hadn't wanted the day to end. The irresistible impulse to stop in that secluded corner of the park had come about suddenly. Not since the days before his military duty had Hunter actually walked through Hyde Park—or any park for that matter. Even the nip in the air hadn't been a deterrent, and Arielle seemed to enjoy it as much as he had.

But he refused to have his impulses causing her ills. He sighed, his thoughts taking another serious vein. If he had felt free to choose his bride without hindrance of his birth, would he have eventually chosen Arielle? No. More than likely, she would have ended up a doctor's wife. Another sigh escaped him and he looked at his pocket watch. The time to depart for the theater had arrived. He got up and went into the hall. "Geoffrey?"

Within hearing distance as always, Geoffrey came immediately. "Yes, my lord?"

"Is the carriage out front?"

"Yes, my lord."

"Very good. Then I'd better make haste to fetch the lady."

11

Glittering lights shimmered off the gilded plasterwork of the theater's reception area. The hum of chatter circulated through the assembled crowd. Every now and then, a burst of laughter floated up. Arielle smiled at the sheer joyousness of the sounds.

To be seen out and about like this with the marquess of Savage would cause no small amount of speculation. Undoubtedly, Hunter knew this as well, but it didn't seem to matter to him as they made their way to the Pembishire box to enjoy the production with Hunter's hosts.

More than once, heads turned as she and Hunter walked by. Lord Twickenbot even stopped them on their way to the box. Arielle stiffened upon sight of him, knowing what was coming and hoping to get away before the man thoroughly embarrassed her in front of Hunter.

"Well, if it isn't the Lady Doctor Stanford," he greeted, deflating any hope of amicability. But that was to be expected. Arielle had refused his son's suit, something her own father hadn't understood at the time. "Taken to coming out unchaperoned now?"

"I beg your pardon, Twickenbot?" Hunter growled, stepping closer to the stout man.

"Beg it all you want, Savage. She had the cheek to turn down my only son for the sake of some silly feminine notion. Perhaps she'll choose you over her doctoring. You're a marquess, after all. I wish you luck, man." Twickenbot stormed away.

Anger flushed Hunter's cheeks and hardened his eyes.

For a moment, Arielle thought Hunter might go after Twickenbot and call him out. His lips thin, he looked at her. "How long ago was this?"

"A-about a year," Arielle whispered, humiliated that Hunter should witness this. He was the perfect paragon of society and she was an oddity. "Maybe I should go home."

His anger lasted a moment longer, then he shook his head. "Don't run, Arielle. You have chosen your course. If that's what you truly want, be true to it. Come. We shall enjoy the rest of this evening."

Be true to what she wanted? Suddenly, she didn't know what that was anymore. At that moment, only Hunter filled her mind. In his double-breasted, wool frock coat with claw-hammered tails that outlined his wide shoulders, he was far more handsome than any man of her acquaintance. Long black trousers clung to the muscles in his legs. His dark hair gleamed against the burgundy of his coat and the white of his waistcoat, and shirt with chitterling ribbings, and stock.

He would have caused a stir all by himself, but the fact that he had an attendant for the evening made for wonderful gossip. He definitely caused a stir in *her*. But Julia Shepperton's reaction at seeing her and Hunter together concerned Arielle the most.

Arielle hadn't seen Lady Pembishire since the night of Julia's party. Then, the countess had been her usual catty, pettifogging self. Arielle could only imagine the blue-nosed harlot's response now.

Their meeting could have been quite amusing, however. Julia certainly wasn't expecting Arielle to arrive with the celebrated marquess. As a matter of fact, from what she gathered, Julia wasn't expecting Arielle to arrive at all. Hunter hadn't had the chance to inform the earl and his wife of their chaperoning duties. The marquess just took for granted that they would do it without any problems.

But Arielle knew Julia, and she knew that she was Lady Shepperton's least favorite person. Her dislike would be taken to new heights when Arielle walked in on Hunter's arm. Julia seemed to have a proprietary attitude where Hunter was concerned.

Hunter paused right outside the Sheppertons' box and smiled at her. "You look absolutely ravishing tonight, Arielle."

"What?" His rich baritone startled Arielle. Nevertheless, she didn't miss the underlying seductiveness. Her face heated and she giggled nervously. "Thank you, my lord," she said in a shaky tone. "You're very kind."

"Are you all right?"

"Yes," Arielle quickly answered. "My mind wandered and for that I apologize."

"That happens sometimes, my lady. Apology accepted."

They pushed aside the red velvet curtains and entered the Sheppertons' private box. A very pretty young brunette sat there with Douglas and Julia, talking with animation and holding a glass of champagne.

"Lord and Lady Pembishire," Hunter said in a cheery voice laced with humor, bowing chivalrously over Julia's hand. Obviously he, too, realized why he had been invited to join the Sheppertons in their box.

Arielle got the impression that Hunter enjoyed besting Julia at her silly games. The low-cut golden gown the countess wore intensified the color of her gold-green eyes. Dark, sweeping lashes, lengthened with false ones, lowered, and she leaned closer, intending to impart something to Hunter. However, the sound of her husband's voice stopped her.

"Hunter, old man." Douglas rose from his seat and shook Hunter's hand in the way old friends do. A tall man in his midforties, Douglas wore his lineage like a proud emblem. Finely chiseled features, dark hair streaked with gray, and a domineering personality made for a very intriguing combination. The earl glanced at Arielle and the same amusement shining in Hunter's eyes lit his own. "So glad you could make it. And you, too, Lady Arielle."

Just as Arielle curtsied to the earl, Julia's gaze fell on her.

"Hello, Lady Julia." This was the woman her father dallied with, who simply hated the ground Arielle walked on, and who wouldn't take kindly to this intrusion. "It's lovely to see you again."

"Why . . . why Arielle! W-what are *you* doing here?" Julia managed, rising to her feet, her voice quivering in surprise.

"*I* invited her, Julia," Hunter put in. "I hope you don't mind?"

Tension thickened in the confines of the red and gold decorated box.

"Er, um, do I mind, my lord? Certainly not," Julia replied, a hint of pink showing through her makeup, giving credence to her faux pas. "Arielle is always welcome."

"Thank you, Julia." Arielle curtsied again, hoping to smooth things over. She didn't want another silly feud to start over something so trivial. Besides, Julia Shepperton was partly responsible for Arielle's very successful debut into society. But much had happened in the two years since, and Arielle didn't think their tentative friendship would ever be reclaimed.

"Please be seated, Lady Arielle," Douglas suggested.

Arielle inched her way next to the all-but-forgotten young woman. A twinge of sympathy toward the disappointed girl shot through her. She was slumped in her chair, clearly embarrassed.

"Allow me to introduce Lady Cornelia Brimly," Douglas said. He frowned at Julia, his mouth tightening. "Our other guest for the evening."

Hunter bowed as chivalrously over Lady Cornelia's hand as he had over Julia's, and brought it to his lips, barely touching it. "My lady," he said, "my pleasure."

That he was a gentleman Arielle had never questioned. That he was a charmer she was discovering every day. Hunter outranked them all.

"Thank you, my lord," Lady Cornelia said stiffly,

barely audibly, the quelling glance she cast at Arielle
meant to intimidate and insult. Tea roses decorated her
mass of hair, piled high on her head. The gown she wore
wasn't as revealing as Julia's but not nearly as conser-
vative as Arielle's—and Arielle's wasn't all that conser-
vative.

Hunter smiled at Arielle, then seated himself next to
her, while Douglas sat on the end next to Hunter. That
put Julia on the opposite end.

Her pretty features scrunched in a frown and she narrowed her eyes at Arielle, before calling out in a loud
whisper, "Douglas!"

"Yes, my dear?"

"Aren't you in the wrong seat?" Julia snapped.

With a great show of inspection, Douglas looked
around. "I don't think so, sweet," he said with forced con-
geniality.

Stiffening her spine and snapping open her fan, Julia
began fanning furiously. She glared at Arielle, the storm
brewing within her easy to sense. "How did you manage
this?" she sneered in a loud whisper, not caring that Cornelia sat between them.

"This?" Arielle asked calmly, feigning ignorance.

"An escort with his lordship, Arielle. I'll never forgive
you for making me look like a fool. I'll ruin you. I swear.
I wonder how it would go over if it were known how
much time you spend in Dr. DeVries's company."

Arielle's calm quickly deserted her, but she drew in a
breath, knowing better than to cause a scene. Yet she resented Julia's insinuations. She resented her blaming Arielle for her devious trick backfiring. The gall of the
woman! "I sympathize with how you feel," she managed
in a steady voice. She looked directly at Julia and used
the same pitch that Julia had, so as not to make Hunter
or Douglas aware of the disagreement. It was bad enough
they had a captive audience in Cornelia, which, of course,
Julia knew when she began her tirade. "We all must take
disappointment in stride. Take a certain gentleman I

know, for instance. His improper dalliances with a certain high-born, *married* woman has me sorely disillusioned—"

Julia paused her fan-wielding hand in midair, the color dropping from her face, giving her a bloodless, ghostly appearance. "W-what?"

"Yes! Can you imagine? I suppose the chippy thinks she's getting away with playing a floozy. How do you feel about that, my lady?"

"W-well—" Julia began.

There was always one friend that knew everything there was to know about you. In Julia's case that friend seemed to be Lady Cornelia, for she was just as ashen as Julia, her eyes as rounded as she stared at Arielle.

"I have forgiven him, of course," Arielle continued in the same unconcerned tone she'd begun with. "Perhaps the tart seduced him. Or maybe he was too lonely to resist her advances. Whatever the reason, it's his affair." She smiled sweetly at the two women. "Just as my escort is mine."

Julia cleared her throat. "Of . . . course. As I said before, it's always a pleasure to see you."

Arielle inclined her head, wondering what made Julia disdain her so in the first place. "Thank you, my lady."

"By the by, Arielle," Julia went on, a smile pasted on her lips. "My boorish husband neglected to introduce my Cornelia to you."

"Julia," Cornelia began, a little weakly, adjusting herself in her seat to better look at Arielle, "it was only an oversight. I'll introduce myself. Hello, Arielle, I'm Cornelia."

"A pleasure, Cornelia," Arielle responded, regretting already her sniping at Julia. Calling her a tart and a floozy might have been out of order, but Julia needed to know that she wouldn't tolerate any threats from her; she would give as much as she got.

But Julia wouldn't forget this evening, Arielle knew. Nor would she forgive her. Tonight's discord would go no further than this box, however.

Hunter's huge hand enfolded hers and Arielle looked up at him. So many rules of protocol had been broken tonight that she couldn't help but smile. But who cared? She certainly didn't. She'd been on the marriage mart for months and for one reason or another had managed to evade the two proposals given her.

It really didn't matter to her what rumors the other gossips of the ton began after tonight. In a very short while, she would be in another world entirely—one of education and discussion, books and societies.

The curtain rose on the stage, revealing actors dressed in various costumes for their roles, and Arielle sighed.

Hunter's hand around hers caused her skin to prickle. With great difficulty, but stern determination, she pushed all other thoughts from her mind.

Her attention focused on the stage—an object that vied with the magnificent man sitting next to her.

12

My Dear Hunter,

Last night was most glorious. Never have I enjoyed an evening more. I must confess it would not have been so had I been escorted by anyone else. Thank you for a perfect outing. However, I must reciprocate with an invitation to dinner with Papa and me. I believe it's high time you met him. Especially since we were undoubtedly seen by potential rumormongers at the theater.

I will tell Papa of our outing without mentioning your intention to aid me with my admission into medical college. He certainly would never understand, as he does not support my dreams.

I will arrange dinner to suit your busy schedule. I hope to hear from you at your earliest convenience.

Yours truly,
Arielle

Arielle took the letter from Georgette. "What do you think?"

Georgie relaxed on Arielle's bed, her pretty deep rose gown spilling over the sides of the bed. They'd retreated here twenty minutes ago. It hadn't taken long before the entirety of her short acquaintance with Hunter had spilled out. Soon after, Arielle was thrusting the letter she'd written last night into Georgie's hand for her to read.

"It's perfect, Ellie," Georgie said, her hazel eyes dreamy. She stretched with contentment, rubbing her hand over the small, almost indiscernible mound of her belly. "And so romantic."

"Romantic?" Arielle echoed, raising her eyebrows. "Really, Georgie, it's only a letter." Quickly, she addressed the envelope, wishing for a faster means of correspondence.

"Only a letter?" Georgie sat up, her black curls bouncing with the abruptness of her movements. "Perhaps the first one might have been 'only a letter,' but not the successive ones. I still can't believe you were brash enough to send him a letter asking his help in the first place."

"Oh, Georgie." Arielle joined her on the bed and bowed her head. "I know. But I was near to desperate."

Georgie put an arm around her shoulder and kissed her on the cheek, much the way they'd comforted each other as young girls. "Ellie, darling, I'm not condemning you. Quite the opposite. I applaud your courage." She paused for effect, waiting for Arielle to look at her. The expected attention came quickly and when it did, Georgie said, "But it appears to have backfired on you."

"How so?"

"From your account, his lordship has yet to truly raise the subject in question. One inquiry, Ellie? There are other schools, you know. In my opinion, he seems smitten with you and is trying to dissuade you from your course without actually saying he's doing so."

"Georgette, really!" Arielle huffed, standing from the bed and walking to the window. Dreary gray skies matched her mood. First, Maisy suggested she rethink her life because *she* seemed smitten with the marquess and now Georgie was telling her Hunter wasn't really keeping his promise to her because *he* was smitten with her. Her cheeks heated at the very idea of Savage being attracted to her.

"Why, Arielle Judith Stanford. You're blushing! Is the attraction between you two mutual?"

"I never said I was attracted to him."

"Neither has he said anything about you, but the signs are obvious. Tell me what has passed between you two. Has he kissed you yet?"

"Georgette, how you do go on," Arielle grumbled, not entirely unkind but not pleased either. She realized she wished she could admit that he had kissed her.

"I'm sorry, Ellie," Georgie said with a laugh, halting next to her, a bundle of energy despite her pregnancy. She put her hand on Arielle's shoulder. "It's just so strange to see you interested in something, or in this case, *someone*, other than medicine."

Georgie was right. Everything else in her life had suffered since she'd really become interested in the healing arts. Once, she'd loved to ride her horse through Hyde Park; she'd enjoyed tending to the hothouse flowers at their country estate; she'd enjoyed visits with Georgie. Sometimes, she even looked forward to seeing her sisters. Always, however, she had an interest in helping the sick. At Hyacinth, her father's huge country home, she'd tended his ill tenants and made elixirs, powders, and balms from the plants she found in the surrounding woods. Somehow, though, she'd resigned herself to the fact that she'd make her debut, enjoy a suitable match with an eligible bachelor, and do what a woman was supposed to do.

Then, just as she made her spectacular debut into society, she'd met Quentin and he fueled dreams she should never have had. Dreams of aspiring to more than the mere lady of the house with a healing touch. Dreams that included making it her profession and becoming licensed. She'd gone after that goal with single-minded determination and swore nothing would stand in her way.

That's the reason she'd contacted Hunter in the first place. But being with him made her remember what she was giving up for an uncertain future. She remembered what it was like to live for the moment and to the fullest. She felt whole, complete, and fulfilled.

She smiled sadly at Georgie. "It wouldn't be wise for me to form a tendresse for the marquess, Georgie," she said softly, not wanting to admit that she already had but knowing she couldn't deny it or act upon it. "Not given my future intentions. His lordship wouldn't consent to a physician-wife. Or one whose parentage isn't sterling."

Georgie snorted. "Have you asked him? Perhaps, if you ask him the right way, he'd give you the very moon and wouldn't care if you were a pauper's by-blow."

Arielle scowled at her friend. Georgie meant well, but Arielle didn't want to hear anything that would give her false hopes. She *had* asked Hunter and already knew his answer regarding his thoughts on her becoming a physician and being a wife. She hadn't mentioned her illegitimacy because she tried to make it as inconsequential as possible to herself. She had the protection of Thomas's loyalty to her mother, so she really didn't have to worry that anyone would discover the truth.

Georgie held up her hands. "All right, I withdraw the question. But perhaps he will endeavor to change your mind, Ellie—"

"Bite your tongue! Nothing and no one will deter me from my goal."

"We'll see, love." She resumed her reclining position on the bed as Arielle returned to her seat. "Ellie," she continued in a more serious vein, "to be loved by someone you love is the closest thing to heaven. I want you to have what Eric and I have."

Arielle's sadness deepened and she passed a tired hand over her eyes. She'd spent the entire night tossing and turning, torn between sending the letter as she'd written it or pouring out exactly what she was feeling in those moments—the same dreamy emotions that Georgie felt for Eric. But she doubted she'd ever experience what Georgie and Eric had together. And, now that she'd met Hunter, all other men paled in comparison.

"Georgie, my friend, I do love you so and I want nothing more than to see you always as happy as you are today. But I fear not even yours will last, if you and Eric don't marry each other posthaste. Your condition is becoming rather obvious."

Georgie positively glowed at the remark, oblivious to the adversity of her situation. Arielle smiled at her friend's happiness.

"Isn't it wonderful, Ellie? Eric and I will soon be parents!"

Shocked at Georgie's words, Arielle shook her head at her friend. She seemed not to care about her impending ruination. "Doesn't your condition concern you, Georgie?"

"Ellie," Georgie said, bounding off the bed and sitting on the edge, next to Arielle so that their knees brushed, "I promised Eric to keep our secret, but I must tell you, my dearest friend." She dropped her voice to a conspiratorial whisper. "We were married a fortnight ago in Gretna Green."

"No!" Arielle squealed, hugging Georgie tightly. "How utterly wonderful!"

"Isn't it, though?" Georgie said, laughing gleefully.

The impulse to host a celebratory ball in Lord and Lady Astor's honor surfaced in Arielle's mind, but then she realized what Georgie had said. The marriage was a secret. "Why the secrecy?"

"Eric and his father are estranged, and he wouldn't have sanctioned our marriage. Eric believes the earl will come around when he learns his grandchild is on the way. I'm sure he will, too."

"I do hope so." Arielle hugged Georgie again and smiled. "Just think, my lady, now I'll have to bow to you."

"Not if you marry Savage," Georgie said, giggling mischievously.

Arielle pinched Georgie. "You're incorrigible, Lady Astor."

"Arielle?" A light tap on the door followed the sound of her father's voice.

"Yes, Papa?" Arielle called as she went to the door and opened it. "What can I do for you?"

Georgie automatically stood and curtsied. "Good afternoon, Lord Stanford."

"Hello, Georgette." Thomas nodded to Georgie, giving her the barest glimpse before focusing on Arielle again. "I didn't mean to intrude, my dear. I didn't know you had a guest."

"It's all right, Papa. If you don't mind, we can talk later."

"Very well."

Thomas sidled another look at Georgie, his eyes straying to the slight protrusion of her stomach. Georgie splayed her hands across her belly in the protective manner she was coming to use more and more.

Thomas glanced at Arielle and then at Georgie again. She smiled brilliantly and nodded her head in confirmation. The viscount's fleshy face pinkened and he released an embarrassed cough, then backed out the door. "We'll talk later," he told Arielle, then hurried down the hall.

Arielle closed the door, then turned and found Georgie doubled over with laughter. "Georgette, you're horrible!" she said, joining her in laughter. "That look on my father's face was priceless."

"He won't say anything, Ellie," Georgette said between gasps. "He would be too embarrassed to."

"Besides the fact that I would have to remind Julia Shepperton that her husband's name is Douglas and not Thomas."

Georgie sobered immediately. She gasped, staring at Arielle in wide-eyed fascination. "Oh, my God! Your father and Lady Pembishire are involved?"

Wrinkling her nose in distaste, Arielle nodded. "They keep your secret and we'll keep theirs. That is until you no longer have a secret. Hopefully by then my father will have seen some sense."

"Oh, such wonderful gossip!" Georgie said with a

mournful sigh. "Imagine what Julia would do with it if she weren't involved."

"I know. Although she did manage to do a little sniping last night."

"She wouldn't be Julia if she hadn't."

"I know. And imagine what she'll do when she discovers the lowly baron's daughter is now a countess-to-be in her own right."

"I never thought of that! She's going to have an absolute hissy fit. I simply must be there when she receives the news."

Arielle laughed. "Come, Georgie, I must have my letter delivered. Then we can chat downstairs over tea."

"A lovely way to top the afternoon," Georgie said, following her through the doorway.

13

Dear Arielle,

    I received your very gracious letter. Needless to say, I was quite flattered by your generous invitation. It's true, the restoration of Braxton Hall does occupy most of my time. However, I will let nothing stand in the way of seeing you again. I am at your disposal, my dear. I only ask that you let me know a day ahead.

                              Yours always,
                              Hunter

"You know she might get the wrong impression, old man?"

Hunter scowled as Douglas Shepperton greeted him with that question. The earl had been situated in Hunter's study and saw the letter that Hunter had penned to Arielle just that morning.

"Yours always?" Pembishire continued, raising his eyebrows. "What the devil do you mean by that?"

His glare deepening, Hunter snatched the letter that his friend held out to him. "Whatever I mean isn't your bloody business, Douglas," he snapped. "Arielle and I are only friends. The lady has aspirations to become a physician."

"You don't say?" Douglas seemed to consider that for a moment.

"I expect this to be kept in the strictest confidence,"

Hunter went on. "The only reason she and I are acquainted is because she came to me for my help to get into the Royal College of Physicians. Once her goal is met, there'll be no need for us to continue our acquaintance."

He frowned at that last bit, the full impact of his own words settling into him. When he'd first reconsidered his decision to help Arielle, it was because of her youth. Now, his reasons were purely selfish. He simply enjoyed her company and didn't want to lose her to what he considered a waste of her life in the first place. However, he'd already set everything in motion with the Board of Regents. He had a request in for an urgent meeting as soon as they reconvened.

Hunter crossed to the liquor table and poured himself a measure of whisky. Tossing it down his throat, he allowed the fiery sensation to roll into his belly. Yet it didn't ease the hollow feeling spreading through him at the thought of never seeing Arielle again. Once she got into the university, she'd be too busy for frivolities. Her studies would consume her time. He'd never know the feel of her lips against his own; the brush of his body next to hers; the ecstatic bliss of lovemaking with her.

"You know I would never betray your confidence, Hunter," Douglas said quietly. He was standing next to him at the liquor table, staring at him in concern. Douglas had taken Hunter under his wing after Proctor died ten years ago. In fact, he'd tried to dissuade him from joining the army without any heirs to the Braxton legacy. It was understandable that Douglas was concerned for him and offered unsolicited advice. "However, tongues will undoubtedly begin to wag, especially after your appearance together. Why put the young lady through that spoilage unduly? Isn't it bad enough her name will be forever tarnished once her aspirations are discovered?"

"There was certainly no harm done—"

"No harm?" Douglas asked incredulously. "When the

two of you were seen arriving together without the benefit of a chaperon in your company?"

Frustrated, Hunter thrust a hand through his hair. Of course he should have known better than to invite her out with him, when she didn't have proper attendance. Being older and wiser, that fault was his. However, he wouldn't take full responsibility. The rest of the responsibility lay with her family, especially her father. Indeed, it was high time he met Viscount Stanford, as Arielle suggested. It was against the mores of refinement to go into the man's home with hostility brimming from him, but he had a strong notion to box the man's ears for his neglect of Arielle.

Now, from what Arielle suggested in her letter, Stanford did not support or understand her dreams. Although Hunter didn't support the idea of her becoming a physician, he understood her desire to find a place where her existence was felt and her opinion respected. Only, Hunter didn't feel entering the male-dominated field of medicine would accomplish that. It would only bring her more heartache and misery. She'd suffer untold ostracism. Of that he was certain. Her way wouldn't be easy.

"I realize you are trying to dissuade her from her chosen path," Douglas said quietly, walking to the huge bay window that overlooked what had once been a clear path to the lake. "But perhaps your reasons are becoming much more personal."

"Perhaps," Hunter admitted, that idea not sitting well with him either. If he couldn't have a stranger wasting her life with a bastard marquess, he certainly couldn't have a woman he'd come to admire and respect do so. But he played a dangerous game and he knew it. "I assure you that she won't enroll in class with a swelling belly. She'll be as intact then as she was the day that I met her."

"Or you could let life's natural progression take place, marry her, and then watch her grow round with your child. And heir," he added for emphasis, looking directly into Hunter's eyes.

"What the devil makes you think I would choose this particular girl as my wife and mother to my daughters and sons? Even if she weren't hellbent on a different path?"

"Tell me that you wouldn't and I'll keep quiet for as long as you continue your association with Lady Arielle." Douglas pointed to the letter before Hunter formed any words to refute him. "That, however, speaks for itself, especially 'I will let nothing stand in the way of seeing you.' And your ending speaks volumes. Am I making too much of it? Or are you making too little of it?"

Douglas walked back to the liquor table and poured out two glasses of whisky. Handing one to Hunter, he smiled mischievously. "Just something for you to mull over, old man. Now, send off your letter and then I'd like to hear about the improvements you're engaging in and if there's anything I can do to help out."

Yours always?

Arielle stared at the closing and wondered at its meaning. Was Hunter trying to tell her something? Was he as attracted to her as she was to him? Whatever happened to "most cordially yours"?

Arielle reread the short note and smiled as she came to her favorite sentence. *However, I will let nothing stand in the way of seeing you again.* Her hand trembled as she sat at her desk and she held the letter against her breast, trying to absorb his essence through the parchment that he'd touched.

She remained this way for a few moments, then she allowed reality to set in. This wasn't going well. Perhaps by gesture, certainly not by deed, she'd conveyed a conflicting impression to the marquess. She definitely was attracted to him and she most certainly harbored dreamy ideas that he'd marry her come what may. Since that was fantasy rather than fact, she wanted nothing more than his aid. When next they met, she'd reiterate that to him.

With a sigh, she stuffed the letter in the pocket of her

calico dress. She'd heard her father return some time ago after having been absent most of the day and decided to go down and chat with him.

She found Thomas at his desk, going over some crucial bills. She stopped in the open doorway.

"Papa, may I come in?"

"Arielle, my dear, of course you may come in." He smiled and closed his ledger. "Have you gotten a reply from his lordship?"

"That's what I would like to discuss with you, Papa." Arielle walked in and seated herself. "I need only to give Lord Savage a day's notice. Will Saturday be convenient for you?"

Thomas swallowed convulsively, his eyes bulging. "Saturday?" he asked in a strangled voice.

Arielle knew her father set Saturdays aside exclusively for Julia. The afternoons he spent with Lady Shepperton sometimes stretched into the evenings.

"If that's not convenient—"

"No! No, Arielle," Thomas quickly stated. "Saturday is perfect. I am anxious to meet Lord Braxton. I am quite gratified that he's caught your interest."

She had an inkling of where this was going, but gave him her full attention anyway. "Really, Papa? Why?"

"Child, this is the first time in over two years that you've been interested in anyone besides Quentin De-Vries. It's rather refreshing, don't you think?"

She shifted her weight and folded her hands in her lap, hoping her look was one of extreme serenity and not the hodgepodge of emotions roiling inside her. "I'll send his lordship a reply, Papa, and pen in Saturday for the dinner date." Not giving him a chance to say anything further, she got up and kissed her father on his cheek. "I'll send Maisy in with tea, unless you have other plans?"

Thomas regarded her, as though he guessed her earlier thoughts of his Saturday rendezvous with Julia. He rubbed a beefy hand across his balding forehead, his look forlorn. "No, my dear, I have no other plans," he said after a long pause. "I would appreciate your company after you finish your correspondence to the marquess."

Returning his smile, Arielle nodded. "Of course, Papa. I would like that."

She returned to her room to pen her note. She would keep it short and to the point. No sense in giving herself or the marquess any hope for a future between them. Choosing her words carefully, she began.

> *Dear Hunter,*
>   *It is my utmost pleasure to invite you to dine at Stanford Manor on Saturday at eight o'clock. My father is looking forward to meeting you. I hope the meeting will be as pleasant as I foresee it to be. Until then, stay well.*
>
>   *Yours truly,*
>   *Arielle*

"Have you gotten your letter off?" Thomas asked a half hour later, when Arielle joined him in the parlor.

"Yes, Papa."

Maisy had already brought in the silver tea service and light pastries. The refreshments sat on the small table, near the brand-new, gleaming piano that had arrived a month ago. Shaking her head at the extravagance, Arielle poured herself a cup of tea, then sat across from her father. He seemed to have aged overnight. His face was lined and his eyes seemed cloudy. With worry? Despair? Frustration? Or a combination of all three? In order to help him, she needed to get to the bottom of his troubles—their troubles, she corrected.

"How are you keeping, Papa?" she asked, allowing her concern to surface.

"Why do you ask, Arielle? Are you looking for someone to practice your misguided skills on?" Thomas asked jokingly.

Arielle laughed softly. "No, Papa," she said. "But it's

hard to hide my concern, when you look so troubled."

Thomas shook his head ever so slightly. "You are quite amazing, Arielle, with your keen perception. If the strictures of our time weren't so prohibitive, you would probably make an excellent doctor."

"Papa!" Her father's words astounded her. He'd never before voiced any positive thoughts on the matter of her chosen vocation.

"But," he continued, detecting the hopeful note in her tone, "there are strictures and laws, and your willfulness to enter the medical profession is not only outrageous but pointless."

"So you keep informing me, Papa," Arielle said, annoyed that she'd allowed herself to fall for her father's bait. It was only another trap to draw her into another quarrel. But she wouldn't allow it to happen. "And I refuse to resurrect this tiresome argument." Standing, she went to the table with the refreshments, set her cup and saucer down, and reached for the teapot. "More tea, Papa?"

"Yes, thank you, Arielle." Thomas leaned back in his seat and stared at the ceiling. "I'm sorry for my outburst, child," he said in a pained voice. "But I find myself overly concerned about finances."

Her father delivered the news just as she was pouring the tea. Her hand shook and she accidentally sloshed tea onto the lacy tray lining. "Oh, Papa!"

Looking at her for the briefest moment, then returning to staring blindly at the ornate ceiling, Thomas said, "Don't be alarmed, child. We won't end up as paupers. So don't trouble yourself."

His tired tone wasn't the least bit assuring, but she kept her deepening concern silent. She didn't want to cause him any additional worry. Pasting a smile on her face, she held out the sugar and lemon–laced tea to her father. "If you say so, Papa. Now, enjoy another cup of tea."

"What would you say to having your sisters and their husbands joining us on Saturday?"

Arielle's heart skipped a beat in alarm and her stomach somersaulted at that thought. Have her catty, gossiping sisters attending dinner with Hunter the very first time he was invited to dine at Stanford Manor? She didn't think so. Their main goal, along with Thomas's, was to see her properly wed. Undoubtedly, the pressure for her to make a decent union would only increase with their father's financial problems. She was the last one left unmarried, the last one with the means to marry a fabulously wealthy and extraordinarily blue-blooded lord.

In other words, if Thomas's debts had truly progressed to a point that was beyond repair, she was his one and only salvation. But she'd never use Hunter in such a way. She'd never sacrifice his friendship for the sake of marriage to him when he was quite aware of her heart's desire. She wouldn't have him thinking she was a milk-brained twit who didn't know her own mind. Or worse, an opportunist who sought to snare him in a trap.

Deviating from the course she'd set with Hunter was out of the question. But deviating from the course she'd set for her life, for her father's sake, was another matter altogether. She'd never allow him to end up humiliated in front of society. She'd do whatever he asked of her to help him out of his financial problems. Even if it meant ripping her very heart out and giving up her own dreams.

She'd do everything Thomas asked of her—except use Hunter. Her sisters' presence would begin just such a chain of events. They could be a devious lot. And she didn't want Hunter to see how they treated her.

"Please, Papa, not this time. Perhaps if his lordship sees fit to grace us again in the future, we'll consider having the family."

An enigmatic smile crossing his features, Thomas nodded. "Very well, child. I understand."

Arielle wasn't sure she did. Her father was being just a little too agreeable, and she wondered what was really going on in his mind. No doubt it had something to do with her. She only hoped it didn't include Hunter.

14

At precisely eight o'clock Saturday evening, Arielle sat nervously with her father in the parlor, as Maisy went to the door and allowed Hunter entrance.

Every confidant footfall she heard in the hallway brought him closer to her and made her anticipation rise, cresting like a tidal wave. Her heartbeat roared in her ears and her breath caught when he stopped in the doorway.

A midnight blue serge spencer jacket, gray waistcoat, and white shirt clung to his massive shoulders and narrow waist. The snowy cravat added elegance to his strong neck and dark gray trousers covered his long legs.

The blue of his eyes burned with an intensity that couldn't be denied, deepening that dark sensuality that Arielle had never been able to ignore. It was this that had drawn her to him in unexpected ways in the first place. And now every hot emotion that roiled between them stood in his chiseled features for anyone to see, raw, bold, and daring.

When Arielle smiled at Hunter, he smiled back, his white teeth gleaming, dimples creasing his cheeks at the full tilt of his mouth. The effect was blinding. He nodded. "My lady," he said, then brought his attention to Thomas.

"Lord Braxton," Thomas blustered, "you grace my home with your presence. Welcome, sir."

"My pleasure, Lord Stanford," Hunter replied, shaking Thomas's hand, his demeanor relaxed and casual. Yet Arielle detected a slight edge to his voice and she wondered at the cause. "Thank you for allowing me to come." He turned to Arielle, bending before her and reaching for her hand. He assessed her appreciatively, his glance touching upon her face, lingering upon the paleness of her bosom revealed in the low-cut neckline trimmed with gathered lace flounces. Matching lace trimmed the wrists of the long-sleeved mint gown that she'd carefully chosen for this evening. His gaze traveled further still to the curve of her waist and the flare of her hips. Then, he met her eyes again. Tiny flames turned his gaze molten, sent scorching liquid through her entire body.

A blush stole into her cheeks at Hunter's torrid look.

"My lady," he said again, only more softly, more intimate. He kissed the back of her hand. "I trust you're keeping well?"

Arielle's smile faltered, his hand warm and masculine around hers. "Yes, my lord. Quite."

"*Hunter,* please," his lordship responded with a chortle.

"Well, *Hunter* it is," Thomas put in, clapping the marquess on his back as if they were the oldest of friends.

Irritation stole into Hunter's languid gaze, and he nodded curtly at Thomas. Her father had an amazing knack for insulting and annoying almost everyone he knew. He'd only just met Hunter, and already the marquess seemed completely put off by him. If Thomas realized this, he'd either be sorely disappointed or greatly insulted. Unfortunately, Arielle guessed it would be the latter emotion rather than the former, which wouldn't sit well with Hunter at all. If only she knew what had transpired to irritate Hunter so, she'd smooth it out somehow.

"Please seat yourself, sir," Thomas offered.

"Thank you," Hunter said with cool cordiality. He sat in a chair opposite Arielle.

"Hunter," Thomas began, seating himself next to her on the sofa, "tell me, when and how did you meet my daughter?"

Hunter swallowed and, after what seemed an eternity, grinned lazily. "Why, my lord, I'm sure if Arielle hadn't explained our meeting satisfactorily to you I wouldn't be here this evening. There's really nothing more I can add to her explanation."

"Ahh, well. Er, my daughter informed me last Thursday that she sent you correspondence congratulating you on your heroic return. She also told me of her disappointment at not meeting you at the Pembishires' gathering."

"Really?" A black brow slashed, his eyes sparkling, his grin widening. "What else did she say?"

Thomas's brow knitted and he cleared his throat. He appeared perplexed at Hunter's amiability, although Arielle wasn't any longer. She realized now that his annoyance toward her father was because her father virtually allowed her to run rampant while he pursued his own interests. She suspected too that Hunter remained silent on the true history of their meetings and correspondences because of her.

But her father wouldn't know any of this, and he wouldn't want Hunter to know that either. As long as he was able to do as he pleased, he didn't care what Arielle did—as long as it wasn't a serious pursuit of the one and only dream she'd ever had.

With the tiniest sparkle of pity for her father, she listened as he blustered his way through the merry chase Hunter's statement took him through.

"You know the rest, Hunter. You sought to make amends by inviting her to the theater."

"And I only wanted to return such a gracious gesture by inviting his lordship to dine with us, Papa," Arielle finished, her voice shaky, hardly able to stop herself from exploding into laughter at her father's confused look. She was confident that he'd believed her explanation in the beginning, but now Hunter's mischievous grin had clearly raised some doubts.

At that point, Arielle really didn't care much about her father doubting the truthfulness of her story. She only focused on this new side of the marquess of Savage. He appeared to have a wicked sense of humor. And even if her father *did* have doubts, he'd never question the marquess.

Maisy's voice intruded, and Arielle looked up.

"Milady, if you are ready, I can serve dinner now," the housekeeper said. "Or if you care to have wine first—"

"Perhaps wine right now, Maisy," Arielle interrupted, not willing to miss a chance to prolong the evening with Hunter.

Maisy curtsied. "Yes, milady," she said, just as the door knocker sounded. "Pardon me."

"Who on earth could that be?" Arielle asked while Maisy answered the knock. She passed an accusing look to Thomas. If he'd invited her sisters against her wishes, she'd never forgive him.

A brief moment passed before Maisy returned and handed an envelope to Thomas. "Beggin' your pardon, Lord Stanford. A messenger just delivered this missive for you, sir."

"Thank you, Maisy." Thomas's expression remained blank as he opened the envelope and read its contents. When he finished it, he folded it neatly, cleared his throat, and smiled weakly at Arielle.

Thomas's sheepish look told Arielle that the message was from one person—Julia Shepperton. The brazen tart.

His jowls florid with embarrassment, Thomas shifted in his seat. "Arielle, my dear, would you mind so much if we pass on the wine?"

Arielle hated that her father would so easily throw aside the plans they had together at the slightest wag from the countess of Pembishire. Did her feelings truly mean so little to her father? He couldn't even recognize how important this evening was to her. "Why, Papa?" she asked, testy and hurt.

"Why, I . . . ahh . . . have an urgent message to . . . ah, meet . . . er, Lord Twickenbot at White's tonight."

Arielle narrowed her eyes at him. "Of all the banbury tales—"

"We can have wine with our dinner, Arielle," Thomas

said quickly to diffuse her rising temper. That his own temper didn't flare attested to his guilt. More than likely, he'd arranged for Julia to send the note to hasten things along. Then, he wouldn't have to give up his plans for the sake of Arielle. "I'm sure his lordship doesn't have time to sit and waste the entire evening with you—er, us, either."

"As a matter of note, Stanford," Hunter said icily, "I have all the time in the world to give Arielle. Something you should try one day."

Thomas rose to his feet at Hunter's unrestrained hostility. "See here, sir."

"See here indeed," Hunter echoed, coming to his feet also, his shoulders taut, his fists balled at his sides. The marquess looked imposing, seemingly made of granite. Fury percolated from him. "You have the audacity to suggest I'm wasting my time with *your* daughter and then have the further gall to become insulted at *my* annoyance."

Thomas puffed up to his full height, further deteriorating conditions already spiraling out of hand. Hunter threw Thomas a fierce look and he wilted.

"You are right, my lord," Thomas said, the gleam in his eyes calculating, considering, looking from Hunter to Arielle and back again.

Seeing the schemes brewing behind her father's patently false calm, Arielle sighed, pasting a smile on her lips. "Hunter, would you mind terribly if we went straight to the dining table?"

"Not at all, Lady Arielle. I am really quite ready to eat."

"Please accept my deepest apologies, Hunter. This . . . ah . . . is really unexpected and most unavoidable."

"I understand perfectly, Thomas," Hunter said. "These things have a way of occurring at the most inopportune moments." He reached for Arielle's hand.

Arielle slipped her arm through Hunter's. "Then shall we retire to the dining chamber, my lords?"

"By all means." Thomas hastily led the way.

Moments later, they entered the room and Hunter paused, his gaze touching every part of the moderate-sized chamber. At first view, the chamber took one's breath away. Pompeian red paint covered the walls. Gilded Palladian plasterwork and tiny mirrors dominated the high ceilings, serving as the perfect frame from the equally and heavily gilded grand chandelier in the middle.

"Quite a spectacular room you have, Stanford," Hunter said, as they took their respective places at the table.

"Thank you, Hunter," Thomas said with a proud smile. "Recently redid the entire town house. Couldn't have it said I was outdated and out of style, you know? Can't find a good match for Arielle if all of polite society believes us to be paupers."

Hunter lifted a brow, a bold, black slash indicating his surprise. "I didn't realize Arielle was in search of a good match."

"Aren't all proper young ladies in search of a well-heeled husband, my lord?" Arielle snapped, angry that her father brought this up in front of Hunter. Glaring at Thomas, she snatched the dinner bell from the table and rang it.

"Even you, my dear," Thomas countered as the door leading to the kitchens opened. The cook and two kitchen maids walked in. He sidled a glance at Hunter. "Meet the right man and you'll forget all about whatever else it is you'd like to do."

"This isn't the time for this discussion, Papa," Arielle said, then fell silent as Cook directed her staff.

With efficiency and quietness gleaned from years of working in noble households, Cook laid dish after dish on the sideboard from the cart she'd wheeled out while a maid poured wine and water into the glasses.

"I'm sure his lordship doesn't wish to be subjected to one of our endless arguments on the course that my life should take," Arielle finished on a heated whisper, not wishing to have the servants gossiping about her. Arguing with her father wasn't anything new. Arguing with her father in the presence of such a prestigious guest was.

"Perhaps, if he knew of—"

"I have no desire to hear this very personal discussion, Lord Stanford," Hunter put in, effectively cutting Thomas off.

Thomas snapped his mouth shut and Arielle mouthed "Thank you" to Hunter.

After serving everyone, the maid departed. Arielle sliced into a seasoned chicken breast and chewed, then asked, "Are you acquainted with Lord Twickenbot, Hunter?"

"I can't say that I am, Arielle," Hunter answered. "Other than what you told me at the theater, I know nothing of the man. Although I met him some years ago." He looked at Thomas. "I trust that Twickenbot is in no distress, Thomas."

His eyes widening in surprise at the rancor in Hunter's voice, Thomas coughed and set his fork aside. "Arrest your worries, Hunter. I have every confidence that Twickenbot is quite up to snuff. However, the sooner I get there, the quicker I'll find out."

Hunter nodded, his nostrils flaring. "Please, don't let me delay you, Thomas." Displeasure rang in his voice. Setting his napkin aside, he started to stand.

"My lord Savage, there's no need for *you* to leave," Thomas said quickly. "Arielle is excellent company. Maisy will attend in my stead."

Arielle exchanged a surprised glance with Hunter. Hurt pierced her, a jagged wound with deep, sharp pain. For his own selfish needs, her father would allow her reputation to be torn to shreds. It was bad enough she'd attended the theater without a proper chaperon, but to entertain an eligible man in the privacy of her home was another matter altogether. She had always walked a fine line with her reputation, but to the ton she was just an eccentric with a wayward view. No one had ever truly witnessed how thoroughly her father disregarded her. And of all the people to witness this humiliation, it had to be Hunter.

It cut deeply.

"Of course, Papa," she said, holding back the hurt in her tone by sheer willpower. "That's very thoughtful of you."

Thomas stood and walked to her, laying his hand on her shoulder. "Arielle, child," he began quietly.

"Please, Papa." Arielle shrugged away from his touch, her throat hurting from the effort to keep her tears at bay. But she never cried over whatever her father did. She wouldn't start now. She was used to this. After all, she didn't hold the highest of places in her father's regard. A watery smile curved her mouth. "You should go. Surely you don't want to be late."

"You are most perceptive, child. I know you understand the importance of this meeting." Thomas stepped away from the table, away from the plate with the forgotten food. "Again, my deepest, most sincere apologies to both of you." He bowed to Hunter, then turned and departed the room, leaving Hunter and Arielle alone.

15

Frigid, damp night air chilled Thomas to the bone and he huddled deeper into the saddle of his horse, his great coat offering little protection against the bitter cold.

He should have allowed his driver to bring him to his destination in the carriage. But he needed the utmost stealth as he made his way to his rendezvous with the countess of Pembishire. This business of bedding another man's wife was risky enough. Added to that was Arielle's astuteness, which he sincerely lamented. Judging by the bitter hurt gleaming from her eyes, she'd guessed the contents of the note.

It never made Thomas proud at having to leave her alone so much. However, he couldn't deny his own needs either. Arielle's four sisters were all married and busy with their own interests. Besides, his four older girls and Arielle were as different as left was from right. Arielle was bold and beautiful, bright and headstrong. The other girls were all perfectly willing to content themselves with the lives that had been predetermined for them.

Sighing, he turned the horse in the direction of the Thames. Perhaps, if Arielle had been more like her sisters, they might have watched over her better than they did. As it was, Arielle's only companions were that wanton Georgette and that bloody Quentin. Neither suited Thomas to keep company with his daughter.

Arielle was too wayward for her own good. Marriage was her only solution. But marriage to whom? Who would tolerate the chit's nonsensical views?

Marriage. If only the arrogant marquess could be persuaded to accept her hand in marriage. . . .

He recalled the look on Arielle's face as Hunter Braxton stood in the doorway of the parlor. He'd never thought any man could put such a dreamy expression in his daughter's eyes. But Savage had.

Marriage.

Marriage to the marquess of Savage. That idea appealed to Thomas more than any others. Arielle needed a strong hand to keep her settled. Besides, she seemed quite taken with his lordship. And he was quite wealthy.

Thomas urged his horse on. He had the perfect reason to coerce a marriage between them, although it hadn't been his intention to begin with. Accusing Savage of compromising Arielle in some way would force his hand. The arrogant marquess needed to be brought down a peg.

Recalling Savage's high position brought to mind a missive he had recently received from the elusive duke of Ridgeley. Thomas had never met the man and hadn't an inkling why he'd gotten an invitation from him to meet with him at his estate tomorrow.

Undoubtedly, the duke had him confused with someone else. However, Thomas would keep the appointment, if for no more than curiosity's sake. It might prove interesting to discover why the duke had summoned him, accident or no.

Right now, though, getting to the warmth of Julia's arms and out of the bitter night air was Thomas's most immediate goal.

Her appetite fleeing at her father's hasty departure, Arielle toyed through the rest of the four-course meal. Still, she managed a smile at the robust appetite Hunter displayed. He sampled all the different foods Cook and her assistants placed before him, all the while praising how delicious they were.

When he touched his napkin to his lips and rose from

the table, Arielle invited him to the parlor for liqueurs.
There, she voiced her displeasure over Thomas's infelic-
itous actions, and apologized for him.

"Arielle," Hunter said in a soothing tone, "I am sure
your father wouldn't have cut short his meal if the matter
wasn't urgent enough to warrant it."

Although thoroughly humiliated by her father's deeds,
she'd regained her composure. Hunter's equitableness
took some of the edge off her simmering emotions. However, in spite of his demeanor, Arielle knew that Hunter,
too, was displeased.

"I'm sure the matter was important, Hunter. My father
would never commit such a social blunder without good
reason."

Rising from his seat across from her, Hunter moved to
the sofa and sat next to her. He took her hand in his.
Without warning, he kissed the back of it. Then, turning
it over, he pressed his lips against the sensitive skin of
her palm.

"Are you as put out over his absence as I am?" he asked
huskily. His eyes twinkling, he glanced over his shoulder
at Maisy, who had situated herself in a far corner behind
them, trying to be as unobtrusive as possible.

Arielle giggled at his words, spoken just for the benefit
of the housekeeper, who chose that moment to excuse
herself and promised to return as soon as possible.

"Terribly," she responded, devouring him with her
gaze, his touch, his nearness all wrapping her in a cocoon
of protection and excitement. She ached for him and the
fulfillment that only he could give her. In medical ter-
minology, it was sexual intercourse. In the frothiness of
a lady's boudoir and the beating of Arielle's heart, it was
lovemaking. "You really are different from who I thought
you were, Hunter."

"Really? And who did you think I was?"

"Not the man that I have seen tonight."

"And what man have you seen tonight, my sweet?"
Hunter asked softly, seductively. He brought the hand that

he'd been holding since he sat down against his lips again. "What man, Arielle?" he whispered again.

His caressing tone sent wet heat spiraling through Arielle's body. "You, Hunter," she said tenderly. "You've surprised me with a kind of freedom I didn't know you possessed."

"It's all because of you, Arielle. I am swamped with obligations. But since I met you, I feel a kind of freedom, a sense of life, of living, I never knew before."

The truth of his words hit Hunter in the gut as Arielle drew in a deep breath. She gazed at him with adoration. Before Arielle, he'd existed merely to fulfill his obligations to king, country, and ancestry. Then, thanks to her sense of independence she'd dropped into his life. Her free-spirited nature allowed her to set her own rules and live her life as she saw fit.

The fact that she didn't have expectations of marriage drew him ever closer to her. Until she was accepted to the school, he could pretend that his dubious past didn't exist and concentrate on enjoying the present.

"I've never met anyone quite like you, my lady. You increasingly invade my mind with thoughts of your free spirit and incredible beauty." Tentatively, he brushed her lips with his own.

Arielle sighed, her breath fanning his mouth, her green gaze burning him with its intensity.

"Arielle," Hunter rasped before closing his mouth with purpose over hers. His tongue lashed out, twining with hers. She tasted like the sweetest of honey and the finest of wines, her lips soft and succulent. Wrapping her arms around his neck, she clung to him like a wild vine, consuming, devouring, seeking. His length hardened, bulged against his trousers, demanded release.

Hunter pulled her closer, onto his lap, wanting to free himself then and there. Her tongue touched his and heat snaked through his veins, filling his groin near to bursting. Her scent exploded in his brain; her taste consumed his better judgment; her response went beyond his most prurient fantasy.

He buried his fingers in the silkiness of her hair, spun gold brought to life. Pins flew everywhere as the heavy mass blanketed them, aroused his senses that much more.

She threw her head back, her legs going around his waist, an instinctive gesture that made him groan. She rocked against him as he pressed his lips against the column of her throat, her most intimate place nestled against his sex. He moved his own hips against her and she moaned, meeting his gaze. Desire brightened her eyes and flushed her cheeks. She bathed his mouth with kisses— his jawline, his brow, his eyelids.

For long moments they remained thus, with Arielle's legs entwined around Hunter's waist, her raised skirts revealing their beauty. Though they were fully dressed, their behavior was scandalous. Scandalous to the point that, had Hunter been willing to subject Arielle to his secrets, he would have gone to Thomas and admitted what had taken place here. The man would have had every right to force his hand in marriage for so thoroughly taking advantage of his daughter.

Not that Stanford would truly give a damn, just as long as Arielle was out of his way. Hunter got the feeling the man disapproved of Arielle's dreams because he felt they reflected badly upon him, not because he truly cared what Arielle did.

"Oh, God," Arielle whispered, the first sign that she was regaining her composure after she'd shattered in his arms. Hastily, she removed herself from his lap and pulled her skirts down. The heat of embarrassment deepened the flush of passion. "My lord—"

Pulling her beside him, Hunter gathered her into his arms. "There's nothing to be ashamed of, darling," he told her. The disturbance between his legs abated slightly, allowing him to shift his weight. He brushed her lips with his own.

"Beggin' your pardon, milord," Maisy squeaked, walking in with a tray of pastries and liqueurs, "you should maintain your distance, sir. Your behavior is inappropriate!"

"Yes, it is, Maisy," Hunter murmured around an ironic smile. If the woman had walked in a few minutes before, she might have cuffed him. And justifiably. At least someone had Arielle's best interests at heart. "For that, I apologize."

"You . . . you're certainly right, Maisy." Arielle patted her hands to her hair. "P-perhaps, it's best if you left us alone for a few moments more."

The housekeeper opened her mouth to protest, but Hunter stopped her before she could.

"You have my word as a former officer in the king's army, that I'll remember my upbringing from this point forward."

Maisy kept her battle stance a moment longer, then nodded. "Yes, milord, milady," she said and went to stand just outside the parlor door.

The moment they were alone, Hunter turned to Arielle. "I won't apologize for what just happened. Not when I want to do it, all over again."

Arielle didn't flinch beneath his gaze. She caressed his cheek with her soft fingertips, then traced the outline of his brow and smiled. "And I want you to, Hunter."

Hunter brushed her cheek for a second, then stood, his heart pounding. "I'd better leave, my dear. It's obvious we shouldn't be alone."

"Of course." Arielle rose from her seat also. "It's best you leave." With wobbly knees, she watched as Hunter donned his great coat, polished beaver top hat, and kid gloves. Dressed for the cold night, he went to the door and turned to her.

"Thank you for your invitation. I will let you know when I hear from the Board of Regents. Good night, sweet Arielle."

Confusion and heat slaking through her, Arielle closed the door after Hunter took his leave and leaned against it.

She'd never understand how the night ended the way it had. It was supposed to have been a cordial evening with her father present to get acquainted with Hunter. Instead, she'd ended up in Hunter's arms, her emotions more in turmoil than ever.

Before meeting Hunter, she'd fixed in her mind what she wanted to be. She still wanted to become a doctor, but, now, she wanted Hunter in her life to share her dream.

An impossible dream, she knew.

Perhaps, if she'd given in to her father's wishes and allowed her sisters to attend the dinner, things would have turned out differently.

As it was, Hunter left saying only that he would contact her when the board reconvened. If she never saw him again, it would break her heart.

Arielle supposed that, knowing what her goals were, Hunter thought to keep his distance. She should've felt honored that he'd allowed his feelings to become so receptive to her.

Walking away from the door, Arielle wondered if, after the incredible chain of events, Hunter might think there were no rules of protocol in the Stanford household.

Tonight, every form of etiquette had been ignored.

16

Ridgeley Court sat atop a soaring cliff that faced the wide, unsettled North Sea. Rolling hills of heather bathed the landscape in purple and led to the sweeping entrance of the red brick structure.

At one thirty the next afternoon, Thomas Stanford's carriage rolled to a stop in Ridgeley Court's driveway. A butler showed the viscount into the south drawing room and bade him to seat himself.

The man bowed. "Forgive me, my lord. The duke will be a few minutes in coming. His lordship asks that you bear with his tardiness."

"Of course," Thomas said, annoyed at the indifferent treatment but having no choice but to accept the delay. When the butler took his leave, Thomas went to the blazing warmth of the fireplace. The chill blowing off the sea dropped the already freezing temperatures to a miserable degree.

Thomas rubbed his arms vigorously, attempting to restore warmth to his body, remembering the heated embrace of a few hours ago, which had warmed him quite well. Yet even the memories of being in Julia's arms didn't help matters. If not for this business, Thomas would still have been in her company, taking turns at pleasuring her and listening to her throaty voice as she talked about everything and nothing.

Her husband had been rusticating at his country estate for over a fortnight and had all but forgotten Julia's existence. And, now, she was angry with Thomas for leaving her as well, to visit with the reclusive old duke of Ridgeley, who hadn't presented himself to the ton in years.

Thomas was already thinking of ways to make this up to Julia. She was in need of a holiday. Perhaps they'd sneak off to Gretna Green for a few nights. While there, he'd focus on nothing but his Julia.

With a disgusted snort, Thomas walked away from his spot near the fireplace. His Julia? She'd never be *his* Julia. She was another man's wife whom he'd happened to fall in love with. There wasn't anything he wouldn't do for Julia, which was part of the reason he was in the bind he found himself in.

Very soon, he'd end up disgraced and humiliated in the eyes of society. He was on the verge of bankruptcy. In the past months, he'd overspent to the point of ruination. He'd wanted to impress Julia; status and affluence meant much to her. It was his willingness to spend on Arielle's debut that had so impressed the countess in the beginning.

Now, he was in a financial abyss that he mightn't ever crawl out of.

Sighing, Thomas glimpsed the decor of the room. Pictures of magnificent ships lined the walls, along with a mariner's map. Someone must have been a seafarer, he thought, strolling around. A gleaming compass caught his eye and he stopped at the duke's desk. Admiring it for a moment, he looked at the miniature ship's bell and other nautical paraphernalia. An array of papers also were scattered on the desk.

Never one to ignore his curiosity, Thomas glanced at the open door to assure himself that his host's appearance wasn't imminent. Then, he brought his regard back to the desk and quickly skimmed through the papers.

Yet Thomas met with disappointment, finding nothing important enough to give him a clue about his host or why the duke would summon him to Ridgeley Court. Pushing aside household statements and other personal letters, he spied a yellowish envelope with a letter partially sticking out. An old letter. That was the first thing immediately obvious.

He glanced toward the door again. Still alone, he extracted the grayish letter without second thought and began reading rapidly. His eyes widened at a most interesting part and he read the statement again. *Your son's intentions were obviously to turn my dear sister into a whore, as she has given birth to his bastard. But Hunter will grow up with respectability. I vow to raise him as my very own. He will inherit my name as well as the Braxton titles and lands. From this day forward, I, Proctor Braxton, am the only living kin Hunter will know. With the closing of this letter, I close the Price chapter in his short life.*

Thomas swallowed hard at this discovery. The marquess of Savage a bastard? It couldn't be! He gazed at the words again and squinted at the faded date. Time and wear had destroyed the exact month and day, but he barely made out the year 1782.

Hunter Braxton, marquess of Savage, and a host of lesser titles behind that, had been born on the wrong side of the sheets. A noble bastard! A bastard that had managed to keep his secret for his entire life. A bastard who would have to pay dearly to keep Thomas's silence.

Of course, Hunter's lofty position and deep pockets should have left him little worry. Yet, the ton were such strange creatures and Hunter really wasn't one of them. He had lived as an outsider for most of his life. Still, he was wealthy, well-titled, and handsome. He would overcome any aspersions against him eventually. On the other hand, a similar discovery of Arielle's heritage could very well ruin her.

Footsteps rustled down the hall. Quickly, Thomas stuffed the letter in his pocket, his hands trembling. This discovery was the solution to his problems. He need only decide how to use it effectively.

Just as that thought crossed his mind, a tall man entered. He had near-white hair and an air of command that even Hunter would be hard-pressed to emulate. Ridgeley's gaze searched Thomas from head to heel, then he nodded.

Momentarily nonplussed at the inspection, Thomas cleared his throat. The cerulean gaze, so like Hunter's, gave credence to the document in his pocket. Thomas's breath caught.

"Hello, sir," the duke greeted with a friendly smile, not at all the man Thomas was expecting. As recluses went, they generally were not so personable, especially blue-blooded ones with bastard grandsons. He rapped his gold and ebony walking cane upon the floor, stepping closer. "You must be Stanford."

"That I am, Your Grace," Thomas replied, wishing for something to pat away the sweat beading his brow. What in bloody hell was happening to him? He had actually stolen someone's personal property. Was he going mad?

The man before him was robust and solidly built, despite his advanced age. His still-massive shoulders hinted at powerful arms. In the blink of an eye, Ridgeley would have Thomas's head on a platter if he discovered the theft. And of course he would discover it. He would miss so important a document if Thomas didn't replace it.

"Forgive the delay, Stanford. I had very pressing business to tend to."

"I didn't mind the wait, Your Grace," Thomas lied. "Although my curiosity is quite profound."

Ridgeley chortled. "As it should be, Lord Stanford." He indicated a chair near the fireplace. "Do seat yourself, sir."

The servant who had shown Thomas to the study reappeared, carrying a tray with a decanter of brandy and two snifters. Pushing the papers aside, he placed the tray on the desk. Afterward, he stacked the papers in a neat pile, then took his leave.

"A very good brandy here, Stanford. Try it," the duke said, pouring a draught and handing it to Thomas. "I pay a handsome price to have it smuggled here. That damnable embargo is the devil's own making." Pouring his own brandy, he sat in the seat at his desk. "Now, then, Lord Stanford. As to the reason I sent for you."

"I'm all ears, Your Grace," Thomas said thinly, the duke's commanding tone making him feel less than worthy of the man's company. He tasted the very good French brandy to fortify his nerves.

"I have just recently learned of my grandson's heroics in service to the king."

Thomas nearly strangled on his brandy. "Your grandson?" he echoed with a sinking heart. Recluse or no, the duke was a very powerful man. If he accepted Hunter back into the fold with open arms, then Thomas's plan would be worthless.

"The marquess of Savage is my grandson, sir," Ridgeley admitted, circling the rim of the crystal snifter with a long finger. Stark sadness clouded the blue eyes. "Although he has no inkling of my existence."

The letter lay heavy against Thomas's chest, the sudden weight nearly suffocating. Guilt guided his hand to his pocket. Monetary need redirected his intentions. Instead of returning the letter to the duke's possession and being summarily thrown out, he brushed his trembling fingers through his hair and said, "I don't understand, Your Grace. What has that to do with me? Do you wish for me to inform Hunter of your existence?"

"That will be *my* duty, Stanford," the duke snapped. "My interest in the Stanfords is in Lady Arielle."

Thomas sat at attention and stared at the duke. The man was just full of surprises. "Lady . . . You know my daughter, sir?"

"I know *of* her, Stanford. She had a spectacular debut. That doesn't go unnoticed. Besides, my grandson has been seen squiring her about. How true is that?"

Surprise stole his voice for a brief moment. Arielle's debut had been two seasons ago. What did the duke know of or want with her? Setting his brandy on the table near him, he finally answered Ridgeley's question. "As a matter of fact, Your Grace, his lordship dined with Arielle and me just last evening. Is that what concerns you?"

"In a way, yes," Ridgeley answered bluntly, leaning back in his seat to stare down his elegant nose. "You see, Stanford, I am an old man. And my grandson isn't getting any younger. Yet he doesn't seem interested in matrimony. Your Arielle is the first and only woman he has shown interest in since his return from the war."

"I didn't know that, Your Grace."

" 'Tis true."

Thomas squinted at the old man, wondering if perhaps he hadn't misjudged him. He still didn't know what he or Arielle had to do with any of this. Perhaps Ridgeley wasn't lucid after all. No sane man would so freely tell the family secrets to someone he wasn't well acquainted with. Stretching his neck from side to side, Thomas asked, "What exactly are you proposing, Your Grace?"

"Since I have long ago given up the pleasures of the flesh, my days of siring are over. But my grandson is in his prime. However, he appears disinterested in carrying on that wastrel's line. Yet, the Ridgeley line is involved, and I don't want *it* to die with him, Stanford."

Left unspoken but quite clear was the fact that Ridgeley wouldn't give two damns if the Braxton line ended.

Thomas nodded. "I understand, Your Grace."

Folding his arms, Ridgeley leaned forward and narrowed his eyes. "I really don't think that you do, Stanford. I think you believe you are talking to an insane old man. Just to make it perfectly clear for you, man, I want you to encourage a romance between my grandson and your daughter, without involving me or yourself."

Arielle married to a marquess, who was sole heir to a dukedom? With his daughter married to Hunter, Thomas's own position would rise considerably. And having a similar background, Hunter might understand Arielle's position if the truth about her birth were ever revealed to *him*.

Marriage between Arielle and Hunter would take considerable worry off Thomas. His last daughter would be safe and secure in a very good union. He would no longer have to worry that she'd waste her life tending the sick.

Lady Arielle Judith Stanford, viscount's daughter, would be a marchioness and future duchess.

Thomas had envisioned just such a union, had even thought to accuse Hunter of compromising his daughter's virtue. But the marquess would never tolerate such a fabrication. What Ridgeley was proposing, however, was something completely different.

It was courtship and society affairs; romance and the first bloom of love between two young people caught in a whirlwind. It was expense and pomp and pageantry. None of which Thomas could afford.

Being nearly penniless, Thomas certainly couldn't afford the lavish wardrobe and the mindless entertainment it would take to keep Arielle and Hunter together. Nor could he pay for Arielle's wedding befitting a union to Hunter.

What the devil could he do to reap the rewards of gaining a wealthy marquess as a husband for his daughter and have his mounting debts discharged at the same time?

"I don't have all bloody afternoon for your answer, man!"

Thomas scowled at the duke's irritation, his self-possession completely regained in the face of these new developments. "No offense meant, Your Grace," he said, just as sharply, "but from what I've gleaned from my brief acquaintance with the marquess, he appears quite arrogant and overly stubborn."

Satisfied laughter escaped the duke. "It gratifies me to hear that, Stanford. That means my grandson is much like his father. And let me assure you, no offense is taken." He sipped his brandy. "Will you lend a hand?"

Thomas swirled the brandy around in his glass, pretending indifference. Perhaps the duke was willing to compensate him for furthering a connection between Hunter and Arielle—compensation enough to free him of all his debts. "It's not my policy to interfere in my daughter's affairs, sir," he said, finishing off the alcohol with one swallow. He swiped his hand across his chin, wiping away an escaping trickle of brandy. Since subtlety wasn't his specialty, he charged forward, heedless of the ramifications. "However, if I succeed in getting them together, Your Grace, what's in it for me?"

The duke quirked an eyebrow, indicating his displeasure. "For you, sir?" he asked with an undertone of cold indignation. "You'll have the satisfaction of seeing your daughter married to the marquess of Savage, heir to John Price, duke of Ridgeley." He let the words float in the air, on a cloud of warning. "Did you have something else in mind?"

Embarrassment heated Thomas's cheeks. Had he become so desperate that he would proposition the duke? "Something else?" he repeated, laughing nervously. "What else could I possibly have in mind?"

"What indeed?" Ridgeley growled. He rose from his seat, leaving Thomas no choice but to follow suit. "Keep me abreast of your plans, Stanford."

Thomas bowed. "I will, Your Grace."

With that, John Price, the duke of Ridgeley, summarily dismissed him.

Ensconced in his carriage for the journey back home, Thomas adjusted the woolen blanket upon his legs. It was bitterly cold outside and the temperature inside the coach wasn't much better. The faint roar of the North Sea reached Thomas through the closed window. He sank deeper into the seats, imagining the frothy foam of the gray waters and the stark beauty of the rocky shoreline.

Untamed beauty that Ridgeley Court faced. Beauty that would be a part of Arielle's life, if he had his druthers.

Thomas felt for the letter he'd stolen. Taking it out of his pocket, he read it again, then leaned his head back.

He contemplated his options, knowing he had but one. He'd be taking his life in his hands because Savage could very possibly throttle him for even approaching him with such a blackmailing scheme.

Yet Thomas had no choice. Not if he meant to see

Arielle and Hunter married, so she would give up her foolish notions about becoming a physician. Not if he meant to keep Julia. And certainly not if he wanted to keep all his worldly goods from being sold off.

Blackmailing Hunter Braxton would set everything right.

Of course he'd never expose Hunter's secret, no matter the outcome. No matter the threats he intended to make. But Hunter wouldn't know that. Hopefully, he wouldn't call his bluff.

Thomas truly didn't care about Hunter Braxton enough to protect him. But he knew what it meant to have a detrimental secret; for that reason, he wouldn't expose Hunter. If Thomas's wife had left behind any such letters, he might just as easily have faced the dilemma Hunter would shortly find himself in.

If Thomas was lucky, very soon he'd have a new son-in-law and a healthy bank account once again. He chuckled. Sometimes, salvation came in the most unlikely way.

17

Dearest Arielle,

My regrets are deep. I had hoped to dissuade you from your course, knowing I have not the right to do so or ask it of you. You deserve a chance at seeing your dreams come to fruition. I am fully cognizant, and living proof of, what unrealized dreams might do to a person.

Because I don't want you to ever face any disappointment, especially by my hand, I've personally arranged an appointment for you to meet with Dean August Shrewsbury early Friday morning. The Board of Regents will abide by his decision in this matter. I attempted to obtain your entrance with this meeting, but the dean assured me this is a routine practice. Beyond getting you an appointment with the dean, there's not much else I can do.

I wish you the best of luck, my dearest. But, for my sake, and quite selfishly for more reasons than you can ever know, I wish your life's course were different. As is often the case, however, we cannot alter our life's journey for another's sake.

I will cheer you on in your profession. I know you will make an excellent physician, so stay your course, sweet Arielle. If you ever have further need of me, I am here for you. I remain always,

Your confidant and friend,
Hunter

"Oh, Arielle!" Georgette whispered, her voice breathy and sad. "Whatever will you do? He would most probably ask for your hand in marriage if you would but give up your quest."

"That I cannot do, Georgette," Arielle said tearily. Rising from her desk, she walked to her window and looked out at the bright day. "I'd never be completely happy, knowing what I gave up for him," she said with a sigh. "Wondering what my life would be like had I followed my dream."

Arielle swiped away the tears sliding down her cheeks. In the week since the dinner party, she'd done little else but think of Hunter and wait for a letter from him. Any letter, even one that expressed nothing but a friendly greeting. She'd finally gotten her wish today. It came with bittersweet happiness, however.

She stood on the cusp of seeing her dream turned into reality. For that she was eternally grateful, never having believed that a respectable school would consider accepting her. In the process, however, she'd lose Hunter. That made this moment as bitter as any elixir she'd ever dispensed.

As if Georgie read her mind, she asked, "If you love him, Ellie, will you be content to live without him? Since when did women have the types of dreams you've lived with for two years? What's wrong with admitting that you realize the extremity of your goal and go to Savage as any other woman would?"

Georgie posed hard questions, ones that needed answers, but Arielle refused to budge. Perhaps, she was different from every other woman in her position. And, perhaps, things would always be the way they were now.

But Arielle wouldn't be content living solely in the shadow of her husband. She needed more in her life. If only Hunter understood that, things might be different between them.

"If he loved *me,* Georgie, he would never have sent

that letter with those demands. Instead, he'd content himself and accept my position."

"Oh, Ellie! Ellie!" Georgie snapped in exasperation. "Must you be so obsessed with becoming a physician? Will you make the biggest mistake of your life and deny your feelings for Savage? There's such rewards to reap in the married state."

"That I do not doubt, Georgie. The rewards must be great for those who want to be in such a state."

"But Ellie—"

"Please, Georgie, let's do change the subject," Arielle declared with impatience, rubbing her throbbing temples. "In his own way, he was trying to tell me there's no future between us regardless."

"Of course, darling." Georgie rushed to her and put her arms around Arielle's waist. "I do wish to see you happy. Either way, I know you will make an excellent physician."

Smiling, Arielle returned Georgie's hug. "No matter what, my dear friend and Lady Astor, you're always there for me."

"Always, Ellie, always," Georgette said softly. She glanced at the timepiece on the mantel. "I must go, Arielle. I have to meet Eric at our town house. He had a meeting with his father today, so I'm anxious to discover if the earl has accepted his son back into the fold." She kissed Arielle's cheek. "We'll talk soon, darling."

"Yes," Arielle said with a sad smile. "Keep in touch, Georgie."

Sitting in the receiving room of the dean's office at the Royal College early Friday morning, Arielle's stomach fluttered at the austere surroundings while she waited for the dean's arrival. His surprised secretary had gone to inform the dean of her presence, as well as the reason for it, and hadn't yet returned.

If Hunter had come with her, she wouldn't have been

as nervous. She had no doubt that he would have attended this meeting with her had she asked, but she hadn't. And why should she? He didn't truly support her dreams. He only wished to fulfill an obligation to her.

But Hunter was a fair man and she was castigating him unfairly. She suspected if she explained how she'd come to this point in her life, he'd better understand her dreams.

When Agatha and Morgan introduced her to Quentin, his fascination with his life's work fed her own dreams. Thanks to the Royal College of Physicians, Quentin was learned, but his own quest for quality led him to the latest advances. His bedside manner with his patients was nothing short of a gift. She couldn't have asked for a better teacher.

Yet those accolades would fall on deaf ears. Laws required her to have more than the knowledge she gleaned from him. She needed to graduate from a respected university and become licensed before her dream turned to reality.

She only hoped Hunter's aid helped her achieve that dream.

Attempting to get admitted into an exclusive and prestigious male school was a shot in the dark, however. More than likely, faculty and students alike would laugh her off the campus. As patients, women were regarded as hysterical and sickly; as practitioners, they were simply viewed as unqualified. But as long as programs continued to deny women entrance, women would continue to be unqualified. Although there were no laws on any books stating women *couldn't* receive medical training, the male-dominated profession simply closed ranks and wouldn't allow it.

It only took *one* forward thinker, however. One liberal-minded, high-ranking university official to give her the chance to take the entrance exam and leave the rest up to her ability and wherewithal. However, as the wait stretched into nearly an hour, she realized that even Hunter's celebrity might not be enough. If Dean Shrewsbury turned her down today . . .

The opening of a door interrupted her thought. A barrel-chested, gray-haired man stood in the entrance, glaring in her direction. Glowering defiantly back at him, Arielle stood and extended her hand.

"Dean Shrewsbury, sir. I have come—"

"Lord Savage has informed us of the reason for your visit, my lady, and I'm sorry to say that I can be of no help."

"But—"

Bushy gray eyebrows drew together, and Arielle swallowed back her intimidation. "Why don't you return to your home and see to your family as befitting a woman?" Dean Shrewsbury said sharply. "Lord Savage extolled your virtues and has vouched for your character. He thinks you have the ability to become a fine doctor."

"Yes, Dean Shrewsbury. All I need is a chance to prove it."

"Lady Arielle, if not for the marquess's request, we would not even have entertained this meeting," the dean all but snarled.

"But I thought—"

"There's no place here for a woman, my lady. We don't need or want you! Please do not further waste my time or yours."

"Dean Shrewsbury," Arielle began in pleading tones, desperate, her dream disintegrating before her very eyes. "Please—"

The man stiffened. "Good day, my lady!"

Before Arielle could respond, the odious man grabbed the doorknob and slammed it shut. Idiot! Buffoon! The urge to shout the names out nearly overcame her better reasoning, but she wouldn't give the dean the satisfaction of knowing how he'd angered her.

Stomping out of the office, she made her way back to her waiting carriage and leaned wearily back. She had known how tough it would be and she realized she'd even expected the insults. What she hadn't known was how much they'd hurt.

But she vowed to continue the pursuit of her dream. Somehow, someway, she'd see it to reality.

18

My Dear Hunter,

Your aid on my behalf was most generous, but, unfortunately, it proved pointless. I was summarily denied entrance to the Royal College of Physicians in no uncertain terms. Because you so willingly lent your assistance to me, I won't prevaricate and pretend that I'm not disappointed. In the eyes of the dean, the university, and the world, my dreams are pointless, laughable, and embarrassing.

It wasn't always my intention to enter the medical profession. Years ago, I hoped to wed as much as any other girl. But as I grew up, I knew I wanted more out of life. What it was, I wasn't sure until my brother-in-law, Morgan, introduced me to a young doctor named Quentin DeVries. In Quentin, I found a soul mate. Not in the romantic sense, mind you, but in the sense that he identified with who I was and what I wanted to become once I saw him in action. I have always possessed a great knack for the healing arts. My father's tenants at our country estate come to me whenever we are there and they have a medical need.

Quentin never saw the perimeters that society deems I have. I tell you this to give you a better understanding of how I came to the point where I am in my life.

I fully understand, my lord, your own views on this subject and yet you consented to help me any-

way. I will be forever grateful to you for that.

I fully intend to stay my course and somehow see my life's dream to fruition. In case you haven't realized it yet, I am quite willful and invariably find a way to achieve my goals.

If you have need of me, the door is always open to you. Perhaps I can pass a decorating tip or two your way. Until next we meet,

> *Yours truly,*
> *Arielle*

Hunter finished the letter and scowled. He should go and have a visit with Dean Shrewsbury. The man had dealt Arielle an unforgiving blow. However, he'd also opened a portal of hope for Hunter. This was his chance to have Arielle as his wife; his chance to trust that all would be well, that love was enough to overcome everything.

He should have been thinking about retribution for Arielle's disappointment. Demanding the dean's resignation. Promising to ruin him. Yet all he thought of was how grateful he was for the man's fortitude. Shrewsbury saved Arielle from herself. He'd given her back to her world of gaiety and laughter and dancing. Shrewsbury had given her back to Hunter.

Oddly enough, *that* made Hunter want revenge. Because now that he had Arielle back within his grasp, there wasn't a bloody thing he intended to do about it.

He looked at the missive again. The pain behind the words of her disappointment was palpable. He promised to help her and he'd failed. And she suffered alone, believing no one understood her or supported her. In all honesty, he knew he didn't support her dreams, but he understood and admired *her*.

Each day away from her filled him with loneliness. He wondered how she fared, what she might have been engaged in at any given moment. He'd almost met her at the college for the meeting with Dean Shrewsbury, but decided against it. If she had wanted him there, she would have invited him.

After the previous letter he'd sent to her, he felt as if he'd be intruding upon her privacy. He felt guilty enough at insinuating she give up what she'd sought for years. To what end? He was reluctant to marry anyone. Even with his vow that he'd never marry, he knew that such a happenstance was out of hand and unlikely. He *had* to marry one day for the sake of heirs, if nothing else. But it couldn't be to Arielle.

That conclusion filled him with a bittersweet poignancy that had his head pounding. If only he could know that the old scandal would never touch her, he would run to her and propose. He'd marry her without the necessary banns, run away to Gretna Green if he had to, then fill her with babies and make her rethink her life's decision. As it was, it took every bit of his willpower not to saddle his horse and ride hellbent for leather to her.

Instead, he made his way to his study and answered her letter with one of his own.

Dearest Arielle,

I am profoundly sorry for the outcome of your interview. I understand what it meant to you to be accepted at the Royal College of Physicians. I mistakenly assumed my position would pave an easier way for you, but, alas, that wasn't the case. Because of the strong will and determination I know you possess, you will not let anything stand in your way, however.

If you are willing, I'd like to meet with you in a few days for lunch or tea. Let me know of your intentions, sweet Arielle, and I'm your willing servant.

Yours always,
Hunter

19

Hunter checked the hinges on the door he'd just hung one final time. Satisfied that it opened and closed properly, he smiled at his tenant, Meg. Blond and brown-eyed, she had been married just under a year and was now expecting her first child. She was positively radiant and he suddenly saw Arielle in her place, heavy with child, *his* child, and married to him.

He had left an opening in his last note for her to send him an invitation, but in the week since he'd sent the letter he had received no word. Each day, stacks of mail arrived and he shuffled through them, hoping to see one with a delicate scroll and a sweet smell. But nothing had arrived so far.

Apparently, she'd made her choice.

"Are ye all right, my lord?"

Meg's concerned voice jarred him. He was gripping the doorknob, his knuckles white because of the tight hold.

He cleared his throat, slightly embarrassed that his mind had been wandering. "Yes, Meg. I'm fine and all finished with your door. Is there anything else that needs my immediate attention here?"

"No, my lord. Ye've spent the bulk of yer day fixin' the leaky roof. Ye also saw fit to put that new door up."

"Will you be all right until Tim returns or should I send Dora over to sit with you?"

"I'm quite fine, sir," she said with a delighted chuckle. "If ye're fussin' over me like this, imagine what ye will do when ye get hitched and yer own lady wife be expec-tin'."

"Imagine, indeed," Hunter said wryly. He collected his great coat, bid Meg farewell, and took his leave.

Not far off, his stallion, Blazer, grazed upon the over-grown weeds. Mounting the horse, he looked around one last time. Even in the dreary, cloudy afternoon, the new door on Meg and Tim's cottage looked welcoming and shiny. There was still much that needed doing, both at Braxton Hall, on the grounds, and at his tenants' cottages and farms.

He'd hire men to clear the grounds and tend to the gardens, but he wanted to see to his tenants himself. Of course, if he needed help, he would hire accordingly. But, for the most part, he wanted to be the kind of landlord his uncle had been—fair-minded, accessible, and friendly. As for his own home, it would take months to complete. He had barely completed the inventory for the kitchen. Before he hired anyone to do work in the manor itself, he wanted to take inventory of each room and see what was needed. Some of the chambers only needed to have a good cleaning before furniture could be returned to them from the attic. In others, painting was the least that needed do-ing.

Proud of his work today, he finally urged Blazer in the direction of Braxton Hall. He frowned at the dull ache in his lower abdomen that had been plaguing him for the past day or two. Whatever it was, he hoped it would go away soon.

Perhaps Arielle could recommend an elixir. That thought crossed his mind so quickly, Hunter knew he wouldn't seriously ask her such a thing. Part of the reason was he still doubted her abilities. He believed that she only sought refuge from a family who ignored her; she didn't seriously wish to forget her upbringing and become a doctor. Besides, he knew he would only be using it as an excuse to contact her again and it was best if he left well enough alone.

Halting Blazer in his curved driveway, his eyebrows rose at the sight of the big gray and burgundy coach parked there. He recognized the vehicle immediately as belonging to Arielle. His heart sped up to a frantic pace and blood rushed through his veins. She'd actually come to see him. She was welcome at any time, but if only she'd sent word, he'd have been waiting for her properly attired. As it was now, he was dusty and sweaty.

He dismounted and started toward the door. He usually saw to the care of his stallion himself, but, just for today, he'd turn his care over to someone else. Hunter reached the entrance door. Just as he did, Vaughn, his new man-servant, swung it open.

"Milord," the big, beefy man greeted, "company awaits ye."

"So I've noticed," Hunter commented, rushing past his servant to get a glimpse of Arielle. Once he saw that she was comfortably settled, he'd excuse himself and clean up. "How long has Lady Arielle been here?"

"There's no Lady Arielle here, milord. 'Tis a Lord Stanford."

Hunter stopped in his tracks. "Thomas Stanford?" he asked, unable to contain his surprise, his mouth drying at the thought that something might have happened to Arielle. "See to Blazer."

He made his way to the parlor, and found Thomas gazing out the window, his hands behind his back.

"Lord Stanford," Hunter began without preamble, "what brings you here?"

Thomas turned, his dark, inscrutable gaze making Hunter distinctly uneasy.

"Is Arielle well?"

"Quite," Thomas answered in a clipped tone.

Noting the coldness in Thomas's voice, the rigidity in his body, Hunter raised a brow, a dark foreboding swirling in him.

"What—"

"The reason for my visit is between you and me at the moment, Savage."

"Indeed?" Hunter said coolly, clenching his fists at his sides, his jaw tautening. His dislike for the viscount was mutual—and obvious. Yet he'd pushed aside his feelings about Stanford because of Arielle. But she wasn't present at the moment, so there was no need for pretenses. "What is your reason for coming to Braxton Hall then?"

"To show you something that should be of grave interest to you."

Thomas extracted a yellowish letter from his inside coat pocket and passed it to Hunter.

Hunter gazed at the letter in confusion.

"Read it!" Thomas commanded, a mountain of smug self-righteousness.

Hollowness entered the pit of Hunter's belly and tiny beads of perspiration formed upon his brow. He stared at his nemesis a moment, before turning away, letter in hand. He didn't want Stanford to see how nonplussed he was, he didn't want him to see the worry he felt. This letter could only be one thing. Proof of his illegitimacy. There was no other earthly reason why Thomas would be so condescending.

Slowly unfolding the old letter, Hunter read the words written on it. Uncle Proctor had written this letter to the duke of Ridgeley, proclaiming Hunter's illegitimacy.

Your son's intentions were obviously to turn my dear sister into a whore, as she has given birth to his bastard.

Hunter fell back as if struck by a physical blow, the impact of these words as brutal, as vicious. His hand shook as he read that sentence over and over again. His body thrummed. His ears rang, the evidence of what he'd suspected all along screaming through his brain.

He was a bastard. He had known it all along. The midwife had told him just that years ago. So why was he so surprised? Why did he feel like his world had shattered into tiny little pieces all around him?

He wanted to weep in shame and bellow in rage. He

walked in circles, pacing, desperate, humiliated. Going to
the window again, he gazed outside, not seeing anything.
Nothing but his life crumbling. Nothing but Arielle's face
looking upon him in pity and scorn.

If Thomas knew, surely Arielle did as well. No wonder
he hadn't heard from her.

He drew in an unsteady breath, struggling to collect
himself and make sense of this. He turned to Thomas.
"H-how did you come by this, and what, pray tell, does
this have to do with you?"

Thomas shrugged, the small eyes in his bullish face
gleaming. "Nothing and everything," he answered, seeming to ignore the first question and taking pleasure in it.
He strolled around the room, as if on a leisure trip in the
park. "It all depends on you."

Hunter's blood ran cold. "What do you mean?"

"How I came by this letter was a stroke of luck, you
realize," Thomas answered with a chuckle. "But how it
will be used is nothing short of a miracle."

"I don't understand," Hunter said. But he understood
quite well. Too well, perhaps. Stanford wasn't the type of
man who would let an opportunity to make money out of
this pass him by. Yet Hunter wouldn't make it easy for
the man. He would pretend ignorance to see just what
Thomas wanted.

"What I mean, my lord, is that the letter has sparked
your *generosity* in asking for Arielle's hand in marriage.
And, of course, as my future son-in-law, you wouldn't
want your father-in-law's property auctioned off, would
you? So besides marriage, I'd consider a thousand pounds
a sufficient gift to me. Isn't it brilliant? This will save the
trouble of a nasty scandal, wouldn't you agree?"

Hunter glowered at Thomas, his head pounding, the
dull ache in his side throbbing. He couldn't quite believe
what he was hearing. "Do you mean to blackmail me into
marrying your daughter?"

Thomas halted in front of Hunter, snatching the letter
from Hunter's grasp before Hunter could react. He stuffed

it into his pocket. "I wouldn't call it blackmail, sir. It's more like . . . like . . . er, top-secret insurance. Information about your *lady* mother will remain top secret, unless you refuse my request and force me to reveal your origins."

"You bloody bastard! You and your marriage proposal can go to the devil," Hunter snarled, grabbing Thomas's ascot and pulling him forward. He needed a plan of defense. Although, beyond burning the letter, he had no idea what that would be. He'd have to kill Stanford to take possession of it again. At the moment, that seemed like the perfect solution. He tightened his hold, his rage overtaking his shock and better sense for a brief moment. Until Thomas began to turn purple. "You have ten seconds to get off Braxton lands, you miserable cad."

Hunter pushed Stanford so hard that he stumbled into the desk. Without another word, he retreated from the parlor and hightailed it down the hall to the entrance door. Hunter was hot on his heels, anger blurring his vision.

"Take heed of what you're risking, Savage," Stanford panted out, running the rest of the distance to his carriage. He pulled the letter from his pocket and waved it at Hunter. "It is your mother's good name you risk."

Hunter made a grab for it, but wasn't quick enough. Before he could pull the door open, Thomas rapped on the roof and the driver started the carriage off at a brisk pace.

Shoving a frustrated hand through his hair, Hunter released a string of curses. This issue had to be addressed with all due haste. In a couple of days, he'd take it upon himself to call upon the man. Maybe they could reach an amicable solution.

Returning to the manor, he slammed the door shut and went back to his office, his concentration gone for anything except the letter proving him once and for all a bastard.

* * *

With the restlessness of a caged panther, Hunter paced the small, opulently furnished parlor at the Stanford town house. He sneered at the fleur-de-lis–designed carpet and the gold satin draperies, resenting Thomas Stanford's ludicrous audacity that much more.

To think Arielle's father would even attempt to blackmail him! Thomas's gall was beyond nerve and cheek.

Hunter's jaw tautened and he eyed a delicate figurine standing serenely on the marble fireplace mantel. He wanted to swipe it to the carpeted floor and crush the hand-blown crystal into a thousand pieces. Just as he wanted to crush Thomas Stanford.

Hunter ached for blood. He ached for restitution. Stanford had effectively quelled Hunter's peace and happiness two days ago with his diabolical demands.

Was Arielle responsible for her father's actions? There was nothing to suggest such a thing.

I invariably find a way to achieve my goals.

Those words from her previous letter crystallized in his mind. Of course she'd never expressed attaining his hand in marriage as one of her goals. *That* would make his suspicions that Arielle was somehow involved more understandable. Yet, where else would Thomas have gotten his harebrained idea?

By her own admission, Arielle knew something prevented a union between them. Hunter refused to believe that Arielle had gone snooping about and dug up the letter her father produced. Would she really do that? Or were her "dreams" all a farce to snare him in her trap?

Thomas Stanford had the means to ruin Hunter and his family. Instead of acting like a raging bull, he should have been searching for a solution.

"Braxton, I see you have come to your senses."

The coolly spoken sentence fueled Hunter's fury and grated on his resolve. But he refrained from turning with lightning speed and striking out at Stanford. He slowly faced the man.

"Actually, Lord Stanford, I have come to offer you an

alternative," he said without preamble, eyeing the rotund man carefully.

Thomas's inscrutability hid any signs of a flexible nature and Hunter breathed in deeply. He needed to find a weak spot, in the event Stanford refused his offer. Thus far, the only thing his solicitor had discovered about Viscount Stanford was that the man had overextended his financial means due to household expenditures.

The knowledge that Stanford's financial woes weren't due to debauchery left Hunter helpless with rage. His own secret was far more detrimental.

"Spill it, young man!" Stanford demanded, with the pretense of an overstuffed dandy. "I don't have all day."

Pacing to the window, Hunter remained silent.

"You are sorely testing my patience, boy."

"As you have already tested mine, old man," Hunter rumbled, clutching the sill and striving for calm. "You are lucky I haven't taken unpleasant measures against you."

"As if you would dare," Stanford shot back. "I would expose your precious secret in a minute if you ever attempted such a thing."

Hating the overly triumphant tone, Hunter finally faced his nemesis. Countless thoughts of hideous revenge surfaced in his battle-weary brain.

"Lord Stanford, what exactly does your daughter have to say about this? Surely, she can't be too happy thinking you are virtually selling her to me." Hunter refused to address Stanford's last inflammatory statement. He'd most assuredly lose his rigid self-control.

"Arielle is well aware of this matter. She wants to wed you come what may."

Hunter raised his eyebrows in surprise. "She has consented to this?"

"Yes, she has," Stanford stated without blinking, staring at Hunter with defiance.

"Will you next inform me that this entire affair was her idea? That perhaps she is at the root of your financial troubles?"

Stanford waved a hand in dismissal and waddled to his desk. "Nonsense, man. Your conjecture is pure rubbish. My youngest is chaste, dutiful, and quite innocent. She would never think to put me in arrears or blackmail you."

The viscount's description of Arielle only served to irritate Hunter more. He himself had detected that and more in Arielle. But it seemed as if he'd overlooked her scheming avarice. Still, he couldn't take Stanford's word for any of this. He'd have to confront her himself. This didn't sound like *his* Arielle. "She sees no problem with your plans?"

"None."

"Well, I am happy to say that I have come with a plan that will save us all heartache and sacrifices." For the first time since the tense meeting began, Hunter smiled and reached inside the pocket of his topcoat. He shouldn't have prolonged this meeting. Nor should he have probed about Arielle. He had come with a solution so he could get on with his life—however devoid of companionship it might be. Pulling out a signed bank draft, he held it out to Stanford. "That should be sufficient funds to free yourself of your creditors as well as give you additional cash to see yourself through until you have restored your own personal funds. In addition, I will personally sponsor Arielle for the next three Seasons and put up a sizeable dowry when and if a match is made. It's all yours, Lord Stanford, if you give up your mad scheme."

Although Arielle had been denied entrance in the Royal College, she'd sworn to try elsewhere. Yet Hunter didn't know what Stanford knew of that. Arielle might have changed her mind about keeping her father in the dark. He didn't want to cause a rift between father and daughter, so he wouldn't broach the subject now. He'd leave well enough alone once he asked why she allowed this—*if* she allowed this.

Stanford stared down at the document for long moments. Uncertainty ran across the man's features, then the viscount heaved a deep breath and closed his eyes, near surrender.

The minutes ticked by, an eternity to Hunter. He believed Stanford only stretched the time out to torture him. The man couldn't refuse a veritable fortune.

Stanford finally opened his eyes. The remorse in the depths of his gaze jolted Hunter. His heart rate increased and his muscles tensed. Even before Thomas spoke and confirmed that he was a candidate for the madhouse with a refusal, Hunter knew what the man would say.

"I'm sorry, my lord," Stanford began in a surprisingly kind tone. "I was terribly wrong about you. I mistook you for just another high-ranking, well-heeled nobleman who wouldn't care about an old man's plight. All the same, I thought you would be good for my Arielle."

"Thank you for the compliment, Lord Stanford," Hunter began cautiously, not trusting the apology he heard. He dropped the bank draft in front of the viscount. "I'm sure your Arielle will find someone more to her liking and everyone can go on as if nothing—"

"That's where you are wrong, my lord," Stanford interrupted, rising to his feet and leaning against the desk. He picked up the bank draft and methodically shred it. "You are quite to my daughter's liking and I cannot toy with her happiness any longer."

"Yet you seek to toy with my life?" Hunter accused.

"I seek to secure *my* life, and that of my daughter's."

"And to hell with how you go about doing it!" When the man remained silent, Hunter cursed. "Am I not right, Stanford?"

"To a degree. Yet I see no reason to explain anything else to you. Now, I want your decision about my proposal this instant!"

Shock paralyzed Hunter. He'd somehow hoped to find a way to save his family's reputation without succumbing to the scurrilous blackmail posed by Stanford. But it seemed it wasn't to be.

Thomas Stanford had discovered the Braxton secret and

meant to expose it if Hunter didn't comply with his wishes. And the viscount meant to do it at any cost.

If only he could discover who and what prompted this treachery. Surely not Arielle. He simply couldn't imagine that. He didn't want to. Yet, he couldn't credit Stanford with plotting all this alone. He'd need the input of someone close to both himself and Hunter.

Which could only mean Arielle.

"I see no other recourse but to comply, my lord," Hunter said without a trace of warmth. He hated Arielle more than he thought possible. She had betrayed him much more than her father ever could. He'd allowed her into his life, his heart, his mind, and she'd betrayed him. He'd never forgive her. "I assure you, you and your daughter will rue the day you crossed me."

"Brave words, but most doubtful," Stanford told him calmly. He headed for the door. "I trust you know your way out. Arielle shall call upon you to discuss wedding plans."

"There's no need," Hunter retorted, convinced of Arielle's betrayal by his blinding anger and her father's words. "It sounds as if you two have this well thought out. You needed only to find your prey."

"Or await his return from service to his country." Stanford bowed. "Good day, Lord Savage."

The bitterness of defeat and the realization that he had given in to Stanford's demands stunned Hunter. In silence, he watched the viscount plod out the door and disappear down the hallway.

It was small consolation to Hunter that he'd had no choice in this situation. His mother had died birthing him. The very least he could do was sacrifice his own happiness to save her good name.

20

"No, Papa, I will not do it!" Arielle stamped her elegantly shod foot for emphasis. Thomas narrowed his eyes and she placed her hands on her hips to forestall another outburst. She really didn't want to defy her father, but she couldn't imagine accepting an offer of marriage from Hunter that came through her father and not Hunter himself. As attracted as she was to Hunter, he wouldn't support what she wanted to do. She *couldn't* marry him.

She just couldn't.

"How dare you defy me?" Thomas shouted, rising from his seat. Anger sharpened his fleshy features, making his bulk all the more intimidating. He stepped toward her and Arielle shut her eyes, closing out his outrage. "You will marry Hunter Braxton, and you will do it gracefully!"

Arielle glared at him, simmering with emotions she usually made herself ignore. "There are times, Papa, when my resentment toward you is as keen as a dagger's point."

"How dare you!" Thomas said through gritted teeth. "After all I've done for you."

"Which is my point exactly, Papa." Blood roared in Arielle's ears, her anger that Thomas would put her in this position and use Hunter in such a way boiling over. "Is it through your regard for me, as you want me to believe, or have you merely tolerated me because of your love for my mother?"

Thomas's look became haggard and he raised his hands in supplication. "How can you say that, child? I have raised you as I've raised your sisters . . . your half-sisters and my own daughters. I love you as my flesh and blood. As my very own."

Arielle wanted to believe that, but she knew better. His treatment of her over the years told her different. "If that is so, Papa, why do you treat me differently from the others? You dare not ask of them what you ask of me. And it's not fair of you."

Thomas released a long sigh. "No, it isn't fair of me. But you are all I have left. You remind me so much of your mother, child. There is still much sorrow in my heart for the love I lost. I treat you differently, Arielle, to keep from treating you *better* than your sisters."

"But why?"

"You're not of my blood. However, like your sisters, you're part of the woman I loved with all my heart. Because of that love, I forgave her indiscretion and could never desert you. I love you as well. Perhaps, I've been harsh at times, but that's only because I want the best for you. For you to marry well, before your illegitimacy is discovered."

"And you've chosen Lord Savage for me to marry," Arielle stated flatly, her tone controlled but cold. Controlled to keep from bursting into tears. Cold because she almost hated him for making her feel so obligated to him. How could she deny him what he asked of her when he had saved her from a lifetime of stigma?

"Yes, Arielle, I've chosen Hunter Braxton for you. You would do well to abide by my decision!"

Arielle stiffened her spine at her father's snarling tone, but she drew in a breath. He'd suffered so many disappointments, Arielle hated to be the cause of another one for him—as much as she resented the predicament he'd put her in.

Presenting her back to him, she looked out the window. Absently trailing the spotless windowpane, she laid her cheek against the cool glass. "What of *my* plans, Papa?" she asked, sounding more caustic than she intended. But she couldn't give up this fight. Thomas had to know that.

"You've always known how I feel about the field of medicine." What he didn't know was the intensity of her feelings for Hunter. He didn't know how much it hurt that she hadn't heard from Hunter herself. Not one word.

"Sometimes we must give up our dreams for reality, Arielle," Thomas said, this time more calmly, his voice just behind her. He patted her shoulders, then gently spun her around. Gazing deep into her eyes, he shook her slightly, then sighed and released her. His shrewd look suggested he had yet to deliver the coup de grace, whatever weapon he was saving for last to assure her capitulation. "I certainly did not mean to disparage your hopes. However, the reality of this situation is, if you *don't* marry Braxton, I will be unable to meet our mounting debt."

"Papa!"

"Don't be alarmed, child," Thomas said with a tender smile, his voice as soothing as warm honey, as though he hadn't just issued a statement to cause the utmost alarm. "I know you will do what's required of you. As unappealing as marriage to Hunter Braxton might be to you, that's how unacceptable debtor's prison is to me."

"Oh, Papa!" Arielle flung her arms around his neck. She knew he would use *something* to force her compliance, but never realized that something would be so dire. "I had no idea."

"I know," Thomas whispered, returning the hug, his arms tight around her, almost as if he held on for dear life. "But I can no longer bear the burden of my own folly, Arielle. And it grieves me to have to demand this of you."

Not as much as it aggrieved her to have to give in. Yet she had little choice as Thomas's only remaining unwed daughter. Resentful of her obligations and her father's demands, she pushed away from him and walked around the study.

It was small and as richly furnished as the rest of the house. She suspected the redecoration and refurnishing had begun her father's financial troubles. He'd spared no expense, demanding the best to satisfy his expensive taste and fine eye for detail. And she loathed to even consider Julia's demands on her father's coffers.

She passed a hand across the Empire-style desk, remembering how happy her father had been when it was delivered from the furniture maker. The entire manor was opulent and showed the time, money, and effort that had been expended on it.

This was the home, along with their country manor, that she had been raised in. Not only couldn't she bear to see her father in debtor's prison, neither could she let the home she'd known and loved all her life fall into the hands of strangers. And heaven forbid Julia Shepperton should find out. The lot of them would be humiliated before the world.

Although it pained her to have to give up her dream, she'd bow to her father's wishes. The Stanfords' reputation was at stake. If she didn't concede, all of society would know they were but paupers in the guise of gentry. She wouldn't subject her family to the humiliation and ridicule of Thomas's incarceration or the loss of their home. Not when there was something she could do to prevent it from happening.

Forcing her sorrow into the core of her heart, she faced her father. "We will not lose anything, Papa," she said, her voice strong, her head held high, though inside she felt empty. "I will consent to become his wife."

"Thank you, Arielle," Thomas responded, barely audible.

Arielle swore mist clouded her father's eyes. But that couldn't be. Thomas Stanford was more stout-hearted than anyone she knew. Yet the despair of revealing their present financial status to her undoubtedly caused him much distress.

Rushing to him, she took his beefy hand into her own and gave it a reassuring squeeze. "Papa, please don't despair. No one need learn of our circumstances. We will arrange one of London's grandest weddings. And your standing amongst your peers will not suffer for it."

Arielle thought of Hunter. From what she knew of him, he didn't easily give his trust. But he'd begun to trust her—enough to admit he was falling in love with her. Now, he'd more than likely think it had been her intention all along to reel him in to wed her. He mightn't ever forgive her and their burgeoning friendship would be ruined forever. Her heart pounded at the very thought of such discord between them. That would be worse than never seeing him again.

Hunter, however, was a reasonable man, and it sounded as if her father had explained everything to him. Surely he knew her sincerity in wanting to become a physician, that her original letter to him hadn't had the ulterior motive of getting him to the altar.

Of course he knew that. He knew her too well not to.

"You're a good daughter, Arielle," Thomas said softly. "You won't regret your decision."

Arielle smiled ruefully at her father. She already did.

21

For the next week, Arielle did little else but focus on ways to get out of the marriage she'd so hastily agreed to. After speaking with her father's creditors, attempting to get a bank loan, and hinting to her sisters of Thomas's distress, she realized she was reaching a dead end.

She knew, however, she couldn't give up yet. Marriage to the marquess of Savage would end her dreams of becoming something other than another gently reared nobleman's wife.

Long before she'd met Quentin, she'd had an affinity to the healing arts. It might have stemmed from her memories of her mother's death after her attending physician bled her to cure a persistent cold. He'd sworn it was the last resort, since the hot poultices upon her chest and medicinal teas had had no effect. Instead, Isabelle died from the "cure" and left Arielle without her guidance and love.

Arielle drew in a ragged breath, tormented by those distant memories. She didn't often admit it, but even now, Arielle missed her mother. She especially wished she were there for her now, to advise her on how to proceed with her life. But since Isabelle wasn't there and her father had already told her what to do, that only left one person to go to—Hunter.

She wanted to know why he'd so readily consented to the marriage. He knew of her intentions. Beyond that, he'd indicated there was something in his life that made a union between them ill advised. Surely he wouldn't ignore those things and suddenly decide to take her to wife.

His reasons for his decision continued to evade her.

And she found it beyond strange that the past two weeks yielded no contact with Hunter. Especially considering the fact that they would be married. Surely there was an explanation for Hunter's silence, which could easily be remedied by a missive from her asking if he were in good spirits.

Quickly, she glanced at the clock and found it to be not yet noon. Today was Tuesday—the day she usually accompanied Quentin on his patient visits. Knowing his routine, she wouldn't start out with him. Instead, she'd pen a note to Hunter, then meet Quentin at Mrs. Beecham's.

In her father's study, pen and paper in hand, she thought, reflecting on what she should write. The entire complexion of their relationship had changed. Without any recent word from him, she wasn't sure what to say. More than ever, their upcoming marriage, and his true feelings toward it, needed settling.

My Dear Hunter,

It has been a fortnight since our last correspondence. I have been so busy, I simply neglected to answer your last letter. However, I miss hearing from you. I am sure your work on Braxton Hall has occupied all your time.

I suppose I should get straight to our business at hand, which I am quite sure you are aware of. My father has informed me that arrangements have been made between you and him for us to wed.

Hunter, as you know, marriage wasn't in my future. Therefore, I implore you to tell me what prompted you to accept my father's proposal, knowing my sentiments. And since you did accept, I think you are remiss in not proposing to me personally.

I would very much like to meet with you to sort out this situation and plan the nuptials. 'Til then,

Yours cordially,
Arielle

Arielle entrusted the delivery of the letter to her livery-man, then left to join Quentin on his rounds. She'd immerse herself in the care of the patients, and perhaps, lose the headache that had plagued her since her father's command that had turned her life upside down.

Reading over Arielle's letter for the third time, Hunter sat stiffly at his desk and rubbed his eyes tiredly. He'd fallen in love with her. Yet he would never look at her the same again. She had betrayed him with her subterfuge.

In the end, however, he'd acquire the wife he would have chosen of his own accord had both their lives been different. Even if Arielle hadn't told him of her medical ambitions, he wouldn't have proposed to her—for the same reason that he was now being forced to marry her.

Why the bloody hell would Stanford insist his daughter marry a man with a background as questionable as Hunter's? Hunter couldn't bear the ramifications of that. Nor could he forget how Arielle felt in his arms, the sweetness of her mouth, the tiny little moans of pleasure she made. No! He refused to dwell on her softness or the fact that just the thought of her caused his blood to heat and his manhood to swell.

Hunter thrust a frustrated hand through his hair and glimpsed the letter again. As she suggested, he should meet with her to discuss their future and propose to her properly. But his pride, his simmering anger, and, yes, his humiliation prevented him from doing so. After all, he was being forced to marry against his will.

How could he ever forgive that?

Expelling an agitated breath, Hunter reached for writing supplies.

My Dearest Arielle, he began, then stopped to contemplate the heading. Dearest? Yes, Arielle *was* dear to him, but she was also a schemer. He could hardly reconcile the scheming traitor with the bright, gentle woman he loved.

Lest she get the wrong impression, he began over again. His heart, however, allowed him to amend the greeting only slightly.

> My Dear Arielle,
> *I've just received your missive.*

Hunter considered that line, pondering how next to proceed. He didn't want to convey any particular emotion to her. Not anger. Nor would he let her see how she'd hurt him. And he certainly wouldn't convey love. She didn't deserve it.

Putting pen to paper once again, he continued without pause, allowing the words to flow out of him. If he stopped to consider everything he was writing, the letter wouln't get finished.

> My Dear Arielle,
> *I've just received your missive. It has occurred to me that perhaps your lost bid to get into the Royal College of Physicians was an omen. Circumstances have a way of interfering with destiny. Had you been admitted, perhaps we wouldn't be heading for the altar.*
> *As for a meeting before the wedding, I'm afraid that won't be possible, as I am overwhelmed with obligatory duties here at Braxton Hall. I have no objections to you planning the affair. Send me the time and place and all the other particulars and I will get there.*
> *Stay well, my dear, and, of course, I'll see you at our wedding.*

> *Hunter*

Hunter paused a second, then sealed the letter. In no rush to send it, he laid it on the desk. His hurt ran deep, but to keep his mother's good name from ruin, he'd marry a doxy.

He'd been squeezed into a neat little trap. Still, the irony of his sealed fate was hard to miss. Refusing to dwell on what he couldn't control, he stood from his seat and fingered the letter a moment.

He left it on his desk and departed the study, not quite able to grasp the fact that in a few short weeks Arielle would be his.

22

"However did Arielle wangle a proposal from the highly sought-after marquess, Thomas?" Julia sputtered indignantly, huffily brushing damp tendrils of hair off of her face to better glare at her lover. Although they hadn't engaged in much conversation in the last several hours, Julia found the information Thomas let slip in between their lovemaking most interesting and quite annoying.

"Er, my dear, that is a question I've been asking myself."

She narrowed her eyes at the discomfort in Thomas's voice. His refusal to look at her confirmed that there was more to this story than he revealed.

Annoyed, Julia lay back on the rumpled white sheets. The scent of sex hung heavily in the coolness of the well-appointed chamber that Thomas had secured for them in Gretna Green. Just over the English border in Scotland, it was a distance from London. The traveling time was of no consequence, however, since the journey assured their anonymity.

Thomas rose from the bed they'd shared for the past two days. She looked into his face, the bulk of his unsightly body unattractive with the completion of their lovemaking.

"Promise me, Julia, that you will say nothing of this until the nuptials are made public."

Delicious malice streamed through her body like wet heat, as intense as her overwhelming sexual needs, fueling

them to the boiling point again. Yet she'd curb her proclivities until she heard the full truth.

"Is Arielle expecting, Thomas?" Anticipation dried Julia's mouth, but she tried to keep it out of her voice. If
her speculations were true, she'd certainly make it her
business to spread the gossip amongst all the ton. She
prided herself on being in the know, and this tidbit about
Arielle was wonderful. The snobbish little twit needed to
be brought down a peg or two.

Of course, being engaged to the marquess would take
some of the bite out of the tale. In effect, it would make
the juiciness of it less bitter. But, until the wedding actually took place, it would damage her sterling reputation.

"Don't be ludicrous, Julia," Thomas answered in annoyance. "My daughter is as pure as the driven snow."

Julia chuckled to hide her disappointment. She wasn't
about to spread false gossip. That could damage her cred-
ibility. "The driven snow? How appropriate. Hopefully,
Arielle lives up to those accolades."

"She will," Thomas assured her. "I know my Arielle."

"But she is acquainted with Lady Georgette Wagner,
Thomas. And the brazen girl's condition is very obvious
now." As was Lord Eric Astor's devotion to her. Julia
suspected that was the reason she hadn't yet been banned
from polite society. But her time was coming, as was Arielle's. Julia would see personally to both.

"I know," Thomas admitted, "but I am not one to pick
and choose Arielle's friends. She and Georgette have been
like sisters since they were children."

Julia stretched her naked form on the bed, weighing the
fullness of her breasts in her hands and admiring the
roundness of them. In her late thirties, she showed no
signs of deterioration. Her breasts were still firm, her belly
flat, and her hips slim.

Now, any man she wanted to satisfy her sexual appetite
was hers, including Hunter Braxton if she set her sights
on him. Yet she'd chosen Thomas quite by accident. They

had shared harmless flirtations for months, then he'd convinced her to sponsor Arielle.

One evening when Douglas left her without giving her the release she so craved, she'd met Thomas at the opera. She'd nearly compromised herself and her reputation by engaging in very intimate touching right in Thomas's box. They'd left before the end of the performance, and ravaged one another as soon as they were in the privacy of his home.

It was a decision Julia thought she'd regret. She'd already had two lovers at the time, as well as her husband, and Thomas was a very unattractive man. But he'd been kind to her. Kinder than any man had ever been to her. Certainly kinder than her handsome husband.

Douglas's attention toward her scarcely existed anymore, leading her to believe that he kept a mistress. How that could be, she wasn't sure. She was the type of woman every man wanted. But Douglas came to her bed once a week, sometimes twice, then left her to her own devices. His times at home were actually more like visits. Except for the brief interludes of their lovemaking, she hardly saw him. All the other times, he claimed to be at his gentlemen's clubs.

She believed that as much as she believed the king to be in his right mind.

She smiled seductively at Thomas, her saving grace, really. He gave in to her slightest whims. Were it not from him, she would have expired of boredom. And she couldn't even imagine what she would have done about her physical needs. Because Thomas was so willing to pleasure her with hands, mouth, manhood, and whatever else she deemed appropriate, she only had him and Douglas in her life now.

Thomas usually started off rather clumsily with the act itself, but, by the end, his performance improved and he got the job done satisfactorily.

She patted the empty spot next to her, fingering her

nest of curls so that Thomas made no mistake what she wanted. "Come back to bed, love."

Sitting on the edge of the bed, Thomas hung his head. "I'm afraid I am spent, Julia," he said, smiling broadly. "You are quite a woman."

"Next time, I'll endeavor to rein in my passion, Thomas." Julia sighed, letting him off for the time being. She was more than sure that he'd shortly find a way to pleasure her. "By the by, what do your other daughters think of Arielle's upcoming marriage?"

"They don't know yet. You're the only person I've told."

"Thomas," Julia purred, running a hand along his back, "I'm honored that you would share such a"—she paused for effect—"delicate secret with me."

"People who care about each other shouldn't have secrets between them."

She frowned at the sadness marring his features. She'd never love him. But her genuine care and concern surprised herself. He had been generous to a fault, gifting her with expensive baubles and trinkets without blinking an eye. He'd even refurbished his entire town house because she'd expressed her distaste over it. Julia really hadn't thought Thomas so affluent.

Everything could be wonderful between them, if it weren't for the snippy, willful little Arielle. She'd tried to befriend the chit, throwing the full support of the Pembishire name behind Arielle's debut. It was a stunning success, and Julia couldn't have been happier. Had it been any of the other Stanford girls, Julia would have summarily declined Thomas's request. Thinking of them made her shudder. A bulldog had better looks than those four Stanford cows. They were the ugliest four women who ever showed their faces in the whole of London. But Arielle was a true beauty. From the night of her debut, Lady Arielle Stanford was admired, sought after, and deemed a diamond of the first water.

Then, Arielle double-crossed Julia by turning down

every suitable prospect that came to her. This after Julia
put such hard work into the ball and got the creme of
society out. No one less than earls or their sons with the
purest of lines had been invited. It was there that Georgette had met Lord Eric and it was there that Arielle's
rebellion began.

Damn the both of them!

Now the little bitch had snagged Hunter. However had
she managed it? By snagging the marquess, she'd
thwarted the plans Julia had for her friend Lady Cornelia
Brimly. Although her own plans for him were not nec-
essarily sidetracked. Lord Savage was only a man and, as
the others before him, he wouldn't be able to refuse Julia's sensual offer.

For Thomas's sake, however, Julia's retribution against
Arielle wouldn't be too harsh. Perhaps a public humiliation of some kind.

Imagining the scene with satisfaction, Julia sat up in
bed and kissed the viscount's fleshy cheek.

"We'd better prepare to return to London, before the
hour grows too late."

"Very well, Thomas," Julia whispered, guiding his
meaty hand to the pulse point between her thighs. "This
will only take a few moments."

Rich masculine decor dominated the bedchamber Arielle found herself in several days later. The floral
print chaise lounge on which Arielle reclined served as
the only evidence that a woman now resided at the town
house. Opened draperies revealed a cold, drizzly day outside, which seemed to be the prevailing weather for the
past several weeks. Arielle prayed that wouldn't be the
case on her wedding day. Such a happenstance couldn't
be a good omen.

Inside Georgie's bedchamber, the mood ranged from
despair to delight. Arielle had been at the Astor household
for an hour and had explained to Georgie all the details

of her hasty betrothal and the arrangements that were being made just as hastily. She already knew the time and
place of her wedding. A wedding that she thought would
never take place to a man who made her heart pound and
her breath catch with the anticipation of his touch.

"Ellie, I don't know what to say," Georgie said from
her place on the big four-poster bed. Sheer blue panels
that surrounded the bed were drawn back for a better
view. "Hunter Braxton! He's rich and handsome. And
sooo eligible."

Arielle waved away her friend's enthusiasm. Georgie
looked well, much better than Arielle expected, considering the difficult pregnancy she was experiencing. She
had sent a note around to Arielle this morning, explaining
that she was ordered to bed by her midwife, because she
had been showing signs of losing the baby. At the moment, however, her mind was focused on Arielle's problems. "Georgie, please."

Sitting up, Georgie rubbed her belly. "What is so bad
about marrying Hunter Braxton, Ellie?" she asked with a
frown. "You're just too stubborn to admit your love for
him."

It was just like Georgie to try and make things seem
so simple, Arielle thought crossly, massaging her temples
and glaring at her friend. "And I won't! When have you
become so bloody practical, Georgie? I don't know how
my father convinced Hunter to agree to the marriage, but
it certainly wasn't Hunter's idea."

"What difference does it make whose idea it was, Ellie?
He agreed. You agreed. Which means you'll own a *marquess!*"

Arielle chuckled at Georgie's gushing tone, but lost her
humor at the thought of anyone attempting to own Hunter
Braxton, the man she'd marry in just under a fortnight.
"*Own* a marquess? You make it sound as though I'll be
acquiring a pet, Georgie."

"You know what I mean, darling."

"Indeed I do, Georgette," Arielle said seriously, gazing

out at the dreary day. "But I wasn't given the choice most women have."

Georgie's raucous laugh surprised Arielle and she quirked an eyebrow at her. "A choice? Whatever do you mean?"

"I mean Hunter didn't propose to me—"

"In essence your father did," Georgie interrupted with a wicked giggle.

"Georgette!"

"Sorry." Georgie raised her hands in supplication, her hazel eyes sparkling mischievously. "Please go on."

"Thank you," Arielle said in annoyance, raising her chin and primly folding her hands in her lap. "If *Hunter* had proposed, the choice would have been mine to accept or refuse."

"But he didn't ask. Therefore, he didn't give you the chance to choose."

"Exactly," Arielle agreed with a nod, satisfied that her friend no longer made light of this serious situation. "He didn't give me the chance to refuse him gracefully."

"Balderdash! You wouldn't have! You love him," Georgie insisted, sounding a little put out.

"Given my proclivities, however, mere love wouldn't make for a successful union between us," Arielle snapped.

"However, all that is moot as it stands, Arielle," Georgette argued, raising her voice in true irritation. "Quite soon, you'll become a marchioness." Lying back on her mountain of pillows, she gazed at the ceiling. "And, in spite of everything, I do wish I could be with you when you marry him."

"So do I, Georgie."

"I'll be there in spirit, Ellie. Wishing I could see the envious looks you'll garner from your female guests, especially from Julia Shepperton."

"Seeing that look from Julia is the only bright aspect to marrying Hunter." Arielle rose from her seat and reached for her reticule, preparing to depart.

"You mustn't leave yet," Georgie said in alarm. "I

asked Verna to bake ginger scones. Your favorite. You must stay for tea."

"How thoughtful you are." Arielle smiled and set her reticule down once again, then returned to the chaise lounge. In truth, she only thought to leave because she didn't want to overtire Georgie. She would prefer staying a while longer to keep her friend company and make sure she was indeed well. Judging by her high spirits, Arielle had no doubt about that. That observation greatly relieved her. They had never discussed her pregnancy in medical terms. Georgie preferred the traditional route of having a midwife tend to the birth of her baby. "Of course I'll stay. I have no other plans for this afternoon."

"Wonderful! I could certainly use your companionship until Eric returns home."

"Where is he, Georgie?"

Georgie heaved a deep sigh. "Visiting with his father. He's truly going to tell him about us today."

"Is he really?"

"Yes," Georgie said with a nod, her loose black hair bouncing softly. "And I am just too overwrought with anticipation."

"*You* overwrought?"

"I can get overwrought." Georgette laughed at Arielle's incredulous tone. "I am more than a little concerned about Eric's talk with the earl."

"What if his father rejects you, Georgie?"

Biting down on her lip, Georgie considered that. Then she shrugged with false bravado and said, "I'll still have Eric and our baby."

Arielle got up from her seat and paced around the room. Touches of Georgie's presence were scattered about. A pair of diamond earrings glinted on Eric's bureau. A delicate, hand-blown perfume bottle stood amongst his writing paraphanalia on the table by the window. A night rail lay atop his sleeping shirt. Would it ever be this way for her and Hunter? Would he allow such feminine reminders amongst his possessions?

Pausing next to the bed and having no answers for her questions, Arielle leaned her head against a post. "Georgie, I hate myself for this, but I envy your happiness," she said on a ragged whisper.

"Don't despair, my friend," Georgie said quietly, understanding Arielle's dilemma through years of acquaintance.

But how could Georgie understand anything? She'd met the man of her dreams and stayed true to her course with him. In the end, she married him and now carried his child. How indeed could Georgie understand Arielle's turmoil? Hunter had met her with a slanted opinion of her and never quite understood her dream. He had shown her the first breath of love, retreated completely, then sent a marriage proposal through her father. Certainly not a way to inspire security.

Georgie patted the edge of her bed. "Come and sit with me."

Obediently, Arielle went and sat on the edge of the bed. She hugged Georgie, who kissed the top of her head and rubbed her fingers through Arielle's hair, as comforting as any mother.

"Darling Ellie, I just know the fates have a unique kind of joy destined for you."

"Your optimism is always so contagious. One can't help but ignore the outrageous aspect of it."

"Good. That means one is not a half-witted ninny."

Leaning back, Arielle smiled. "Let the fates bring what they must. But not before Verna serves my favorite afternoon repast. Where in heaven is that woman?"

"She'll be here. But first, you must tell me what it's like to be kissed by Hunter Braxton."

Feeling decidedly better, Arielle went back to the chaise lounge and stretched out. "Let me see," she said with flourished drama, her hand on her breast, "where shall I begin?"

* * *

Later, in the privacy of her bedchamber at Stanford Manor, Arielle answered Hunter's cordial response to her request for a meeting.

Dear Hunter, she began, then paused, frowning at how distant her greeting sounded. It was such a contrast to her previous greeting of *Dearest Hunter* or even *My Dear Hunter.* Yet, given their unknown future together, she no longer felt comfortable with such a personal greeting.

Melancholia descended upon her at the thought, but she knew she had to face her current circumstances with fortitude and determination. Hopefully, she and Hunter would work through their problems once their marriage took place.

With a sigh, she returned her attention to the letter, leaving the greeting as she'd written it and continuing from there.

> *I was sorely disappointed by your refusal to meet me to discuss our wedding, but I understand your previous obligations must take precedence over nuptial arrangements.*
>
> *As for my lost bid to get into medical college, I have certainly lamented that. I think it prudent to inform you that matrimony will not dampen my passion for helping and healing the sick, however.*
>
> *As indifferent as it seemed, you requested information about the wedding ceremony. Please be at St. Paul's Cathedral for ten A.M. on the twenty-fifth of March. Following the nuptials, a wedding breakfast will be held at Stanford Manor. If you have any concerns, please feel free to call on me.*
>
> *Until our next meeting,*
>
> >   *Cordially,*
> >   *Arielle*

23

Intricately carved domed ceilings rose high above Hunter, seeming to aspire to the heavens. Huge columns supported gilded archways. Sunlight blazed through the windows surrounding the dome of St. Paul's Cathedral, gleaming down upon the guests sitting in the hard wooden pews and crowning his bride with a golden aura as she advanced toward him.

Rigid with anger, he stood at the altar, watching her, hating her, loving her, needling her, wanting her. But she knew his secrets. And she'd gone along with her father's schemes to get him here. Married and several thousand pounds poorer.

She reached the first step and his fists clenched at his sides. She paused, hesitating, recognizing his fury. A grim smile touched his lips, his sweeping glance purposefully cold. She'd wanted to wed him at any cost. She'd have to live with the weight of her decision for the rest of her life—and his as well.

For the better part of three weeks, he'd waited to receive any word from her. An apology. A note proclaiming her father's demand had been a farce. A letter expressing that she loved him despite his being born a bastard.

The only thing he'd gotten was a few brief words from her, giving him the time and date of their wedding, and her adamancy about her passion for the healing arts. Nothing more. Now, for the rest of his life, he had to face her, knowing she knew all his ugly secrets. Knowing she'd used those secrets against him.

Viscount Stanford rose from his seat on the first pew, interrupting Hunter's thoughts. He heard titters filtering through the huge crowd; Arielle remained rooted where she stood. Hunter glared at Thomas, daring him to take another step. The old viscount cleared his throat loudly, his face flushing. He took heed, though, and didn't move any further. For the briefest of moments, Hunter cheered Arielle's mortification. He reveled in her embarrassment. She'd wanted him enough to blackmail him. She needed to suffer through this fiasco and feel the pain of betrayal.

Arielle made it to the second step, having one more before she stood next to him. Vulnerability and fear radiated from her. Satisfaction arced through him. On the heels of that came waves of guilt. He wanted no woman to fear him, especially not Arielle, who would be his wife very shortly. What had she to fear from him anyway? They'd become friends over the weeks since meeting. Friends and nearly lovers.

Hunter thought about ending the torture, then and there. He could walk away and never look back. Stanford had already paid off his debts with the bride-price he'd demanded from Hunter. Hunter could walk away and threaten to expose the man's missed appointment with debtor's prison if he revealed the Braxton secrets.

But what purpose would that serve? The viscount was bound and determined to see Arielle wed him; he'd expose Hunter's secrets if the wedding didn't take place. Then, two families would be destroyed and humiliated.

Cursing softly, Hunter strode forward and grasped his bride's small, gloved hand. He ignored the delicate, whispery touch of her soft fingers, the trembles in her body as he stared at her, the fragrance of rose water drifting in the air around him.

The dim lighting at the sanctuary's altar, and the white, heavy lace veil covering her face, didn't lessen her exquisite beauty. The veil added etherealness to her finely carved features and satiny skin. The blond highlights in her hair shimmered beneath the lighting, but the emerald of her eyes was hidden.

His heart beat a little faster. She was moment's away from being his wife. His wife. One day, out of familial duty, he would have married someone.

Now *Arielle* would be his marchioness. *Arielle* would own his heart. *Arielle* would produce his heirs. *Arielle* would know his scorn.

Tonight, he'd bed her. Tomorrow, he'd pretend she didn't exist. It was the least that she deserved after playing him for a fool.

Satisfied with his plan, he released her hand and moved to the right of her. He gave the barest of nods for the bishop to begin.

"Dearly Beloved, we are gathered here today . . ."

Hunter allowed the words to trail away, his returning fury barely contained. The only involvement he wanted in this ceremony was to say the words he had no choice but to say. He could have accepted an *arranged* marriage. But a *forced* marriage was unforgivable. And she'd wanted this. The obvious care and planning put into this day made that fact apparent.

The wedding was a blatant spectacle. No expense had been spared. Grudgingly, he admitted to himself it was the most beautiful, tasteful wedding money could buy. Even if it was his own. And even if it wasn't under the circumstances he'd imagined. Especially to Arielle.

If she'd objected to the marriage in any way, she wouldn't have put on such a display. One day, if he ever overcame his anger enough to speak to her at length, he might ask her why the lavish ceremony.

The monotonous tone of the bishop droned on, grating on Hunter's anger, increasing it to a fever pitch. But the moment for his answer finally came.

"Do you, Hunter William Braxton, marquess of Savage, earl of Toomsley, Viscount of Brigsten, take Arielle Judith Stanford to be your lawfully wedded wife? To love

and honor, to have and to hold, from this day forward 'til
death do you part?"

Hunter sidled a glance at the white organza-and-lace-
clad figure. She barely reached his shoulders; tempting
curves outlined her slender body. Silent and solemn, she
stood unnaturally straight next to him, as if she were a
soldier in Wellington's army. He clenched his jaw. How
would they ever get through their wedding night when
she seemed as frightened as a rabbit trapped in a snare?

Ignoring the pleasant scent of rose water and the
woman it emanated from, he stared straight ahead, answering the bishop in a clear, clipped voice. "I do."

For a moment, Arielle thought he would refuse. But
the strong, deep voice spoke with an underlying men-
ace hard to ignore. She closed her eyes, the words washing over her. She came ever closer to her own acceptance,
which would bind her for life to Hunter Braxton, the marquess of Savage.

Savage. Maybe fitting with the detestable looks he
threw at her, but certainly not for the man she'd fallen in
love with. Least of all did the name fit the *way* he looked.
Handsome beyond her wildest dreams, he was tall, broad-
shouldered, and slim-hipped. In his regimentals, he presented quite a dashing figure. His sinfully black hair
gleamed like onyx and the brilliant blue eyes that haunted
her dreams now bore into her like shards of ice.

Detecting the disdain in them, she shivered, the facts
worse than she'd imagined. This man detested her.

She stiffened her shoulders, wondering what motivated
him. Surely, she had nothing to bring to the union. Lord
Savage was a marquess, a decorated war hero, and out-
rageously wealthy. In short, a man who could pick and
choose any woman he wanted—and one who would be
an asset to him.

He could do much better than a penniless viscount's
daughter with unseemly medical ambitions.

Once she made the decision to go through with the wedding, she'd spent as recklessly as possible, hoping the marquess would become so annoyed with her careless disregard for his wealth that he'd beg off. The grand wedding she'd promised her father could've been given for half the money she spent. But her plan failed. Now she stood here, minutes away from becoming the next marchioness of Savage.

"Do you, Arielle Judith Stanford, take Hunter William Braxton, marquess of Savage, earl of Toomsley, viscount of Brigsten, to be your lawfully wedded husband? To love, honor, and obey, to have and to hold, 'til death do you part?"

Arielle's knees threatened to buckle; she swayed upon her feet. As he had done a moment ago, Hunter took her hand and held it tightly. She should run now, before she responded.

Mrs. Beecham came to mind. There was also the hackney driver who Quentin said had a tumor of the stomach; she thought too of the young wife who had miscarried all six of her babes, growing weaker each time she got with child.

Arielle knew she could be a help to each and every one of them. She'd learned a lot from Quentin. With her knowledge, she might have been accepted into a medical school one day.

She might have even acquired her father's assistance once he saw how truly determined she was and how needy the families she helped. Thomas wasn't a bad person. He was just an ambitious one.

"My lady?"

Hunter tightened his hold on her and Arielle took a deep breath. She had no choice but to marry Hunter, she reminded herself. Every other plan she'd conceived of to help her father out of his debts had failed.

She had no choice.

"I do."

The bishop uttered a few more words, binding her for

life to the marquess, before he said, "You may kiss the bride, my lord."

The statement echoed in Arielle's brain, and she stiffened even further. This wasn't a love match. Hunter wouldn't do such a thing. His hesitation bespoke shame. He released her hand, then turned and lifted her veil. His disdainful gaze traveled over her forehead to her eyes and nose and lips.

The bishop cleared his throat. Hunter smiled, giving his features a brief boyish charm. When he leaned down to kiss her, Arielle pulled away. Their marriage was such a mockery, but her feelings weren't. She could never hide her love for him, if he touched her so intimately.

For endless seconds, their gazes locked.

"Madam," Hunter murmured with ire. His hot breath fanned her earlobe as he spoke for her benefit alone. "This is no way to start a marriage."

Before Arielle responded, he lowered his head again, this time finding her lips. Glimpsing his simmering anger, the gentle contact surprised her. She sighed against his mouth. Immediately, Hunter broke the brief contact. His remote look hurt.

Hunter held out a scarlet-clad arm to her and she grasped it. Together, they started back down the aisle.

The brilliant sun still gleaming through the dome windows didn't alleviate the fear in her of what was to come later. Her new husband seemed ruthless, if not altogether heartless. But this wasn't the man she'd gotten to know. The man she'd fallen in love with had been so solicitous of her feelings. He'd been charming and funny and seductive.

This man, however, was an angry stranger. She worried that he might be brutal with her in the bridal chamber. The minute kindnesses he'd shown to her these past weeks might have only been for show. But she wouldn't believe that, for the sake of his debts, her father could sacrifice her to an unkind man, even if he happened to be well-heeled.

Her worries were unfounded, she told herself, holding on to Hunter as they made their way through a sea of well-wishers toward the brightness of the morning and their waiting coach.

Once they were secure in the coach, Arielle sank back in the leather seat, warily watching Hunter, who sat across from her. Angry resentment punctuated the silence. She glanced out the small window, willing herself to remain calm.

This wasn't the wedding she'd dreamed of, despite the fripperies and flowers and food. Despite the showcase planned for their breakfast. But it was the only wedding she'd ever have. She must push aside her apprehensions and pretend enjoyment of her grand day. Then, she'd endeavor to be a model wife and forget the circumstances surrounding her marriage.

It wouldn't do for the gossipy rumor mill of the ton to speculate on her nuptials. If only she and Hunter had met to discuss today, they might have come to some sort of agreement on how to act in front of everyone. But Hunter's last letter to her had summarily dismissed such an idea, even as he hinted that their marriage might have been destiny.

"How are you, my lady?"

She gazed at him, into his cerulean blue eyes, refusing to look away. She didn't want him to know how much he intimidated her and how she resented him then. "Well, my lord."

He nodded, the answer seeming to please him. Still, he scowled. "Good."

She folded her hands in her lap, stifling the urge to gnaw at her fingertips. "And you, my lord?"

A brief smile touched his well-shaped lips at her flippancy. He shifted in his seat. "Do you really care, my dear?"

"I would not have asked if I didn't."

Narrowing his eyes at her, Hunter chuckled without humor. "I'm touched."

Anger heated Arielle's cheeks at his sarcasm. "Why ever did you consent to the union between us, my lord?"

"You are as well informed of those facts as I am, my lady. Don't insult me further by posing such a question.".

"I won't pose any more questions to you, insulting or otherwise."

Blindly watching the passing scenery, Arielle pretended not to notice Hunter's cold gaze upon her. She pretended the routine river traffic on the Thames was an absorbing sight. But she did relax a measure. A man as resentful as he was wouldn't want to touch his new wife in the marriage bed.

She'd enjoy her wedding breakfast with a lighter heart and worry about the rest of her life later.

24

A quarter of an hour later, Arielle and Hunter entered the reception hall at Stanford Manor, where a trio of musicians played a celebratory tune. Delicate pastries, tender meats, fresh fruit, warm breads, and various other foods ladened the refreshment tables. Waiters circulated amongst the guests, carrying ornate silver trays filled with glasses of champagne and wine. Garlands of roses adorned the columns in the hall, while big bouquets of flowers graced the tables.

Hunter's cold accusing eyes strangled her rising joy at finding everything as it should be. Arielle winced at her husband's indignation. Perhaps she had gone overboard for the wedding, especially when her father didn't have a shilling to buy a periwinkle, let alone fund this display. This was just one more thing she and Hunter would have to deal with. Smiling with sweet satisfaction to her guests, she pushed aside her disappointment. She'd thought Hunter would have been pleased by everything.

"Arielle, my dear!" Julia rushed up to the two of them and curtsied delicately. "You made a most beautiful bride."

"Thank you, Julia." Arielle forced a smile, recovering from her shock at Julia's false gesture. With her position as marchioness this was expected from an earl's wife. But Julia's hypocrisy galled Arielle. She knew Julia would've preferred to trample her than bow to her.

Julia looked exquisite as usual. Her chestnut hair framed her delicate features and hazel eyes gleamed with

an unknown light. "This wedding was such a surprise."
She smiled, a cat's smile that told Arielle to beware. "You
should have told me several weeks ago at the theater. I
would have announced it then. But I should say, you and
Dr. DeVries appeared to be such an ideal . . . couple.
Everyone thought you would eventually wed each
other—"

Hunter quirked an eyebrow at Arielle, curiosity spreading across his features. Embarrassment coursed through
her. Although she clearly remembered mentioning Quentin to Hunter in a letter, to have him brought up with such
innuendo might further strain her and Hunter's relationship.

Their acquaintance had started off friendly enough and
their growing friendship had begun to blossom into something far more powerful. But it was becoming clear to
Arielle that Hunter Braxton was quite a complex man.

Damning Julia's negligible comment, Arielle scowled.
She had a few negligible comments of her own she could
make, but she would never dare expose her father. "Julia,
really! Your comment is beyond tasteless."

Julia laughed shrilly. "Well, you never did mince
words, did you, darling? But you shouldn't be shy about
DeVries. Everyone thinks you've made the better choice.
Lord Savage is a dream. I hadn't the faintest notion that
he was back in circulation!" She transferred an appreciative glance to Hunter. "I hope you don't mind my assessment of you, my lord."

Hunter's expression closed at the invitation in Julia's
eyes. "Of course not, madam." His intense, inscrutable
gaze raked Julia, his husky tone only adding to his aura.

Arielle's intuition pricked her senses, sending chills
down her spine. She saw the subtle play between Hunter
and Julia and suddenly felt their acquaintance went deeper
than a mere flirtation. Julia glowed from Hunter's dark
sensuality, sidling closer to him, her breasts caressing his
arm. Arielle's cheeks burned with anger and humiliation.

"I should warn you, however," Hunter continued, "that

I've never succumbed to flattery or assessment before my marriage to the marchioness and I vow I won't start now that the event has taken place."

His iciness surprised both Julia and Arielle. His abrupt change made Arielle wonder to whom did he direct his ire.

"Oh!" Julia's hands flew to her chest. "I never meant to flatter you—I mean—"

"It's all right, Julia," Arielle inserted quickly, hiding a satisfied smile, relief flooding her. Julia seemed genuinely perplexed. At least Hunter had spared Arielle his anger. "Hunter never meant to offend you, as I'm sure you never meant to . . . seem, uh, *assessing* of him. We *both* know what you meant." Turning to Hunter, she met his amused glance. She smiled back at him, his appeal hard to ignore. "I forgot to tell you that Lord Pembishire was unable to attend the reception."

Hunter nodded, facing Julia. "I heard that he was in convalescence from a riding accident. Please extend my well wishes to him. You and Douglas must attend a dinner when he is fully healed. We have much to discuss."

"Of course, my lord," she cooed.

"And forgive my facetiousness. As Arielle said, I never meant to offend you."

"You *didn't*, Lord Savage," Julia responded, clearly pleased by Hunter's remorse and invitation. Douglas needed to keep a rein on his bloody wife, Hunter thought. She was loose-moraled and arrogant, and Hunter could hardly abide her. He only did so for Douglas's sake. Yet Julia had better endeavor to pay Arielle the same respect he always accorded her. Or suffer the consequences of insulting his wife. Never mind that he and Julia had courted twelve years ago, he would tolerate no interference from her in his life now.

Other guests began gathering around them, awaiting their turns to congratulate the bride and groom. A stout-bodied fop walked up to him with an extended hand. Past-

ing a smile on his face, Hunter held on to his patience by
sheer will.

"Lord Savage, I'm Malcolm Bronson, barrister." The
brightly attired man pumped his hand vigorously. "One
of your new brothers-in-law. Let me be the first to com-
mend you on your excellent military record."

"Malcolm is Emma's husband," Arielle clarified.

A moment later, the rest of his new in-laws made themselves known to him. Viscount Laurent Cabot and his
wife, Ellen, were the least likeable of Arielle's family.
Baron Sidney Collins and Baroness Kate would always
be welcome in his home. Of Dr. Morgan Wilford and his
wife, Agatha, Hunter hadn't an opinion. They just blended
into the background of the brood. All extended a warm
welcome to him and praised his battle record.

Hunter really hadn't prepared himself for such mundane compliments about his military accomplishments. Or
the boring morning he saw ahead of him. He was amongst
people he hardly knew; Arielle's family, whom he really
didn't want to know. Not after the way the marriage had
come about.

"I'm pleased to meet you all, but do have pity and
allow me a moment on the dance floor with my bride."

"How insensitive we've been," the unwavering Julia
said. "Of course you must have your due, my lord. But
please indulge us a moment longer. I noticed at the ceremony no ring was presented. Was that some significant
gesture we should know about?"

Julia *was* brash and her remarks were intended simply
to goad him. Arielle's fingers tightened on his arm and
he glanced at her. Her unease was palpable, but he forced
himself to ignore her distress. It might have been from
Julia's inappropriate question, but he doubted that. If it
had been, Arielle would have set the woman in her place,
however sweetly. He felt it was her apprehension about
how he'd reply. With only a few words, he could let it
be known what a sham this *happy* celebration truly was.

"Lady Pembishire," he responded in a light tone, "I was

in such a rush to claim Arielle as my bride, there was no time to procure a ring that adequately expressed my feelings for her."

"How romantic!"

"Isn't it?" Viscountess Cabot remarked, giving her youngest sister a cool glance. "And to a marquess, no less. My dear little Arielle, you truly amaze me."

"Ellen—"

"Well, she shouldn't, Ellen," Kate snapped, interrupting Arielle and kissing her cheek. "She has beauty to put you to shame and a sweetly angelic disposition. Lord Savage would be a fool not to have fallen madly in love with her."

"You should be ashamed of your snide remark, Ellen!" Emma huffed. "Especially on Arielle's wedding day. Where is your tact, *Lady* Cabot?"

Hunter looked at the other sister—Agatha—and waited for her to speak. She merely shrugged, a sheepish look upon her face. Having heard enough, he began to pull Arielle out of the tight circle. "If everyone is through throwing sallies at one another, I'm sure you'll excuse us."

"We shall be returning to our country manor in two days," Ellen went on, craning her neck as Hunter continued his stride. "I hear your own estate isn't far away, my lord. I should like to give an intimate dinner to welcome you into the family."

"Lady Cabot, I shall leave the discretion of acceptance up to my wife," he called over his shoulder.

Without another word, he led Arielle into the ballroom. The musicians noted them in the center and they slowed down the reel they'd been playing. Like the Red Sea, other dancers parted, standing on the sidelines to watch the newlyweds in their first dance together.

Hunter hated that he and Arielle were the objects of attention, but it kept his mind off how he felt with his arm around his beautiful bride. The music kept his mind off the hot need coursing through him, the desire to sweep her up and lose himself in the sweetness of her body.

Closing his eyes, he sighed against her hair, closing out the curious gazes of his guests.

The music from the orchestra lulled them into a brief truce. The applause as Arielle pirouetted before resuming her place in his arms brought about a feeling of oneness. Her sweet scent intoxicated him. Her fresh beauty enthralled him. And her softness as she moved in his arms fascinated him. That combination made it virtually impossible to distract himself from the fact that she was now his.

She appeared completely confused and totally vulnerable. She'd used the ruse of becoming a physician to get him to the altar. Her uncertainty had to be another deception.

"Are you enjoying yourself, my marchioness?"

"Yes. Very much."

The sound of her low, throaty voice excited him, sent tingles to his loins. Pushing the feeling aside, he glanced pointedly around the room, his seething anger returning. God help him, she'd deceived him. He hoped her hard-won titles pleased her. "You should. Such a fabulous display should please any bride."

Arielle nodded. "Yes. It should."

Hunter chuckled without mirth, annoyed at her frugal words. "Your enthusiasm overwhelms me, my dear marchioness."

Sea green eyes flashed indignantly. "Please call me Arielle," she said through gritted teeth. "Not *marchioness!*"

"My mistake, *Arielle*. With our marriage taking place with such haste, one would think you couldn't wait to claim the title."

Biting down on her lip, Arielle very carefully and very deliberately ground her foot upon his. He misstepped his dance movement, then tightened his hold on her.

"I, my lord?" she sneered, preventing him from warning her not to do such a thing again. "I couldn't claim that title without your permission *and* cooperation. Were you in such a rush to give it away?"

"Point well taken, Arielle," Hunter conceded. The musicians drifted into another tune without pause, saving him from completely letting his guard down. He gestured for the other dancers to rejoin them on the floor. "Care for some champagne?"

"Yes."

Others took to the floor as they walked hand in hand to one of the refreshment tables, where glasses of wine and champagne stood.

Hunter handed a glass to Arielle. She took a sip and perused the room. Her attention focused on a young man with dark hair and black eyes. A hint of a smile curved her mouth and the young man barely nodded.

"Friend?" Hunter's question garnered her attention.

"Who?" Her hand trembled, and the glass she held shook, a betrayal of her surprise at Hunter's observation.

Hunter quirked an eyebrow, that lone gesture enough to convey his disdain for deception.

Arielle tasted her champagne again, then raised her chin. "Yes."

"Dr. DeVries, I presume?" he asked, remembering Julia's words.

"Yes. Dr. DeVries." Resentment echoed in her voice and marred her features. "I should like to introduce Quentin to you, Hunter. We are old friends."

"Of course," Hunter said cordially, refusing to acknowledge the displeasure he felt at the way Arielle's face lit up. "Over time, I expect to meet all your friends and acquaintances." He followed Arielle to where DeVries stood watching Arielle like a lovesick fool.

"Hello, Quentin," she said, stopping just inches from him. "I'm so glad you were able to attend."

Quentin bowed, as unsure as Arielle of what to do next as he looked from her to Hunter and back again.

What had passed between them, for both Arielle and Quentin to display such nervousness? Hunter wasn't big on rumors. For the most part, they were embellished and spread without regard to accuracy. It seemed in this case, however, the countess mightn't have been far off the mark.

"Hello, my lady," Quentin said finally.

Arielle laughed, giving in to her urge to hug him. "Dear Quentin, that's not necessary. We've known each other too long for such formalities."

Shifting his weight, Quentin smiled, but didn't touch Arielle. "I know." He darted his eyes between them. "But your circumstance has changed."

"But *not* our friendship," Arielle emphasized, looking at Hunter for confirmation.

Creasing his lips in a hint of a smile and placing a possessive arm around Arielle's waist, Hunter focused an icy gaze on DeVries. "Certainly not that."

Annoyance flickered in Quentin's limpid gaze, and Arielle scowled at Hunter. Her brilliant eyes flashed dangerously, but she held her temper in check.

"Hunter, I would like to introduce Dr. DeVries to you," she said into the silence.

"DeVries," Hunter said with a nod.

Quentin extended his hand. "How do you do, my lord? It's my pleasure to meet you."

"Same here, Dr. DeVries." Hunter shook Quentin's hand. Only his good breeding allowed him the show of manners. He wanted to escort DeVries to the door and command that he never return. Such a display, however, wouldn't do.

A few more awkward moments filled with tiresome comments lapsed before Quentin excused himself to go to the refreshment table, pleading a need for a drink.

"How could you?" Arielle snapped once her friend was out of earshot.

"How could I what?" Hunter asked, feigning boredom. But she wasn't stupid by any means. She knew he'd deliberately made Quentin feel uncomfortable to discourage any invitation she might extend to him to visit their estate.

"Quentin is—"

"A friend," he completed for her, "who must know his boundaries." When she would have argued more, he raised a hand to forestall her. "We can discuss this on another occasion, Arielle. We have a long day ahead of us and an even longer night."

She went completely still at his statement, the hand holding her glass pausing in midair. Wide, misty eyes studied him. The thought went through his mind that she might not be an innocent. Perhaps that was why Stanford had been so hell-bent to rid himself of her.

A new sense of determination to fulfill his husbandly duties surged in Hunter, one that had nothing to do with her father and everything to do with his pride.

"I—I don't understand, m-my lord."

"I believe you do, my lady. But in the chance you are speaking the truth, I am referring to our time in the bridal chamber later on. Surely your father had someone explain the basics to you?"

A blush stained her flawless ivory features and she shook her head. Setting the glass down, she said, "I am a patron of the healing arts, my lord. I know how the body functions."

"Then I needn't be concerned."

"I should have known you had lulled me into a false hope. We barely know each other. We cannot—"

"We can and we will, Arielle," Hunter snapped, hating the urgency in her voice, the unease in her eyes. "We've known each other long enough. Although, the length of time a couple is acquainted has nothing to do with when they become intimate. However, I will not have it said that this is a marriage in name only. Prepare yourself for the inevitable, madam."

Tears glistened in her eyes, but instead of succumbing to them, she blinked furiously and drew in a deep breath, then completely changed the subject. "I don't understand where my father could be. I haven't seen him since we left the church."

"I'm most certain he's somewhere about," Hunter told her. "He'll find his way to you soon."

The weight of the world seemed to descend on his wife's shoulders, if the anguish in her eyes were any indication. After tonight, he'd have to steer clear of her for his own sanity. He wouldn't abide telling himself he was angry and resentful of their forced marriage and then not proving the point with his actions.

Just as the thought crossed his mind, Thomas Stanford finally made his appearance. Looking directly at them, ignoring the well-wishers as he passed by, Thomas barreled toward them with purpose, his features haggard and wrought with worry. When he reached them, he pulled Arielle into his arms and hugged her.

"I'm so proud of you, child," he said, his voice taut with anguish.

Arielle lowered her eyelashes. "I did it for you, Father."

"I know. And I'm forever grateful to you." Stanford gazed at Hunter and cleared his throat. "Congratulations, my lord."

Aware of the crowd around them, Hunter bowed with rigid anger, feeling completely betrayed. If Arielle had been against her father's wishes at all, this display wouldn't take place. "The pleasure was all yours, Stanford." He swept Arielle with a cold glance. "And yours, of course, my dear," he added, insulted at her words. He had known Arielle had only gone along with her father's plans to further her own. "If you will excuse us?"

He didn't await Stanford's reply, but guided Arielle back onto the dance floor. After participating in another dance, more of her family members surrounded them. She really was from a large bunch. Hunter hoped he wouldn't have to suffer their presence very often. He had always been a very private person. He couldn't imagine his deeply accustomed privacy so abruptly ending.

They remained for another hour before Arielle's weariness reared itself. She'd probably been awake most of the night and half the morning in dread and anticipation. He certainly had been. When she stifled a yawn with her gloved hand, he said their good-byes, then guided Arielle toward the waiting carriage with the Braxton coat of arms gleaming in gold on the door.

Searing anticipation removed the sharp edges of Hunter's anger, leaving him somewhat empty and drained. Yet his desire for Arielle overrode those emotions. As the coach rolled away, he thought of all the ways to put a young wife at ease in their bedchamber.

25

"I must thank you, madam, for putting on such a spectacular display."

Sinking deeper into the leather seat of the coach, Arielle pulled the lap rug around her legs. She eyed her husband, searching for traces of sarcasm in his features. His words sounded so sincere. Naught more than that impossibly inscrutable gaze met her and she nodded. "Thank you, my lord."

"It was a wonderful accomplishment," he continued, a small smile creasing his mouth. "And you made quite an extraordinary bride. You will be the talk of society for months."

Listening to him, Arielle shifted her weight. She didn't want to be the talk of society. Instead, she wanted her safe, secure world back, where she was a dutiful daughter to her father and a cherished friend to Georgette and Quentin. Change, even in its smallest amount, was insufferable to her. The only change she'd ever looked forward to was becoming a doctor, not a *wife*. Changes brought complications to ordinary routines. In a matter of weeks, her entire life had changed forever, the comfort of her routines all but forgotten.

"Where have your thoughts taken you, Arielle?"

She closed her eyes at the sound of Hunter's voice. It was so pleasant this time, so masculine, its soothing gentleness washing over her like a fine mist. It almost sounded as if he wanted to make amends for his hostility.

"I was thinking how much my life has changed."

"Is that a good thing or a bad thing, my dear?"

She opened her eyes again. The concern in his voice contrasted with the cool irritation on his face.

"I've always detested change, Hunter. If not for my father's request, I never would have consented to marry you."

The wide shoulders she'd been ignoring stiffened and he narrowed his eyes, his nostrils flaring. A brutal mockery invaded his features. "Then I suppose I should applaud your sense of *duty* to your father as well, my lady."

Raising her chin defiantly, she folded her arms. "You make my duty sound like an ugly crime, my lord."

"Duty is a commendable trait. Sacrificing your life for it is not."

"This from a decorated officer in Wellington's army? You wouldn't have sacrificed your life for duty to crown and country?"

"That is quite different, madam, and well you know it."

"Is it?" Arielle asked bitingly, annoyed that he might be right.

"Yes, madam! It is. Giving up your life, your happiness, for family duty is tantamount to giving up your soul. You haven't been true to yourself. Giving up your life for crown and country when you do it freely is a personal choice that is quite honorable."

"Are my intentions no less honorable for wanting my father happy? It is change I abhor, not duty."

A frustrated sigh escaped Hunter and he shoved a hand through his thick black hair. "Change is an inescapable part of life," he said, more calmly. "Change is the only constant, as a matter of fact."

As he spoke with such conviction, she pretended not to notice anything about him. Not his discarded coat lying carelessly next to him. Or the tanned, hard chest peaking from beneath his unfrilled white shirt. Or the long, muscular thighs bulging in the white breeches and the gleaming black boots crossed at the ankles.

"So it is," she said softly.

"What is it about your life that you wouldn't want changed? There's always room for adjustments."

He didn't sound scornful or disdaining, just interested.

"My life was perfectly settled until the offer of marriage came about," she said, her bitterness coming through, knowing there was nothing he could do about her dreams and desires, now that they were already married.

"In other words, you had no intentions of ever marrying."

"Of course, my lord. What girl doesn't wish to wed?" She swallowed hard. "But I wish to become a physician. The first licensed female doctor in Britain. You know that, Hunter."

Hunter snorted and glanced out at the passing scenery. His chiseled profile etched itself into her memory. As the silence grew, so too did her unease. He was fully aware of her dreams. But as the marchioness of Savage, he'd expect her attitude to change. "Hunter, I—I—"

Hunter raised a hand to halt her flow of words. "There is certainly no turning back, Arielle. I do hope you remember your duties as my marchioness, which do not include pursuing a physician's license. Forgive my bluntness, my dear, but I'm sure you understood what you were giving up when you decided to bow to your father's wishes."

She didn't have a response to his truthfulness. When her father made his demands, she knew what she'd give up and that's why she'd fought so hard against it. Deciding to push aside the conversation for the moment, she focused on the passing scenery. If they continued in this vein, it would only lead to a terrible argument. She suspected the duties he referred to principally included her producing an heir and she really had no choice but to fulfill that obligation to him.

"Here we are, milady," the maid cheerily announced, arriving at a dull wooden door upstairs in Braxton Hall.

The hectic pace of the preceding weeks, the strain of the past hours and the uneasy expectation of what was to come converged on Arielle at once. She barely smiled. Exhaustion drained her last bit of strength, stealing away her ability to respond to a simple pleasantry.

Quietly, she followed the maid into the room, finding only a huge tester bed and a small stand with a pitcher and washbasin on it. She drew in a deep breath.

Having only just arrived at Braxton Hall, Arielle was in no condition to make a true assessment of what needed doing. Hunter had disappeared as soon as the maid had come to bring her to her room. Perhaps he'd been embarrassed at the state of his manor, although she'd already seen it and knew the reasons for its condition.

Still, the entire manor went beyond simplicity to unwelcoming and bare. Her new husband *had* been away for the last several years, so she couldn't entirely fault him. Hopefully, he'd allow her to rectify the situation as soon as possible.

What she could fault him for, however, was walking away without even a proper introduction to the staff.

"Is there anything ye be needin', mum?"

Besides escape? Arielle thought with despair.

"I'm fine, thank you," she said, not glancing over her shoulder. On trembling legs, she approached the bed. A rapidly waning sun stole the last vestiges of light from the chamber. Sooner than she wanted, Hunter would come to claim his husbandly duties.

Nausea threatened to choke her and she swallowed deeply. She couldn't imagine making love to Hunter with such a tremendous division between them.

"I shall return in a few minutes with a lamp, mum," the woman said quietly, her underlying kindness almost Arielle's undoing. "His lordship has also instructed me to help ye into your night rail. Is that acceptable?"

"Y-yes."

"If ye should need anything before my return, milady, the connecting door there leads to the marquess's room."

Arielle glanced in the direction the maid indicated. Heat crept into her cheeks at the thought that Hunter would be on the other side of the door as she undressed in preparation for their consummation. He might even grow impatient and burst in before she completed her toilette.

She closed her eyes, barely noticing the maid's departure. The man she had married was such an enigma to her. Which, of course, was just as it should be, given that they were virtual strangers.

Placing her head in her hands, she shivered, the cold draftiness of the room finally seeping into her bones.

Everything was unfamiliar to her, she thought bitterly. The lack of warmth, both literally and figuratively, at Braxton Hall. The sparsity of furnishing. The terrible silence, heavy with tension.

But this was what she had agreed to for Thomas's sake. These deprivations were part of her duty to her family. As the last unwed daughter, she had been the only one who could help her father.

It didn't matter that Ellen, Emma, Kate, and Agatha probably wouldn't have done the same had they been in the position to. Well, maybe to become a marchioness they might have, especially Ellen, but certainly not out of any loyalty.

She had done what she'd had to do. She had changed her entire life because she couldn't refuse her father. Now, she had to make the best of that change. She had had no choice in the matter. She could have refused, but she owed Thomas Stanford a great debt of gratitude for the honorable way he'd handled her mother's terrible indiscretion and claimed Arielle as his own. Marrying Hunter actually freed her of her debt to Thomas. He no longer had authority over the course of her life.

Hunter listened as the door opened and closed for a second time and surmised Dora was returning to Arielle's bedchamber.

Dressed in a dressing gown and edgy with anticipation, he prowled the length of the floor, the minutes moving at a tortoise's pace.

If he and Arielle hadn't parted on such a strained note, he would be better off. Instead, he'd rudely left her to her own devices upon their arrival. That certainly wouldn't have relieved Arielle's anxieties. It would only have added to them. He needed to remember that he had to take care with her inexperience. He had to treat her with kid gloves and forget what had taken place.

Most importantly, he needed to ignore his anger and remember that he loved her.

This, after all, was his fault. He had mocked Arielle's so-called duty, but that was exactly what had driven him to marry her, only he'd claimed it was loyalty to his mother's memory. But it was family duty as well, which meant he wasn't so different from Arielle.

Besides, he was the marquess of Savage; he *should* have been able to find a way to put an end to Stanford's lunacy with a more concerted effort.

Was it only the need to protect his mother's good name that drove him? Partly. But, in truth, he really wanted to take Arielle to wife.

He had always been so ashamed of all the implications that entailed the Braxton secrets; secrets that had guided his entire life; secrets that had never allowed him to grow close to anyone for fear of being a handicap to any confidant if a scandal ever broke. Ignoring his own needs, he had learned to exist in a solitary world, relying on no one but his beloved uncle for advice and companionship.

For a long while, a wife had been out of the question. He had actually considered letting the line die out with him. It might have been better for all concerned.

Then, the Stanfords had entered his life and he'd waged a meager fight against them. And the very liabilities that hadn't allowed him to take a wife had now seen him standing at the altar of St. Paul's.

There were any number of things Hunter might have

done to stop his wedding. He could have gone and personally paid off Thomas's debts. The man couldn't have been heartless enough to continue with his blackmail if Hunter had rescued him.

Of course, Thomas could have. Viscount Stanford had been determined to see Hunter marry Arielle. Whatever he had yet to discover about Arielle, Hunter knew she wasn't a wilting flower. She didn't hesitate to express herself. Maybe Stanford needed someone to come in and take a firm hand with her, given her proclivities.

That, however, had been *his* job as her father. He couldn't really expect Hunter to bring her around and remove her desire to become a physician.

And quite a noble desire, even if it was misguided. However, there were any number of charities she could involve herself in if she needed to extend a helping hand to others. But that's all she could do as a woman, and a nobly reared one at that. A midwife, too; not a licensed physician, practicing and treating all sorts of ailments.

A grim smile touched his lips and he gazed at the closed door again, shaking his head in amazement. She had arranged an impeccable wedding. Without her sense of refinement and knowledge of the social graces, she couldn't have done it. He grudgingly admitted that he wouldn't have wanted his wedding any other way. Although he was too pigheaded to admit that to Arielle right now, he decided it had been the perfect ceremony for the marquess and marchioness of Savage.

Arielle's hallway door closed again. Knowing Dora took her leave, Hunter's throat went dry at the thought of how Arielle must appear, dressed in some virginal white garment, her hair hanging loosely about her shoulders, her skin perfumed with an evocative fragrance.

He breathed in deeply. The time had come for him to face Arielle again, the woman who was now his wife.

26

A sudden knock on the door startled Arielle to her feet. "Er . . . a moment, please." She smoothed out the satin wrap she wore over the matching night rail, then nervously patted her hair. Taking a deep breath, she went to the door and opened it. Her breath caught and her heart tumbled.

Hunter took up nearly all the space in the portal, his massive shoulders and tall, strong body devastating and alluring. Shot through with gold threads, the black drooping gown he wore added luster to his inky hair. The look in his eyes as his glance roamed over her reminded her of a storm-tossed sea, intense, fascinating, and dangerous. Passion and hunger filled the unnerving gaze.

Powerfully vital and handsome, Hunter stood there with a heedless grace. Without warning, he took her hand into his own and placed a delicate kiss on the back. "My lady."

"My lord," Arielle managed, stepping aside to allow him entrance.

In the span of one day, she'd witnessed his anger, his consideration, and even his appreciation. But it was this tender, seductive side that might put her at risk of having her heart broken. Although she'd decided to make this union work, her heart raced as if she had already succeeded.

Hunter stood looking at his bride. How could such an angel be so deceiving?

Shimmering like golden silk, her hair fell down her back. An oval face framed exotic cheekbones, a dainty nose, and full lips. Her face, with its flawless, glowing complexion, was so lovely, it left him breathless. The look of angelic vulnerability in Arielle's features touched something deep within him. It was the same look she'd worn the day he met her and it had the same effect upon him now that she had become his wife. She was absolutely heartbreaking.

She had the face of an angel and the heart of a gold digger.

A frown marring his features, Hunter drew in a deep breath. He wouldn't let his emotions obscure the real reason he'd been trapped into the marriage.

She'd appeared so forlorn on the trip to Braxton Hall, he'd wanted to comfort her. Turmoil surged inside him. She wasn't supposed to elicit such tender emotions. He wanted his anger toward her and her father to remain uppermost in his mind. He wanted to bed her and be done with it. In the core of him, however, he knew his determination to bed her wasn't mere lust.

It was desire. It was need. It was love.

After he performed the husbandly duties that wouldn't leave a doubt about the validity of their marriage, however, he'd leave Arielle to her own devices. Whatever she wished to do was fine with him, as long as she left him alone. It was the best course for all concerned.

The only circumstance he wouldn't tolerate was infidelity. To have his peace, he'd even allow her to tend the sick on his estates.

He closed the door with a firm thud. "Are you rested, madam?"

"Yes, quite. Th-thank you, my lord."

Seized by apprehension, Arielle braved a shy smile. Hunter's presence was overpowering, the frown on his features daunting. For long, awkward moments, they stood facing each other.

He walked to the bed, leaving her to follow behind him. Glancing at the bareness of the walls, the floor, and the Spartan furniture, he settled his gaze upon her.

"I take it nothing is in the order of your liking, Arielle. I have not had the time to hire a full staff." Considering he had come to bed her, he attempted to be as cordial as possible.

To Arielle, Hunter spoke the words with a wry non-chalance that belied the arrogant set of his features, the careless stance of his body. Summoning the courage stolen by his unyielding look, she went to where he stood. "I have no complaints, my lord. With your permission, I will furnish the house."

He narrowed his eyes at her, his jaw tautening. "I have looked forward to doing that very thing for quite some time, my dear. Before your father came up with his idea, I had planned to reside here at my seat until such time when Braxton Hall was once again the glorious home I remember. However, under my direction, I will allow you some part of the restoration."

Arielle discerned his bitterness and fury, despite his outward cordiality. She saw the anger in the two unforgiving bits of blue ice that were his eyes, daring her to gainsay him. She knew she was overlooking the vital piece of information causing him to act in such a manner, but at the moment it was hard to think about anything other than his cold words and his bracing nearness.

"My lord, forgive me for pressing the issue, but we need to settle what place I have at Braxton Hall—"

"That of my wife, Arielle, and a wife's duties."

"Hunter," Arielle said with a deep intake of breath, her indignation at his stubbornness rising. She had a lot to be bitter about as well. "I no longer have my work with Quentin to absorb my free time and Georgette has been ordered to bed—"

"DeVries?" Hunter asked sharply, ignoring her reference to this Georgette as his frown turned into a glower when she nodded.

"Yes, *Dr.* DeVries. I don't have access to him, or his patients, or even the medical books he gave me. Furthermore, you're being vague about my role here."

"You should have thought of your position before you accepted your father's proposal. As for DeVries, what exactly are your feelings for him?"

"He's like the brother I never had, Hunter, and a dear friend."

He couldn't very well deny the sincerity in her voice, the earnestness of her gaze. As much as he wanted to. Still, he couldn't fully trust her either. "If you say so, my dear. Know this, however; I refuse to be cuckolded. I require an heir and I refuse to have his lineage in question. Whatever your feelings for DeVries, bury them."

"For what? To sit and dawdle in a corner? Our patients—*his* patients—expect to see me."

A dangerous glint lit Hunter's eyes. "Listen and listen well, Arielle. For his sake, don't dally with him. Do I make myself clear? Julia Shepperton made some very unseemly references to your acquaintance with DeVries. How accurate was her statement about speculation on a marriage between you and the doctor?"

"There's no truth whatsoever to that statement, Hunter," Arielle snapped. "Because of our mutual interests, Quentin and I are friends. *Only friends.*"

Hunter shook his head, Arielle's vehemence convincing him of Julia's flagrant intent to create a rift between them. The countess was in the know. She wouldn't have dropped such doubt into Hunter's mind without specific purpose and he had a bloody good mind as to her intentions.

Shamefully, Hunter had fallen right into her trap and questioned his wife like she was a spy caught behind enemy lines. "I'm sorry." He drew in a great intake of air. "I thought . . ."

Hunter's voice trailed off and Arielle wondered exactly what he had been about to say. She opened her mouth to question him, but he abruptly drew her into his arms and lifted her chin with his index finger, placing a tender kiss upon her lips.

His endless gaze stripped her bare, divesting the last of her outrage, but creating sudden nervousness.

The mistrust in the depths of his eyes warred with the desire there. Trembles careened through her, thoughts of chores and furnishings, heirs and others tossed away.

His hands touching her shoulders, he lowered his mouth to hers. "Unfasten your wrap, Arielle," he whispered, claiming her lips in a tender kiss.

He traced her lips with his tongue, tantalizingly persuasive, masterfully demanding. Her mouth parted beneath the sweetness of it all and his tongue brushed hers. A slow heat in the pit of her belly spiraled lower. She wrapped her arms around his neck and he swept her off her feet and into his strong embrace.

Sliding her fingers through his hair, she caressed the nape of his neck, and returned his kiss, desire coursing through her. Hunter's lips turned hungry and ravishing. She moaned at the urgency, quickly losing herself in the intensity of it.

Until he set her on her feet again and began unfastening the bow on her night wrap, his lips still locked to hers, she'd completely forgotten his request. He slid her wrap down her arms and it slipped to the floor. She made a desperate attempt to recover it, but Hunter stopped her. Nothing but her night rail remained and she felt naked before his hungry gaze. It mortified her.

Stepping a few inches away from him, Arielle crossed her arms over her chest.

Hunter dropped his arms to his sides. "What is it?" he asked, concerned.

"I—I . . ."

Her glance traveled the length of his body and her eyes widened at the bulge in the lower half of his dressing gown. It dawned on her with horrified fascination that that was the only thing standing between him and his naked body.

Heat scalded her cheeks, and she spun away from him. Before she knew what was happening, Hunter snaked his arms around her waist and pulled her up against him. His manhood pressed against the small of her back. She whimpered.

"Don't be afraid, Arielle," Hunter whispered. "I know it's your first time and I promise to be gentle. Turn around and face me."

Slowly, Arielle turned. A gasp stuck in her throat when she saw the magnificent nude body before her, the dressing gown pooled at his feet.

Standing stock-still, Hunter allowed Arielle to peruse his body. The blush staining her cheeks told him to give her as much time as she needed to compose her delicate sensibilities. However, he seriously doubted her composure would be regained quickly, given that she was viewing a naked man for the first time. And given that that man had an erection he was intent on sharing with her.

When her trembles ceased and her gaze melded with his, Hunter finished undressing her. While in the process, her eyes never left his face.

He'd thought to join her in a glass of wine, but the sight of her nude body was intoxication enough. Her long hair draped her shoulders like a golden shawl, contrasting against the delicate paleness of her skin.

Hunter slid his hands down her arms, then caressed her small, round breasts. "Such loveliness," he murmured, before taking one into his mouth.

Arielle's knees buckled and she clung to his bent shoulders, gasping. Desire replaced her fear; she threaded her fingers through his silken locks. Delight pierced her and her being smoldered, ready to erupt into flames.

"Oh, Hunter," she whispered and laid her head on his chest.

In response, he lifted her up, carried her to the bed, and set her down upon it as tenderly as if she were a newborn babe.

He kissed her eyes, her cheeks, delving into the recesses of her mouth. He glided his hand over her stomach to the moist throbbing ache between her thighs, eliciting a need that was both unfamiliar and frightening.

Every touch, every caress, scalded her skin. Every brush of his lips awakened a new want.

When his fingers found her erect bud and he began massaging her wet heat, she nearly buckled off the bed. Encouraged by her response, he slipped his finger inside her and she moaned with pleasure.

Hunter raised his mouth from hers. "Arielle," he said hoarsely, "I'm going to enter you now. Just hold on to me if it becomes painful."

Arielle couldn't understand how what she was experiencing would transfer into any pain. Maybe Hunter meant an easing of the overwhelming heat that burned her body and scalded her loins.

He bent his head again and kissed her deeply. Returning his kiss, she wrapped her arms tightly around his bare back. In a fog, she felt the weight of her husband on her body as his knees spread her legs apart. His manhood pressed against her femininity and she whimpered. Without warning, the pleasurable touch became a powerful thrust into her center.

A surprised cry escaped her lips. She stiffened, tears flooding her eyes and streaming down her cheeks. She pushed against his chest, but he didn't budge. He remained encased firmly inside her.

"Forgive me, Arielle. I didn't mean to hurt you."

"L-leave me alone," Arielle sobbed.

Hunter held on to his control by a thread. She was so hot and tight and as soon as his shaft touched her, he realized inching into her wasn't an option. He regretted taking her the way that he had, but he hadn't wanted to give her time to think about what was happening.

"The worst is over, my dear," he said in a breathless rasp. "I promise you'll feel pleasure again." Slow, gentle movements into her hot wetness punctuated his words. "Oh, God, Arielle, you feel wonderful."

Like the pain, the feverish tingles caught Arielle by surprise. Blood rushed to her woman's place, inflamed by Hunter's heated, provocative thrusts. Unknown sensations rippled through her; she moaned with pleasure, trying to comprehend the depths of such rapture. Grasping for an incomprehensible deliverance, unable to hold on to the sensations fanning into each part of her, her world exploded around her in brilliant rainbow colors. Her heart pounding, she held tight to Hunter.

The smoothness of Arielle's legs, the silkiness of her flesh, sent tremors of excitement through Hunter's already feverish body. Passion like he'd never felt before threatened to wrestle his self-control away. Exhilaration seized him and her moan urged him to new and greater heights. Searing, primordial ecstasy sent him over the edge. His release came in explosive waves and a loud groan escaped him. He gave a last powerful thrust and his body quivered involuntarily before he collapsed on top of her.

After a few minutes, Hunter withdrew and rolled to the side. Another few minutes of silence passed before he swung his legs over the side of the bed and stood, his back to her. Purposefully, he kept his thoughts at bay, shaken by what had just happened between them.

How would he ever be able to deny his love for her when he wanted to keep her in his arms forever? Yet, she wanted no part of such sentimentality. She didn't want to be his marchioness.

She wanted to be a physician and saw him as a barrier to those dreams. But he could no more explain to her now why he'd accepted her father's blackmail than he could explain to her weeks ago why he felt they wouldn't have suited.

Arielle scrambled for the covers to conceal her nakedness as Hunter recovered his own dressing gown and put it on.

"Are you all right, Arielle?" he asked without turning to look at her, his head bent.

The distant tone of his voice hurt Arielle in the wake of their intimacy and she sank deeper beneath the covers.

"Arielle?"

"Yes, I'm fine," she replied quietly.

"Very well." He started for the connecting door. "I'll see you in the morning, my dear," he said upon reaching his quarters. Without another word, he closed himself inside and latched the door.

An arrow pierced her heart at the sound of the lock clicking into place. The evening had meant naught but an obligation to Hunter. She, on the other hand, had submitted without protest. She felt used and disgusted.

Once they'd abandoned talk of what their future held, he had been gentle and patient and tender. So much so that she hadn't even known she was being seduced. She realized when she saw him tonight, she'd thought an emotional bond would be forged after they shared their bodies. But she'd been in error and she was now irrevocably linked to him.

Indeed, she'd keep his home for him and be the proper wife he no doubt expected her to be—until such time as she could once again focus on her own priorities, that is. In the face of his latest insulting snub, however, she'd never again allow herself to be seduced by Hunter Braxton.

27

Half asleep, Arielle stirred in her bed, a smile curving her mouth. In her dreamlike state, she felt sensual and sated. She hugged her pillow tighter, the image of cerulean eyes and inky hair crystallizing in her mind. Sliding her hand over the spot next to her, a cold, empty space greeted her. Another, less desirable memory formed at the fringes of her thoughts. Something wasn't right, something that hurt deeply, but she couldn't remember what just then, didn't *want* to remember.

Coming fully awake, she glanced at the open door that connected their two chambers. Realization hit her full force. Last night, Hunter had left her after consummating their marriage and closed the door between them, overwhelming her with hurt in the process. This morning, the door gaped open as if in invitation. What was he trying to tell her?

A frantic knock on the door to the hall interrupted her thoughts. "My lady?"

My lady. The marchioness of Savage. Not Lady Arielle Stanford, viscount's daughter, but Lady Arielle Braxton, the marquess of Savage's wife. *Hunter's* wife.

The evidence of her encounter with her husband showed not only in the stains on her pristine white sheets, but in her nudity. Heat warming her cheeks, she pulled the counterpane over her bare breasts, her nipples tingling.

The pounding came again and the urgency of it finally got through to Arielle. "Lady Braxton, come quick!"

Scrambling out of bed, Arielle ran her fingers through

the tangled mass of her hair. She ignored the stiffness of her limbs and the soreness in the place between her thighs as she hastily threw on her night wrap and opened the door.

The woman from last night stood there with a worried frown. A drab gray uniform hung on her small, birdlike frame. Warm, honey-colored eyes stood out in an otherwise nondescript face defined by brown hair streaked with gray. Upon seeing Arielle, she curtsied. "Beggin' yer pardon, milady. I didn't mean to wake ye."

Arielle regretted not knowing the woman's name. But, last night, when the maid had come to help her, she'd been filled with tension and fear at what would pass. She mightn't have remembered her name even if she'd been told.

"It's all right. Is there a problem?"

"Yes, mum," the woman said anxiously, wringing her hands together. " 'Tis one of the tenants. His wife is in labor and—"

"I'll be but a minute," Arielle said breathlessly.

"May I help ye dress?"

"Yes . . . er, what is your name?"

"It's Dora, mum."

Arielle beckoned her in. "Then do enter, Dora, and help me to prepare."

Heaving a deep sigh, Arielle went to her unpacked valise and threw it open. She quickly chose what she'd wear. After she'd dressed, she stood impatiently while Dora buttoned her up, glancing around the room to take her mind off how slowly Dora seemed to be going. Dust hung on the heavy draperies and small stand. The washbasin atop it sported a large crack down the side. And, for the first time, she noticed a small chair, in a deplorable state of disuse, in the far corner.

Shaking her head, she smiled with a new sense of determination. She meant to turn Braxton Hall into the home it should be for the marquess of Savage.

"His lordship's manor begs for my attention, Dora, and

I shall need your help. As soon as I see to . . ."

"Meg, mum."

"Meg. Direct the servants to the study for a meeting.
What position were you hired for?"

"Er . . . the housekeeper, mum."

"Excellent. For the most part, then, the upper servants
have been hired. I hope Lord Savage leaves it to you to
hire your staff. I wouldn't want you in charge of servants
that are disagreeable to you. In the meantime, we will do
what we can. Now—"

"Forgive me, mum," Dora interrupted. "But do ye think
Lord Savage would want ye to do any menial tasks?"

"I am unsure what his lordship wants," Arielle said with
more force than she intended. Even though she'd leave it
to Dora and the others to see to the hiring of a kitchen
staff, the housemaids, and the butlers, her own days would
be fully occupied if Hunter chose not to hire the livery-
men, the groundskeeper, and his own manservant himself.

"Milady," Dora began, digging inside her apron pocket,
"I almost forgot. His lordship asked me to give you this."

Arielle reached for the envelope Dora passed to her. "A
letter?" she asked in confusion, wondering what Hunter
would put into words that he couldn't say to her in person
now that they were married.

"Yes, mum. A letter."

Arielle was written across the front of the envelope in
Hunter's familiar, bold handwriting. A bittersweet smile
tugged at her mouth. It was with a letter that their acquaintance began. How could she have foreseen from that
letter, as short time later, she would be married to him?

She opened the letter and quickly read it.

Arielle, my dear,
    My upbringing deserted me last night. Forgive
me such inconsideration of your well-being. Al-
though I was cognizant of your comforts, even I
realized how I trod upon your feelings. I was a spe-
cial kind of cad and I apologize for my behavior.

I will endeavor to be more civil to you in the future. Although our connecting door will be closed at times, I assure you, it will never be latched again. And, my dear, I was remiss in not telling you how impressed I was by the exceptional way you arranged our wedding nuptials and feast. Your efforts and taste did perfect justice to our station. Thank you again. I'm sorry I couldn't be mindful of you this morning. I have an early appointment with my solicitor. Acquaint yourself with the servants. 'Til I return later,

Hunter

Hunter's words were cordial, and he had apologized in no uncertain terms. She hadn't the time to further analyze, however. She needed to get to Meg as soon as possible. Stuffing the letter inside her dress pocket, she drew in a deep breath. Just from this small courtesy, her pulse had quickened. Wanting to get control of herself, she glanced at the ceiling.

The cracks in the plaster immediately caught her eye and she lowered her lids, thinking about the insurmountable tasks ahead, thinking about her husband. She knew then that her mind wouldn't soon be free of him, if ever.

She would extend open invitations to her sisters and her father. She would send for the finest interior designers, the most acclaimed landscapists, and the best furniture makers to help get the house in order. She'd visit the tenants on the estate, and, most of all, she'd continue her friendship with the one person who understood her best— Quentin—and she'd do it all with or without her husband's permission.

"Push, Meg!"
Arielle gave the directive to the young woman who lay in childbed. It was eleven that night and Meg

had been in labor for nearly fourteen hours, but the babe's head had finally crowned, which meant it would be over soon.

"Breathe," Arielle instructed, encouraged by the glistening crown peeking out. Meg drew in deep drafts of air, then released them. "Push again, harder."

Meg screamed but complied with Arielle's request. "My lady, I feel like I'm being torn in two!"

"It'll be just fine," Arielle said softly, sweat beading her brow. "Bear down with all your strength and push again."

Meg arched her back and did as she was told, the keening wail accompanying her actions reverberating through the small house and echoing in Arielle's ears. And yet it was successful. Into Arielle's hands slipped a baby girl. A gentle slap on her buttocks and the baby let out a scream that rivaled her mother's. The tiny new life flailed her arms and legs, not in the least pleased to have escaped the warmth of her mother's womb.

"It's a girl," Arielle said softly. Quickly and efficiently, she cut the baby's umbilical cord and cleaned her up before wrapping the squirming bundle in a blanket and handing her to Meg.

It didn't take long after that for Meg to expel the afterbirth or for Arielle to assist in cleaning her up. Once she did, she left the new family alone and started back to Braxton Hall, as exhausted as if she'd given birth herself but still exhilarated from the experience.

She rubbed her neck tiredly as she made her way to her bedchamber. She stopped in her tracks when she saw her husband sitting in the chair, glowering in her direction.

"Where have you been?"

"Seeing to Meg Henderson," she answered, her tone neutral. "She had a baby girl."

Hunter rose to his feet, the top buttons on his nightshirt gaping open, revealing a hard, muscular chest. "I will say this one time and one time only, Arielle. I do not want you playing doctor or midwife ever again. You made the decision to become my wife and forsake all else. Never forget that."

Before Arielle could respond to his acrid command, he crossed the room to his own chamber and slammed the door.

Early the next morning, Arielle rose from her bed, tired and agitated. She'd had a restless night, thinking of her husband's command. Was he so against her tending the sick that he'd even deny her bringing a new life into the world? She wanted to talk to him, but there was no answer to her knock.

She turned the knob and found it unlocked. Opening the door, she peeked inside, but found the room empty.

"Milady?"

Despite her melancholy mood, Arielle smiled at the sound of Dora's voice. It was so friendly and warm, which she needed right now. She walked back into her own bed-chamber.

"Come in," she called.

Dora pushed open the door. "Milady, I've a bath prepared for ye in the bathing chamber."

A bathing chamber? Impressive. "You are quite intuitive, Dora. I'll meet you in there. In the meantime, please make sure a basket of food is sent to the Hendersons for the next several days."

"Aye, mum," Dora said and left Arielle alone.

After completing her ablutions, Arielle allowed Dora to help her into a high-necked navy blue dress accented with a white lacy apron. Immediately afterward, she went downstairs to the study.

The chamber's musky, closed-in smell sent a distasteful frown across her face. On her tour with Hunter, things hadn't seemed so completely bare. At that time, however, she'd been enthralled with the man.

Now, heavy gold draperies had been thrown back to

reveal a partly sunny day. The study's parquet floor gleamed brightly.

Beatrice and Dora awaited her and, after a few brief words, Arielle discovered that Vaughn had been drafted by Hunter for the day.

"Very well," she said with a sigh, considering her husband's removal of the only manservant presently in his employ another obstacle. "We'll just do what we can between the three of us."

"Aye, mum," Dora said with discomfort.

"Mistress, if you don't mind, we would like to air out the rooms. This one especially." Beatrice gazed about with disapproval. A robust woman of middle years, she had a no-nonsense attitude that Arielle immediately liked.

"Of course." Going to the floor-length window nearest her, Arielle eased it open.

Without hesitation, Beatrice and Dora followed suit, quickly raising all six windows in the room. Cool, cleansing air washed in, bringing with it the scent of dewy grass and wildflowers.

Arielle lifted a sheet from the couch and discovered a blue-and-yellow-striped giltwood chaise lounge. Running her fingers along the silk upholstery, she found it in near-perfect condition. She couldn't wait to see the home in all its glory. "I assume his lordship has brooms and such?"

"Yes, mistress." Beatrice removed the protective covering from the huge mahogany and satinwood desk and bookcase that dominated the far wall of the room. Her eyes widened at the intricately carved piece. "All of which are in the storage rooms near the carriage house."

"I see." Arielle scanned her memory for the location of the carriage house and realized she'd never toured the grounds. "How much of the property have you seen?"

"Not much, mum," Dora answered, helping Beatrice to fold the sheets they'd removed from the desk and bookcase. "What we have seen is in bad need of refurbishing."

"Yes, mistress," Beatrice interjected, laying a folded sheet on the desk. "Dora and me only just came here."

"And Lord Savage was in a foul disposition, mum," Dora said, her gaze darting from Arielle to Beatrice and back to Arielle again. She recovered the sheet Arielle had removed from the couch and began folding it with Beatrice's help. "He ordered the house be put to rights with all haste."

"How did he expect the two of you to accomplish it? The condition of Braxton Hall is quite regrettable and the furnishings are sparse."

"Perhaps they are stored, mistress," Beatrice offered, her task complete.

Arielle nodded thoughtfully. "Perhaps they are," she agreed. "Lord Savage shut the house down during his tour of duty. Perhaps he stored the furnishings. I'll search the attic for anything useable—"

Dora gathered both sheets in her arms, then paused, her arms overflowing. "Will ye be needin' any help, mum?"

"Yoo, mistress, One of us could go up there with you. It's probably dark and dusty."

Arielle smiled. "Thank you both, but no, I'll be fine mucking about up there. I'll give you a call if I have need of you."

"Yes, mistress." Beatrice started for the door.

"I thought Beatrice and me could endeavor to spruce up yours and his lordship's bedchambers."

"Very good, Dora. I was about to suggest that. Since we are pressed for time, I will join you in the kitchen in three hours to prepare our evening meal." She wouldn't speculate on whether or not Hunter would join them. Even if he didn't, she, Dora, and Beatrice still had to eat.

"We won't hear of it, mistress," Beatrice began sternly.

"Aye, mum! A lady such as yerself in the kitchens?" Dora placed a hand on her heart, her eyes widening in true horror. "I think not."

"I know well my place in this household; however, basic necessity demands I forsake my status for the time being. I appreciate your concern, but I will do what must be done until we have a full staff and that's final."

"But his lordship will be awful angry, mum."

"I will deal with Lord Savage when he returns," Arielle assured her. "Now, we have work to do."

"Yes, mistress," Beatrice said with a stern nod, though approval gleamed in her eye.

Dora curtsied. "Aye, mum."

She waited until the two women departed before she retrieved an oil lamp, lit it, and stepped into the hallway, then made her way to the sharply curving iron and stone staircase. The third flight led her to the servants' quarters, a dark, dreary, and dusty area that made Arielle believe in ghosts. She wondered how Dora, Beatrice, and Vaughn could sleep up here.

As quickly as possible, she found the steps leading to the attic. Unadorned windows allowed the outside light in. She smiled in satisfaction as her gaze met sheets gray with time and dust, outlining huge pieces of furniture. Excited at her discovery, she set the lamp down on the windowsill

A happy laugh escaping her, she piled the sheets in a corner one after the other, uncovering beautiful articles too long concealed. The furniture needed cleaning to restore them to their original sparkle, but they were lovely pieces, deserving display in the light again. She marveled at each object, fingering them with rising anticipation. Even the new and latest trappings at Stanford Manor couldn't compare to the exquisite things stored here.

A Grecian couch, matching armchairs, wing back chairs, a lady's dressing table, drawing room furniture, two cheval mirrors, a circular bookcase, and an old library table were just some of the treasures stored there. But her most prized find was the sixteen caned beechwood chairs and huge dining table.

She spent most of the day opening boxes and trunks. With each new discovery, she hoped to find another hidden treasure to display in the manor. Over the hours, she coaxed porcelain vases, ornate silver pieces, intricate candelabras, even fine paintings from their hiding places.

"Mum, I can see how enraptured ye are here. We wouldn't mind terribly if ye chose to remain."

Arielle raised her head at the sound of Dora's voice. She glimpsed herself in the cheval mirror and saw the black smudges on her cheek and forehead. Tendrils of hair escaped her single plait and framed her face. But her eyes were languid and content. Her look wasn't only from the pleasure of her discoveries in the attic or her sense of achievement. It was because of Hunter and the way she'd felt in his arms. It was the note he'd written that morning apologizing for his behavior. Even though last evening he'd expressed his displeasure over her aid to Meg, she had a sense of belonging here at Braxton Hall, that she'd finally found a place where she was truly important. Besides, it wasn't as if she'd really heed Hunter's demands. She smiled at Dora. "Thank you. I think I shall remain, but if you need an extra hand in the kitchen, please call me."

"Aye, mum." Dora seemed relieved as she left Arielle alone again.

Arielle chuckled softly. Dora and Beatrice really had nothing to fear. They worried overmuch about Hunter's reaction if he came and found her working along with them.

She was certainly enjoying what she was doing. The solitude she found there, while discovering each new treasure, was akin to the satisfaction she felt reading a medical book or searching for an answer to a patient's woes.

Only now, the face of her husband once again intruded upon her serenity. The remembered feel of his lips on her breasts, the heated madness as he drove himself into her.

Immediately, she reproached herself and the liquid heat pooling between her thighs. She wouldn't do this. She couldn't. Leaning back against the dining room table, she stared at the wall, seeing nothing but her father announcing her engagement to Hunter.

Thomas had had something to do with Hunter's decision to marry. It was so like him to twist events so her

life would go exactly as *he* saw it. If only she could discover what her father had said to Hunter for him to consent to marry her. Every time she thought about it,
embarrassment stole her happiness.

Hunter could have had his pick of the crop of young
noblewomen—or old ones, for that matter. Yet he chose
her because Thomas had wanted it that way. Why? Did
he know of the circumstances of her birth? No, he never
would have wedded her if he did.

Arielle wasn't a brainless fool. There was more to this
story beneath the surface. Hunter's anger and actions suggested his hand had been forced. Just as hers had. Knowing her father, whatever he'd said to Hunter couldn't have
been good. It could only have been one thing. Blackmail.

The horrible thought bubbled up from somewhere deep
inside. No, how could that be? Blackmail for what? It was
beyond reason and logic that Thomas would do such a
thing. He had absolutely no motive to blackmail Hunter.
Thomas couldn't possess any knowledge so horrible about
a man as rich and powerful as Hunter Braxton that it could
change the entire course of his life.

If she had any type of courage, she'd confront Hunter.
But she was afraid to hear the awful, ugly truth. She was
afraid she'd discover Hunter would never have married
her had it not been for Thomas's coercion. If she ignored
everything, she might have a decent life.

She passed a tired hand over her eyes, her head pounding from her speculations. These possibilities could be
considered later. She'd come up here to take stock of the
furnishings, not contemplate her marriage.

For several more hours, she managed to lose herself in
that happier task until hunger and exhaustion forced her
to call it a day. By now, the light from outside was fading,
leaving only the meager lamp flame to illuminate the attic.
She stretched heartily, her muscles aching from moving
the heavy boxes.

Though it was past time to leave, she noticed a superbly
carved, highly polished wooden trunk in a corner. She

didn't recall uncovering it, yet she must have, because it wasn't blanketed with dust.

Tingling with curiosity, she stooped down and lightly ran her fingers over the carvings. What could such an exquisite item be concealing? Moving her neck from side to side to get the kinks out, she decided it wouldn't hurt to investigate.

Lifting the lid, a distinct but faint scent of lavender floated to her. The feminine effects inside surprised her. She'd never considered Braxton Hall as another woman's domain. Although surely it must have been at one time. Undoubtedly, Hunter's mother had lived here. The tarnished silver-handled mirror with a richly ornate matching comb and brush attested to *some* woman's presence. White porcelain doves, wrapped in silk, rested in a crystal bowl. Next to that lay several packets of letters, neatly tied together with brightly colored ribbon.

Bold, heavy penmanship with the words *To My Dearest Beloved* graced the top envelope. A quick inspection found seven packs of envelopes, all with the same greeting as the first one. Intrigued, she stared at the letters— and sat them back in their place of concealment. They were love letters, maybe even for Hunter. She had no right to intrude upon the private words.

With a decisive thud, she closed the lid and stood. If they belonged to Hunter, it might be a good idea to read one. It would give her further insight into his character. And she wanted to discover everything there was to know about him. His foibles and fancies. His dreams and desires. There was only one way to do that, and that was to read a letter.

Hmm. One. Reading one wouldn't hurt.

Then, she'd walk away and read no more. But she'd reserve that pleasure for tomorrow.

28

"Arielle?" Arielle stirred, stretching her perfect limbs with drowsy awareness. Hunter hated to awaken her, but he had no choice. He was leaving shortly and didn't want her to find him gone after they'd parted company so angrily. Yet how could Arielle think to follow her dreams and be his wife as well? This was her doing. *She'd* connived to become the marchioness of Savage. Now, she had to play the part.

"Arielle, I hate to disturb your sleep," Hunter said again, feeling awkward watching his beautiful young wife throw the bed cover aside and arch her back.

Arielle sat up in bed and blinked. "H-Hunter?" she said, her tone husky with sleep. With one last stretch that left Hunter's mouth dry, she slid out of bed and took her night wrap off the chair.

"Let me help you with that." He took the robe out of her hand, then held it while she slipped her arms through it and secured the tie around her waist.

"Thank you, my lord." Nervously, Arielle ran slim fingers through her blond hair, sleep-tousled and inviting.

"There's not much you can do to improve on perfection."

Arielle smiled at him, her cheeks pinkening. "What a very nice thing to say."

Hunter hated the wall that stood between them. From the moment they met, they'd always had more than enough to say to one another. Even now, most of what stood between them could be cleared up with a conversation. If only he wasn't so ashamed and angry that she knew him to be a bastard. He would give anything, do anything, to have had that secret kept from Arielle.

He wasn't sure why it was so important that she see him in such a favorable light. He only knew that it was. Now, he was not only a bastard to her, but, after the other night, a tyrant as well.

Arielle shifted her weight, her arms folded, her fingers clutching her robe. "I forgot to thank you for the letter you left for me the day before yesterday. I appreciate your candor."

So she had received the letter. His heart beat a little faster because she mentioned it to him. Perhaps it did matter to her. Of course, he'd acted such an ass two nights ago, she couldn't mention it to him. A bittersweet smile curved his lips. "I negated everything by making demands on you. I realize now that without your assistance Meg and her baby could have died."

Hope brightened the emerald eyes that invaded his dreams. "Oh, Hunter!" Arielle gasped, reacting to words she seemed to have misconstrued.

Hunter raised his hand, forestalling any other misconceptions. "Please don't misunderstand me, Arielle. You are a marchioness. My wife. Perhaps I was harsh with my demands and could have put them a different way, but those are my wishes, my dear."

"I see," Arielle responded in a crisp, cool voice, turning away from him. "Is there anything else?"

"No," he said softly, her arrow-straight back and stiff shoulders indicating her anger and disappointment at his words. But he didn't want to leave on a sour note. There'd be time enough to discuss this. "Except I'm afraid for the next few days I'll be staying in London."

Arielle faced him again and gazed into his eyes. "London?"

"Yes. Amongst other things, I have another appointment with my solicitor." He refrained from telling her it was to have her name added to the Braxton family documents. As his wife, she had a claim to all Braxton hold-ings. He just couldn't bring himself to tell her this when there was so much tension between them.

"Of course." Unable to contain thoughts of the Bee-chams, she mentioned the family to Hunter, hoping he might consider looking in on them in her stead.

"I'll return in a day or two," he added when she fell silent, not commenting upon the Beecham's plight.

"I will be seeing to the attic in the meanwhile," she said, disappointed.

"Of course." He echoed her earlier statement, lifting his hand to touch her satiny skin, smooth out her silky hair. As abruptly, he let his hand fall back to his side. Trust between them was more important to him than a brief touch here and a stolen kiss there. "Have a good morning, Arielle."

With that, Hunter departed his wife's company before passionate desire overtook his better reasoning.

29

She had been looking forward to this time since yesterday. With a lit lamp next to her, Arielle settled herself on the floor in front of the trunk and lifted the lid.

The faint lavender fragrance invaded her senses once again as she glanced at the contents inside the trunk, delicate and unerringly feminine. That piqued her curiosity most of all. She wanted to know to whom they belonged.

Hesitating only a second, she took out a bundle of envelopes and inspected them. She turned the neatly tied packet this way and that. Guilt filtered through her. This was someone's private belongings—meant for their eyes only. She really didn't have the right to invade these letters.

Judging by the yellowed paper, however, some time had gone by since anyone had gazed at them. What harm would it do to read them when they sat here apparently forgotten and ignored?

She reminded herself that the letters' contents might give her more insight into her husband's character. That thought eliminated entirely the guilt engulfing her. Learning anything about Hunter justified her curiosity.

Without further ado, Arielle untied the pink ribbon around the envelopes and haphazardly picked one out to read. She opened it and unfolded the page inside.

She scanned the words and her breath caught as she searched for the author of the love letter. She read, fast and furious. Then, as the meaning hit her, she started over at a much more sedate pace.

Dearest Beloved,
*   I cannot wait to next hold you in my arms again*
and share the passion of our love. To feel the beat
of your heart close to mine and the softness of your
lips against my own. I will write no more at present,
but demonstrate my feelings when we are once
again together. Until that time, I remain,

                    Your devoted servant

Arielle folded the letter and held it. Her heart reveled
in such passionate words. Who *were* they? Could such
love—the type of love that flowed through these missives—really exist between two people? The type that she
wanted to share with Hunter. The feelings that *she* already
felt for Hunter, but had no earthly idea how to express or
make mutual.

With shaking hands, Arielle reread the letter. Could it
be a letter from Hunter to some woman he fancied? No,
it seemed he more than fancied her. It was a letter to
someone dearly loved. Yet it didn't make sense that he
would save letters he'd written to someone else. He must
have been the recipient.

Glancing at the letter again, she noticed a faded date in
the corner. She moved the parchment closer to the light
and squinted. *November 20, 1781.*

Relief flooded her and she laid the letter down. Hunter
couldn't have had any involvement in this letter. He
hadn't yet been born when it was written.

She drummed her fingers against her thigh, completely
overtaken by curiosity. Reading *one* more couldn't hurt.
Hunter didn't want her to overwork herself. What better
way to pass the time than this?

Carefully, she chose another envelope and opened it.
This letter began as the first one had.

Dearest Beloved,
*   Since meeting you a fortnight ago, I have been*

*unable to keep my wits in order. The suddenness of
my attraction to you has turned my normal activities
wrong-side out. As dotty as it may seem, I have
fallen in love with you. I implore you, grant me the
privilege of your adored presence once more, so
that I may gaze upon your loveliness. I eagerly
await your reply and will remain, always.*

Your devoted servant

Arielle drew in a deep sigh, wishing she could have
met the author of such beautiful words. Maybe he would
have had some advice for her with her own marriage to
Hunter. Did Hunter know the letters existed? He must.
They were in his house, after all.

She glanced toward the door, torn between decency for
others' privacy and her intrigue. She decided to resume
her duties of inspecting and uncovering the remaining furniture. Reluctantly, she stood and stretched out the kinks
in her lower back.

Dearest Beloved . . .

The two words ran across her mind, drawing her attention back to the trunk. Blast it, anyway! If only she knew
who the parties involved were, she doubted her urge to
continue reading would be so overwhelming.

She would love to be someone's "dearest beloved." A
bitter laugh escaped her. She would love to be *Hunter's*
"dearest beloved."

*Since meeting you a fortnight ago, I have been unable
to keep my wits in order.*

It had actually taken a fortnight for him to admit that?
The day Arielle met Hunter her wits had become severely
out of order.

*The suddenness of my attraction to you has turned my
normal activities wrong-side out.*

Arielle scowled. It was as if she were still reading the
letter and not standing in the midst of furniture that
needed her attention. The words rolled through her mind,

striking a chord so deep within her she was momentarily immobilized.

She too had become attracted to Hunter. It had been sudden, unanticipated and frightening. She hadn't expected to feel that way in his arms and her normal activities were most definitely turned wrong-side out because of it.

He had the ability to provoke her temper, induce a smile, increase her heart rate.

As dotty as it may seem, I have fallen madly in love with you.

She could agree wholeheartedly with that statement. But how could she ever express that to Hunter? It had been nearly six weeks since she'd received any letters free of tension from him. She'd enjoyed reading them, enjoyed answering them. They had in effect been part of their courtship period, but he'd turned into a man she didn't know.

I implore you, grant me the privilege of your adored presence once more, so that I may gaze upon your loveliness.

For the first time since she'd started analyzing the letter, Arielle giggled. She imagined Hunter's reaction if she went to him and "implored" him for the privilege of his adored presence, so that she might gaze upon his . . . handsomeness. He *would* think her dotty.

I eagerly await your reply and will remain, always, your devoted servant.

Judging from the stack of letters, the devoted servant had apparently received the reply he'd sought. Weighing the differences between this letter and the first one she'd read, it seemed as if this letter had been the one to start the correspondence, though the date was completely faded.

Undoubtedly, his words had touched his dearest beloved as deeply as they touched Arielle. What woman wouldn't have been moved by a man claiming himself her "devoted servant"?

A deep, abiding sadness welled within Arielle. She missed corresponding with Hunter. If they had continued in the vein in which they had started, perhaps *their* letters might have become as passionate and romantic. Then again, she wasn't the type of woman who inspired such adoration.

The sun had shifted and the shadows in the room had changed position, indicating it was nearing the evening hour. She sighed, not in the least interested in unveiling the furniture. Instead, she read the letter again. Perhaps it was just the inspiration she needed.

Two days later, she went into her bedchamber and drew in a deep, sad sigh. Hunter still hadn't returned and she missed him terribly. After reading the letters in the attic, she realized what an integral part of her life Hunter had become. They'd only been married for several days and she'd barely seen him in that time. She knew he was purposely avoiding her and she knew that he'd never know what she felt if this continued. What better way to tell Hunter all that she wanted to express to him—than by writing him a letter.

At Hunter's desk, pen and paper in hand, she wrote:

Dearest Hunter,
    All this is very new to me. If I have yet to please you as a wife, I hope that I will be all that you expect of me. I should hope that you would instruct me in all things in the ways of lovemaking to your liking. I want to please you during our beddings, for you certainly please me. I do not wish to appear a wanton woman to my husband, but you made me feel such ecstacy in the bridal chamber. This kind of letter from a lady of my station must appear most irregular, my lord, but I only wish you to know my true regard toward you. I am quite proud to be mis-

tress of Braxton Hall and prouder still to be your wife.

   However, my inclination toward becoming a physician is still as keen as ever. I want you to be aware that as much as my heart is set in that direction, I am fully cognizant of my duties toward you and our home. I will not pretend that my desire for practicing medicine has disappeared. It never will. But I want you to know how important you and your needs are to me.

                      Your servant,
                      Arielle

Arielle read over the letter to make sure it was as she wanted it to be. Her fingers trembled by the time she finished. Leaving such a note for Hunter was risky indeed. It might turn him further against her. But she had taken risks before. She had risked everything—reputation, family, and friends—for the sake of obtaining entrance to a university. Could she do no less to win Hunter's love? Everything else would fall into place in due time.

As Hunter told her in a letter weeks ago, circumstances had a way of interfering with destiny. Perhaps, it had been her destiny to marry Hunter.

Hunter needed to know that he was as important to her as anything else. Hopefully, this letter was a start.

30

Braxton Hall loomed against the horizon of the cool night as Hunter made his way to the stables astride Blazer. Parapets from the original hall rose mightily to the sky, a reminder to Hunter of the history of his home. Over the years, the estate had been remodeled and enlarged to keep with the times. But it wasn't his home that occupied his mind in the last few days. It was Arielle. He was anxious to see her.

He'd completed his business a day earlier than he'd anticipated, and found himself unable to stay away from her. There were quite a few distractions to be found in London, but he hadn't been interested in any of them.

At first, he'd told himself it was because he could finally get serious about the refurbishing of his estate. But somewhere between London and Braxton Hall, he stopped fooling himself. He *was* quite serious about his estate, but he wanted to see Arielle more. He wanted to make her laugh, to watch her eyes sparkle with merriment and darken with passion.

He wanted to make her love him. But would she ever? Could she ever, given her knowledge of him? *She* was still devoted to becoming a physician. He just couldn't allow that. He couldn't allow her to spend her days toiling over the sick and infirm. To be fair to himself and his rising guilt, he'd felt the same way upon first meeting her. He knew too, however, that had she been the unattractive spinster he'd expected, he would have made every effort to help her achieve her goals.

It was completely unfair of him to feel such a way, but no one ever said the world was a fair and just place. And that self-admittance wasn't providing answers to the tension Arielle's determination was creating. What should he do? She had enough to resent him for. Why in the devil would he give her something else?

Not having an answer to that, Hunter dismounted Blazer, relinquished the reins to the groomsman, and hurried to the manor. Finding all quiet inside, he went to his bedchamber and noticed the connecting door to Arielle's bedchamber slightly ajar. He pushed it open a little wider and stopped in his tracks.

Arielle lay sprawled on her back asleep, covered to her waist, one hand above her head. She looked like an angel surrounded by a cloud of golden silk.

The sight caused a sharp, wistful intake of breath. Hunter had an urge to rush to her and take her in his arms. To make her realize how much he loved her. But she didn't love him. And he'd already debased himself by giving in to Thomas's blackmail. He wouldn't add further humiliation to that by confessing his love to her and have her laugh in his face.

Pride stiffened his determination and he backed out, then pulled the door closed. He began disrobing, fatigue settling in to the core of him with abruptness. He needed rest. Then, he could put everything into proper perspective once again.

And then he saw it.

An envelope with his name written in Arielle's hand. He glanced toward the door. What could she have put in a letter that she couldn't say to his face?

He opened the letter and read it, not quite knowing what to make of it. Arielle had expressed her feelings quite eloquently. She didn't want to appear a wanton woman to him. Of course she wasn't wanton. She merely desired him as much as he desired her. The very thought made his blood heat and his manhood harden.

He'd thought to stay away from her. He didn't want to

coax her to do something she wasn't really interested in doing. But he could make love to her every day, if that was her heart's wish. He wanted more than just a physical relationship with her, however. He wanted her loyalty, her understanding, her love.

Thrusting a hand through his hair, Hunter glanced at the letter again. As he had suspected, she still had hopes of practicing medicine. She had to know what an impossible dream that was. Anger began to bubble to the surface, but it quickly deserted him, leaving a dull ache in his heart. He did love Arielle so and perhaps expressing their feelings through letters would draw them closer. Maybe writing their opinions instead of voicing out loud harsh words that would surely lead to disagreements was an option, if not a solution. And maybe . . . just maybe . . . he could find a way to tell her himself of his background. He wanted her to know that for the first ten years of his life he'd had no idea of his illegitimacy and how that knowledge had affected him. Perhaps then she could come to understand him better and accept him.

Glancing toward the door again, Hunter went to his desk. He couldn't leave her letter unanswered, not now that he'd recognized this as the means to forge a bond between them.

Twenty minutes later, Hunter stood beside Arielle's bed. He leaned down and kissed her forehead, her long-lashed, closed eyelids, and finally the tip of her pert little nose.

She stretched, her eyelids fluttering open.

"Arielle," Hunter whispered, desire tightening his loins.

A dreamy emerald gaze met his own and he swallowed hard.

"Yes?" she murmured, not fully awake, her mouth soft and inviting.

"I read your letter."

As if he'd doused her with a bucket of cold water, Arielle sat up and gasped. "Oh! I—I . . ."

Chuckling softly, Hunter laid a hand on her shoulder

and guided her back onto her pillow, wanting to lie next to her and fold his arms around her then and there. "It's all right, sweetheart. I believe you expressed a desire to please me?" he asked, not wanting to ruin this moment and mention anything else she wrote.

The color in her cheeks deepened to rosy red. With all her daring, she was still somewhat prudish. Although the first part was what he'd focus on tonight, he loved the way she'd expressed herself in the entire letter. Reaching down, he lifted her off the bed. "I believe your instructions in pleasure should have its start in my bedchamber, my dear," he said, carrying her across the sill of the connecting door to his room.

*A*rielle, my dear wife,
  I returned a day earlier than I had expected to. I was disappointed to find that you had already bedded down for the night. I sorely missed you while I was away. Considering our somewhat strained parting, I didn't know what to expect from you upon my arrival. Still, I anticipated seeing you.

However, I did not expect a letter from you. I am fortunate to have a wife who can be so free with her feelings. Sometimes, it's easier to express one's emotions on paper. The spoken word can never be recalled. The written word can always be erased, analyzed, and rewritten. Rewritten in such a way as to spare another's feelings.

Arielle, you've made your desires known to me. I can act upon the former, for my passion is as deep as your own. I cannot, however, lend my agreement to the latter part of your letter. You must not take my wishes so much to heart that it prevents us from bridging this gap between us.

I need a wife, Arielle, along with understanding and the passion you spoke of in the letter. I don't need a physician. If my bluntness offends you, I am

*asking in advance for your forgiveness. There is a
lot roiling inside me that needs sorting. It would
grieve me greatly if I gained your scorn in face of
all else.*

*Thank you for taking care to pen a letter to me,
my dear. Correspondence was once a regular thing
between us. I have sorely missed receiving your letters.*

*I will see you at breakfast, Arielle. 'Til then, I
remain,*

*Yours,
Hunter*

Arielle sat on the side of her bed, close to tears. After
being with Hunter for the entire night, she hadn't realized
he'd had time to write anything. But she'd found the letter
moments ago when she returned to her bedchamber.

Until then, she'd thought Hunter's response to her letter
was the tender ministrations he'd rendered to her during
their lovemaking. Which in part it had been. It was, after
all, what she'd requested.

Still, it aggrieved her that Hunter refused to consider
her eternal longing to become a doctor. But how could he
begin to comprehend such yearning? He was a marquess
and a man of the highest standards. Honored and respected by his peers, he had naught to worry about except
restoring Braxton Hall.

Melancholia settled into her. She had respectability.
She had the protection of the Stanford name. On occasion,
she remembered her true heritage, but never gave it much
attention, especially since she'd decided to pursue her
own dreams and not worry about marriage. She really had
no reason to worry that she could one day be exposed.

But along with her and Hunter's tenuous relationship
came growing concern. What would he do when and if
he discovered her illegitimacy? Surely, a high-born nobleman such as he would set her aside.

Arielle glanced at his letter again. He said he'd missed her letters to him. Maybe she could find a way through her letters to tell him of her secret. Maybe he'd even understand and not demand a divorce. She only wished he loved her as much as she loved him. Then, of course, it wouldn't matter to him. He was self-assured and confident and he didn't allow anyone else's opinions to affect him. Because of that, if she had his love, then she'd have his loyalty and protection. Of course, had *he* been illegitimate, it certainly wouldn't have mattered to her.

With a heavy sigh, she stood from her bed. She must put on a pleasant face. After last night, Hunter would expect that. In all probability, he was already seated at the dining table and awaiting her arrival for breakfast.

Crossing the room, she pulled the bellcord for her maid to assist her in her toilette, wondering what the day would bring.

She thought of how she'd felt in his arms last night. Her heart pounded with bittersweet poignancy and a question rose in her mind. How could anything so right possibly go so wrong?

31

As Arielle walked into the dining room she looked beyond the French doors to the lake and hunting grounds. A thousand shades of green dotted the landscape as the new leaves on the numerous trees made the transformation from winter barrenness to spring beauty. The maze was again the intricate artwork it had once been instead of the overgrown square of greenery she had found upon her arrival.

As Arielle approached the table, Hunter rose from his seat and she smiled brightly.

"I lost myself many a day in that maze when I was a boy," Hunter commented wistfully. He pulled out her chair and kissed her cheek. "Good morning, Arielle."

"Good morning, Hunter," Arielle responded. "I'm sure there are many interesting stories to hear about your childhood."

Hunter's expression closed and he shook his head. "Not really, my dear. I was merely making a comment."

"Of course," Arielle said softly, refusing to make an issue of whatever it was that disturbed him about his childhood. Instead, as she slid into her seat, she changed the subject completely. "Why didn't you wake me?"

Hunter chuckled, the sound filled with relief. "After last night, I thought you'd want a lie-in."

Heat suffused Arielle's cheeks. "Hunter! The servants."

At that moment, Dora and Beatrice bustled in and began serving breakfast. In a few short moments, they excused themselves, leaving the remainder of the food covered on the sideboard.

"Now where were we? Oh, yes, about last night—"

"Yes," Arielle interrupted, surprised at the mischief lightening his tone. "About last night. It was wonderful." She sighed and met his curious gaze with her own. "I read your letter this morning. I fully understand your need to have a wife to perform specific duties and I cannot disdain your honesty. But I implore you to have an open mind for my interests."

"Arielle," Hunter began without rancor, "it's doubtful that I will ever agree with your sentiment about becoming a doctor. But I promise you, I *will* give it some thought on your behalf and try to see the matter from your viewpoint."

His generosity warmed her whole being. She hadn't thought he would ever reach such a point. Even though he still hadn't conceded, it was a small victory on her behalf. "Thank you," she said, unable to suppress a smile.

He returned the smile and proceeded to eat breakfast.

Later that morning, Arielle listened while Hunter explained to her his chores for the day, which included securing building supplies for some of his tenants. She really had no objections, since she was anxious to get back to the trunk in the attic. As soon as he departed, she rushed upstairs.

Dearest Beloved,

Be wary, my darling, lest you lose your heart to me, as I have lost mine to you. You must be made aware of the consequences of our actions. For when next we meet, I intend to possess you fully. I want to know the wonder of making love to you and taste the sweetness of your kisses.

If you deny me my desires, it will aggrieve me, but I will understand. However, if you will be my love, I will pledge to you all that I am. I love you, my dearest heart, to the depth of my being. With all my life, I await your reply and remain,

Your devoted servant

She randomly chose another letter from the pack. This would be the last letter she read, she vowed. She certainly couldn't waste hours in a stifling attic when there were so many other things to be done.

Dearest Beloved,
  My thoughts are never far from you. And my body constantly responds to them. My need for you is all-consuming. My love for you is eternal. We are soul-mates, my darling, and I cannot wait to reveal our secret love and wed you. 'Til next time, I'll meet you in my dreams.

Your devoted servant

Heat flushed Arielle's skin. Her stomach quivered and her intimate area throbbed.

"Hunter," she whispered, ready for him, needing him. She wanted him to crave her kisses as the stranger had craved his love's.

She wanted him to be devoted to her and to love her with such passion.

"Milady?" Dora's voice penetrated Arielle's amorous thoughts and she jumped as the partially ajar door opened wider. "Are ye in here, mum?"

Feeling like a child caught doing mischief, Arielle stood abruptly and held the letters behind her back. The heat of embarrassment crept up her neck.

"Y-yes, Dora," she called. "I'm over here in the corner. How can I help you?"

"Well, mum, we all mucked in on the receiving chamber and it's quite up to snuff, milady. Ye should just see it."

Arielle managed a smile, the letters burning her fingers.

"I'm sure it must be wonderful. I'll be down straightaway, Dora. I—I have a few more sheets to remove."

"Oh, mum, that's why I'm here. I can do that. Vaughn and the other lads are ready to take the furniture down and set them in place, so ye and his lordship can seat yer guests proper-like when ye entertain."

"Sterling, Dora," Arielle said with a chuckle, sweeping the friendly woman with an appreciative glance. "I'm sure Lord Braxton will be most grateful for your expediency. As I am."

Dora beamed. "Aye, milady."

"Go and get the others," Arielle told her, wanting to buy time. "I'll instruct them about what needs to be brought down."

"Aye, mum." Without another word, Dora turned and hurried to the stairs.

Alone again, Arielle forced her thoughts back to order. In her view, the last letter she'd read was most erotic and quite poignant.

Placing the letters back inside the trunk, she dropped the lid shut, then leaned against it. She could no longer avoid the fact that she needed to know the words of *all* the letters. To give herself a chance to read more of them, she would make the trunk be amongst the last pieces of furniture removed from the attic.

It was clear that she'd read from two different periods in the couple's relationship. The letters obviously hadn't been placed in the order in which they had been written, which made them all the more appealing to Arielle.

Besides, one of them might very well reveal the lovers' true identities.

32

"Milady?"

To pass time, Arielle was sitting in the room she planned to make her medical library, penning a note to Mrs. Beecham to inquire after her health. Hunter had been gone for hours and she missed him dreadfully.

"Yes, Dora?"

"Sorry to disturb ye, mum, but ye have a visitor. Would ye care to receive him?"

Automatically, Arielle passed a hand over her dress and her hair, then nodded to Dora. "Show him in," she instructed.

"May I present the duke of Ridgeley, milady?" Dora introduced.

Arielle stared at the stranger.

"Would you bring in some tea and pastries, please, Dora?"

"Aye, mum," Dora said, leaving her post by the door and disappearing down the hall.

The cerulean gaze, so like Hunter's, made Arielle's breath catch. She swallowed. "Please excuse my appearance, Your Grace," she began with a curtsy.

"So Hunter is not here at this time?"

The familiarity in which he said Hunter's name, as if they shared some connection, caught her by surprise. The more Arielle compared Hunter to Ridgeley, the more she gleaned a resemblance.

"No, Your Grace. At the moment, he is in the back fields. Would you care for a seat, my lord?"

"Yes, child." For the first time, Arielle noticed his gold and ebony walking cane, which aided him as he made his way to the sofa and sat. "You are most gracious."

"Thank you." Arielle sat across from him as Dora walked back in with the tea. She waited in silence while the housekeeper served them, then once again took her leave. "Is there something you needed from Hunter?"

"Only a visit," Ridgeley responded, dropping a cube of sugar into the cup of steaming liquid.

Arielle considered his enigmatic statement, knowing there was more to this call than he wanted to divulge to her. She bit into a piece of gingerbread cake, unsure of how to view the man across from her. "Should I send warning to Hunter, Your Grace, that you seek his company? Or should I welcome you into my home?"

Ridgeley paused as he set his tea on the table, then hooted with laughter. "You are as tart as Roxanne, I see."

Arielle didn't take offense at the statement, not when it was uttered with such amusement. Yet her curiosity was roused, since she had no idea who Roxanne was. "Roxanne?" she echoed.

The duke nodded, moisture forming in the blue eyes. "My son's wife, my lady. Both long deceased but still sorely missed. She was the mirror of grace and he was the quintessential rake who fell madly in love with her."

It almost sounded like the couple from the letters. "Did Hunter know them?"

"Fenton and Roxanne?" Ridgeley shook his head. "No, I'm afraid not. My son was killed a day after his wedding and his wife died in childbed. As a matter of speaking, your husband doesn't know me."

Not taking her eyes off the man who had grown so melancholy, Arielle set her own cup and saucer down. "You have my condolences. It seems as if you are not yet over your profound loss, Your Grace."

The duke of Ridgeley sighed, his shoulders heaving as he stood. Maybe it was his remoteness that reminded her yet again of Hunter, but whatever it was she couldn't deny the thought that her husband was related to this man.

"I shouldn't have come. I can only imagine how Hunter would receive me."

Arielle came to her feet. "He would have welcomed you, my lord," she assured him, wondering why indeed he had come.

He must have seen the question in her eyes, for he said, "I came to congratulate him on his marriage as well as his heroism. I . . . my own grandson was lost to me some years ago by the vicious bitterness of his mother's relatives."

"Your thoughtfulness is commendable, Your Grace, albeit confusing. I still haven't grasped the real reason for your visit."

Ridgeley bowed and placed a gentlemanly kiss upon her left hand—the hand that should have had a wedding ring upon it. If he noticed the lack of that symbol, he remained silent. "Time will reveal my reason."

"Please, feel free to call here whenever you wish," Arielle said with another curtsy. "I'm certain Hunter will be as pleased as I am to make your acquaintance."

"Thank *you* for your graciousness, my dear, and I most certainly will take you up on your offer in the very near future."

For several minutes after the duke's departure, Arielle remained standing. She had no idea what Ridgeley was about, but it clearly did not include harm to Hunter.

33

Dearest Arielle,

Once again I've returned to find you asleep. I have no wish to absent myself from you so frequently. But, alas, Braxton Hall must be restored, which, as you know, is why I have been so busy. Braxton Hall's restoration is not a matter of life and death, however. I believe it's more imperative that we get to know each other better.

I want you to accompany me to London later today. I know you have been extremely busy with the interior of the estate, but that's why I employ servants. I will not have my wife overworked, lest she would have to minister her skills of medicine to herself.

As I promised, my sweet, I have thought long and hard on our conversation about medicine. While we are in London, if it pleases you, I would not be averse to accompanying you to visit your former . . . patients, are they?

I will reiterate that you don't misconstrue my meaning—you already know my feelings. The only way I can understand your passion for the healing arts is to try and get a firsthand view. Perhaps, then, discussing it won't make for such a volatile subject.

When you awaken, I will probably be giving instructions to the men I hired. I will be ready to depart shortly thereafter. I implore you to be ready also.

Your dedicated husband,
Hunter

Her heart thumping with anticipation, Arielle sprang out of bed, and immediately summoned Dora and Beatrice to help her pack.

She folded Hunter's letter and promised herself to reply as soon as time permitted. After only receiving two letters on two consecutive mornings, she was coming to expect such from him. Their correspondence was indeed opening windows of communication for them. It made it easier for her to understand how the anonymous writer of the letters in the attic grew so close in accord with the recipient.

Taking her night wrap, she slipped it over her sleeping gown and made her way to the bathing chamber.

Several hours later, Arielle found herself with Hunter at his town house in Park Lane on the western border of Hyde Park. Passing clouds stole away the slight warmth of the day. The shelving slopes of grass and tall trees within her view looked inordinately green, kissed with the newness of springtime.

Arielle was delighted to accompany Hunter to London at his request. He had business interests in the city that he had to see to and he hadn't wanted to leave her behind at Braxton Hall, which thrilled her to no end.

Immediately upon arriving, Hunter gave her a tour of his town house, and now they sat in the study, where burning lamps and a blazing fire created a lazy atmosphere.

"What is your preference, my lady? Brandy or tea?" Hunter asked, sitting next to her on the sofa, her scent of rose water fluttering into his senses.

"Hot tea would be superb at this time, my lord."

Hunter summoned Geoffrey. He, along with Wilfred, now remained permanently at the town house, since Hunter had hired a staff for Braxton Hall. The two ancient men were loyal and efficient and Arielle knew how genuinely fond her husband was of them.

The servant bowed to Arielle when he entered the room. "Welcome, my lady."

"Thank you, Geoffrey." Arielle glanced around, then nodded at the gleaming freshness of everything. "The town house is lovely. I should like to open it for a ball and show it off."

Although she spoke to no one in particular, Hunter realized Arielle was complimenting Geoffrey's care of the house while Hunter had been gone.

The retainer realized it as well. His moustache wiggled as his mouth curved into an embarrassed smile, a blush stealing into his normally staid expression.

"That is an excellent idea, my lady," Geoffrey said softly, looking at Hunter. "Sir, would you like some refreshments for you and Lady Savage?"

"Yes, hot tea would be excellent."

"This really is a beautiful chamber," Arielle commented after Geoffrey left.

"I think so," Hunter returned, perusing the clouded plaster ceiling, buff-colored walls, and fine appointments with a critical eye. He tried to discern what had made the biggest impression on Arielle. Had this been his first visit here, he wouldn't have been able to make a decision. He thought everything was lovely. "Would you change anything about it?"

"Not at all," Arielle said.

"Thank you. It pleases me that you like the house, especially since it's also yours to enjoy," Hunter said with a smile. "You are lovely, Arielle," he told her softly, abruptly changing the subject. She wore a high-neck muslin gown with a puff top where ties at the upper arms anchored the long fitted sleeves. Pearl beads on embroidered silk disks trimmed the velvet tunic that was over the gown. The upswept, tightly curled ringlets of her hair deceived the eye. Hunter knew quite well the length of the silky mass. "I must endeavor to keep you in the latest fashions."

A liquid flame intensified the sea green of her eyes. But Geoffrey's return with the tea stopped any response. He placed the tray on the cart near the sofa.

"Would you like me to serve, Lady Arielle?"

Arielle moved with fluid grace to the tray. "If you don't mind, I would like to serve his lordship."

Satisfaction lit Geoffrey's features. "Not at all, milady." Smiling at Hunter and dipping his head, he departed the room.

"I take it he's pleased with my request," Arielle said with a chuckle, deftly picking up the silver teapot. She held a cup filled with steaming tea in one hand and a lump of sugar in the other. "One lump or two?"

"None."

Her eyebrows lifted as she handed him his cup of tea. "Really? I take three myself," she finished breezily, dropping that amount into her own cup.

"Sweets for the sweet," Hunter murmured.

Her cheeks stained with a very becoming pink, Arielle returned to her seat.

She was an extremely beautiful creature, and gracious. Sea green eyes gleamed in a perfect and delicate face. Not for the first time, Hunter wondered how such an occurrence had taken place. Thomas Stanford was a big, meaty figure with starchy hair and an overbearing manner. And Arielle's sisters? He'd be less than a gentleman to admit what he thought of their looks.

Stanford had chosen Hunter's bride well. The man had chosen the daughter to most torment him, the daughter who had the ability to leave him guilt-ridden and regretful of his treatment of her. Arielle acted as if she truly loved him—as if she wanted him and not his fortune. If Arielle had conspired with her father against him, why did she gaze at him with such wistful longing and loving tenderness? Why did she prick *his* conscience and tug at his heart?

"I have seats for the theater tonight. I thought we'd stay in London a fortnight and absorb some culture."

"I would love to absorb London culture with you, Hunter. Unfortunately, I didn't bring any evening gowns with me."

Rising to his feet abruptly, Hunter grabbed her hand and pulled her up. "That can be easily remedied," he said. "I'll have Geoffrey fetch your coat and bonnet, then we'll go to Regent Street and visit some of the shops. Can you do with a new wardrobe?"

Arielle merely nodded.

In all of her memory, no one had ever taken Arielle shopping for clothes. Growing up, her sisters had selected her gowns, giving her no choice. When Arielle became older, she ventured to the shops alone, where she engaged in the selections on her own. Maisy went with her once and threw in a comment or two, but never with the personal interest Hunter now took in the entire process.

Arielle proudly stood in a gown of gold gossamer sarcenet, cut daringly low. Madame Sanfert beamed with approval when Hunter nodded with satisfaction. The modiste had showered them with attention from the moment they'd walked in an hour ago, no doubt relishing the fact that they had chosen her very fashionable shop.

Arielle smiled and twirled in the gown she modeled, having a particular affinity for it. Not only did it make her feel utterly feminine and entirely risqué, she enjoyed the way Hunter's eyes darkened as he watched the gown cling to her body.

She smoothed the gown on her backside and looked over her shoulder, her hands outlining the curve of her bottom. "Do you really think it's appropriate for me, my lord?" she asked sweetly.

Hunter's half-lidded inspection slid over her, as seductive as the most urgent caress, as smoldering as the hottest

flame. Her being filled with anticipation and she turned
around, caught at her own game.

"That gown was made *especially* for you, my dear,"
Hunter replied in a deep voice.

"Shall I have it packaged for you, milady?" Madame
Sanfert inquired, a knowing smile wreathing her pow-
dered features.

Hunter stroked his chin. "Do you see anything else here
that interests you, Arielle?"

The two ready-made opera gowns and three dinner
gowns she'd already chosen came to her mind. Before
they returned to Braxton Hall, six additional gowns,
which had to be created especially for her, would be
brought to the town house. Now, he wanted to purchase
more? "You're very generous, my lord. But I feel my
wardrobe is more than adequate."

"Are you sure? We've only bent our steps to seven
stores."

"Quite, my lord," Arielle reassured him. "I am quite
finished with shopping for the day."

Hunter turned to the modiste. "Yes, madame, you may
package the gowns Lady Arielle chose and have them
delivered to my home on Park Lane."

After scribbling down the address, Hunter and Arielle
stepped out into the bustling activity of Regent Street.
Stationary vehicles monopolized the center of the
crowded street, jammed with carriages, gigs and ba-
rouches. Conversation buzzed in the air, a great gabble of
indistinguishable chatter from the scores of people milling
about.

Remaining close to Hunter, Arielle followed him as he
snaked through the confusion and made their way to the
curricle. She wanted the afternoon to go on forever, but
they reached the town house not long after.

Once there, Hunter easily alighted from the curricle,
then turned, slid his arms around her waist, and lifted her
down. A brisk breeze passed around them, swirling
through the tall, ancient trees in the park across the lane.

"Are you cold?" he murmured against her hair, one arm still protectively around her as they reached the entrance door.

Nestled in his arm, Arielle leaned her head against his shoulder. "And tired."

Before he had a chance to use the brass knocker, Wilfred opened the door. "Then you'd best go upstairs and rest," Hunter suggested, nodding to Wilfred as he led Arielle upstairs to her bedchamber, still with his arm around her waist.

"In the course of reviewing your records I came to the same conclusion you did. Braxton Hall and your other estates are in excellent financial condition, my lord," Eric Peabody announced.

Hunter had hired the solicitor upon his return to England and was quite satisfied with his performance. Leaving Arielle resting, he had come to settle his wedding expenses as well as do something on Arielle's behalf. She had told him not long ago about a family she had been caring for, the Beechams. Even though she couldn't practice medicine, he knew it was important to her to help in other ways. "I thought so too. The estate manager did an excellent job while I was away."

"That he did, milord. Even your exorbitant withdrawal several weeks ago didn't hurt you."

At the unwelcome reminder of Thomas's greed, Hunter paced to the window.

"I have another withdrawal to make that I am entrusting you with." He turned to Mr. Peabody and briefly explained the matter of the Beechams to him.

"I need fifty pounds delivered to Mrs. Portia Beecham on the first of every month," Hunter concluded.

"That is quite a sum, Lord Savage!" Mr. Peabody blurted, his eyes wide.

"I can very well afford it, Mr. Peabody. Along with the bank draft, please include a letter explaining that you have discovered that her deceased husband was recently awarded a settlement. As Mr. Beecham's widow, she is now entitled to that money."

"Your generosity—"

"Is of no consequence. Just do as I ask."

"Aye, my lord."

Hunter grabbed his top hat from the chair and placed it on his head. "I have taken up enough of your time, Mr. Peabody. I think I shall take my leave for the day."

"Of course, my lord," Peabody answered with a cordial nod.

A stack of paperwork spread before him, Hunter rubbed his eyes, unable to concentrate as he contemplated the long day's events. He hadn't seen Arielle since they'd returned from buying the dresses and he thought if she was still resting now, three hours later, it might be best not to disturb her. He'd thought an outing together to the theater would be nice for both of them. Yet he didn't have the heart to wake her, so he thought it best to amuse himself for the rest of the evening.

Pushing his work aside, he called Geoffrey to bring his coat and hat.

Not long after, he found himself at White's, reclining in his seat, only half-interested in the games going on around him.

"Savage!"

Hunter scowled inwardly when he looked up and saw the voice belonged to Viscount Laurent Cabot. He really was in no mood to entertain one of Arielle's brothers-in-law.

"Cabot," Hunter acknowledged grudgingly, tasting his brandy. He cursed under his breath as Cabot joined him at his solitary table. Shrewd brown eyes assessed him.

"It is quite a surprise seeing you here so soon after your nuptials." Cabot took a drag of his cigar and released the smoke in a curly plume. "How does the lovely Arielle fare?"

"My wife is sterling," Hunter said without inflection.

"Ellen is in the country," Cabot rambled on. "I believe she intends to pay Arielle a visit."

"Arielle will be glad to see her," Hunter said, resigning himself to Cabot's presence. At least the pomposity that Hunter had noted at the wedding breakfast was missing tonight. "The family seems close."

"They dote upon the old man. Especially Arielle. His every wish is her command."

A fact that Hunter already knew with confusing clarity, if the exorbitant wedding bills he'd settled were any indication. "Did you stop over to warn me of that, Cabot?"

Cabot laughed. "I'm sure you've found it out for yourself, Savage. Arielle's loyalty is as legendary as her beauty."

"Is it now?" Hunter asked, raising his eyebrows. "Perhaps I hadn't heard about either because I've so recently returned to the country."

"Perhaps." The viscount shrugged. "And perhaps not. Few people who haven't actually met Arielle believe she's as exquisite as rumor has it."

Hunter held any comment he might have made in reserve.

"I almost fainted myself when I first saw Arielle," Cabot continued without encouragement. "You should feel lucky to have won her hand."

He knew he was quite lucky, although her hand had been forced into his. Still, he didn't like the way Cabot sounded—like a moonstruck puppy—as he spoke of Arielle. "You are a happily wedded man speaking of another's man wife, Cabot."

Embarrassed laughter greeted that statement. "That I am, old boy. But you have the gem—"

"Savage! Cabot!"

Wondering who would next see him, Hunter smiled as the earl of Pembishire approached.

"Hunter, what in the name of king and country are you doing in the city when you are so newly married?"

"Bloody hell, man! Is my wedded state anyone's business?"

"Trouble with the lovely Arielle so soon?" the earl asked, his eyes twinkling.

"I thought you were in convalescence," Hunter grouched, Julia Shepperton's words returning to him. The countess had said her husband was in the country nursing a broken leg. "Why aren't you in bed somewhere?" He should have known he would get no peace wherever his friends congregated. Especially Douglas.

"Julia and I had a row," Pembishire said in a hoarse whisper. "She came to London on her own for the ceremony and spread that cockamamie story about my broken leg. I apologize, my friend, for not showing up, but I couldn't tolerate my wife's company just then. No slight intended."

"I see," Hunter said, understanding well his friend's dilemma, being married to Julia. From what he'd gathered about her, she was more than willing to pass her time with another man. He'd never tolerate a loose-moraled wife, no matter how beautiful.

"She's back at the estate now, isn't she?" Cabot asked, smoothing down the ruffled hair at his nape.

"Which is why I'm back in the city," Pembishire answered with a laugh. "My mistress is ever grateful to Julia's usual inattentiveness."

Hunter snorted and the two men gazed curiously at him. "I suppose you have a mistress as well, Cabot?"

Uncertainty flickered in Cabot's features and he leaned back in his seat. Instead of answering, however, he posed the question of Hunter.

"And you don't, Savage?"

"Why should he? He's just back to the country and newly married. He has no need for a mistress just yet," Pembishire declared.

"And I won't ever have need of one," Hunter snapped.

"So you say now, my lord," Cabot returned, splaying his fingers on the table. "But Arielle is a Stanford. A sweet disposition disguises a sharp-tongued, iron will. As much as her beauty might bring a man to his knees, I have no doubt that she is as shrewish as her sisters. If I may be so bold as to point out, Hunter, after less than a month of marriage, you are here and she is someplace else."

"Laurent," Hunter began in snarling tones, "you overstep—"

"Three years ago," Pembishire interrupted hastily, trying to avert an argument between the two men, "a fellow I knew back at university offered for Arielle."

"By Jove, Douglas! She was fifteen at the time," Hunter said incredulously. "I never took you for the type to approve of a full-grown man wedding a mere child."

Color suffused Pembishire's face. "Damn it, Savage, you know that I do not. He was pressing for a betrothal, not an immediate marriage!"

"This is the first I'm hearing of that," Cabot said. "Ellen never mentioned it."

"That's because Thomas adamantly refused."

"Really?" Hunter asked, intrigued. He knew that Twickenbot's son offered for Arielle a year ago, but this was the first he had heard of this older suitor. "Was Stanford saving her for anyone in particular?"

"Not especially," Pembishire answered. "He said he wanted her to make the choice of who she'd wed on her own. That's why everyone was in such a state of shock when word got out that you and she were to marry. No one realized you knew each other."

Hunter debated on how much to tell Douglas in the presence of Laurent. Certainly, he couldn't divulge the blackmail, but a small explanation would ward off any unsavory rumors. "Thomas and I reached an agreement on her behalf." He pinched the bridge of his nose and sighed. "Her father said she insisted on marrying me. It was past time that I wed, and, I admit, I found myself deeply in love with her."

"You would have been a fool not to," Pembishire stated stoutly. "She always did have a touch of the romantic about her. I guess she'd heard about your exploits on the Peninsula and wanted you for herself."

"Perhaps so," Hunter said quietly. A twinge of envy went through him. Both these men apparently knew a lot about Arielle, and seemed genuinely envious of him for having caught her eye. "Tell me, gentlemen, is there anything else that I should know about my bride?"

"Other than the fact that Quentin DeVries is in love with her?"

Hunter glowered at Laurent. "Yes, you ass, other than that, though I know better. You wouldn't like it very much hearing that another man was in love with Ellen, would you?"

A twinkle lit Cabot's eyes and he hooted with laughter. "If only I could be so lucky!"

"Do you ever have a serious thought in your head?" Hunter bit out.

"We've told you everything there is to know about Lady Arielle, Hunter," Douglas said. "The rest, my lord, is up to you to discover."

34

It was past midnight when Hunter returned to the town house. He hadn't meant to stay out so late, but ended up having quite an enjoyable time, despite his annoying friend and equally annoying brother-in-law.

Tired now but wanting to look in on Arielle, he went to her bedchamber and rapped softly on the door. When no immediate response came, he opened the door and looked in. Soft lamplight and the low embers of the fireplace cast a glow about the room, and moonlight spilled through the opened drapes, adding extra brightness.

Partially covered, Arielle lay sprawled on her back. Her head rested on the pillow, her gold hair spread over it and spilling around her, like shimmering silk.

Hunter's breath caught and his mouth went dry. He stepped fully in and closed the door, clicking the lock into place, then he moved closer to where his wife lay. He studied her breasts. The memory of how they felt pressing into his chest as he made love to her sent a hot rush of blood to his manhood. He chuckled softly. Was she accustomed to sleeping naked or did she expect a visit from him?

Whatever the answer was, he didn't want her embarrassed to see him there gawking at her person, so he pulled the covers over her chest and sat on the side of the bed.

Glimpsing the note she'd pinned to his pillow, he reached for it. He shouldn't have been surprised, he thought with a chuckle. Arielle was doing this often and he enjoyed each and every one.

> *Hunter, my dearest,*
> *If I am asleep when you return, please wake me.*
> *I want to tell you how much I missed you while you were gone. I am lost in a wonderland that I never want to be rescued from. Unless you are my rescuer. You are my destiny. My all.*
>
> > *Yours eternally,*
> > *Arielle*

Hunter's blood warmed. How could she not be sincere with such words? He ignored the doubt he felt toward her; the fear that she could never really love him; the worry that she'd only married him out of duty to her father.

Her letters, her *love letters*, convinced him that she loved him and wanted him no matter what.

Gently, he shook her shoulder. "Arielle?" he said softly.

"Umm." Arielle stirred, bringing one arm above her head. In the process, she exposed one breast again, a rosy nipple beckoning him.

His heart pounding, his nether region growing fully, Hunter brushed her hair back from her face. "Arielle," he whispered, "are you awake?"

Arielle opened her eyes, dewy green from sleep. Her gaze met his, searching his face. A dazed smile curved her lips and she didn't appear at all regretful of her undressed state.

"Hunter?" she murmured dreamily.

"Yes, my angel?"

It took a moment for Arielle to answer; in that moment, her position dawned on her. She sat up abruptly, bringing the blankets with her to shield her bare breasts. Her eyes widened. "Omigosh! W-what are you doing here?"

A vague smile touched his lips at her modesty. She still

wasn't accustomed to being nude around him.

Hunter waved the letter at her. "I take it you forgot our engagement," he whispered, kissing the tip of her nose. "Shakespeare at the Globe?"

"Oh!"

"It was a long day for you, sweetheart. You've been asleep for hours and I'm just returning from my club. I hadn't the heart to wake you for the theater. There'll be other nights. I merely came to look in on you. I didn't mean to startle you. But perhaps I can rescue you from oversleeping."

Again, their gazes met, melded, mesmerized.

Large, liquid sea green eyes gleamed with awareness and anticipation, and dropped to his lips. Her fingers fidgeted with uncertainty at the covers shielding her breasts.

"Let go of the covers, Arielle," he urged, his tone one of heated seduction.

As though in a trance, her regard never leaving his face, Arielle's grip on the counterpane loosened; it slipped from her hands.

"You're so beautiful," Hunter whispered thickly.

Cupping one breast, he lowered his head and flicked his tongue over her hardening nipple. When he closed his mouth fully over the breast he held and began suckling it, little breathy sounds escaped Arielle's lips.

"Hunter," she whispered, her head thrown back, her mass of hair hanging loosely about her and brushing his cheek.

Hunter stood abruptly from the bed and, moments later, he'd rid himself of his clothes.

Arielle's heart fluttered wildly in her chest, the hammering beat of it throbbing in her ears. Her breasts still tingled from Hunter's sensual touch. Burning need rushed through her being, exploded in her center, pushed away her lingering doubts.

"I must confess, I much prefer spending the evening alone with you," he said, drawing her into his arms.

"So do I."

Hunter kissed her throat, sliding his lips to her ear and nibbling on her lobe with drugging tenderness. Every hot kiss he bestowed, every spot he touched, scalded her. His lips trailed across her cheekbone, down the column of her throat, caressing her like a velvet whisper, consuming her like the brightest fire.

He cupped both breasts, kissing one and then the other, laving her nipples until they stood out, pebble hard. Arielle's nerves rippled deliciously, tearing a gasp from her throat.

"I want to love you properly, my sweet," Hunter said hoarsely. "I want to make love to you as a man in love with his wife."

"Yes, Hunter, I want that too," Arielle managed weakly.

Holding her tightly, Hunter's mouth found hers again, her sensitive breasts pressed against his bare chest, stirring her blood to a fever pitch. He slid his hand between her thighs, his fingers teasing before slipping between the folds of her flaming center. Finding her erected bud, he massaged it, slowly, provocatively, maddeningly.

Arielle arched her back, gasping. "Oh, God, Hunter! Oh, please!"

"Tell me you like it, my darling," Hunter rasped, massaging her faster, his assault ruthless, licking her nipple again, to the rhythm of his hand.

Arielle tried to speak but the rush of sensation stole her breath.

Kissing her tenderly, Hunter removed his hand and took her into his arms again. His phallus pressed against her thigh.

"Touch me," he whispered.

Arielle looked at his manhood. Tentatively, she slid her hand across the long, slick length of it, circling her finger around the thick tip.

Hunter closed his eyes and groaned. "Ahh, yes," he murmured as the pressure of her fingers increased. He allowed her to pleasure him a moment longer, before he grabbed her hand, his excitement increasing. "Not yet."

Rising up and seizing her mouth, he tasted her again. Over and over, he kissed her. Entwined in each other's arms, nothing else mattered, not the past or the future, only this moment in time and age-old need.

As Hunter kissed her breasts, moving his mouth to her navel and tracing the indentation of it with his tongue, red-hot hunger ignited Arielle's senses. Her body shook with anticipation, cried for relief. But Hunter was relentless. His lips flirted with the downy bush between her thighs, kissed her aching flesh. His tongue parted her folds and encircled her bud in a searing, searching touch that sent excruciating sensation careening through her.

He thrust his tongue into her opening, and she jerked against the delicious pain of his kisses, drawing her knees up to allow him the utmost access. He sucked her, leaving her defenseless, her body moving convulsively, half-crazed. Unbridled pleasure rushed through her.

Arielle tugged at Hunter's hair, grabbing, reaching for anything to grip as sheer ecstacy threatened to steal her very soul. The friction of his mouth against her sent her into a frenzy and wet heat flooded her thighs, uncontrollable moans escaping her throat.

When she thought she might expire, Hunter retraced his paths upwardly, along her body. He found her mouth again, delving deeply into her warm recesses, allowing her to taste the glistening muskiness upon his lips. He kissed her wildly, urgently, hungrily. Raising himself over her, he spread her thighs, his organ throbbing with need. He locked his arms around her thighs and pulled her forward, impaling her with his silken rod of steel, filling her completely.

"Arielle, my sweet, sweet Arielle. You're s-so hot."

Their two sexes ground against each other, soldered together with slick fire, joined to the very hilt. The feel of him inside her was like the sweetest ambrosia, gratifying and delectable. Hunter devoured her mouth as he thrust inside her, deep and demanding, his strokes stealing her reason.

She whimpered, wrapping her legs around his back, kissing his broad chest, now beaded with sweat. She flicked her tongue over his nipple, kissed the hollow of his strong neck. And still his endless thrusts continued, causing her body untold heat, bright and fiery.

"You feel so right, so w-wonderf-ful," Hunter said in broken tones. "So wonderful."

Arielle didn't bother to respond, nearly succumbing to the joy of the intense pleasure pounding through her body. She thrashed her head about, moaned from somewhere deep inside, moved to his rhythm, unable to comprehend the depths of such excruciating rapture.

Flames of brilliance lapped at her sanity. Pins and needles pricked her with overwhelming sensations. Hunter's movements became unforgiving, each scorching push into her more powerful and rapid than the last. The flames became the light; the pins and needles, stars.

Arielle's fingers dug into Hunter's back and her thighs tightened around his driving hips.

Hunter pumped one last furious stroke into her, then she felt the swift stream of his release. With a deep moan, he collapsed on top of her. A moment later, he slid off her and pulled her flush against him, holding her tightly. Brushing damp strands of hair from her face, he kissed her on the forehead.

"We'll make the theater again before we return to Braxton Hall," he promised, between breaths.

"If I had my preference, I would have chosen our time together here," Arielle whispered, kissing the hollow of his neck.

35

Upon first sight of the run-down hovel in the East End, Hunter frowned. He had heard about the poverty-stricken, but hadn't ever seen their living conditions. But his gently born wife visited here to tend people who really mattered to her.

Wrinkling his nose at the horrid stench assailing his senses as he halted Blazer and dismounted, he made his way to the door and knocked. A moment later, a fragile-boned child answered. Smudges stained the boy's cheeks and nose. Well-worn clothes hung on his small body.

He looked Hunter up and down, his eyes rounding.

"And you are?"

"Tory, sir."

"Are you Mrs. Beecham's son?"

Tory nodded. "Aye. Me ma is sleepin', you know?"

"Who's at the door, Tory?"

The owner of that voice appeared. Hunter didn't need two guesses to know that the young girl with pretty features and reddish blond hair was Maura. Her affectionate smile faded as she caught sight of Hunter. Work-roughened hands flattened over her belly and she stared with mistrust at him.

"And who might ye be, sir?"

"Hunter Braxton. The marquess of Savage," Hunter answered, trying to inflect a bit of warmth into his voice, instead of the irritation he felt.

Tory and Maura gasped in audible unison.

Maura, the first to recover, dropped into a deep curtsy. "Lady Arielle's husband?"

"Yes, one and the same," Hunter answered. This wasn't going well at all. His discomfort came through in his stilted words and stiff movements. Suddenly, he had no earthly idea why he'd come here, where he felt so out of place. These visits couldn't have been easy for Arielle. "I came to see how Mrs. Beecham fares." He swung his gaze between Maura and Tory before settling on the girl. "And you, my dear. I hear you are . . ."

His voice trailed off and he felt heat creep up his neck. It didn't matter that Maura wasn't a gentlewoman, he had no business speaking so freely about such a delicate matter as her pregnancy.

"Expectin', my lord?" Maura finished, amusement lightening her query and curving her mouth.

"Yes."

"Aye, I am." Her smile faded and she shrugged. "I'm three months gone. Dr. DeVries has been seein' to me and he says the babe is progressin' fine."

Hunter swallowed hard, taking in Maura's appearance. She looked as malnourished as Tory.

"We was hopin' to see Lady Arielle soon," Tory said softly. "Is she well?"

Maura sent her little brother an abashed look. "Don't go askin' Lord Savage that, poppet. It ain't proper manners, Tory."

"Tory's question didn't offend me, Maura," Hunter reassured her. "He has every right to want to know about her. You all do. My wife is fine. She sends her regards," he added quickly.

"Tell her I miss her, my lord," Tory said.

Hunter nodded. He wouldn't soon forget those huge, sad eyes in the small face. "By all means, son."

A door opened from inside the house and Maura looked over her shoulder. "Would ye like to meet my mother, Lord Savage?"

"Of course."

When Maura and Tory escorted him into the small space, he felt like an oversized Olympian.

"Mum, this be Lady Arielle's man," Tory announced proudly, taking Hunter's hand into his own grimy one. "He come to look in on us for her."

Mrs. Beecham bowed deeply. A small cough escaped her. "Yer lordship, I never would have imagined ye comin' to my end. If ye truly come to bade Lady Arielle's words my way, then ye are a jewel and quite deservin' of her."

At that moment, Hunter didn't feel deserving enough. He'd remember this day, when this destitute woman said his wife's name as if she were her savior.

"Would ye care fer a seat, my lord?" Mrs. Beecham asked, indicating the threadbare couch. "Maura can serve us a spot of tea."

"I can't stay," Hunter said.

"I haven't had tea in ages," Mrs. Beecham continued. "But this morning, a post came for me and it had a bank draft in it. A near fortune," she whispered conspiratorially. "The note in it said it was from a settlement for my deceased husband. So we will have real tea, my lord!"

His solicitor had seen to the matter promptly, Hunter thought with satisfaction. He couldn't have imagined the happiness Mrs. Beecham would feel because she'd have tea. Not after having everything at his beck and call his entire life.

"I'm happy for you." However lame the words sounded, he was sincere. Hunter hastily turned toward the door. "I'm sure Arielle will pay you a visit soon."

"She's still allowed to come here?" Maura asked incredulously.

"Maura!" Mrs. Beecham scolded. "Mind yer manners, child."

"Aye, Mum."

"There's no harm done, Mrs. Beecham. Your children are truly lovely."

"Oh, you haven't met the rest of them, my lord," Maura

put in brightly. "They would have ye tearin' yer hair out."

Hunter smiled at the girl's fondness as she spoke of her younger siblings. She was going to make a wonderful mother. Walking toward the door, he dug into the pocket of his waistcoat and pulled out a pound note.

"Please, my lord, it ain't proper!" Mrs. Beecham said.

Hunter stuffed the bill into Tory's hand and smiled again. "I gave the blunt to your son, ma'am. Not you."

Before the woman could answer, Hunter hurried out the door.

Awakening the next morning, Arielle was disappointed not to find Hunter lying next to her. She blinked at the morning sun shining through the window.

She could have remained in his arms forever, listening to his words of endearment, making love with him.

Arielle ran her fingers across the place Hunter had lain and sighed wistfully. She loved him, but she wasn't sure what good that was. They'd made love last night, perfect, wonderful love. Yet she didn't know if his tenderness had come from the heart or if mere lust guided him.

Glancing at the side table, she saw an envelope with Hunter's familiar scrawl on it. *For My Dearest Arielle.* With anticipation, she picked up the letter and opened it.

> *My dearest wife,*
>
> *Words cannot begin to explain the bliss I experienced with you last night. Arielle, we have reached a place in our marriage where we should be open with each other upon our return home. For now, we are on holiday, away from the pressing chores of Braxton Hall.*
>
> *I must tell you of the joy you bring me, despite my reservations of so many things about our marriage. I am glad you consented to become my wife. I can hardly imagine another woman in my life. You're perfect for me.*

> *I have an errand to see to, my Arielle. I know*
> *you planned to visit your father today. Stay as sweet*
> *as you always are.*
>
> Until later,
> Hunter

Arielle clutched the letter to her breast, sighing dreamily. Hunter loved her! In so many words, he'd said so. She was perfect for him. Still, she must find a way to make him confess his love to her. With another sigh, she slid out of bed to prepare herself for the day ahead.

Arielle arrived in Grosvenor Square later that morning. A light drizzle plagued her short journey, and, by the time she stepped out of the coach, she felt wilted and depressed over the need to confront her father. Still, it was necessary. She needed answers.

"Arielle, what a surprise, my child," Thomas said five minutes later, a happy light entering his eyes. He gazed about. "Have you come with your husband?"

Without answering immediately, Arielle led the way to the sofa and they both sat. A blazing fire warmed the room, taking away the morning chill.

"Hunter is off in the city."

"Then matters are going well with you, I gather?"

"Better than expected." Arielle smiled. "Papa, I need to ask you a very important question and I need your complete honesty."

Thomas stared at her for long moments, his haggard features growing wary. "What is it?"

"What did you say for Hunter to agree to the wedding?"

"Oh, child." Her father rubbed his temples, then took her hands into his own. Dread welled within her at his look of regret. "Where can I even begin?"

"With the truth?" she suggested in a neutral tone, her heart pounding.

Thomas stood and made his way to the window, his shoulders drooping. Turning toward her once again, his look turned almost defiant, increasing Arielle's dread. "What makes you think there is something more to say on the matter?" he said sternly.

"Because of your brief look of remorse. Because Hunter had other plans and obligations that took precedence over a hasty marriage."

Thomas shrugged arrogantly. "A man is entitled to change his mind," he snapped.

Her simmering anger spilled over and she rushed up to Thomas. For so many years, she'd thought she was supposed to do as he asked because of what he'd done for her. But, in the end, he'd set trap for her and she'd fallen right into it. At this moment, she was angry with him for pulling her strings and making her feel obligated to him. "You're certainly right, Papa. A man is entitled to change his mind, but Hunter wouldn't have," she said through clenched teeth, tears burning the backs of her eyes. "His mind was set to do other things and marriage was not in the immediate future. Now, I want the truth! I insist on it! I deserve it!"

Thomas's gaze touched her rigid stance, the pounding pulse at the base of her throat, the tears glistening in her eyes. But Arielle knew he couldn't see the piercing hurt that she mightn't ever get over. The only thing he saw— the only thing she wanted him to see—was her angry determination.

She met his glance and held it, refusing to look away, refusing to give over. Finally, Thomas's features clouded with regret again and all irritation disappeared. He drew in a deep breath. "Yes, Arielle. You deserve to hear the truth from me. The truth is, I blackmailed Hunter. I swore that I'd expose things I'd discovered about him, leaving him no choice but to comply with my demands or face embarrassment and social ruin. The truth is, I forced both of you into this marriage. I can only hope that you'll find it in your heart to forgive me."

Bile rose in her throat at her father's words. Tears of anger burned her eyes and she backed away from Thomas, her body shaking in outrage at how Thomas had toyed with their lives for his own sake. Hunter had every right to hate her. As she'd long ago suspected, blackmail had brought her and Hunter together and the humiliation it caused him underscored their marriage. "How dare you! How could you?"

"Arielle, please, listen—"

"Listen? To what?" she asked bitterly, finally understanding Hunter's attitude toward her. He had never wanted her in his life and now she knew why.

How could she ever face Hunter again? Yet how could she ever leave him when she found herself so deeply in love with him?

Before her father could say any more, she gathered her gloves and reticule and headed for the door.

"Arielle, wait!"

She didn't stop. Instead she ran to the carriage and instructed Wilfred to leave with all due haste.

Had her father even considered what effect blackmail would have on her union? Apparently he hadn't thought beyond his own debts. He didn't care about the misery he'd inflict on either her or Hunter.

Considering what she now knew, Hunter had been more than considerate toward her. He was the most innocent of all and still he had managed to express tenderness toward her.

As a child, her father had been her very own hero, her knight in shining armor not only to her but to her four sisters as well. He had soothed the grief upon their mother's passing when Arielle was only six and too young to understand the finality of death. She had preened beneath his compliments and wallowed in his attention.

Then, her sisters, Thomas's real daughters, had begun to grow up and leave her behind.

From Arielle's twelfth birthday on, she had watched her sisters depart; and with each successive year, her father's attention had been turned away from her to follow the women who shared his blood. As a result, she'd devoted herself to him in an effort to reclaim her father's attention.

Her only hope now was for Hunter to be a very understanding man. An explanation of why she'd so readily accepted her father's demand to marry him might set everything on the right path.

Or he might view her as a manipulator and scorn her even more.

"You never cease to amaze me, Hunter," Arielle said two hours later, as they sat beneath a tree. No sooner had she returned home than Hunter whisked her off for an outing in the park.

"How's that?" Hunter asked, tracing his thumb around her lips, his head resting in her lap.

She fought to keep her control, Hunter's innocent touch wreaking untold havoc on her. "As of late, I don't know what to expect from you."

Expelling a long breath, Hunter sat up and looked thoughtfully at her. "What can I expect from *you*, Arielle?" he asked in a quiet, serious tone.

"Me?" she retorted in surprise. "I don't understand. Haven't I demonstrated to you my determination to please you? I've worked diligently to help restore Braxton Hall—"

"Yes, you have," Hunter interrupted, "and it's going to look far better than I remember it."

The sad, longing smile he accorded her took her aback and her heart turned over in her chest as she realized she'd caused the look.

Arielle's face heated with shame. "I—I think I know what you're getting at, Hunter. I didn't please you last night. I really don't know about life in that manner, my lord. If you could teach me, I'll try to do better. I—"

A searing kiss, deep and soul-searching, stopped her rush of words. Her skin prickled and her toes tingled.

"Last night, my lady, you took my breath away. I can hardly express my enchantment with you," he reassured her. "Hopefully, we have a lifetime before us to correct any mistakes we may have made. Didn't you read my letter?"

"Yes, Hunter," Arielle said breathlessly. "I read it. Hopefully, we have a lifetime before us."

"I take that to mean there's a chance we *will* be together a lifetime."

"Of course!"

Hunter stroked his chin. "Then, my sweet, the time for us to talk is overdue."

"What about?" Arielle asked, dread filling her. Her father had already admitted that he'd blackmailed Hunter. Since she had never doubted that she'd be married to Hunter for life, he apparently was having second thoughts.

"I need to know what you actually know about me," Hunter said slowly, choosing his words carefully. "Why you were so compelled to marry me."

"I only know what my father told me and what I've heard through the ton," she quickly added, seeing the frown marring his face.

"What *have* you heard through that rumor mill?"

"Just that you proved yourself courageous and honorable in the military."

Hunter's expression grew unreadable. "What exactly did your father say to you about me?" he asked in a noncommital tone, leaving her unsure if he had a genuine desire to know and understand or if he was looking for fodder to use against her.

"Arielle?"

"As I told you before, my father was indebted," she answered, knowing it would be hard for him to believe that she'd had no knowledge of her father's plans. "He said you'd recently left the military and wanted a wife to run Braxton Hall. In order to get me, you were willing to compensate my father for his loss of me." She tugged at a lock of hair. "At first, I refused."

Stunned silence met her admission and she saw the furious working of his mind. If she'd refused her father's request, Hunter had to know that she'd had no part in the blackmail.

"You refused?" he finally repeated with incredulity.

"Yes."

"Why?"

"Because I wanted to pursue my dream. But my father's revelation about his plight convinced me to do otherwise. However, I developed a distinct dislike for you since you accepted my father's marriage proposal for me instead of asking me directly."

"And now? Do you still dislike me?"

"Only sometimes," she admitted.

"I see. Why did you finally decide to marry me?"

"To keep my father out of debtor's prison. He swore our wedding was his only recourse."

"You gave up your own dreams for your father? Are you sorry you married me?"

Arielle shook her head slowly. "To save my father, I would do it all over again."

"Does that include marrying me?"

"I haven't decided yet," she said with a giggle.

His eyes gleaming with amusement, Hunter grinned. "Fair enough," he conceded. "While you think on your decision, we should go to the Emporium for a spot of tea and a bite to eat."

"My sentiments exactly," Arielle agreed, rubbing her belly. "I am famished."

Shaking his head in bemusement, Hunter got to his feet. "First I nearly freeze you and now you tell me you are about to succumb for lack of food. Are you sure you're up to being with me?"

Arielle laughed. "Quite sure, my lord," she said, placing her hands in his and allowing him to help her to her feet.

Together, they gathered their things, then made their way to the carriage.

Whatever else she'd expected from her explanation, it

hadn't been unheralded acceptance. She'd hoped he would at least declare his own feelings, if not outright understanding.

She supposed, however, it would take time for Hunter to readjust his perception of her.

36

After two spectacular weeks in London, Arielle and Hunter returned to Braxton Hall once again. Hunter resumed the daily chores that took him away for most of the day, while Arielle went back to her duties as mistress of the estate. It was an easy rhythm that they fell into and one that she enjoyed. At night, they shared each other's company at dinner, then retired together and made love.

Still, Hunter held back a tiny part of himself from her. She had no doubt that it was because of the scurrilous position her father had taken to have the marriage take place in the first place. When the time was right, she'd sit Hunter down and clear the dissension between them. But first, she had to gain his complete trust. She had to let him know, through words and deeds, how much he mattered to her.

Since their arrival home, they had continued leaving letters for one another. She made it a point to write one at some point during each day. Hunter seemed to do the same, for every morning she found a note beside her pillow.

She and Hunter still argued over her desire to become a doctor, however. Even now, plagued with stomach pains for the past two days, he refused to allow her to see to him. He swore if he needed a doctor, he'd find a *doctor*.

The man was completely pigheaded and insufferable on that issue. Every time he raised her hopes, he found a way to dash them.

For distraction Arielle went to the attic and settled next

to the beautiful trunk to begin yet another letter between
the mysterious lovers.

> *Dearest Beloved,*
>   *I fear I am ruined with the love I bear you. I
> tremble with my need for you and cannot describe
> the complete joy I experience in your presence.
> Even so, I cannot tell you of the oneness I feel when
> we are joined in passion. I love you, dearest angel.
> Everything you do and say is a balm to my soul. I
> will hold on to our time together as I hold on to
> life. 'Til we meet again, my love, I remain,*
>
>   *Your devoted servant*

Arielle refolded the letter with shaking hands to put it
back in the envelope. She held it for long moments, staring at the yellowed enveloped as if in a trance.

These letters from Devoted Servant to his Dearest Beloved were so poignant it made Arielle want to weep.
They described her own feelings about Hunter so accu-
rately. Did such letters enhance the love between the
strangers? Would letters in kind facilitate a true and last-
ing love between her and Hunter? They'd reached a point
now where they expressed their physical feelings with
tender ardor. But she wanted them to meld their physical
feelings with their emotional ones.

With a heavy sigh, Arielle closed the trunk. Chores
awaited her. In spite of Hunter's edict to let the servants
handle them, Braxton Hall was her home. She would see
to it herself.

For now, she'd desert her letter reading, but promised
herself to pen a similar one to Hunter.

After their two-week stay in London, she'd decided it
was time to return to Braxton Hall and tie up the loose
ends. Finish the restoration of the manor, so she could
commence entertaining. She thought it high time she and
Hunter returned to society.

37

The western sky slowly changed from an enticing golden red of sunset to the grayish dusk of evening.

Astride his black Arabian stallion, Blazer, Hunter grimaced, waving his hand and urging Vaughn to Braxton Hall's carriage house. An oddly out-of-sorts feeling plagued Hunter. Dizziness suddenly attacked him and pain careened through his belly. He blinked to clear his eyes, tightening his hold upon Blazer's reins, his skin percolating with warmth.

Vaughn, astride another horse, finally passed Hunter, chatting nonchalantly with one of the four servants that had accompanied them to look over the grounds. Barely able to stay in the saddle, Hunter spurred Blazer toward the stables. He dismounted, only to realize that he was unable to stand any longer.

"Milord!" Vaughn sank down beside Hunter and put a thick arm around his shoulders. "Milord! Are you not well?"

"I'm feeling out of sorts, Vaughn," Hunter managed weakly, swallowing against the dryness of his mouth. Out of sorts was an understatement. He'd never felt worse. He placed his own arm across his servant's shoulders, not wanting to alarm his staff. Or Arielle. "Lend me your assistance, if you will."

"Certainly, milord."

Relying on Vaughn's strength to help him up, Hunter stilled his movements once on his feet again. The exertion had only worsened the nausea and dizziness. A few moments passed before his head cleared and he was able to proceed without aid. "I can probably reach my bedchamber on my own strength. However, in the event I'm wrong, I want you to walk inside with me."

"Of course, milord."

Moving slowly and without aid, Hunter reached the door to the kitchen and opened it, stopping in shock. The large dresser was now bedecked with crockery and kitchen utensils. The painted walls had been scrubbed and the stone floors gleamed from hard work, reflecting in the shining copper pots hanging from ceiling hooks. Even the windowpanes were clear and sparkling.

Dora sat at the long wooden table paring apples, while Beatrice stood at the range, stirring the contents of a large pot on the fire. Noting his presence, Dora rose from her seat, her eyes wide.

To banish the tension, Hunter nodded to Vaughn. "It's been a long day."

"Yes, my lord," Vaughn commented. "That it has."

"See to it that the carriage horses are watered, fed, and brushed down. And take extra care with Blazer."

"I'll start with Blazer, milord."

"Excellent. Have the new people settled in their quarters yet? I want them to meet Lady Arielle as soon as possible. But she may be asleep at this late hour."

Vaughn smiled. "Yes, my lord."

He shifted his heavy bulk and continued. "If that be the case, sir there's always tomorrow. About food for the new staff, my lord, no one has eaten since half past the noon hour—"

"By God, they must be famished!" Hunter interrupted, swaying on his feet and grabbing the dresser to steady himself.

"There's a plentiful supply of food here, my lord," Beatrice said, staring at him with raised eyebrows. "Lady Arielle insisted we prepare a substantial amount."

"Very good," Hunter said, impressed by his wife's instinct. "I'll be in my bedchamber. Carry on," he said, dismissing Vaughn, his mind insistently straying to Arielle and remaining firmly away from the throbbing pain. He refused to have anyone fussing about him unnecessarily. He'd ask Arielle to discreetly send for a doctor and be done with it.

He reached the end of the corridor that connected the kitchen and empty dining room. Holding tightly to the banister, he went up, reaching his wife's door shortly thereafter.

His head was pounding like a drumbeat and his heart was racing a rapid tattoo. He knocked. "Arielle?" He leaned against the door, panting for breath, his body heavy.

The rich baritone of Hunter's voice slammed into Arielle's senses. Uncertainty made her hesitate and a moment later, she heard his footfalls drift away from her bedchamber. Then, his own entrance door opened and closed.

Really! Hunter needed to learn patience and control his temper. She wasn't a bird to flit and fly about at his slightest whim. He hadn't given her time to open the door to him.

She opened the connecting door between their rooms in time to see Hunter slump in a heap atop his bed.

"A-Arielle."

Arielle's hand flew to her chest, her eyes widening at the sight of her husband's inert form on the bed. "Hunter!" she gasped, rushing to his side.

"Arielle," he groaned in a whisper. "I—I am bereft of my strength. S-something is terribly amiss."

Placing her hand on his forehead, Arielle found it unusually warm. "My God, Hunter! Where have you been?"

Hunter attempted to sit up, but his efforts failed him.

"No, my love." Arielle's concern resounded in her shaky voice. "Lie still. You have a fever. Let me help you undress." She stood and pulled him into a sitting position, straining against his weight. He tried to aid her as she unfastened his shirt, but his hands dropped to his sides.

Working quickly, her belly knotting in fear, Arielle finally succeeded in freeing Hunter of his garments. He leaned wearily against the pillows.

She took his hand in hers and drew in a heavy sigh. "Hunter, you have a fever. Please, tell me how you feel. Are you in pain?"

"Yes, Arielle," Hunter answered in a weak tone. The contrast to his normally commanding voice made her heart ache. "My lower abdomen. The pain is excruciating."

The last postmortem exam she'd watched Quentin perform came to Arielle's mind. The subject had been a patient of Quentin's and the man had died of perityphlitis.

If the man had had his appendix surgically removed, his life might have been saved, Quentin had explained to her.

Surgically removed? The mere thought filled Arielle with dread. The procedure had never been done. And being a surgeon was a far cry from being a physician. Still, perityphlitis killed.

Dread filled Arielle. "What else, Hunter?"

"I—I'm nauseous, weak, and dizzy. Even as I recline, my head still spins."

Arielle placed her hands under the cover and laid her hand against Hunter's abdomen. "Tell me if it hurts where I touch you," she said, applying pressure to Hunter's stomach.

"Stop!" Hunter pleaded at the barest of touches. "Please," he said, his eyes bright with pain and fever.

Arielle touched his forehead again. "Oh, Hunter."

"What is it, Arielle?"

"You have all the symptoms of perityphlitis. Acute perityphlitis."

"W-what does that mean?"

"My love," Arielle began softly, fighting back tears, "it means you are very ill."

Hunter drew in a ragged, painful breath. "Then we must summon your doctor friend posthaste. I am in great pain."

"I know. However, there is not enough time to summon him. You require surgery immediately or you will die." Trembles seized her voice and her body as she spoke those words to him.

Hunter, dead? Her vital, virile husband gone? She couldn't imagine it. She had to do everything in her power to save him, but knew that one mistake would be deadly. As it was, Hunter would risk all sorts of infections after the surgery. Yet, they were in the country, away from the fetid humors of the city. Had they been in London, Arielle mightn't have risked the unheard-of procedure.

"You can't be serious," Hunter whispered after a moment of stunned silence. "Are you telling me I'm dying?"

"No! I won't let you die! Hunter, I will send Vaughn to fetch Quentin with all due haste. But you will not last until he arrives."

"Then why summon him? What are you trying to say to me?"

"That you must trust me," Arielle blurted, before she lost her nerve, before it set in that she was the only one, at the moment, who had a remote chance of saving her husband. "You must trust me to do the surgery."

Hunter chuckled. "I'm damned either way," he said, his bitter words slicing through Arielle. She would save him, whether he believed it or not.

She swallowed, the pulse point at her throat beating fast. "Please, trust me."

Raising a hand, Hunter brushed away the tears staining her cheeks. "Don't cry, Arielle," he rasped, "I—I have the utmost faith in you. Truly. I have never questioned your ability. I have only questioned your reasoning."

Arielle threw her arms around his neck, trembling. "I'm grateful that you trust me," she said between sniffles. "But the legal ramifications of what I must do to save your life are staggering. Not only am I not licensed, as the law requires, I have not set foot in one accredited medical class." Her sobs deepened and she hugged him tighter. "I have only seen Quentin do this once as a study. The thought of having to cut you terrifies me."

Through a fog of pain, Hunter realized Arielle needed reassurance. At this moment, she was his only hope. He didn't have a physician and Quentin was miles away in London. Doctor DeVries might or mightn't reach him in time. So he had to trust Arielle with his life. He didn't want to die. "Arielle, I trust your abilities. You are intelligent. I'm sure DeVries knows this, which is the reason he took you under his wing. You *have* to do this, Arielle."

She disentangled herself from him and nodded. "I know what must be done, Hunter," she whispered, her eyes watery and haunting. "I will face whatever consequences that need to be faced to save your life."

"I won't allow them to punish you," Hunter grunted, another sharp pain hitting him. "DeVries would lose his license and face charges as well. Of course, if I don't survive this, I'll have no say in the matter."

"Please don't jest, Hunter," Arielle scolded, her skin chalk white as if she were the patient, instead of him. "This is too serious. Your life is in grave jeopardy and I'm so frightened for you. For us. But we must not waste any more time. Every moment lost lessens your chances for survival."

"I know." Grimacing in pain, he closed his eyes. "Proceed, my love, and be true to your calling."

38

After summoning Dora and Beatrice to assist in preparing Hunter for surgery, Arielle retrieved her black
bag from her bedchamber. Since Quentin had gifted her
with it, she'd only used it occasionally. Mostly to dispense
medicine and lance nasty boils. She'd never actually used
any of the lethal devices that Quentin had put inside the
bag.

Recalling the reason Quentin's patient died, Arielle's
heart pounded with fear. The man's symptoms had been
the exact same as Hunter's. Nausea, fever, pain, and vom-
iting. He'd died within hours after his appendix ruptured
and poisoned his system.

God, what if she couldn't save Hunter? Then, she'd be
without the man she loved; she'd bring disgrace upon her
family. She might even face murder charges. What was
she doing? Was she insane? She'd only seen this procedure performed once—and on someone already deceased.

Suddenly, she was furious with Hunter. If only he'd
allowed her to examine him sooner, she could have sent
for Quentin in time. Quentin would have known what to
do; he'd have been there to look at other options that
might have saved Hunter's life. Arielle knew only one.
This dangerous, illegal, unheard-of one.

She and Quentin had only discussed other treatment
options during the postmortem exam on the patient's cadaver, not actually implemented them through practice or
study. To make this surgery a success, she needed to recall
the preciseness of the incision Quentin made. And al-

though his deceased patient's appendix had already ruptured, she recalled the way Quentin cut away the infected
tube without damaging the cecum.

That incision, however, was relatively easy, since the
patient was already dead. Hunter, on the other hand, was
alive. How could she perform this surgery on her husband?

Repeating to herself that she must separate the personal
relationship from the professional one over and over
again, she signaled the women to help lift Hunter from
the bed. He grimaced in pain as they placed him on the
makeshift table covered with clean white sheets.

"It'll be over soon, my love," Arielle soothed in a surprisingly strong and steady tone considering the rawness
of her emotions.

Sweat beaded Hunter's brow, but he managed a weak
smile as he whispered, "I know, sweet Arielle."

Arielle settled him on the improvised operating table,
covering him with a sheet. Opening her bag, she took out
a bottle of chloroform and a pad. She set both items next
to Hunter, then stroked his damp hair. "Hunter, I'm going
to put you to sleep now," she told him softly, then took
a few seconds longer to explain her procedures to him.

"Do what you will," he whispered.

The sound went through Arielle. This was a do-or-die
situation. "I will make you better," she told him with soft
confidence then placed the chloroform-soaked pad over
his nose. Not long after, he drifted into a peaceful sleep.
Satisfied at Hunter's unconscious state, Arielle made the
sign of the cross. "God give me courage. Guide my hand
through a safe and true course." Breathing in deeply, she
pulled the covers down to shield only Hunter's groin.
Then, she fished out a bottle of alcohol and the sharp
surgical instrument that she never thought she'd have to
use.

Before she might lose her nerve, she made an incision
on the lower right side of Hunter's stomach. The blood
swiftly seeping from the cut nearly daunted her. Queasi-

ness roiled in her belly, but she ignored it. Stemming the blood with her metal clamps, she went in deeper until the vermiform appendix came into view. Angry red and swollen to the bursting point, infectious mucus filled it. She clamped off more blood flow, then used gauze to soak up the blood around the engorged tube.

She drew in a rapid, ragged breath. The dangers Hunter faced having his abdomen laid open and susceptible to infection frightened her. After the surgery was over, he might die anyway. What had she been thinking? She wasn't a surgeon or a physician. She was only a woman, who'd gotten caught up in her own selfish dreams. Now, she was using her husband as an experiment. She should have waited for Quentin.

She'd never forgive herself if she proved responsible for Hunter's death.

"Ye can do it, milady," Dora softly encouraged her, as if she knew the struggle Arielle faced at this crucial time.

"Aye, milady," Beatrice said. "His lordship wouldn't have let you cut him had he not believed in you."

Arielle nodded, their concerned voices spurring her on. She knew the worst was yet to come, however. She still needed to slice away the tube without nicking the organ attached to it *and* without causing the tube to rupture.

Holding her hand steady, Arielle guided the scalpel to her target. With a swift, precise motion, she snipped the tube off the end of the cecum and clamped it. Then, she lifted out the appendix and dropped it into a metal pan, still intact. That done, she worked rapidly, removing the clamps and sealing off the blood flow. She closed the incision and put a sulfur poultice over it, before sealing it.

"Let's put him in my bedchamber," Arielle instructed. "His lordship's chamber needs tidying up. And please let's get his night shirt on."

"Right away, milady," Dora said, pride clear in her voice.

"Thank you both," Arielle said, her voice cracking, her

worry and dread as a concerned wife creeping back into her. "I—I must clean up. Dora, after you and Beatrice finish assisting my husband, please prepare some broth. His lordship may be a little hungry when he awakens."

"Aye, mum," Dora said.

With practiced expedience, they went about their tasks collectively. Sometime later, with Hunter secured in her bedchamber, Arielle sat in a chair next to the bed. Fixing her gaze on his sleeping form, her body began to tremble. In awe and fear of what she'd done, her eyes watered and tears cascaded down her cheeks. Leaning her head on the bed, she wept unashamedly.

Unexpectedly, she felt a gentle caress gliding over her hair. She raised tear-filled eyes and gazed at her husband.

"There now, my mercy angel," Hunter murmured, groggy and weak. "There's no room for tears."

Arielle smiled tremulously. "How do you feel, Hunter? What I did just settled into me."

"What you did was nothing short of miraculous, Dr. Braxton. You should be very proud. As proud as I am of you. I feel so much better. Although I still feel pain, it's a different kind of pain. Mostly, I am very tired."

"So am I," she said with a relieved chuckle. Hunter *sounded* strong, despite his haggard look. She supposed surgery did that to a person. "Mind if I join you?" she asked, turning down the covers next to him.

"I can't think of a more rapid cure," he told her wearily as she snuggled in next to him.

39

"It's amazing, my lord," Quentin remarked after completing his inspection of Hunter's incision.

Arielle watched as Quentin applied a fresh poultice and clean bandage to Hunter's cut. Quentin had arrived an hour ago, just after dawn broke, prompting Arielle to reluctantly leave the warmth of her bed and the nearness of her husband. From what he said, he hadn't slept in over twenty-four hours. His red-rimmed eyes attested to his lack of sleep and his stubbled chin added to his run-down appearance. Still, he hadn't hesitated to come straight up to the bedchamber and see to Hunter. If it hadn't been for just such dedication and thirst for excellence in him, she never could have learned as much as she had from him; she never could have saved Hunter.

Rubbing her neck, she leaned back in the chair she'd taken next to the bed and gazed tiredly out the window. A cloudy, damp morning greeted them and made her long to return to bed. She needed sleep herself, having had a restless night, checking Hunter every so often. But she couldn't return to bed. Even with Quentin's presence, she still had to see to her husband's well-being.

"Lady Arielle has performed an operation not even I have had the chance to do," Quentin continued, his amazement coming through in his tone. "Or any other *surgeon,* to my knowledge. And she has done it well."

"In all truthfulness, Quentin, my courage almost failed me."

"But it didn't," Hunter rasped, his face flushed with the

pain of Quentin's examination. "Of which I am eternally grateful." He looked at Quentin and smiled weakly. "You should be proud of your student, Dr. DeVries. You've done an excellent job of teaching her."

Embarrassment knotted Quentin's brow. "Indeed I am, Lord Savage. And completely wonder-struck."

"Is there something I should do in the follow-up, Quentin?"

"Just keep doing whatever you've been doing, my lady."

Hunter chortled weakly at Quentin's formality. "Under such special circumstances, Quentin," he began around a cough, "I think it's all right to dispense with any formalities. Please call me Hunter and my wife—"

"Dr. Braxton," Arielle jested. "My husband has," she finished, joining them in laughter.

"Arielle," Quentin said, his gaze serious as it settled on her. He folded his arms and leaned against the bedside table. "Hunter will need a lot of rest before he is fully healed. And I'm sure you will make an excellent care giver."

"You can be assured of that," Arielle told him, as serious as he. "Now, please, Quentin, go down and make yourself comfortable. I'll see to Beatrice or Dora getting your breakfast. By then, a bedchamber for you to rest in will have been tidied up."

"Thank you, Arielle, but I cannot stay. I still have patients in the city I must see to," Quentin said with a yawn.

"Perhaps another time, doctor," Hunter told him. "Thank you for coming out."

"It was my duty, Hunter," Quentin said, "and my pleasure. Have a pleasant day, both of you."

Arielle walked to the door with him and opened it. "Thank you, my friend," she said, hugging him tightly. "I'll see you soon. Good-bye."

"Good-bye, Arielle." Quentin kissed her on the cheek, then walked the few steps down the hall to the staircase and descended.

* * *

After three weeks of caring for Hunter, his amazing progress gratified Arielle. During his recuperation time, they had become as they were before their marriage.

They were friends again.

Sitting beside his bedside Arielle prepared to begin reading another act from *A Midsummer Night's Dream.*

"Arielle!" Hunter growled.

"Please, Hunter, don't interrupt. It's impolite," she said, trying to keep a straight face, knowing it would annoy Hunter. Her activities weren't restricted and still the daily reading she did to break the monotony for Hunter was beginning to drive her mad. She could only imagine what it was doing to Hunter. She opened the book wider, balancing it on her knees. "Now, where was I?"

"Arielle Braxton!" Hunter fairly snarled, swinging his legs over the side of the bed. "I want out of this bloody bedchamber. I want to go into my own room. I want to bathe and dress and ride over my lands. And I want you with me."

All pretenses aside, Arielle laid the book on the table and stood as Hunter came to his feet. Hands on hips, she blocked his way to the connecting doorway.

"Really! If you think I'll allow that you're badly mistaken."

Hunter looked down at her, frowning. "Oh?" he said, hauling her against him. Covering her mouth with his, he kissed her deeply, fervently, leisurely. "Umm," he murmured. Abruptly, he stopped and stared ahead.

"W-what?" Arielle managed weakly, worried that he might be in pain, clinging to him to keep her knees from buckling beneath her.

"Nothing."

"Nothing?"

"I don't feel anything. Nothing at all."

Because she still felt their relationship wasn't what she wanted it to be, Arielle automatically assumed he meant he hadn't felt anything from her touch. The words sliced through her. How could he not feel anything when she wished to kiss him for hours more. "How dare you!" she said with indignation, pushing out of his embrace.

"I don't mean the kiss, my love," he said with a chuckle. "I'm sure the evidence of your power over me speaks for itself."

Arielle's gaze strayed to his private area, where a bulge protruded from his nightshirt. Heat burned her cheeks and Hunter's chuckle erupted into a laugh.

"How wonderful you look," he said. "However, I meant I am quite up to snuff. No pain of any kind." He caressed her cheek. "Send Vaughn up to assist me, my lady. Afterward, I'll have him saddle Blazer and the new mare I acquired for you."

"Then I'd better put myself to rights also. But you must promise me, if you experience any discomfort at all you will inform me."

Hunter laid his hand over his heart. "I promise."

Arielle watched him walk a little unsteadily to his bedchamber. Then, she crossed the room on her way to seek out Vaughn.

The letter she'd written to Hunter, twenty days ago, caught her eye and she picked it up off the floor under the bed, where it had lain unnoticed since this ordeal began. She smiled, deciding this would be the perfect time to write him a note and then slip both to him.

Hunter, my dearest love,

How can I tell you of the dread I felt at the thought of never having you in my life again? Of never feeling your warmth, your touch, or thrill to your kisses? Without you, I am a shell. Not even my passion for medicine would fill it, my dearest beloved.

I am yours always,
Arielle

Hunter watched in fascination as the letters slid slowly under his door. Chuckling to himself, he bent slowly and picked them up. His recovery was remarkable, he thought, wondering what he would have done without Arielle there.

He had been so incredibly unfair to her, when he should have been thanking daily whatever star had sent her to him.

Swallowing hard, he opened the first letter and read. She was a shell without him? His heart swelled with emotion at those words and he breathed in deeply. Whatever he'd been expecting to find in this envelope, it hadn't been this. Words of encouragement, perhaps. Even of friendship, but never anything expressing such heartfelt fear. And maybe even love.

But how could she love him? He hated that she knew his secrets. He hated that her father had used them against him. It left Hunter feeling unworthy of her. He owed her his very life.

Gazing at the second letter, he wondered what he'd find in it. He couldn't imagine this note touching him any deeper than the first one had. Without further ado, he carefully opened it.

Dearest Beloved,
I am compelled to tell you of my true emotions. I cannot describe the sheer ecstasy I feel in your presence. I've come to cling to your every word and I cherish our time together.
London was a marvelous balm to my soul. I want to please you as you have certainly pleased me. I want to be all things to you in all ways. Thank you for a most wonderful and auspicious holiday.

Your devoted Arielle

The words jumped out at him, piercing him like Cupid's arrow. By God, she pleased him in every way possible and he needed to let her know that. He needed to start treating her with more reverence. Treating her like the woman he loved.

The knock on the door signaled Vaughn's arrival to aid in his dressing.

"Come in," he instructed, hardly able to contain his impatience at having his ablutions completed. Afterward, a tour of the grounds would be the beginning of showing his love the whole of his estates.

40

For the rest of the afternoon, Arielle floated on a cloud. She walked along the stone pathway to the stream not far from the carriage house and gazed over the clear, placid water. Alder and birch trees shaded her from the sun. The smell of wildflowers sweetened the air and the activity of the workers in the distance punctuated the dreamy silence.

Hunter wasn't fully recovered, but things couldn't have turned out any better had she planned it. She smiled and watched as a pair of merlins landed on a tree branch, lingering for only a moment before taking flight again.

Tonight, everything had to be extra special—from her hair right down to her attire. Because tonight, she intended to reach into the core of Hunter's heart and repair the remaining damage to their relationship.

The shadows of evening dissolved into the dark of night as Hunter pulled out the chair to the right of his own. He gazed about the dining chamber in awe. The results stunned him.

The striped tan and green wallpaper and dark green woodwork had been washed down; the sixteen chairs brought down from the attic had been meticulously polished. Candles sparkled against the glistening brilliance of the two intricate crystal chandeliers. The draperies had been shaken out and rehung and now pooled upon the gleaming hardwood floor, the Axminster carpet hung out and freshened, then brushed.

It wasn't long before Arielle made her entrance into the dining room. Wine and water glasses, already filled at her instructions, stood before two place settings. Covered silver dishes sat on the sideboard, enticing aromas filling the air.

Finding everything to her satisfaction, she glided to the table as Hunter stood, her heart pounding with the cadence of a drumbeat. Tall and magnificent, there was a rakish air about him this evening. His gaze rested on the smooth, soft globes of her breasts, visible in the low-cut gown she had chosen. Images of his big hands upon her mounds as he caressed and tasted them rose in her mind. Her flesh prickled as though she were already back in his arms relishing more of his lovemaking.

Pasting a guileless smile upon her lips, Arielle leaned forward in her seat.

"I think you are most considerate to join me tonight, Hunter," she said softly, grasping his hand and squeezing it tenderly. "Considering the tiresome day you had."

"I wouldn't have passed up this opportunity no matter what."

Hunter's gaze feasted upon her lips again, then traveled back to the mounds of her breasts. She walked to the sideboard, the heat of Hunter's regard warming her. She lingered over the scallop and oyster dish, stole a bit of the stuffed artichoke and forcemeat, savored the scent of the pea soup with bacon and herbs, and considered forgoing everything else for a taste of the lemon pudding pie.

"Where should we place the tapestries and paintings, Hunter?"

For long moments after her question, silence ensued. Unable to temper her curiosity, Arielle turned and gazed at Hunter, only to discover him staring at her, hot intensity upon his features.

She swallowed, her throat suddenly dry.

"Did you hear me, Hunter?"

Color tipped into his cheeks. "Er, I'm sorry, my dear. I must confess my thoughts have a way of straying from their original subject." Straightening in his seat and reaching for his wine, he cleared his throat. "What were you saying?"

Arielle smiled as she prepared two plates of food. "Just that we should agree on where the tapestries and paintings should be hung. I think the study is an ideal place."

Hunter frowned as she placed the food in front of him. "The study?" he echoed, waiting while she returned to her own seat with her bowl. "One of the tapestries should hang over the fireplace in the drawing room. The other will go in my bedchamber."

She tasted her soup and nodded. "All right, my lord. This is why I suggested you help me in restoring the manor. Perhaps it would be wise if you suggested a place for the vases and paintings and—"

"Arielle," he interrupted, swallowing his food, "the tapestries carry a special meaning for me. They once belonged to my father. However, you may do as you wish with the other objects."

"I—I didn't know the sentiment they held for you, Hunter. I am glad I asked your advice. Did you have a close relationship with your father?" Arielle went on innocently, realizing she knew little about his family, other than the fact that they had been aristocrats.

"About as much as you have with yours," he snapped.

Ignoring his irritation, she laughed with abandon. "Absolutely close, then, my lord?"

Tasting his wine again, his look turned inscrutable. "Are you deliberately baiting me, madam?"

"No. Why would I?"

Hunter considered her carefully before lowering his gaze. He traced the rim of his glass with his finger. "Suppose I admitted to you that I never knew my father?" he asked quietly.

Arielle sat motionless. He posed the question without any inflection in his voice, but she knew it was of the utmost importance to him. She chose her answer carefully. "Even if such a thing were true, Hunter, you would still be the same man I married."

He digested her words and then nodded thoughtfully. "What exactly did you know about me on our wedding day?"

"Before I met you, I'd heard bits and pieces of your life. Tales of your exploits on the battlefield. I remember hearing of your sadness when your father died and then, a year or so later, you joined the army." She searched the vestiges of her memory for other facets, uncomfortable beneath his intensity. "I didn't hear much regarding *you.*"

"And who am I, Arielle? An easy mark? A gullible fool?"

"Of course not, my lord! You are simply a man, a powerful, virile man."

Hunter drained his glass. "Exactly what was your father's request? Why in God's name did you consent to his schemes?"

"I wouldn't call his need for money and the decision you two made that we marry a scheme, Hunter. As for my consent, I couldn't very well watch my father go to debtor's prison when I had the means to prevent that from happening."

"Marrying me was your means?"

"Yes," she answered softly. "At the time, I saw no other recourse than to do what my father asked of me."

"If you had to do it all over again, would you?"

"Would I marry you? Without hesitation. But not simply to please my father. I would do it because of the man that you are."

She hated to see the shadows of pain in his eyes and decided to change the subject. Knowing of her father's blackmail added to her doubt about ever forging an unhindered relationship with Hunter.

"I ordered the entire manor to be refurbished before any furniture was set out," Arielle explained, the animation in her face brightening her already sparkling eyes. "But I don't mind if the staff deviated from my original order. As a matter of speaking, I could have easily stopped them." Her fidgeting hands left tracks on the shining table. "I hope it is to your approval?"

He smiled, at loose ends. Her joy at the results of the hard work evident in the chamber appeared as deep as his pleasure and surprise. And as genuine. "It more than meets my approval," he answered. "In the years gone by, Arielle, I merely sat in here to eat."

Arielle's fingers touched the point lace of her bertha. "Thank you, Hunter," she murmured. Her succulent lips formed a moué and she regarded him with mischief. "So you did not capture your surroundings back then?"

"Hardly," Hunter responded, caught off guard by her charming flirtation, lambasted by her utter femininity. She had changed into a muslin dinner gown with a silk embroidered leaf pattern. Undoubtedly because it was the proper, perfect thing to do as a marquess's wife. He allowed his appreciation for her to show as his gaze slid downward before settling on her face. He gave her a pointed look. "But I can assure you, Arielle," he said huskily, "my surroundings were never as lovely as this. *Everything* in this room tonight is lovelier than I've ever seen it."

A blush stained her cheeks, but her stare became as assessing as his. She worked the muscles of her throat, at a loss for words, and he smiled again at their seductive play. But he didn't want doubts to intrude and mar the settled rhythm their marriage had fallen into because of his illness. He didn't want to prove that he was still the proud, unmovable ass of his youth. He wanted to show that he was the forgiving, battle-worn soldier of adulthood.

He took her hand into his own and pressed his lips against the white of her skin. "My compliments to you, my lady, for a superb job."

Uncertainty creased her lips and played in her eyes. Briefly, she tightened her hand in his, then removed it completely. "The staff is to be complimented, Hunter."

Her soft, carefully chosen words disquieted him further. He could very well give in to the urge to completely forget the way their marriage started, but what would become of them if anyone else ever discoverd the Braxton secrets? She had gone to great lengths to get his titles. Her father had even refused a fortune on Arielle's behalf. But if word ever got out about exactly how Hunter's family had acquired the precious titles, Arielle would no doubt be humiliated.

As long as the scandals remained secret, worthy of blackmail, she didn't care. But would she stand in Hunter's corner if everything were somehow to come out?

"I must speak to you, Hunter."

Hunter nodded at the urgency in her tone and leaned back, weary of his misgivings. "You have my full attention, Arielle."

She leaned forward and dropped her voice to a whisper. "I have been thinking about that family I once told you about that is in dire need. I—I was wondering, my lord, if you would be averse to me extending a helping hand?"

"In what way, Arielle? What is it you would like to do?" If she had asked him for the shirt off his back, he would have agreed to it.

"A small, *anonymous* donation, Hunter," she said in a rush. "Mrs. Beecham suffers from a wracking cough. Her six children are undernourished and the eldest, as you know, is with child."

"Yes, I recall. And what of Mr. Beecham? I don't believe you said."

"Deceased. Killed in a hackney accident a couple of years ago."

"A donation is all you're asking for?"

She considered his question then shook her head.

"What else?" he prompted.

"Your permission to continue their care, especially Maura's. She's only fifteen and is uncomfortable with Quentin. They are Quentin's patients, but Mrs. Beecham has allowed me to assume some responsibilities for her care."

"And if I agree to your continuing those responsibilities, then would Quentin remove himself?"

"No."

"And if I don't agree?"

Arielle shrugged. "I suppose I would finally learn the meaning of being dutiful to myself. Even if it didn't meet with your approval."

"Meaning you would defy my directive?"

"If I didn't agree with your directive and had the means to defy you, yes."

"What am I to do with you? You are quite a handful, aren't you?"

Arielle blinked. "Am I? I never heard such an opinion about me expressed, Hunter."

"Shocking."

Arielle laughed again and threw her napkin at him, which Hunter deftly avoided by tilting his head. "You are lampooning me, sir."

"Hardly. I neglected to tell you that while on our holiday in London, I met the Beechams and set aside a monthly stipend for them—"

In a heartbeat, Arielle shot out of her chair and rained kisses all over his face. "Thank you, my lord."

Unable to help himself, Hunter laughed. "You are an amazing creature, Arielle. You must be the one responsible for the gray in Stanford's hair."

Arielle joined him in laughter. "I'm afraid not, my lord. When he didn't need my involvement in one of his activities, he barely noted my existence."

His laughter died as she fell silent. Perhaps he had mistaken her reasons for marrying him. Stanford might have wanted his money and the prestige that having a daughter wed to a marquess afforded him, but Arielle needed an escape from her inconsiderate prig of a father.

Whatever Arielle's reasons for going through with the wedding didn't make it right. Now, he needed to remove the threat of further blackmail by Stanford. To do that, he needed the letter the viscount had in his possession.

"I suppose, Lady Savage, I have no choice but to agree to your demands. I will have my solicitor keep your identity a secret from Mrs. Beecham. As for you caring for Maura . . ."

"Yes?"

"I cannot stop you."

"Indeed," Arielle replied, not losing her animation. "And I thank you. Now that we've settled that, I noticed that you have many beautiful things, Hunter—"

"I believe now that we are married, you may include yourself as a possessor of those belongings."

"You are most generous," Arielle said, lowering her lashes and turning her attention to her food. For a moment, she chewed thoughtfully. "There was quite a lot of furniture in the attic. Did you purchase any of it yourself?"

"A few pieces," he said, pouring himself more wine. "But you're welcome to peruse the shops in London if you wish to buy more."

Arielle's sidelong look was unreadable. "I can assure you that once the furniture is all brought down and put in place, not even a nook will be exposed for more." She ate more of her food, then said, "I suppose you must have forgotten what's up there."

"Actually, Arielle, I don't know what's up there."

"I beg your pardon? How's that possible? Surely you would know your own belongings."

"You seem alarmed," he said with a chuckle. "It was previously my late uncle's—er, father's. I always meant to uncloak the mystery of his belongings."

Hunter hated what he'd almost let slip. He hated that his late uncle hadn't really been his father. That knowledge had helped to shape the man he had become. Not knowing much about his own sire had somehow robbed him of his true identity. He wasn't sure if his parents had been married or not at the time of his birth. And his uncle

Proctor had refused to talk with Hunter about the man who had stolen Roxanne's heart.

He supposed Arielle knew that truth, as well, but he didn't care to spread such tales himself—or expand upon them.

"You certainly do not suffer from an abundance of curiosity, Hunter," Arielle said good-naturedly, not commenting upon his change of wording if she'd noticed. "I would have scrutinized the attic long ago."

"Then hopefully you're curious enough for both of us, to compensate for my lack of inquisitiveness," Hunter said. "And you're free to explore at will."

"What if I should discover anything of importance, Hunter?"

Hunter shrugged, sure that all of his documents were secure in his study. He didn't believe that anything stored in the attic could hold any danger to him or his family. "Use your own judgment, Arielle. No need to notify me about each and every discovery. You can discern what's important and what's not."

"Of course, my lord." Arielle leaned back, satisfied at how the evening was progressing. Whatever had wrought the change in Hunter was most welcome. Tonight's interlude left no doubt that she wanted Hunter's love.

She smiled as he spoke again.

"Would you care for more wine?"

"Yes."

They fell into an amicable silence and Arielle refilled their glasses, then served the scallops and oysters along with the stuffed artichoke. She mulled over their conversation.

Hunter had mentioned an uncle and a father in one breath, as if he'd been covering a slip-up. And yet what man could mistakenly refer to his uncle as his father or vice versa, unless some great intrigue were taking place?

If she knew nothing else, she knew that Hunter had secrets. Secrets that were detrimental to him—and to her

now that she was his wife. Tonight, he'd tried to tell her
something.

Now, she had but to figure out why whatever she'd
known about him *before* their marriage was so important
to him at present. Important enough that her father had
blackmailed him.

Leaving Hunter to mull over some of Braxton Hall's
records, Arielle retired to her bedchamber much later.
Only moments after entering, she noticed a letter on her
turned-down bed. With happy anticipation, she hurriedly
opened it and began reading.

Dearest Arielle,

*I can hardly ignore my pounding heart when I
think of you. Or the wonder my eyes behold at sight
of you. My sweet Arielle, I do not want to be unhappy and yet I am.*

*There is much that stands between us. But I lack
the courage to rectify such ominous shadows. Because we are what we are, perhaps our problems
will never be solved. That aggrieves me. With such
a prospect, how will we ever know true love?*

*It's a durable fire, this true love, able to with-
stand the most formidable adversary. At risk of incarceration, you put yourself in peril to save my life.
The fire of gratitude for that act burns eternally in
my soul for you.*

*Although I have disparaged your ambitions, I was
surprised by the sheer joy I felt at your skill. Yet, I
am sorry to say, I still disapprove of such an aspi-
ration for my wife. However, it is with reservations
that I reluctantly lend you my support.*

*Arielle, my dear, I may not always be happy, but
I want to see you happy always. I've decided to
build you an infirmary right here on Braxton lands.
Perhaps then I will be able to see firsthand what*

*inspires such passion in you, for I realize that you
are not only determined, but somehow compelled to
lend your assistance to the sick and infirm.*

*You are to be commended for your compassion.
As soon as time permits, I will begin work on your
building. It would please me greatly if you won't try
to rush me. It will be started and finished in due
time, I promise. For I most rightly praise you for
your talent. I must end now, my sweet. I will place
this on your pillow 'til next time.*

*Yours forever,
Hunter*

Realizing tears were sliding down her cheeks, Arielle
brushed them away. Thrilling amazement went through
her at the thought of Hunter building her an infirmary.
Yet her heart twisted in pain. What made her husband so
very unhappy? She thought she knew what shadows stood
between them. Her father's blackmail. But what in God's
name did Thomas have to blackmail Hunter with?

Perhaps, if she confessed her love for him to him, he
would respond in kind.

"Arielle?" Hunter's voice floated through the closed
connecting door.

Hurriedly, Arielle folded the letter and placed it under
her pillow. "Yes, Hunter, do come in."

Hunter opened the door and stood in the doorway. His
smoldering gaze raked her. "I was hoping to persuade you
to come into my bedchamber. I want you tonight. I need
you to be close to me."

Without another word, Arielle rose off the bed and went
into his arms.

41

"I'm thinking her ladyship will be most pleased, my lord."

Hunter nodded at Vaughn's words, then gazed at the large building again. Against the light glimmering from the torches, the freshly whitewashed outbuilding, complete with new roof, windows, and doors, gleamed. The inside still had work yet to be done, but he'd promised Arielle an infirmary and an infirmary she would get. He only hoped she liked it. "I hope you're right, Vaughn."

Hunter paced the length of space in front of the building and then back again. The structure sat on the fringes of a stand of trees, atop a heather-clad hill that gave way to a rolling meadow. Still, the building itself was stark and cold. Though it would house the sick, Arielle liked warmth. "Adding a portico will be our next project after the inside is completed. On the morrow, borrow one or two grounds keepers from whatever they're doing for Arielle. She likes flowers, if what she has done around the manor is any indication. Have them add window boxes."

"Yes, my lord."

"In a couple of days or so, I will be unavailable. I'll expect you to oversee things for me during that time."

"If you'd prefer, my lord, I can take care of everything as I did while you and Lady Savage were away."

"No," Hunter said with a decisive shake of his head. "I want to be involved in the day-to-day activities of this whenever I am here. You and the men you hired did an excellent job. Which couldn't have been easy to do; judging from the sterling condition Braxton Hall is now in, Arielle kept everyone busy."

"That she did, my lord," Vaughn said with a pleased smile. "But we all managed just fine."

"Yes, you did," Hunter agreed. "I think we're finished here. You can head for Braxton Hall. I'll see you tomorrow."

"Yes, my lord."

Left alone, Hunter studied the building one last time, trying to gauge Arielle's reaction. He hadn't any idea how much the project meant to him. But he valued both their growing closeness and her remarkable healing knowledge, and he realized everything had to be just so before he allowed her to see it.

Out here, lost in the country, it was so easy to forget everything and believe the melting look in her sea green eyes. It was easy to remember that she said she'd marry him again, if she had it all to do over, because of the man that he was.

The more he thought about it, the more he realized that Arielle acted as if she'd known nothing of Thomas's demands. She'd acted as if Hunter and Thomas had come to an agreement to pay off Thomas's debts, and she'd gone along with it out of familial duty.

Thoroughly exhausted, he made his way to the manor. Reaching the entrance hall, he looked around proudly. In the month since they returned from London, Braxton Hall's restoration had advanced with amazing expediency. Inside, work was completed, and not much was left to finish on the grounds either. A fortnight more work on Arielle's infirmary would see her dream of caring for the sick and downtrodden come true. Arielle was even in the final stages of planning a fabulous dinner party to take place three days hence. The only thing left to do was send out the invitations. "Arielle?"

"My lord Braxton," Beatrice said, coming up behind him.

"Yes, Beatrice?"

She curtsied. "Her Ladyship is having a look-see in the attic, my lord."

"Really? I thought everything had been cleared out."

"Well, almost, my lord. But there are still a few items left, among which is the beautiful trunk my lady likes so well."

"A trunk? That's interesting. Thank you, Beatrice. I'll just go to the attic and find my wife."

"Yes, my lord," Beatrice said, then started back toward the kitchens.

Wondering exactly what drew Arielle to the trunk, Hunter went straightaway to the third floor. Given the cloudy, drizzly day, the light in the attic was scant, but he couldn't miss the beautifully carved trunk in the corner. An oil lamp sat there, and the flint with which to light it, but no Arielle.

Most convenient, Hunter thought, squatting down and lighting the lamp. An image of family secrets buried inside made his hands tremble. He dreaded the shameful tidings the trunk would reveal. Having no choice now but to see the matter through, he drew in a deep breath and raised the lid.

He frowned as the faint scent of lavender wafted into his brain. In surprise, he stared at the silver mirror, matching hairbrush and comb, and the other obviously feminine belongings. Several packets of envelopes, neatly tied together, sat beside some unbound ones in tidy stacks.

Hunter blinked, then picked up one of the untied letters. A chill danced along his spine and he glanced around, half expecting to see the owner of the pleasant scent. An owner who obviously wasn't his uncle.

He was losing his wits! No ghosts occupied the attic. Chuckling softly, he returned his attention to the letter and lifted it out of the envelope. He unfolded it and began reading.

Dearest Beloved,
Be wary, my darling, lest you lose your heart to me.

Love letters? Hunter quickly scanned the remaining words, then placed the aged parchment aside. Love letters.

Grabbing the other unbound envelopes out of the trunk, he read the letters one by one. There were never more than two paragraphs in a letter. The wordings were short and poignant—and very passionate.

He knew Proctor's penmanship. The letters were not in his uncle's handwriting and the contents of the trunk clearly belonged to a woman. But what woman? He'd always known his uncle to be a bachelor, although persistent rumor had it that his young wife had died in child-bed after delivering Proctor's stillborn son. But this had supposedly happened years before Hunter's birth, and the faded date on the letter stated the year as 1781. The year before Hunter was born.

Uncle Proctor had told Hunter that he was the son he'd never had. He'd adopted Hunter upon Roxanne's death and raised him as his own. Yet the letters and other contents of the trunk had to have significance. They must be letters from Proctor to his lost love. For some reason she must have returned them to him.

Hunter fingered the letters, his mind working. He struggled to remember an incident. A woman. Conversations about a deceased wife. *Anything* that would bring light to the mysterious trunk and its cache of love letters.

A sterling realization broadsided him. Upon his return from Waterloo, he had not been remaining out of sight just to restore Braxton Hall. He had been hiding more from the prying eyes of society.

He hadn't wanted to circulate amongst his peers and wonder when it would be discovered that the man the aristocracy knew as Hunter Braxton's father was actually his uncle. He couldn't bear to have it whispered that more than likely Roxanne had died birthing a son she had no father for.

Those discoveries would only lead to the most detrimental one of all. Yet he'd realized he'd actually enjoyed the company of Laurent Cabot and Douglas Shepperton.

It had given him a feeling of belonging and a sense of self. Which he mightn't have ever chanced had it not been for his marriage.

And now this new demand upon his tentative happiness. The demand that he confess all to Arielle. The demand for honesty. The demand for trust. But would he still have a marriage after he told Arielle of his past?

Maybe she'd confess her love to him. Perhaps she'd forgive him the stain on his family name. Or perhaps that was just wishful thinking.

He glanced at the letters again. How could he tell her of his anguish? If only he could put into words his shameful secret.

Hunter paused. Maybe that was the answer. If she accepted his secret, she'd come to him with open arms, without regret. Or she'd pen her disfavor to him and break his heart.

Arranging the letters as he'd found them, he closed the lid on the trunk, snuffed out the lamp, and went downstairs.

In his study he took out pen and paper.

He had no idea what he'd write, but if the letter would be cause for losing her, he refused to spoil her moment of glory at her party. Which meant he wouldn't give it to her until after the festivities.

42

Attired in the gold crepe gown Hunter had purchased for her, Arielle made her way to the parlor, where some of her guests were already assembled. She saw Hunter and smiled. Extraordinarily handsome, he looked every bit the king of his domain. His black evening attire made his appeal devastating and sinful. Proud to call him hers, she blew him a kiss and shook her head, the reason for his mood immediately clear. Julia Shepperton had him cornered, and whatever it was she spoke of, Hunter found most unappealing.

She and Hunter were finally hosting their long overdue dinner party. Their dining table had been set for twenty-two, space enough for her family and a few friends, including a very expectant Georgette, who hadn't as yet put in an appearance.

Going to where Hunter stood, Arielle slipped her arm through his. Julia's haughty gaze roamed over her. The epitome of womanly perfection in a midnight blue gown, the countess threw her black sash over her shoulder. Baring her teeth in a semblance of a smile, she curtsied to Arielle. "My dear little Arielle," she purred, "you look smashing. It seems country life agrees with you."

"Perhaps we should try it, sweet," Douglas Shepperton piped up, walking to join them when he saw Arielle. "I would kill to have anything agree with *you*." He turned to Arielle. "My dear, you are ravishing." He bowed low and kissed her hand.

"Still no ring, darling?" Julia sneered, raising her brow, undaunted by her husband's flippancy.

"My dear Julia," Hunter began with a tight smile, "since you're so much more concerned about a ring than Arielle is, I should tell you the diamond cutter I hired has informed me that he has begun work on the stone, just arrived from Africa. As soon as it's set to my specifications, I'll contact you so that you can see me present it to my wife."

Arielle swallowed a laugh. "How perfect."

Her eldest sister, Ellen, seated nearby, swept Arielle with a scornful glance and said, "You were always such a charmer, Arielle."

Arielle's humor faltered and if Hunter hadn't tightened his hold around her, she might have attempted to cover herself from her sister's glare. In Madame Sanfert's shop, the gown she now wore had seemed perfect for just such an evening as this, if a little daring.

Her breasts felt as if they'd spill free from the low-cut gown at any moment. The gold crepe chemise gown revealed and concealed, its gossamer satin slip caressing her body. Grecian sandal-slippers covered her feet. The combination was utterly feminine. Hunter's appreciative glances spoke volumes. Still, she felt exposed and vulnerable beneath her sister's disdain.

"You do look quite lovely," Ellen conceded into the silence.

"Thank you, Ellen," Arielle said quietly, wondering where Georgie might be when she noticed her sister Kate and her husband, Baron Sidney Collins.

"Arielle," Kate gushed, rushing up to embrace Arielle. "I've missed seeing you at the town house. I'm so glad that you finally decided to entertain!"

"I have missed going, Katie," Arielle confided. "Now that Braxton Hall has been put to rights, I will have more time to visit and have visitors. I would adore to have you over often."

Of all her sisters, she and Kate were closest. That wasn't to say she didn't enjoy Agatha's and Emma's company as well, because she did, but for the most part they were possessed of a serious nature that drove Arielle to distraction. Ellen, however, had always been jealous of Arielle, sometimes viciously so. As a result, Arielle had as little contact with her as possible. "You and Emma are welcome as well, Agatha."

"We would like that, Arielle," Agatha said shyly, from her seat where she sat with her husband, Dr. Morgan Wilford, near the window.

"Remember your other guests, Arielle," Julia commanded. "We have a lot to catch up on with you, darling."

"This is a beautiful house, Arielle," Emma greeted as she and her husband, Malcolm, walked in.

"Thank you. We put a lot of work into it," Arielle admitted, her voice inflected with pride at what she'd accomplished working alongside the staff and Hunter.

"This dinner is perfect to show it off," Kate said.

"The hunt also crossed my mind," Arielle commented. "Hunter has been away a long time, and a few well-placed invitations might reacquaint him with his old acquaintances and neighbors."

"Perhaps I will organize a hunt soon."

"That's a sterling idea, Hunter," Laurent said. "A hunt will give you a chance to get to know the family even better."

"Something I've been salivating to do, Laurent," Hunter commented dryly, "ever since the day I married Arielle."

Douglas laughed heartily and clapped Hunter on the back. "Arielle, please don't exclude me from that hunt. I want to witness the family bonding."

"Really, Douglas," Julia said in a pique, "maybe you *should* attend that hunt. You may learn something of family bonding."

"I'll get permission to attend," Douglas snapped, glaring at Julia.

Swinging her gaze from Douglas, Julia harrumphed. Her glance collided with Arielle's.

"I wonder what's delaying my father," Arielle said pointedly, watching with satisfaction as Julia's face reddened. With a swish of her skirts, she walked away from the group and went to the liquor table on the opposite side of the room.

Just then, Georgie came in on Eric's arm, followed by Quentin and Thomas. Their arrival halted further conversation.

"Well, you stragglers!" Arms outstretched, Arielle embraced Georgie. "Georgie, I'm so glad you are fit enough to come."

"Oh, pshaw, Ellie! I couldn't miss your first dinner party. Especially since I missed your nuptials."

Lord Eric Astor leaned down and planted a kiss on Arielle's cheek. "I couldn't keep her away, Arielle. I hope this isn't a mistake."

Georgette chuckled, her cheeks glowing with happiness. "He's such a worrywart. How can I go wrong with two healers on hand?"

"Two?" Arielle and Eric chorused.

"Ellie and Quentin, of course," Georgie clarified.

Arielle hugged Georgie again. "Thanks for the support. Let me greet my father and Quentin and then I'll introduce you to Hunter."

Soon everyone in attendance found themselves seated in the beautifully restored dining chamber. Happiness touched Arielle as she watched Hunter beam at each compliment on the restoration. Still, the hostility emanating from him toward her father was palpable. Nonetheless, Hunter exhibited amazing control and rigid politeness to Thomas.

Julia, on the other hand, flirted brazenly with both Thomas and Quentin, the only single men in attendance. If her intentions were to get a rise out of Douglas, she failed miserably on that account.

Arielle couldn't conceive of Douglas's obliviousness when everyone else was so aware of Julia's disgraceful display. Even Arielle's father seemed embarrassed and put off. It suddenly dawned on Arielle that it wasn't blindness on Douglas's part. He just didn't give a damn what Julia did.

Sympathy for both her father and Julia careened through her. Now that she looked closer, she saw they were both thoroughly uncomfortable. She really shouldn't have invited them to the same gathering. She wouldn't have been able to justify either omission, however. Douglas was one of Hunter's best friends and Thomas was her father.

"Ellie," Georgie began, "you were so thoughtful to hold dinner for my sake. Since that is the case, will you please have it brought out before I starve? I'm famished!"

Chuckles rippled amongst the guests.

They all finally sat for dinner and were served with the utmost speed and efficiency. Arielle gazed down at the gold-rimmed plate piled with mutton surrounded by spinach and topped with buttered cauliflower. Another plate revealed seasoned boiled potatoes and pickled beets on the side. Biscuits and freshly churned butter followed.

"You and Beatrice spent a lot of time in the kitchen today?"

"Aye, mum," Dora confirmed as Beatrice made her appearance holding a bottle of wine. "Beatrice left the mutton to me at my request and—"

"And you did just fine, Dora," Beatrice said as she began filling the wineglasses that had been placed on the table earlier. She lifted the pitcher of water from Dora's tray and topped the water glasses as well.

A stretch of silence ensued as the two women went about their duties.

Hunter noted the fresh, starched uniforms they wore

and the obvious pride they took in their work. He lifted
his glass in salute to Arielle, crediting her for the servants'
appearance.

Blushing, Arielle followed suit and picked up her glass
of wine, then took a delicate sip. "Papa, I know how you
like mutton. I hope you enjoy tonight's fare."

Thomas smiled for the first time that night. "Excellent,"
he said, raising a forkful of lamb.

"I must say this was worth coming out for," Ellen commented, swallowing her own bit of lamb.

Arielle merely smiled at her sister.

"Um," Quentin said, drawing everyone's attention. "I
know Morgan will be interested to know what a capable
healer Arielle is."

"Quentin!" Hunter rumbled.

"I'm sorry, my lord," Quentin said with a shrug. "But
I know you are as proud of Arielle's achievement as I
am."

"What is it?" Georgie exclaimed.

"It's wonderful," Quentin continued. "She performed
emergency surgery on Hunter and saved his life!"

For a moment, Quentin's announcement met with
stunned silence. Then, everyone erupted into conversation
at once.

Hunter watched the disbelief on his guests' faces. In
that moment, he also saw the respect mark those same
faces which had so disdained Arielle in the past. He never
loved her more than at that moment, for she handled all
the accolades with dignity and aplomb.

Douglas cleared his throat. "What a treasure you've
found, my friend," he said in a serious tone.

"I'm hoping his lord and ladyship like gooseberry pie?"
Beatrice walked in, interrupting any further comment.
"It's what Dora and me will be serving for dessert."

Hunter exchanged glances with Arielle, his mouth pulling into a slight frown of distaste. She covered her own
mouth with her hands and he winked at her, grateful for

the interruption, even if he did hate gooseberry pie.

"Gooseberry pie is my favorite, Beatrice," he said, dissembling for this moment, unwilling to lose the humorous moment. He was also sure that Arielle would make it known not to prepare it ever again. "And you, Arielle?"

Arielle released the laugh she'd been holding in. "Just what I was hoping for. I hope everyone else is in accord." Everyone nodded in agreement. "Then, I'll ring the minute we're finished this course."

"Yes, mum," Dora said happily, following Beatrice back toward the kitchen.

"What do you say we make our escape right after we finish this course?" Arielle asked Georgie in a dramatic whisper, once the servants made their departure.

Georgie giggled. "You're horrible, Lady Savage!"

"Am I to understand that you detest gooseberry pie as much as Georgie does?" Eric asked with a mischievous grin.

"Probably more so," Arielle acknowledged, picking up her glass and tasting the wine again. She looked at her scowling husband. "Although I don't think it's as much as Hunter. So, Lady Astor, are we in agreement that we should leave *before* they come in search of us?"

"Certainly not! We shall sit through this entire fiasco. If you don't have enough control over your staff to keep them from preparing a dessert that gives you the chills, then you must suffer the consequences."

"I'll remember that," Arielle said glumly, before she and Georgie shared laughter.

The leisurely meal lasted another hour, and, not long after it ended, Georgette and Eric departed, leaving Arielle bereft of a true friend. She conceded that after Quentin's revelation of her medical accomplishment, however, she'd gained a new respect from everyone. Even Thomas appeared to have accepted that her dream hadn't been a frivolous one. The men hadn't yet retired to the drawing room for after-dinner liqueurs and cigars. It appeared as if they wouldn't, because most of her family seemed ready to depart.

"Don't look so forlorn, Arielle," Julia snapped, not long after Georgie took her leave. "The woman put herself at risk as it was, coming to your party."

"Must you always be so logical, Julia?" Kate asked, annoyed.

"Well, someone has to remind our little sister that she has other guests," Ellen put in sarcastically.

"Well," Agatha began in her quiet way, "Georgette isn't the only one to beg off. Arielle, I have a wicked headache, darling. I'm afraid I must leave as well."

"Hunter, it has been a long evening. Why don't you and the other gentlemen retire to your drawing room. Vaughn has brandy and cigars waiting for you."

Thomas came to his feet. "I'm afraid I must pass, Hunter. I came with Quentin, and he appears ready to depart."

"Please forgive my early departure, Arielle, Hunter," Quentin said, having also stood. "But I have a patient to see to before I retire to my bed tonight."

"I understand, Quentin," Arielle said, surprised that Thomas would cross the room with Quentin, let alone the countryside.

Douglas joined the group at the entrance door, and cleared his throat. "Dr. DeVries, my wife appears peaked. Would you object to escorting her back to town?"

An audible gasp escaped Julia.

"That is," Douglas continued, sweeping his wife with a cold look, "if Lord Stanford doesn't mind."

Arielle gulped down an astonished breath, as stunned as everyone else. Her only thought was that the earl of Pembishire knew his wife had cuckolded him with her father and he would call Thomas out for it.

"Lord Pembishire!" Thomas snarled.

Or it could be the other way around, Arielle thought, near panic.

"The carriage belongs to Dr. DeVries," Thomas continued. "I can only abide by his decision. However, if it were left up to me, I would insist Lady Pembishire depart as she came. With you."

Douglas chuckled without humor. "Very well, Stanford. The lady shall indeed depart with me."

Uncertain what to do, Arielle embraced her father. "Good night, Papa. Have a pleasant journey."

"Hunter," Douglas said, holding out his hand, "I'll see you in the city at White's." He grabbed Julia's hand. "Come along, my lady."

Meekly, Julia went to stand beside Douglas, her face chalk white. "Arielle," she said in a small voice, "you've been a very gracious host. Thank you for inviting me . . . us."

"It was a pleasure having you both, Julia. Please take care." Arielle tempered the urge to embrace the countess. The pity she felt for Julia almost overwhelmed her. Douglas had succeeded in thoroughly humiliating his wife, although she'd brought it on herself with her earlier disregard of him.

In moments, everyone else crowded the door, wraps and coats in hand. After a few minutes of hugs, kisses, and praise, some false, others genuine, Arielle found herself alone with Hunter.

"All in all, my lady, I think it went quite well."

"Hunter, it was horrible!"

Hunter lifted her up and swung her around, then planted a kiss on her lips. "Yes, but it's over."

"There's nothing amusing about it, my lord," Arielle lamented. "Julia and my father have been found out. My sisters . . . well, they will never change—"

"You worry too much, sweetheart. Next time, plan your guest list more carefully. Make sure to include Georgette at all functions. I really like her."

Arielle laughed. "Well, perhaps something went right after all."

"And don't forget your partner in medicine, Dr. De-Vries. He has turned out to be quite likeable." Still holding her, Hunter bent his head and slanted his mouth over hers. "Now, my lady, can I persuade you to put the festivities behind you and accompany me to my bedchamber?"

Arielle smiled and took his hand in hers as he set her back on her feet. "As you wish, my lord."

43

My Dearest Beloved,
I sought you in my dreams and found you in my
soul. I was born to be yours. And now my heart is
lost in a maze of love as I go madly about seeking
the heart of my true love. With open arms and open
heart, you gave me my reason for being. I crave
your kisses, my angel. My heart beats with the ca-
dence of desire for you. As I sleep, I dream only of
you and remain,

Your devoted servant

Arielle sighed, deeply shaken. She wished Hunter
thought of her in such a loving, poetic way. She kept
telling herself that he loved her. Her life should be perfect.

Her infirmary was nearly completed. She was the wife
of one of the wealthiest nobleman in the realm, whom she
adored.

A week had gone by since her party and she'd missed
reading the letters. She and Hunter had been invited to
Kate and Sidney's estate two days after the dinner party,
then to Quentin's parents for afternoon tea. It seemed
everyone wanted to reciprocate her and Hunter's invitation.

Weariness had already set in at just the thought of the
myriad balls and parties that they would attend in the
coming week, but she was determined to see Hunter back
in society's fold again.

Even if she had to skip a few days of reading the letters. And even if she thought she must be losing her mind, finding something vaguely familiar about the handwriting in this letter that she hadn't noticed before. She just couldn't discern what it was. She shouldn't waste her time reading the letters of strangers, yet they drew her to them. Of all the letters she'd read, this one touched her the most.

She put it back inside the envelope, noticing how much fresher the letter appeared than the envelope. She studied it, searching for a date, looking for any clue explaining why this one struck such a chord within her.

She could write something like that to Hunter. Something from the heart. Something that would reach deep into his soul and show how much she truly loved him.

> *Dearest Hunter,*
> *I thirst for your kiss and ache for your touch. I crave your wit and cherish your soul. I am beguiled and bewitched and honored to know you. Keep me in your heart always.*
>
> *Arielle*

Her heart thumping, Arielle left the note in plain view for Hunter to see. He always went to the study before retiring. Hopefully, he wouldn't overlook this.

Arielle had been asleep last night when Hunter retired. Upon awakening this morning, Dora had informed her that he was again at the infirmary. She carefully looked around, and sound disappointment hit Arielle at not finding a response to her letter.

Dejected, she completed her morning routines and returned to the attic and read the few remaining letters, deciding to join her husband later at the infirmary.

In the attic, she went through her usual ritual of lighting her candles and the oil lamp and lifting the letters out of her beautiful trunk. Frowning at the arrangement of her letters—she swore they'd been arranged differently—she decided to tell Hunter all about it and have the trunk moved into her bedchamber. Shrugging away the oddity, she started to open an envelope, but was interrupted.

"Beggin' your pardon, mum," Dora called from the bottom of the stairs to the attic.

"Y-yes, Dora?"

"There's a messenger from Dr. DeVries waiting to see you."

Arielle jumped to her feet. "Quentin?"

"Aye, mum. Says it's urgent. Maura Beecham just died in childbed."

Without further ado, Arielle rushed downstairs and summoned Hunter. She explained to him what had happened and, immediately, Hunter prepared them for a trip to the city.

All things considered, Portia Beecham was handling the loss of Maura remarkably well. Arielle made this private observation three days later, as she and Hunter stood in the Beechams' hovel on a cold, rainy morning after having left the simple burial. As usual, the rest of the children had scattered to the four winds after their sister was laid to rest, leaving Tory and Portia to return to the house with Hunter and Arielle alone.

The moment Tory had seen her this morning, he ran into her arms, throwing his own thin ones around her neck in a heartfelt hug. The child was still small for his age, but Quentin was right—the money Hunter was sending had done a world of good.

The house glowed with the light of extra candles and a small fire blazed in the hearth. Mrs. Beecham and Tory had put on some weight and the mourning clothes they wore might have been cheaply made, but they were new.

Standing in the eerily quiet house now, Hunter grasped

Portia's hand, surprising Arielle as much as his offer to come and pay their respects.

"You have our deepest sympathy, Mrs. Beecham," Hunter said.

Swallowing hard as tears gathered in her eyes, Mrs. Beecham gave him a watery smile. "Thank ye, milord. I only wish there was somethin' I could have done. Dr. DeVries did everythin' in his power and still it wasn't enough."

"Is there anything we can do for you now?" Arielle asked, wondering what, besides time, would ease her pain.

Removing her hand from Hunter's grasp, Portia went to the sofa and sat. "I had intentions of accepting your invitation to move Maura, her babe, Tory, and the others onto your estate, my lady. But now, what's the use? She's gone, so I'll stay."

A knock prevented Arielle's response to that emotionless statement.

"Answer the door, poppet," Arielle instructed Tory, releasing the child's hand.

When he did, Quentin stood on the other side.

Quentin paused on sight of Hunter, his hesitation clear. "Hello, Hunter. Good of you to come."

"Quentin," Hunter greeted. "Arielle and I were on the verge of trying to convince Mrs. Beecham to return with us to Braxton Hall. Perhaps you can add your shilling's worth and assist us."

"Hunter, that is most generous of you," Quentin responded.

"Mrs. Beecham," Arielle said, walking to where Portia sat dejectedly. "There's a new infirmary on the estate and there are several empty cottages that I know of. You must come for the sake of the other children and yourself." Tears slid down the woman's cheeks, but she remained otherwise unresponsive. Arielle took her into her arms. "I can't begin to imagine your pain because I have never suffered such a loss. I was so young when my mother died; any grief I felt is only a vague memory. But Maura meant a lot to me as well and I cannot express my deep pain at her loss. Yet we all have to go on—"

"But she is here," Portia said softly.

"Yes, she is," Hunter said. "Her presence is everywhere in here because of the times you spent together. Yet she lives in your heart. And as long as you are alive, she will go wherever you go."

"Portia," Quentin spoke up. "Listen to them. On behalf of Arielle, I implore you to take the offer up."

"All right, ye all win. I will go."

"You won't be sorry," Arielle promised. "Now, relax yourself and Tory and I will prepare a meal for us to enjoy. In the meantime, Hunter and Quentin will keep you company."

Standing with purpose, Arielle smiled sweetly at Hunter. Amused incredulity played about his features and he shook his head in resignation. As she passed by, he leaned down and whispered in her ear,

"Come tonight, I will show you just how unhappy I am with your request, my lady."

"Come tonight, my lord," she whispered back, "I will simply have to make you forget your unhappiness."

She glided away, the passionate promise she'd made hanging between them.

Moments after Arielle climaxed, Hunter groaned one final time as he exploded inside her, trembling in his release, his being weightless and sated. Breathing heavily, he rolled over onto his side and drew her into his arms.

Her passionate surrender never ceased to thrill and amaze him. Each time they made love, she gave more and more of herself, leaving him powerless in the wake of her response. The primordial, wild abandon she showed in bed enamored and delighted Hunter.

He was convinced Arielle knew nothing of his background and he wondered if she had read his letter. When she reiterated the reason she'd married him, all misgivings of her character was removed, creating an almost perfect union.

They had passed a singularly depressing evening at Portia Beecham's house. The grief that Mrs. Beecham had held inside was starting to pour out `of her, and in an attempt to cheer her, Quentin and Arielle went out of their way to talk about the times they'd spent together with the family when Maura was alive.

"I've been thinking about hosting another dinner party while we are in London, Hunter."

Arielle's voice surprised him. He thought she'd fallen asleep. "Another dinner party?" he echoed.

"Yes. A small one. I'm not sure if my sisters and their husbands are in town, but, if they are, I'd like to invite them again."

"Your father as well, I take it?" Silence met his question. Hunter supposed she mulled over how best to get his compliance. But he wouldn't argue the issue. It would only be one evening. "If that is your wish, my lady, then by all means do so."

"What is it you have against my father?" Arielle asked quietly, hoping he would open up to her in person.

Something in her tone sparked a thread of intuition in him and he gazed down at her. "Toward me, he isn't the kind, loving man you know and admire. He—"

"Is a blackmailer."

Hunter went still at her bitter, angry words. She removed herself from his arms, threw the covers aside, and got out of bed. Moonbeams cast a silvery glow about her, shimmering off her golden hair and pale skin. She paced, as he often did in his agitation.

"I know all about it, my lord. I can't tell you the shame I felt and still feel at his tactics."

"But you had nothing to do with Thomas's blackmail."

"Simply by agreeing to his demand, I am guilty. I should have questioned him then, instead of now. It would have made our lives so much easier."

"I'm sure it would have."

Arielle had been through a lot, so Hunter couldn't fault her for speaking her mind. He would work to make her happy and erase the pain he had caused her in the beginning as well.

Getting out of bed, he went to her and gathered her in his arms. "Arielle, we *are* married now and I don't regret our troth."

"Nor do I, Hunter, and I promise to make the best of our life together."

Arielle rested her damp head on his chest.

His body hardened as he remembered just why she perspired. "I'd also like to invite the earl of Pembishire and his wife," he said hoarsely, the scent of sex hanging in the air adding to his rising desire.

Arielle groaned audibly and pressed her body into his, placing a hot kiss in the hollow of his neck. "We can't very well not invite them. In spite of everything, they are our friends. At least Douglas is." Flush against the wall, she pulled Hunter into her arms and slanted her mouth over his.

"No fair, my lady," he said, after the kiss had ended, raising her up and pulling her legs around his waist. His manhood rested at her slick, scalding entrance. "You like Douglas. I detest Julia."

"I have a story to tell you about Julia that might lead you to rethink your notion, Hunter," Arielle whispered. "So tolerate them both for that evening. I'll make it worth your while." To demonstrate her gratitude, she tightened her arms around him and pushed herself forward, impaling herself to the hilt of his throbbing sex.

"God, Arielle!"

"Tell me," she commanded, her hand reaching between them and massaging his heavy sac.

"Invite anyone you want."

With that declaration, he closed his mouth over hers and showed her the same amount of passionate mercilessness that she had just shown him.

* * *

After several enjoyable weeks in London, where Arielle and Hunter attended a whirlwind of dinners, teas, and plays and hosted their own dinner party, they returned to Braxton Hall with the Beechams and Quentin DeVries in tow.

In London, they had been the golden couple, the events leading up to their abrupt wedding shrouded in romantic lore and heartfelt mystery. Hunter knew when the Season finally began in several weeks, the uproar that had started with their venturings into society would turn into pandemonium. Even his sisters-in-law and their husbands were likeable sorts, if one were gracious enough to overlook Ellen Cabot.

Unbelievably, Hunter actually looked forward to the commotion. He had developed a friendship with Laurent Cabot and Sydney Collins, Kate's husband, and had reestablished his acquaintance with Douglas Shepperton. Julia Shepperton fell into the same category as Ellen, but Arielle managed them quite nicely.

He could have almost called himself happy. Quentin helped Arielle set up and arrange the equipment for their practice at the infirmary.

Since their return to the country, Arielle spent most of that time in the company of Quentin. Hunter had looked in on them three times yesterday and twice today. Each time, he found them arguing some point about where the books should be placed on the shelves, how many attendants would be needed, and who would work to oversee the place in Quentin's absence.

The conversations thoroughly bored Hunter, so, after a few minutes, he left. From the way things sounded, his wife intended to make this a well-staffed, accredited place that was within the boundaries of the law, which meant she wouldn't be able to "practice" there. The knowledge intrigued him and he couldn't wait to see what she had in mind.

At loose ends and refusing to look in on her again, Hunter recalled the letters stored in the attic. Without second thought, he made his way to the third floor and paused at the entrance. Next to the empty oil lamp sat a half-burned candle. Going to the trunk, he realized Arielle had been up there again, reading the ardent letters.

He smiled, thinking of all the ways they'd made love. Those letters were a food to her passionate nature, he was sure. For all the wonders it did, she could have the trunk brought to her bedchamber and read them all day.

Opening the lid, he rifled through the contents of the trunks more carefully. The mirror, comb, brush, and a little jewel box, all tarnished and silver, still lay there. Next to those things were the letters, stacked to one side in two piles. This time they were all unbound, with one stack being shorter than the other. Still, their neatness made it hard for him to discern which stack had been read.

Not wanting to upset her arrangement, Hunter decided to read from the higher stack. He picked up the other items and replaced them before disturbing the letters. When he came to the jewel case, however, he thought better of it.

It was a tiny, intricately designed box, and his curiosity got the best of him. He sprang the latch and the lid flew open. Inside sat the most exquisite ring he had ever seen.

A white pear-shaped diamond was set in the center; several smaller diamonds encrusted a thin yellow gold band. In the sparse light of the attic, the ring sparkled like the sun's reflection on a dewy rose. It was obviously an expensive item, worthy to give to a cherished loved one.

Hunter didn't know if his uncle had had a secret affair and had bought the ring for his lady love. The ring, however, was small enough to fit Arielle's tiny finger; and Hunter did love and cherish her.

Taking it out of the jewel case, he placed it in his trouser pocket, then he laid the case back on top of the mirror, brush, and comb he'd already placed inside. Unable to put off reading a letter any longer, he got an envelope from his chosen stack, extricated the letter, and began reading.

> Dearest Beloved,
>   Your angelic face puts sunshine in shady places and warmth in my heart. Tomorrow we meet again. We will share our bodies, molded together as one, fashioning the pleasures borne of our forbidden love. I love you and will always hold your loving heart close to my own. 'Til we meet again, I remain,
>
>   Your devoted servant.

Such passion. So unlike the reserved man he remembered his uncle Proctor to be. But if it wasn't his uncle who wrote the letters to his dearest beloved, who then had?

Searching for answers, Hunter rummaged through the trunk again, careful not to disturb the letters, but found nothing else inside to give him a clue.

He quickly read over the letter again.

Borne of our forbidden love.

Forbidden love?

Proctor had kept most people at arm's length and had a no-nonsense overbearance that left most people wholly frustrated or completely intimated. Proctor Braxton, the marquess of Savage, wouldn't have involved himself in a forbidden love.

Given that, what would make Uncle Proctor keep these things? There were only two people in the world that mattered to the man: Hunter himself and Proctor's sister, Roxanne, Hunter's mother, whom Proctor often described as willful and headstrong, and the rest of the world knew as sweet and gentle. She was a woman ruled by passion, Uncle Proctor had fondly complained, instead of practicality.

"My God!" Hunter whispered, his insides turning cold.

Forbidden love! Who else could these things have belonged to except his mother? There was no other reason that Proctor would have kept them.

He regarded the trunk with reverence and awe. He had never known Roxanne, but these were her things. Even though the letters confirmed his belief that he had been born a bastard, they also attested to the fact that he had been created out of love.

He fingered the ring in his pocket, its discovery that much more significant now that he realized it had belonged to his mother.

Needing to know more, he went back to the trunk and read some of the letters at random. All of them began with *dearest beloved* and concluded with *your devoted servant*. They left positively no clue to the identity of the writer or recipient. With each one he read, however, there was no mistaking the love they bore each other.

If the woman in question was Roxanne, then the writer had to have been his father. But how could that be? Surely, in the years Hunter was maturing, his uncle would have mentioned that he had keepsakes from Hunter's parents in his possession.

His mind in turmoil, Hunter dropped the lid on the trunk and stood. When he'd first discovered the trunk, he hadn't taken as much time to inspect it, but now its intrigues fascinated him. Uncle Proctor couldn't have let this languish all these years without telling Hunter, if the trunk had been Roxanne's. He wouldn't have.

Pinching the bridge of his nose, Hunter looked at his pocket watch. The time had gotten away from him. Arielle's return from the infirmary with Quentin was imminent, so Hunter decided it was time to start back downstairs.

Unanswered questions bombarded his thoughts. Yet there was no doubt in his mind that Dearest Beloved and Devoted Servant were his parents. His confusion now centered around his uncle's reasoning. Why had Uncle Proctor stored the letters without Hunter's knowledge? At

some point, he could have alerted Hunter to the fact that
they were there.

All the letters he'd read reflected in some way his feelings for Arielle and paralleled his emotions. The writer
and recipient of the letters were obviously very much in
love and it was also obvious that their love was kept secret
from everyone else while they were alive. Their beautiful
letters were the glue that bonded them together, despite
opposition from others.

Hunter decided that he, too, would let his letters make
known his love for Arielle. His uncle's words came back
to him about Roxanne, as if the man stood there and whispered in Hunter's ear.

Passionate, willful, and headstrong. Like Arielle.

He'd write his wife a letter. He indeed had much to
say.

44

My Dearest Beloved,

You have waylaid my heart with your exquisite charms. Your eyes, like the stars of a cool twilight, scatter my wits to the heavens. Yet you are unaware of my turmoil.

I want to feel you beneath me, quivering with pleasure, and giving me the same. I want to relish your softness, taste your sweetness. I need you, sweet one. Take me into your heart and say you love me as I love you.

There is much to be said to you, my dearest beloved, but my courage yet deserts me. My sweet jewel, I have seen the love that shines in your eyes. And I know it shines for me, something my ragged soul desperately clings to.

My darling, I long to hear you whisper you love me. Nothing else can equal those words from your lips. This mysterious thing called love fills my heart with profound joy. I love you, my angel, my love. My dearest beloved.

> *To the love of my life, I remain,*
> *Your devoted servant*

Pressing the letter to her breasts, Arielle sighed. Such great love. Such devotion. She knew Hunter loved her. If only . . .

She halted her thought. She wouldn't linger on "if

only." That her husband carried a tendresse for her had become evident in his actions. During the day, he could barely see to his own work for looking in on her and Quentin. He made it a point to have dinner with them, even if he was grimy and dirty from some repairs he involved himself in at a tenant's house.

On those occasions, more often than not, he had Tory in tow. A few times, the other four Beecham boys and Mrs. Beecham had come to dine with them as well. Arielle knew he made those overtures to the family for her sake.

And, in the quiet of night, when everyone else was settled, she and Hunter lay in a haven of love, sequestered in his bedchamber until the light of morning crept in and the process began all over again.

Love for her shouldn't have been long in entering Hunter's heart. Yet he still held something of himself back, as if he were afraid to get too close to her. The thought frightened her immensely. She hoped she wouldn't have to settle for his kind regard toward her for the rest of her life.

With a sigh, Arielle took up another letter.

Dearest Beloved,

Words cannot express the pride and joy in my heart at your good tidings. I'm going to be a father! We must prepare for marriage with all due haste. Come to me, my love, so we can plan without interference from our families.

I belong to you, my darling, and you belong to me. Forever. I love you. I love our child. Until we meet, I remain,

Your devoted servant

Brushing away a tear, Arielle smiled. She hadn't realized she was weeping, but the letters always touched her to the core—this one especially. The devotion her lovers bore each other had created a new life. Their love was ultimate and eternal. Through the child, two great souls had merged as one and lived on. Somewhere, someplace, their legacy lived, a greater person for having had such parents.

If she had learned anything from the letters besides how to express herself intimately, it was what a rarity it was to find true love. She wished she'd discovered the couple's identity, but it seemed as if it wasn't meant to be. She had read only half the letters so far, however, so maybe there was hope yet.

"Arielle," Hunter began as they sat in the parlor later that evening, having after-dinner liqueurs.

Hearing his cross tone, Arielle giggled. She had wanted to expire in humor a half hour ago when dessert had been served. The crestfallen look of distaste on his face had truly been priceless.

"Arielle . . ."

Laughing harder, Arielle raised her hand in protest. "I know what you're going to say, Hunter. But I merely forgot to tell Beatrice and her assistants about the gooseberry pie."

"I hope you enjoyed it, you little witch."

Arielle shrugged, sipping her sherry. She eyed him innocently. "It was palatable, for a change. And you? How was the forkful you tasted while Dora and Beatrice watched over us?"

Hunter laughed. "I see you're enjoying this."

"You sent them away, Hunter," Arielle reminded him, another giggle escaping her. "They didn't see you dispose of their work so thoroughly. Now, they'll think you enjoyed it and will take it upon themselves to serve it often."

Drinking from his brandy snifter, Hunter frowned at her.

"All right, all right," Arielle conceded quickly. "I promise I won't forget to have Dora take it off the menu."

"May I have your word on that, my lady?"

Arielle saluted him. "You have, sir!" she barked out.

"You are a bloody hellion, you know that?" Smiling sadly, Hunter absently traced his fingers along the outline of the glass, a touch of sadness spreading across his features. "How does it go at the infirmary?"

"Wonderful, Hunter. I'll always be grateful to your generous consideration of my needs. Of my dream," she added with enthusiasm. "I may never become a licensed physician, but you've given me the next best thing. If I haven't said it before, thank you. It's all too much."

"And how's Quentin working out? His absence is quite notable tonight. Was there a rift between you?"

"Of course not. He has returned to London for the weekend. Were it not for Quentin's presence at Hunter's Haven—"

"Where?"

"Hunter's Haven, the infirmary, my lord. Now, please don't interrupt me—"

"You named your infirmary after me?"

"You're still interrupting, Hunter," Arielle chastised, draining her glass and standing in one motion. Grabbing Hunter's nearly empty snifter, she went to the liquor table and refilled their glasses. "Now, where was I?" she said, handing Hunter his drink and then returning to her seat. "Oh, yes. Dr. DeVries is doing an enormous amount of work. Without him, the task would be difficult."

"I'm glad he consented to work with you."

"Hunter, you thought of everything, even down to the large coach you've provided for transporting patients from London. Two are set to arrive tomorrow. And if Mrs. Beecham is any indication, the country air and the proper nourishment they get from the infirmary will do wonders for them."

Flexing and unflexing the muscles in his arms, Hunter clenched his teeth, then sighed. "I've noted you've spent all your time at the infirmary."

"Well, I'm needed there," Arielle responded neutrally.

"After all, we've only just been opened three weeks. I don't mean to neglect you, my lord, if that's what you're getting at."

"Of course you don't, my darling. Anyway, you make up for your absence in my arms at night."

Lowering her head, Arielle fluttered her eyelashes, casting a half-lidded flirtatious look at her husband. She drank from her glass, then licked her lips to remove the remnants of the sherry, allowing her tongue to linger as her gaze met his. "Don't speak so loud, my lord," she whispered throatily. "The servants might hear."

"Heaven forbid," Hunter mocked, sprawling his long legs before him in masculine carelessness, the swell in his trousers easy to discern by his position.

Her gaze lingered upon his growing hardness, wet heat pooling between her thighs. Agitated, she finished her sherry, warmth rushing through her body.

"Getting back to the subject I'd begun, sweetheart," Hunter murmured, his voice as smooth and galvanizing as hot molasses curling around her belly. "You must have completed your chores in the attic, since you have not been up there in a while."

Her thoughts on something far more pleasurable than the contents of the attic and moments away from closing the doors to engage in it, Arielle straightened in surprise.

"Oh, that," she responded, belatedly realizing Hunter had referred to her as "my darling," an endearment written in one of the recent letters. Her heart pounded all over again and the dream of "if only" returned. "As I've said, I've been preoccupied with the infirmary. However, there are things up there that still need sorting."

"No doubt there are. When were you last up there?"

"After Quentin left this afternoon, I latched down the clinic and mucked about a little in the attic."

Hunter straightened in his seat. "This afternoon?"

"Yes," Arielle answered, breathless at his sudden interest. "Would you have cared to accompany me?"

"Perhaps another time. Oh, I almost forgot to mention

that there are some forms on my desk to be filled in for medical supplies—"

"The infirmary's first documents!" Arielle said gleefully, genuinely happy.

"You can fill them out later. Now, milady, it's time to replace thoughts of your infirmary with thoughts of your poor neglected husband."

Arielle chuckled. "As you wish, my lord," she said, going into his arms.

*H*unter, my dearest,
    Thoughts of you brighten my dreams by the light they make. I marvel at what is transpiring between us. You are the wonder of my days and the joy of my nights. Let us find a common ground, my love, to come together.

Your devoted Arielle

Hunter read the short note left on his bed, wholeheartedly agreeing with the written sentiments. Arielle had become the wonder of his days and the joy not only of his nights but of his life. Preparing to depart the chamber, he looked at Arielle. His sleeping angel. He wouldn't waken her. Their night had been filled with long, lazy lovemaking. She was probably tired.

As he departed the chamber, however, he vowed to bring himself and Arielle together in a common . . . no . . . noble ground.

45

Dearest Beloved,
   My love for you has turned my normal activities wrong side out. I know that you love me as much as I love you. But I fear to lose that love if you knew of my background. I have reason to believe that I am illegitimate. Some nobleman's by-blow.
   My only love, the name I have given to you is not even mine to give. I pray this revelation doesn't cause you to detest me. I love you madly and as dotty as it may seem, I would whither like a rose on a bush if you left me. With all my love, I wait your decision. As always, I remain,

Your devoted servant

For long moments, Arielle held the letter. When the tears blurring her vision blocked the words on the paper, she folded it and put it back inside the envelope. She knew. Everything was becoming clear. Her marriage. Hunter's anger. She loved him and would stay with him under any conditions.

He hadn't known how to approach her with such painful information. She must be careful how she responded to him.

Deciding to read only one more and leave before someone came in search of her, she opened another envelope.

My Dearest Beloved,
   Today, I wandered aimlessly around my estate,

wondering how you fared, wondering if you thought of me at all. Is there a small part of your heart that you might share with me? I am desperate for your love. Don't let me languish in this Never Land.

This is so hard for me to write, my darling. But I must make you aware of my feelings. I must go now. There are tasks to see to. Know that I love you and will do so for all time, into the nimbus of the ages, and the depths of forever. And I remain, always,

Your devoted servant

Words, even thoughts, failed Arielle at the moment. All she did was feel Hunter's pain, for she recognized his handwriting. How she loved him! She'd find a way to ease his heartache and make him realize it didn't matter to her if he'd been born a serf. It suddenly dawned on her that the first letter she'd taken up today had been written in Hunter's hand.

He'd said he loved her!

The barrenness of early spring had turned into the lush, green beauty of approaching summer, drenching the landscape with nature's perfection and ushering in the season of hope and renewal.

Having no reaction from Arielle over the letters he wrote thoroughly irritated Hunter. Undoubtedly, she'd read them. Was she aware of the difference in them, however? Would she tell him he'd misrepresented himself and want to end their marriage?

With that thought, Hunter downed the rest of his brandy. What he really needed was scotch.

"Hunter?" Arielle's soft voice floated to him from the doorway in a whisper.

He looked up. Her eyes were as vivid as an emerald ocean, sea green, moist, and wide. A transparent pink dusted her pale complexion and her delicate mouth trembled.

"Arielle?" he asked hoarsely, rising to his feet.

Going to where she stood, Hunter took Arielle's hand and led her to the sofa. "Why are you weeping, sweet?" he asked, his voice laced with concern.

Arielle held out the letters she clutched in her hand. His heart raced as he noticed his letters for the first time.

"D-did you write these?" she asked tremulously.

"Yes, my love," he replied raggedly, his voice as soft as hers, "I did."

At his admission, Arielle flung herself into his arms and hugged him tightly. "Oh, Hunter," she wept, "I've loved you for so long, I don't care about your past. Or that you're illegitimate."

Anxiety flickered through him. She *had* read his letters. Drawing in a deep breath to get control of his spinning emotions, he knew he couldn't turn back now. He had run away once. He wouldn't do so again. Not when he risked losing Arielle's love if he did so. "I don't remember when I fell in love with you, Arielle. But I didn't know how to say it. I was afraid you'd reject me."

"Reject you?"

"Yes."

"Oh, my love, my foolish, foolish love," Arielle said, half laughing, half crying. "I could never reject you."

Hunter kissed her then, tenderly and longingly, deeply and hungrily. He kissed her until his doubt and fear were assuaged, and until he realized he really didn't need scotch. Arielle's confession of trust for him was all the opiate he needed. "I'm sorry for not responding to your last letter. As much as I realized that you were trying to convey your true feelings to me, I didn't dare trust that they were true."

"As true as the night sky is," Arielle said softly.

Giving her one last kiss, he took her hand and led her up the stairs to express his love in a most desirous way, by resting between her silken thighs.

* * *

" **A** re you telling me you're not Stanford's daughter?"
Hunter asked incredulously, the next morning. He
and Arielle had had a late lie-in, after an ecstatic night of
lovemaking. In as delicate a way as possible, he'd asked
Arielle why she alone amongst her family possessed such
great beauty and she'd broadsided him with her stunning
news.

A might hesitant at first, she finally told him. "My
mother committed an indiscretion with the too-handsome,
womanizing Lord Wharton. My father . . . Thomas . . .
forgave Mama because he loved her and steadfastly refused to set her aside. Mama died when I was six and
Thomas raised me as his own. My father never once made
me suffer. But it was just another reason I wanted to
please him so dearly."

"Goddammit, Arielle!" Hunter snarled. "That bastard
blackmailed me into marrying you because of *my* illegitimacy—when you were a by-blow yourself! Get up!" he
instructed, sliding out of bed. "Get dressed. We're going
to Stanford Manor. I'll explain what I know of my sordid
life story on the way there."

46

S everal hours later, Hunter brushed past the butler at Stanford Manor and stormed into the parlor, holding tightly onto Arielle's hand. He found Thomas entertaining a rather distinguished-looking gentleman, but Hunter didn't care. He was angry enough to spit fire. Releasing Arielle's hand, he advanced toward Thomas in threatening strides.

Arielle rushed ahead to stand between him and her father. "Hunter, please! This can wait until later. Lord Ridgeley is—"

"Excuse me, Arielle," Hunter said, pushing her aside, his dark, angry expression silencing her. He refocused his gaze on Thomas, who stood mere inches from him, his skin drained of color beneath Hunter's towering rage.

"You bastard!" Hunter snarled. "Your circumstances were hardly different from mine. Yet you held over my head the threat of exposure for my questionable parentage. A parentage as questionable as Arielle's." He landed a solid punch to Thomas's jaw. The viscount reeled backward, sprawling onto the sofa behind him.

"No!" Arielle screamed, grabbing his arm as Hunter grabbed Thomas by the collar and dragged him to his feet. "Stop it, Hunter!"

"Arielle—"

"Enough!" a heavy, booming voice commanded, cutting through Hunter's fury.

Momentarily surprised at the interruption, Hunter looked at the owner of the voice. He'd only given the man a cursory glance upon arrival. Now, he realized the sharp-featured, blue-eyed nobleman bore a strange resemblance to himself. And this man was definitely part of the aristocracy. Every refined nuance of him bespoke his heritage. "Who the hell are you?"

"What are you doing here, Your Grace?" Arielle asked in clipped tones, ignoring Hunter's question.

"Your Grace?" Hunter echoed.

"Sit down, both of you!" the man commanded in a tone that brooked no disobedience. When Hunter pushed Thomas away from him and seated himself on the sofa, a modicum of satisfaction crossed the eerily familiar face. "Thomas, are you all right, sir?"

Standing with his hand on his jaw, his clothes disheveled, Thomas nodded with as much dignity as the situation allowed him. "Certainly, sir."

Arielle went to her father and touched his sleeve. "Father—"

"Go sit with your husband, Arielle," Thomas instructed,

Sighing and glaring at Hunter, Arielle seated herself next to him.

His wife's displeasure made him feel a tad foolish. He'd allowed anger to overrule his upbringing and acted like a low-class hooligan. In spite of Thomas's vile acts, he was still Arielle's father—or the man who had raised her—and she loved him dearly.

"You are more beautiful even than the last time we met, Lady Savage," the duke said, placing a kiss on Arielle's hand.

"The last time you met?" Hunter drew his eyebrows together in confusion. "Arielle, are you acquainted with this man?"

"Yes, Hunter," Arielle answered. "He came to Braxton Hall weeks ago."

"Why?" Hunter asked, deadly calm, directing his attention to the tall white-haired man.

The duke rested his blue gaze on Hunter for an eternity. In that time, Hunter realized he glimpsed a mirror of how he'd look years from now. He saw the same wide shoulders, which age hadn't touched, and the same intense, cerulean eyes set in his face.

Mist filled the old man's eyes, and he blinked. "Would you care to answer that, Thomas?" he asked, without turning away from Hunter.

Thomas cleared his throat. "No, Your Grace. I don't feel qualified to answer such a provocative question."

Hunter rose to his feet, struggling with the reality of a shared connection to the duke and in no mood for posturing. "Someone had bloody well answer!" he snapped.

A faint smile touched the man's lips. "Sit down, Hunter," he said gently. "You're past due an explanation." As Hunter obeyed, the duke gazed at Arielle. "Do you love your husband?"

"Yes, Your Grace, very much."

"And he, you, I suppose?"

"More than words can say," Hunter put in, unsure of where this conversation was leading. "Not that it's any of your deuced business."

"No, it isn't," the duke agreed with a robust laugh. "Allow me to introduce myself to you, Hunter. I am John Price, duke of Ridgeley." He walked forward and stopped before Hunter, putting him in the unenviable and unprecedented position of being looked down upon. "Your grandfather," he added into the silence.

"Oh!" Arielle gasped.

Hunter looked at Thomas, and Thomas nodded. He went rigid, digesting the information. Anyone acquainted with him *and* Ridgeley would notice the striking resemblance between them. Yet at the moment, Hunter couldn't think of John Price as His Grace or his grandfather.

"Don't blame Thomas entirely," John began. "It was my suggestion that sent him to you with his ultimatum. I also armed him with most of the information by planting the letter."

"You?" Hunter asked, his pain growing. "Did you think it was a jest toying with our lives?"

"Of course not," John said, walking away from him. Arms behind his back, he paced. "As my heir, I needed you to wed. I am also quite aware that Proctor would have rather had you believe you were born a bastard than allow me into your life. He and I shared a deep-seated bitterness that began when he was a young man. I was well into my thirties then and he just invested with his titles. We fell in love with the same woman, the woman *I* married and he loved the rest of his life. It seemed, however, our families had a destiny together. Years later, Roxanne and Fenton, my beloved son and your father, fell in love. If things had been different between Proctor and me, we mightn't have forbidden their romance. As it was, after a lengthy affair, they had no choice—your uncle and I still left them no choice—but to run off to Gretna Green."

"A-are you . . ." Hunter swallowed hard. Since he was a child, he'd believed he was the product of an illicit affair. Even the letters he'd discovered in the attic had suggested such. "Are you telling me that my parents w-were indeed married?" he managed in broken tones.

"Quite," John told him wryly, walking a hole in the carpet.

Until then, Hunter hadn't realized what a nerve-wracking practice he had. Watching John Price pace back and forth was both frustrating and irritating.

"What do you know about the Braxton family secrets?"

"Not much," Hunter admitted. "Only that they were damaging and had the power to ruin the family. I grew up almost a recluse. Whenever Uncle Proctor and I came to London, we invariably stayed at the town house and didn't venture into society for the most part. I made tentative steps into the ton after his death, but I was never . . . comfortable. At any moment, I expected someone to remember something and expose me to the world."

"So you left?" Arielle queried softly.

"Yes."

"You handled it as best you could," John said. "As to the secrets, many of your contemporaries know nothing about them. Those of us in the old guard remember the rumors."

"By all means tell me," Hunter said, emotionless. "Then I have questions of my own."

"In the first years of the last century, a murder happened. Lord Savage's murder has never been solved."

"Lord Savage?" Thomas echoed.

John nodded. "The ninth marquess of Savage, to be exact. As far as the Crown knew, he left no heirs. Everyone thought the line ended upon his stabbing."

"Apparently, it didn't. I am living proof."

"Yes," John agreed. "However, your great-grandfather came out of nowhere. He had never been heard of before."

"That's not atypical, Your Grace," Arielle told him, her eyes following his annoying movement. "A very junior branch of a family can inherit if the deceased doesn't have a male heir."

"True enough, and there should be some sort of proof, but six weeks after Lord Savage's murder, Christopher Braxton petitioned the Crown as a long-lost relative of the marquess and was granted the titles. *No one* had ever heard of a Braxton branch of the family."

"This is impossible!" Hunter said. "I can't believe you're standing there telling me such a twisted fabrication. If no one had ever heard of Mr. Braxton, why was he granted—"

"Who knows? Blackmail, perhaps?" John answered with a sardonic laugh, gazing at Thomas. "My point is, *I* remembered the unproven rumors of how the Braxtons had come by the titles by nefarious means. Coupled with mutual enmity toward Proctor, I didn't want my son marrying into the family. I considered them murderers, thieves, liars, and blackmailers."

"And the Ridgeley line was unscathed?" Hunter snarled, Price's snobbishness angering him.

"Probably not. But I never knew anything about such damaging secrets. I'm sure this is hard for you to swallow, so why don't you ask me the questions you had?"

As much as Hunter wanted to delve into the convoluted tale he had just heard, he did have other, more pressing questions regarding his parents. "Where was my father during the years of my youth? Where is he now? And why did he leave my mother?"

The pacing stopped and a haunted look softened the duke's commanding presence. Hunter almost felt sorry for him.

"Your father died accidentally the day after he and your mother returned from Gretna Green."

"Why now, after all these years, have you decided to seek me out?" Hunter asked with bitterness. He'd suffered the question of his birth nearly all his life and this man had had the wherewithal to set matters right long ago. As had his uncle Proctor, who had chosen to let Hunter suffer because of a feud he had no part of, one that should have ended upon Ridgeley's marriage.

"I only learned of your whereabouts some months ago, son," John answered. "In my grief, I said some very unkind things to Roxanne, which included the word *fortune-hunter*. She fled to Proctor and told him of my hurtful words. It was just an added bone of contention, and upon her death he sent me a missive stating that you had been stillborn as well."

A ragged, choking sound caught in Hunter's throat. He was vaguely aware of Arielle flinging her arms around his neck.

"Hunter," she whispered, "I don't know what to say."

"Then may I say something?" Thomas asked, stepping forward and sitting in the seat across from them.

"Yes," Hunter agreed, drawing in a weary breath.

"I beg both of your forgiveness," Thomas implored in a rush. "My actions, as well as His Grace's, hurt both of you, and I am truly sorry for my part in the scheme."

Tears streaking her cheeks, Arielle rushed into her father's arms and kissed him. "Father, don't despair. If it wasn't for that scheme, I never would have married Hunter."

Knowing the truth of that statement, Hunter cleared his throat. "Please *don't* despair, Thomas," he reiterated. Too many lives had been ruined or made miserable within his family by unyielding vengeance and inability to forgive. He had once been as overweening, but knew he couldn't let it rule his life. He smiled at his father-in-law, realizing for the first time the type of man Thomas truly was. "What you did for Arielle and her mother makes you a good and kind man. A gentleman of the first order. I thank you for my wife and I'm sorry that I lost my temper earlier." Everyone laughed, easing the tension as he turned to the duke. "Your Grace, I mean no disrespect, but you'll pardon me if I don't start our relationship by calling you Grandfather right away."

"I expect no less from you, boy," Ridgeley said. He touched his waistcoat, then dug inside and pulled out an envelope. "I have a letter from my son to your mother, which you might be interested in reading. It begins with 'dearest beloved,' " he said, taking on a faraway look. "I suppose that's what Roxanne was to her 'devoted servant'—that's how Fenton signed his letter to her." He laughed, then turned serious again. "I deeply regret my actions with your mother, Hunter. It's obvious she and Fenton were very much in love."

"The letters in the attic!" Arielle exclaimed excitedly. "I finally know where they came from!" She slanted a shy smile at Hunter. "Most of them, anyway," she clarified.

"There are others?" John asked in surprise.

"Yes," Hunter murmured, wondering if perhaps saving the letters had been Proctor's restitution. Knowing of Fenton and Roxanne's love, his uncle had likely saved the letters for Hunter as proof because he couldn't bring himself to confess his role in keeping them apart.

"Hunter," John began, "you are a product of the Braxtons and the Prices. You are free to carry either name and, whichever you choose, you will always be my grandson, my only link to my lost son. If you choose Price, there'll be gossip. But it will die soon enough. Besides, I'm quite sure many wouldn't dare cross me."

"Thank you, sir," Hunter said, standing. "And now if you don't mind, Arielle and I will retire to my town house." He held out his hand to Ridgeley and inclined his head. "Pleasure meeting you, Your Grace." Glancing at Thomas, he accorded him the same courtesy, then he took Arielle's hand and led her from the parlor.

Hunter disengaged himself from Arielle's arms and got out of bed. He went to his trousers and dug in the pocket.

It was the wee hours of the morning. Only the flames from the fireplace and a low-burning lamp provided light. They had been awake most of the night alternately contemplating the incredible turn of events with each other and making love. Arielle couldn't believe her good fortune. She had a wonderful husband, with titles too numerous to mention—titles from both sides of his family. And when the day's occurrence sank in for him, he'd realized he had a grandfather to share his life. Perhaps a son or daughter as well, if her calculations proved correct.

"Arielle?" Hunter said, returning to the bed and taking her hand into his. He slid a ring onto the third finger of her left hand.

She gasped in surprise, lifting her hand to inspect the gift. The diamonds caught a ray of the meager light and sparkled with magnificent brilliance. Her overly emotional state of late sent a rush of tears to her eyes and she looked in question at Hunter.

"I found it amongst my mother's things in the attic, my love," Hunter explained with a quiet vulnerability like a little boy waiting for acceptance. "I realize now it was the wedding ring my father gave to her at their ceremony." He cleared his throat. "Would you accept it as your own symbol of our vows?"

"Yes," Arielle whispered without hesitation.

"You are my dearest beloved, Arielle. You are so much like the woman my uncle Proctor described my mother as being, it is easy to understand how my father became her devoted servant, as I am now yours. I love you, now and forever."

"Through the nimbus of the ages?" Arielle said with a watery smile, remembering his own words of devotion. Once, before she had known their identities, she had envied the love Roxanne and Fenton shared. Now, she and Hunter's feelings mirrored that of his parents and gave life to their beautiful letters. "I love you as much, my lord, and I am honored that you'd give me your mother's ring."

Unprotesting as he guided her back onto the pillows, she planted a tender and stirring kiss on his lips. But, for the moment, their bodies were sated. Flinging an arm behind his head, he rested on the pillow.

"Has the discovery of having a grandfather made you happy, my love?" Arielle asked, snuggling her naked form closer to his bare flesh.

"Stunned is more the word, my angel. But it's something I can get used to."

She circled her fingers on his chest, unsure if he'd had enough surprises for the day or not. "Do you think you're up to more good tidings?"

Raising himself, Hunter rested his elbow on the bed. His head on his hand, he looked at her. "Always."

"I've missed my monthly, Hunter," she whispered. "But," she quickly added when she saw his eyes widen, "I'll need a few more days to be absolutely positive."

"Arielle, my sweet, sweet love," Hunter said, his voice cracking. "You're going to give me an heir?"

"Yes, Hunter. I want to so badly."

"Then, dearest beloved, by all means, let's help it along," he said, enfolding her into his arms and slanting his mouth over hers with a love that reached the nimbus of the ages and the depths of forever.

She had sought him in her dreams and found him in her soul. Her devoted servant, indeed.

$\mathcal{A}$UTHORS' NOTE

Until the mid-nineteenth century, women in the healing arts were typically midwives, who acquired their knowledge through oral tradition and simple apprenticeships, assisting more experienced counterparts. Such as Arielle's informal training with Quentin.

Unlike Dr. Quentin DeVries, who was more than willing to share his knowledge with Arielle, the male-dominated profession helped to mold contemporary medical ideas that embodied the social attitudes of the day about women. Medicine as a whole came into its own, disengaging from the religious superstitions that had delayed advances. However, women were generally viewed as susceptible to disease and illness. First and foremost, because of their gender, and second, if and when they stepped outside of the boundaries of their conventional roles.

Of particular note are four women who made great strides in the field, when women were relegated to the background of the profession as patients and practitioners—Trotolla di Rugerio, Hildegard von Bingen, Elizabeth Blackwell, and Elizabeth Garrett.

Trotolla, an eleventh-century Italian physician, is credited with writing the first complete work on women's health. German-born Hildegard didn't attend medical school, but wrote medical books recognized as the most intensive and greatest works on the healing arts to come out of the medieval period.

In 1849, Englishwoman Elizabeth Blackwell graduated

from the Geneva Medical School of New York, becoming the first woman in America identified as a qualified physician. When Elizabeth Garrett received a diploma from London's Worshipful Society of Apothecaries in 1865, she received the same distinguishment in Britain.

The first published account of a successful appendectomy is listed as 1886 by surgeon Rudolph Kronlein, although his seventeen-year-old patient died two days later. Well into the nineteenth century, inflammation of the appendix was called perityphlitis, a term of unknown origins. In the interest of the book and Arielle's character, we took literary license and had her perform the surgery.

Please write to us at P.O. Box 8815, New Orleans, LA 70182-8815. Or e-mail us at *smintch@aol.com.* And visit our web page at: *http://www.tlt.com/authors/christinehol-den.htm.*

HIGHLAND FLING

*Have a Fling...Every Other Month with Jove's
new Highland Fling romances!*

<u>*January 2002*</u>
Laird of the Mist
by Elizabeth English
0-515-13190-3

<u>*March 2002*</u>
Once Forbidden
by Terri Brisbin
0-515-13179-2

All books $5.99

TIME PASSAGES